"What a good read of landscape and treatment ... native issues and people. I loved the ambiguity and subtlety of the various relationships, as well as how Pryce handles the thoughts and feelings of both male and female characters."

Robert Cowan
Author, Local Historian and
Chair of Enderby & District Heritage Commission

"The wealth of knowledge on which Pryce draws is obvious. The narrative she produces is entertaining and extremely instructive."

Charles Hayes
Editor, South Okanagan Review newspaper, 1981-1996,
Author and Historian

"Pryce's novel portrays realistically the lives of both men and women, white and native, involved in ranching and the fur trade over a period of more than a century. Her work fills a hitherto unmet need in the historical literature of the area."

John Ortiz
Okanagan Historical Society

"As a native of the Okanagan, I really like the way Pryce depicts the valley; as it was and as it has changed. When Pryce writes about ranching and horses, she writes with an authority that comes through to the reader."

A. David MacDonald
Author & Educator

OTHER WORKS BY ELIZABETH PRYCE

WAGON TRAIN OVER THE MONASHEE

by DOUG COX AND ELIZABETH PRYCE

OKANAGAN ROOTS

by DOUG COX with ELIZABETH PRYCE

SKAHA CROSSING

Vol. 1

Elizabeth Pryce

ELIZABETH PRYCE

ACKNOWLEDGMENTS

Recognition is owed to the late Dorothy and Doug Fraser of Osoyoos, who reviewed the first draft and encouraged me to continue; the late Charles Hayes of Okanagan Falls, for initial editorial assistance; Elsa Lewis in Oroville, WA, for research assistance; A. David MacDonald in Penticton, for editorial assistance on the third draft; and Robert Cowan in Enderby, for his encouragement and editing the fourth draft. Special thanks to Gillian Veitch in Kelowna for her patience and edit of the final draft.

Grateful thanks to my husband, John Bork, and our daughter, Sandra, for their encouragement and faith in me to write the SKAHA trilogy.

All of the characters in this book are fictitious and any resemblance to actual persons is coincidental.

Cover: "The Twin Falls", by Jill Leir-Salter
Illustrations: Michelle Edge and Gillian Veitch
Production & Editing: Gillian Veitch

Note for Librarians: a cataloguing record for this book that includes Dewey Decimal Classification and US Library of Congress numbers is available from the Library and Archives of Canada. The complete cataloguing record can be obtained from their online database at:
www.collectionscanada.ca/amicus/index-e.html
ISBN 1-4120-3785-9
Printed in Victoria, BC, Canada

TRAFFORD

Offices in Canada, USA, Ireland, UK and Spain
This book was published on-demand in cooperation with Trafford Publishing. On-demand publishing is a unique process and service of making a book available for retail sale to the public taking advantage of on-demand manufacturing and Internet marketing. On-demand publishing includes promotions, retail sales, manufacturing, order fulfilment, accounting and collecting royalties on behalf of the author.
Book sales for North America and international:
Trafford Publishing, 6E–2333 Government St.,
Victoria, BC v8t 4p4 CANADA
phone 250 383 6864 (toll-free 1 888 232 4444)
fax 250 383 6804; email to orders@trafford.com
Book sales in Europe:
Trafford Publishing (uk) Ltd., Enterprise House, Wistaston Road Business Centre,
Wistaston Road, Crewe, Cheshire cw2 7rp United Kingdom
phone 01270 251 396 (local rate 0845 230 9601)
facsimile 01270 254 983; orders.uk@trafford.com
Order online at:
www.trafford.com/robots/04-1600.html

10 9 8 7 6 5 4

INTRODUCTION

This is not a story concerned with the politics of our country or specific historical events of the century it spans. It is a chronicle of the lives of fictitious characters in a setting based on Okanagan history.

The settlement, *Skaha Crossing*, is created on a great expanse of rolling hills and flat lands west of Skaha Lake. To this day, the area remains relatively barren save for ranging cattle. The McAllisters and all the novel's characters are real only to this story. With the exception that the author has extended the life of Spokane House by five years, all dates and names are authentic to the best of her knowledge and research. The Indian settlement at Okanagan Falls was not a village with a chief but a special salmon fishing place shared by the Okanagan bands.

The name *Okanagan* is spelled many ways. Okanogan is the accepted spelling of the early fur depot, Fort Okanogan, located at the confluence of the Okanagan and Columbia rivers. Okanagan is the name of the Interior Salish Indian tribe. Some historians claim the band took its name from Okanagan Valley, Okanagan River and Okanagan Lake, whereas others contend these areas were named after the tribe. Generally, the word is spelled with an 'a' north of the current Canada-US border and with an 'o' to the south. Place names Penti'ktEn, Sxoxene'tk^u, Soi'yus and others have special meanings to the Okanagan Valley and are referenced in The Salishan Tribes of the Western Plateaus by James Teit and Franz Boas.

Several sources were invaluable: Okanagan Sources, compiled and edited by Jean Webber and the En'owkin Centre in Penticton; Enwhisteetkwa, by Jeannette C. Armstrong of the Penticton Indian Band; Soft Gold, by Thomas Vaughan and Bill Holm, Oregon Historical Society Press; Okanagan Historical Society annual reports; The Old West series from Time Life Books; and the National Geographic Society. Many local and provincial publications were constant research sources, as were personal interviews and early photographs and maps.

SKAHA CROSSING is the first part of a trilogy of historical fiction set primarily in the Okanagan Valley in British Columbia, Canada.

E.P.

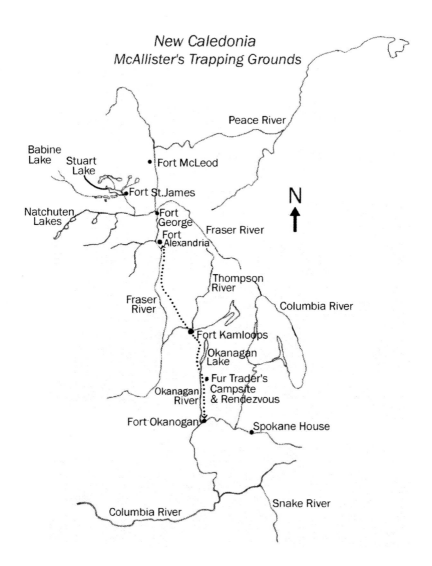

New Caledonia
McAllister's Trapping Grounds

Peace River

Babine Lake

Stuart Lake

Fort McLeod

Fort St.James

Natchuten Lakes

Fort George

Fort Alexandria

Fraser River

N

Thompson River

Fraser River

Columbia River

Fort Kamloops

Okanagan Lake

Fur Trader's Campsite & Rendezvous

Okanagan River

Fort Okanogan

Spokane House

Columbia River

Snake River

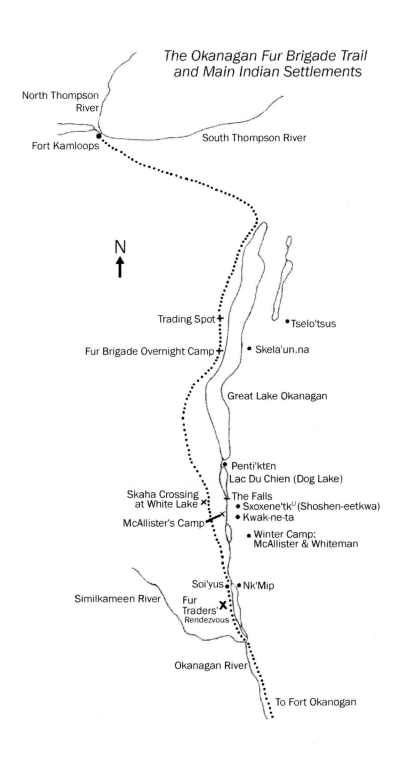

The Okanagan Fur Brigade Trail
and Main Indian Settlements

North Thompson River

Fort Kamloops

South Thompson River

N

Trading Spot

Tselo'tsus

Fur Brigade Overnight Camp

Skela'un.na

Great Lake Okanagan

Penti'ktɛn

Lac Du Chien (Dog Lake)

Skaha Crossing
at White Lake

The Falls

Sxoxene'tk^U (Shoshen-eetkwa)

Kwak-ne-ta

McAllister's Camp

Winter Camp:
McAllister & Whiteman

Soi'yus

Nk'Mip

Similkameen River

Fur
Traders'
Rendezvous

Okanagan River

To Fort Okanogan

FORT ST. JAMES

1

The Canadian wilderness was vast in 1815. It was a territory of extremes in climate and terrain and presented a wide opportunity for the early explorer and fur trapper whose basic nature knew no fear and recognized no law but his own.

In the complicated web of waterways of central Canada, Indians of the Cree, Iroquois and Huron nations roamed the land and vied with French voyageurs in the trading of furs. Upper Canada soon became dotted with forts where there was brisk and often heated trade between Indians, fur trappers and the Hudson's Bay Company.

On a wintery afternoon, Duncan McAllister, a Scots-Canadian, and his young son paddled their light canoe across a lake, entering the narrow river at its confluence. Canada's northern wilderness surrounded them, seeming to lock them safely into its great, protective body in the approaching evening. Only the rhythmic dipping of the paddles could be heard in the stillness. The man and his boy pulled their craft ashore and set about preparation of their camp for the cold night ahead.

McAllister moved about the riverbank gathering dead branches for a fire in preparation of the evening meal. With a great yearning for adventure and challenge, he had travelled extensively in Upper Canada, but lately his thoughts had strayed to the Hudson's Bay Company's expanding fur trade in the Pacific region.

Possessed of the essentials of survival, McAllister's senses were finely tuned to every threat to his safety. No Indian or animal could cross his trail without discovery. He had the ability to live off the land and supplement his basic diet of dried salmon with game, wild fruits and roots. With herbs, he dressed his wounds and eased his pain. Years of hard-learnt experience perfected his skills and taught him the many dialects necessary to live among the Indians.

With him travelled his young son. Almost from the cradle, David Rayne McAllister's education was the woods, the rivers and their inhabitants. Fleet of foot and ever wary, young McAllister was well trained and could bring down a deer with an arrow as well as anyone. He became exceptional with a knife and gun. He had canoed with his father down endless rivers with the silence of the vast forest on either side of him. He was at home.

He knew the value of beaver and how to trade with Indians. Young Rayne had learned to get along with the Indians, for he had been raised among them. And he knew they stood back into the deep forests watching, as did the deer and other creatures, as he and his father passed. Sometimes at night the wolves watched too and their chilling howl sent shivers along his spine.

That evening while camped on the shore of the narrow river with the cold November night surrounding them, Rayne whispered to his father, "Sometimes I'm afraid, Father."

"The wolves?"

"The wolves." Knowing the animals were just beyond their firelight, the boy could sense their sharp, watchful stare upon him, their eyes bright red dots in the dark.

They sat together in the circle of light from their fire and his father said to him, "Well, he is a fierce one, but he stands in awe of us. He is also afraid of our fire so let us bank it up for the night and crawl beneath our robes where it is warm." Moving to drag in several lengths of logs, McAllister placed them into the fire at angles which would ensure a bright flame while they slept.

McAllister assured his son. "We'll be safe." The confident smile which flashed across the trapper's weathered face brought a return grin from the boy.

A bright, full moon shed light through the trees of the thick forest. Beyond their camp the water moved quietly and smoothly past them to the shimmering lake beyond. Looking upward from his bed upon the ground, the boy watched the changing patterns made by the tall trees against the silvery light of the night sky and the cloud formations which moved across the moon's lighted path.

Buried beneath the hides and warm beside his father, Rayne persisted. "Why is the wolf afraid of our fire?" He knew that his father had laid his gun close by as he did every night.

"Because it confuses him. Do not fear him too much. If an animal knows you are afraid then it becomes brave. Now go to sleep." McAllister pulled the thick hide over his son and patted the top of the boy's head where it stuck out from beneath the cover. "We have a long river ahead of us and I want a strong lad awake at the end of the paddle tomorrow." Tugging thoughtfully a moment at the length of his red beard, the seasoned trapper settled himself comfortably upon the robes and hard ground beside his son.

Young Rayne, now ten years old, snugged himself deeper beneath the warm buffalo hide, feeling protected with his father close beside him. He knew his father to be a brave man and he taught himself to be nothing less. He learned all about the marten, mink, lynx, fisher and especially the beaver, becoming familiar with their habits, homes, and tracks. He knew which was easiest to trap and how to set the traps properly. With his father he skinned, stretched and packed the hides into tight bales for transport. He had learned to manoeuver the canoe: how to portage, run the rapids, ride the currents to advantage, and where to hide it when necessary.

McAllister would often flash his broad smile and tell his son, "You make your Mama proud."

"Mama isn't here," was the boy's detached reply in which a hint of loneliness lurked.

"She knows anyway."

The boy could not mourn a mother he had never known. She had departed this world at his birth and therefore, for him, she had never existed. He had known only a succession of Metis and Indian women whom he had come to trust through their gentle care and attention. They clothed him in soft skins, decorated him with bright beads and quills, hung feathers from his fair hair and bones around his thin neck. Moccasins kept his feet warm in wintertime. At night he slept comfortably beneath the thick buffalo robes obtained in barter with a small band of wandering Cree from the flatlands. Rayne considered his only true friends to be the birds and animals which he had cleverly learned to imitate.

However, Rayne's life was very different when, during the summertime, they lived at trading posts. Interaction with other youngsters and schooling became a daytime experience, while at night he preferred listening to the men in their talk of hunting and survival. His father never chased him away to his bed, but let him linger and learn. Regardless of how much fun he had at play with his classmates he felt a bit of a loner for their experiences were opposite during the winter season. They remained at the fort while he travelled into the wilderness and fell behind in his studies.

In 1818 the McAllisters began their travel westward and wintered at York. There, an opportunity presented itself and young Rayne took full advantage. The Chief Factor's wife, the local school teacher, took a liking to him for he reminded her of the son she had lost to an accident and who she greatly missed.

Suddenly, Rayne was no longer spending his evenings listening to the men. Instead he could be found seated at the kitchen table in the small house of the Chief Factor receiving extra study in necessary subjects, plus a rough fluency in French.

One great advantage derived from such attention was a polishing of his natural eloquence of speech. Perception was at its best in Rayne and the written word soon developed a fuller meaning of life for him. His mastery of the English language would stand young McAllister in good stead throughout his life, especially in the field of bargaining and understanding his opponent.

Fort St. James

However, as well educated as Rayne became in his youth, he was still a trapper's son and the rivers were his life. He was more comfortable with the Indians, having lived his life near their camps. Sometimes the children Rayne encountered on his journey west from post to post taunted him by saying that he was more like the Indians than the Indians themselves. At one post, they gave him the name Many Rains. It had no meaning and was only the envious, childish mocking of the sound of Rayne.

2

In the footsteps of the early explorers, trappers and traders migrated to the west. The quiet waters of Stuart Lake, the challenge of its river, the Stuart, and the bountiful harvest beckoned fur traders from across the nation to this wild, uncharted expanse of land.

So it was in 1820 when Rayne McAllister was fifteen years old that he travelled with his father from the familiar rivers, forests and trading centres of Upper Canada to the wild and exciting frontier of New Caledonia. There a trading post had been constructed above the shore of Stuart Lake nineteen years before by the men of the North West Company. Originally known as Stuart's Lake Post, it was renamed Fort St. James following the merger of the major fur companies. Trapper Duncan McAllister's continued quest for adventure had led them to this western fort.

Rayne remained relatively undisturbed by the change. In fact, he considered it a challenge and felt that since the years of his youth were nearly behind him, the experience of a new land and post was a welcome one. Although Rayne was the youngest man on the post, he fit in well. His maturity was commendable. Perhaps the quiet manner with which he conducted himself made the difference in acceptance among the men.

His father's instructions in survival were endless. "It matters not if you can pack ten pelts or fifty, but whether you do it without complaint," the trapper lectured. "When a man whines about the hardships in life which he himself has opted for, he finds himself booted out of camp. There are other jobs to be done in the world besides trap furs, you know. 'Tis all a matter of choice." Then, tugging at his thick, curly beard, a grin playing about the corners of his mouth below his mustache, McAllister added, "Time will teach you that, lad!"

Sitting near the table in their cabin on a quiet morning at Fort St. James, Rayne watched his father sharpen his knife. He drew out his own double-edged weapon which he had won from a confident Assiniboine brave.

McAllister pushed back his chair, turned the knife several times before his eyes, then rose and strode toward the doorway.

Rayne followed. With the rays of a bright morning sun bouncing off his fair hair, he grinned with great respect across into his father's face. "Toss you!" Rayne challenged impulsively.

From the entrance to their cabin, McAllister's hearty laugh boomed out into the air as he threw back his head and waved an arm upward. "You're on! For what?"

"Anything. Nothing. It doesn't matter," Rayne faltered suddenly. "I just want to toss you."

The tall trapper looked across at his fair son. He smiled. "Aye, think you can beat me, lad."

Rayne watched his father's face. Deep blue eyes twinkled from beneath McAllister's brow where thick locks of curly red hair fell. A wide smile, allowing a show of even teeth, beamed from the midst of his heavy beard, equally as red. Rayne knew he was being studied by his tremendously competent father. "Maybe I can," he half whispered daringly. "Someday I have to, Father, or I won't live long."

Duncan McAllister thought about that statement. "That's the truth. Well now, we'll do it." He drew his knife, ran his thumb along the edge of the sharpened tip and, stepping down from the boards of the walkway, winked an eye indulgently at his son. "The price of the first made beaver this season. That's a handsome sum, my boy."

Rayne looked sharply across at the trapper. "The first made beaver," he agreed and turned his eyes toward the edge of the forest of spruce and tall pine. They walked across the compound, passing through the palisade entrance toward the edge of the clearing before the forest. "D'you see that Lodgepole with three knots facing us? Centre between top and second. Okay, Father?"

McAllister grinned expectantly. "Centre 'twixt top 'n second it is," he repeated. "Three times then." Removing the wide, red sash from around his thick waist, he placed it upon the ground, thereby marking the line from which they would throw their knives.

A crowd soon gathered behind them. Men clad in traditional Indian tunics and breeches, or loose white shirts and baggy wool trousers, their waists wrapped with colourful sashes, watched the two McAllisters from the edge of the compound. Aside from a few initial cheers, all were silent and expectant.

Duncan McAllister was the unchallenged champion on the post. The trapper tossed first and retrieved the knife from the centre. Rayne carefully placed his moccasins against the sash, raised his knife, studied the target for a brief moment and threw. It deepened his father's mark. He walked up for the weapon and pulled it from the tree.

McAllister glanced at his tall son, raised a quizzical eyebrow and ordered, "Next two knots, centre!"

Rayne nodded, his mouth tight, eyes strained in concentration.

McAllister tossed. The knife centered swiftly, quivering

momentarily in the bark of the tree.

Rayne threw once more and deepened his father's mark again. His heart skipped. In his anticipation he dared not look across at his father.

The trapper pulled at his beard in thought and studied the tree. "Five inches above knot number one," he ordered brusquely.

Their knives flew menacingly through the air and once more Rayne's double-bladed weapon deepened the cut that his father's knife had caused. They turned to each other, smiled and shook hands.

McAllister told his son, "We split the catch. You are not better, my boy, but you have become as good as this old man." He strolled toward the Men's House with an arm across Rayne's shoulders, the gesture pouring confidence into the younger. He felt very proud of the fair-haired, handsome, tall young man he had sired. Indeed, McAllister thought now, he shows the promise of a survivor!

"Next, it'll be the gun," Rayne stated quietly without glancing across into his father's face, for he knew the surprise that would register there.

The fur man looked around, grabbing playfully at his son's wavy hair in a show of affection and laughed boisterously. Striding across the grassy yard, his arms swinging at his sides, he grinned knowingly and called back to Rayne, "And then, I suppose, I can go to my grave knowing that I have left a man of substance to carry my name through those glorious pages of history you studied! I've taught you how to stay alive and you've been listening, lad." From the steps of their small log cabin, situated beside the Men's House, he said further, with seriousness lacing his words, "This is all I ask of the time that's left to me. All who will know you, will know you for the survivor that you are!"

It was a kind of prophecy and Rayne, watching his father turn on the steps and disappear into the dark interior of their home, did not shudder from the impact of its meaning. The men of the fort who had witnessed the contest now filed past him, talking in low tones on their way back to the Men's House, leaving Rayne with his private thoughts on the matter of his future.

Fort St. James was quite different from the old forts of eastern Canada where often the families of the trappers and traders dwelled and one might occasionally be invited to hear music, even dance a bit, and be the lucky recipient of a smile from a fair young lady. Few white women were to be found on this post, mostly those within the families of the Chief Factor and the Chief Trader. Often, though, the factors travelled alone in the west, preferring to leave their women located on posts wherein lay a greater degree of safety and comfort than the forts of New Caledonia provided.

Fort St. James was the hub of the western fur trade. Not only did the post handle all the business of trade for the entire north-western region, but conducted a fur trade of its own with the local Carrier Indians. The natives spent most of the fall and winter season trapping the area surrounding the fort, bringing in the pelts of mink, lynx, marten, otter and beaver during the early spring months of March and April. They traded at the post store for provisions manufactured in eastern Canada and Europe which were imported by the companies of the fur trade. Furs were transported by pack train to Fort McLeod enroute to the east, and supplies were brought back by the same route.

Eventually ships sailing the Pacific Ocean delivered to the western ports trade goods, household supplies and staple foods such as sugar, tea, coffee, salt and various grains. By means of exchange the Carrier Indians of the Stuart Lake area, as was the case with all Indians who came into contact with the fur trade, were able to benefit personally by trade without disruption to any great degree of their cultures.

The Carriers, the most numerous and progressive of the Northern Athapascans, were settled in the middle area of the interior of New Caledonia. Their hunting grounds surrounded Stuart Lake with outer boundaries pressing those of the Bella Coola, Kwakiutl and Tsimshian bands on the shores of the Pacific Ocean, the Babine and Sikani to the north, the Interior Salish in the southeast and the Coast Salish in the southwest. The fur trade in North America continued to expand, necessitating penetration into these native hunting areas. Misunderstandings developed between the Indians, who fiercely guarded their territories, and the fur-greedy white men who steadily encroached upon them.

At the Fort St. James trading post, fear of native uprising brought about the building of heavy palisades with corner bastions. Even a cannon was installed. Night patrols were initiated. Throughout the dark, still nights, guards made regular checks on the boundaries of the enclosed compound.

At the time that the fur trade in the west was reaching its height there were only about 1,500 Carrier Indians in New Caledonia. They lived in permanent villages and left their dwellings only in organized hunting and fishing parties or on berrying expeditions. The exception to these habits was the taking of furs to the post. By 1826 the initial fear of the white strangers had worn off and they no longer considered the bearded, light-skinned hunters, who sometimes dressed in tanned hides identical to their own, as species of a supernatural race. Year by year they had learned to accept the strangers who intruded into their territory as traders like themselves and even allowed some of them to enter into family relationships and marriage.

The isolation of New Caledonia contributed loneliness and exhaustion to an individual's life there. Part of its harshness was in the shipment and distribution of the furs and trade goods. This was heavy work. A route from the north to the south of New Caledonia had been established in 1821. The size of the pack trains was increasing with the number of furs which were brought into the post. And often, added to the harshness of the elements, food became so scarce that rabbits and horse meat became a supplement to a diet of dried salmon and berries.

Agriculture had been tried as early as 1811 and had fared miserably. Finally, only turnips could be grown successfully in the depleted soil. Late winters afforded little chance of a mature summer garden. Poor soil also contributed to the poverty of agriculture. The inability to grow their own food placed increased demands upon supply pack trains into northern New Caledonia.

It was evident to Duncan McAllister that Fort St. James had been successful with a reasonable turnip yield, but with little else. In 1826 while some attempts were still being made to produce vegetables, Rayne expressed a desire to develop a small garden on the slope behind their cabin. McAllister, however, preferred to encourage a greater interest in canoe-making and leave the cultivation of carrots, cabbages and turnips to those with less imagination.

Most of the local Carriers travelled in bark canoes, but some of them used dugouts. Such dugouts quite impressed McAllister and, following their procedures, he busied the mind and hands of Rayne throughout the summer months. The making of a canoe was an art, he declared, emphasizing the importance of such transportation in its relation to the fur trade.

McAllister instructed his son thus, "Find a good cedar if you can. If you carve it yourself, you fit it to suit your supplies, your furs and you. You know its weight and the paddle fits your hand just right. There's no way you will ever lose it. I 'ave taught you to run the rapids," he continued seriously, rolling his r's. "Because you had to save your hide once, you'll never let a tipping happen again!" Studying the expressionless contours of his son's youthful face, McAllister issued this warning, "Aside from your knife, your gun and traps, the canoe is the most valuable thing you will own. Make a poor one and you'll drown. Carve a good one, you'll sail."

Cedar in northern and central New Caledonia was sparse, and a tree thick enough for carving was difficult to find. However, through persistence, McAllister located a log of sufficient size and soon the burning and chipping of the inside began. Rayne laboured many weeks hunched over the sharp blade of an adze, but when the steaming and spreading was finished and the proper hollow achieved, the canoe was a heartening sight. It poured confidence into his being and caused a restlessness within, a longing to be gone upriver, an eagerness to begin the season of trapping.

In the fall, when the trapper and his son set out for the hunt, they navigated the waterways that seamed the northern New Caledonia trapping areas in a steadier, more durable and roomier craft than before their arrival in the west when only light birch bark patches had been the available material for building. During their travels upstream, the sixteen foot canoe, tipped on its side, provided ample shelter from the elements at each overnight stop. Much heavier than the rounded birch bark canoe, this dugout often made portaging difficult.

Even though they had accepted the presence of the strangers, the northern Indians still felt some resentment toward the coming of the white man to their land. As the McAllisters travelled upstream each year into the spectacular scenic and abundant hunting areas of these Indians, they took careful note of the villages they passed along the way and the approximate number of inhabitants, at least those which they could see.

The homes resembled large earthen mounds arising from deep dug out holes in the ground and were covered with tree branches, patches of sod and thick moss. Along the shoreline the men of the tribe, tall and straight and dressed in soft hide costumes, watched in silent agitation as the trappers in their canoe passed the village.

The women also watched in quiet resignation. Perhaps they realized something of the eventual change which these fair-skinned strangers would impose upon their ancient way of life. They stood back from the shore near their sod covered huts. They knew they caught the eyes of the strangers with the thick layers of beads across the shoulders of their dresses and the many strands of their necklaces which hung to their waists, the silver pieces that glittered brightly in the late fall sun.

It was because of the women that the name "Carrier" had been given by the earliest fur traders and explorers to this Dene tribe (the Denes were a breakaway branch of the Athapascan Indians.) The women had been noted to carry the bones of their cremated husbands on their backs during the mourning period of one year. This followed an elaborate ceremony in which she was forced to lean over the flames toward the corpse, until sometimes she would be so burnt herself as to leave patches of discoloured skin. This endurance attested to her devotion to her departed mate. Such an attachment could not escape the attention of the white man, who naturally considered all the benefits of having a Carrier woman permanently lodged in his cabin at the fort or his hut along some river.

Although McAllister had been told the story of such cremations, he had only once during his years in Carrier territory, seen a widow acting according to custom. In fact, the only Carrier women he had actually met were those few who had become wives of trappers and traders and lived with their men at the fort or in camps near the fort. Such a marriage formed a necessary alliance with the native bands and afforded those trappers more relaxed movement among the Carriers in their hunting grounds.

On a few occasions McAllister had spoken of such logic to his son, adding, "If I took an Indian wife, life would be much easier for both of us, and damned little trading would be necessary." At times the younger McAllister had cast a hungry eye about the area for a likely wife for himself, but had not given the matter the serious quest it needed, out of a reluctance to accept the added burden of a family.

Often of late, the old trapper had studied his son and considered the life they shared together. He had summed up each hour of contemplation with the decision that it was now time for them to part. His son was no longer a boy, had not been merely a boy for several years, but had reached manhood with the best preparation possible to survive on his own.

"Perhaps," McAllister decided aloud to the company clerk one day, "after this year I will stay at the fort and be content to work for the Company, and keep warm and comfortable in my cabin when the snow flies and the lake freezes." And just maybe, the old man smiled, remembering his own days as a young hunter, Rayne will build his own cabin and find himself a woman to live in it.

In 1829, the McAllister men entered the waterways of the northern New Caledonia fur trapping areas in separate canoes. Along the Stuart River to its junction where the flow continued southeast to Fort George and the Fraser River, Rayne followed behind his father's craft. Then, as planned, the old trapper changed his own course to the west. He wished now to be alone and had emphatically stated this to his son. Had it not been that they travelled in familiar country on rivers near Carrier camps, which had in the past shown some friendliness, Rayne would not have left his father at all, for deeper within Carrier country there still prevailed a strong feeling of resentment toward intruders.

As Rayne contemplated his father's decision, there developed a study of the old man almost for the first time. It was surprising to Rayne to observe that this man, who had guided him thus far in life, now appeared quite old. The hair that had only three years before been thick with auburn curls was now generously laced with white, was noticeably thinner and hung loosely to the old trapper's shoulders. Fine lines about McAllister's blue eyes and those curving around the corners of his mouth spoke of weariness. Could it be, Rayne considered now, that I have never given thought to his age? Have I never noticed how his step has slowed or that I now do most of the packing and unloading, while he struggles with our meals over the campfires? Why have I not reminded myself that he was getting older each time he spoke of being another year on, and lately of his sixty-nine years? And in his contemplation, he failed to understand his father's wish to make this last trip alone. Perhaps to prove that he could still do it, had what it takes yet, to trap through a tough season unassisted? It was suicide, he reluctantly decided.

To his father, Rayne mentioned the cold winter ahead, the gathering of firewood and the building of a winter hut, to which the crusty old McAllister replied, "I've got my buffalo hide, and no cold'll penetrate that. It's time you quit dragging me about this territory with you and hunt on your own." During that particular moment, McAllister could not look at his son, for he had created a situation his pride would not now allow reversed.

Their parting was swift, sudden and too cordial for Rayne, who had become thoughtful of the situation and determined that this moment must surely be as traumatic an experience for the old trapper as for himself. For Rayne it had been a lifetime of comfortable companionship together. Impulsiveness overtook Rayne and he raised a hand to draw his father's attention once more.

"Who thought up this separation?" he called along the shoreline. "Not I! Do you really wish to be alone? What if something happens?" An icy chill seized his spine at the sound of his own words.

McAllister scoffed loudly, reminding his worried son, "I have endured more trials in my time than you and ten like you together will in yours! Now be off with you!"

While that emphatic statement may have been stretching the truth, it nevertheless got the point across. For the first time in his life Rayne McAllister left his father and, against his better judgment, bid the old trapper farewell. He moved upstream alone, paddling toward the Natchuten Lakes. They had made their plans to meet in mid April at this same junction. Young McAllister's concern was not with his own safekeeping but with that of his father who now stood alone on the chilly riverbank, an arm extended upward in farewell.

Clad in elk hide tunic and breeches, wearing moccasins and leggings of moose hide laced up to his knees and a cap of fine beaver, Rayne flung a cape made from the sea otter over his shoulders and settled himself more comfortably in his canoe. In the ends of the craft he had stored his food supplies, bedding, extra ammunition, trade goods, ropes and traps. He placed his gun across the wooden bench and from his belt, hung the sharp knife encased in rawhide.

Fort St. James

As he disappeared up the river, thick with early morning mists rising to meet the warm rays of an autumn sun, Rayne McAllister was the true image of the fur trapper and trader of his era.

3

The long, harsh, bleak winter brought Duncan McAllister much loneliness without his son beside him. A strange emotional pain often assailed him. It was a feeling he had never encountered within himself before, not even when his wife died twenty-four years before in childbirth. Then, he had been caught up in the vitality of youth and the challenge which life presented to his adventurous nature. With his youth far behind him, McAllister now contemplated his lonely position and questioned why he had insisted that Rayne leave him.

Each morning when he went out to look into his traps, he wondered at the wisdom of his decision and the isolation of his life alone. As he plodded over the steep banks of crusted snow where his snowshoes hardly left trace of his passage, he wished for his son at his side. With hands stiff and painful from the bitter cold years of working in icy waters, he skinned and stretched the beaver he caught, lashing the hides tightly to the wooden frames with thin elk thongs.

As winter wore on and his supply of dried salmon and berries dwindled, the steady diet of boiled beaver meat gave rise to intestinal problems. He was forced to travel twenty miles downstream and barter for more fish with a group of Carriers camped there. But the Indians, too, were perilously thin as winter lingered, and could offer the lone trapper little more than six pieces of hard crusted salmon which had been over-smoked and which they were glad to give away.

He remained at their fire for one night. In the late, cold hours an old woman brought a cup of thin tea made from the dried shoots of juniper root sprinkled with a few crumbled pine needles for added flavour. A killing drink by McAllister's standards, he nevertheless swallowed it and was appreciative of its warmth.

When the woman had replenished the fire and left him, McAllister lay upon the cold ground wrapped in his buffalo hide. Watching the flickering red and yellow flames, he contemplated the Carriers.

Beside the campfire McAllister slept restlessly, his peace broken by the wanderings of his mind as it dwelt upon the people amongst whom he stayed and also by the aggravating, persistent barking of a camp dog which was soon quieted by the quick thrust of an impatient brave's knife. In the morning a small portion of the freshly roasted dog meat was offered to McAllister for the day's first meal. Although his stomach rebelled at the taste, the gesture of hospitality in the Carrier's kind sharing was not to be shunned and so was accepted with a gratefulness limited in enthusiasm while the curious Indians watched his every bite.

In two days, when McAllister returned to his own camp and checked his traps, he found them to be full. He interpreted this to be a sign that, after four seasons in their territories, the Carriers had finally accepted his presence among them. No longer would he be dogged by uncertainty regarding their temperament or the raiding of his traps. Essentially, he knew the Carriers were a peaceful lot if left alone but their hospitable disposition could at times give way to sudden bursts of violence when much blood would be shed for little reason. He had not actually witnessed such incidents. The stories had come to him second hand but he did not doubt them.

McAllister's movements among the Carriers had been relatively free of harassment and he was very grateful for their generosity with the fish. He determined that those six sheets of dried salmon may just save his life this season.

During the thaws of March, the snow was reduced by the ancient process of melting during the day and freezing at night. The river shoreline where McAllister had set up his winter camp became a perilous doorstep over which he must tread to reach his traps.

On the last day of March, while lifting a load of bales into his canoe, McAllister slipped on a rock. It happened without warning. His head struck the side of the cedar craft, plunging him into a state of dizzying pain. Unable to control his reflexes, McAllister slid into the water of the swirling river. He felt the cold surround him, encasing his body in its stiff, icy grip. He fought to catch hold of his canoe, but darkness overcame him and he slipped further into the river. Water moved along his chin, soaking into the thick beard as he suffocated into unconsciousness. His life was very quickly drained. The river claimed him.

One week later, some Carriers stumbled across the body of Duncan McAllister. It had been pushed ashore by the moving ice flow and left exposed to view. As the Indians stood over the body, discussing the incident among themselves, McAllister's lifeless, open eyes seemed to warn them to commit no mischief, to return his body to his son at the fort for proper burial.

Fearing the worst from their chief should their negligence bring a reprisal, the Carriers loaded the body of the trapper into a canoe for transport. The hazardous journey down the river now clogged with a breaking ice pack, took several days. Their arrival at the fort was almost unnoticed. As they paddled their crafts alongside the long, wooden wharf which jutted out into Stuart Lake, it was mid afternoon of the seventh day of travel.

Suddenly the sound of gunfire reached their ears. In the distance, toward the west side of the high palisade rode a small contingent of Hudson's Bay Company officers, guides, wranglers and hunters, preceded by a young bugler, who would soon fall into disfavour for the awful crackling sound which came from the instrument at his mouth. A deep, furrowed frown registered on the brow of the Chief Factor.

The Indians, now squatting in easy comfort on the wharf, watched with curiosity as the procession moved toward the fort. Fur-clad men and decorated horses clattered their way over the still frozen ground, around the corner of the palisade toward the main gate, to the accompanying sound of cannon fire from the corner bastion above them. Warily, the Carriers remained close to their canoes which were now tied to the half-submerged wooden pilings of the dock. In the bottom of one lay McAllister's body.

The time involved in getting the Hudson's Bay horsemen and the Company's Chief Factor, his wife and daughter, and the accompanying pack train into the enclosed and guarded compound of the Capital of the western fur trade, seemed immeasurable to the Indians. At one point in the elaborate proceedings they had almost given up hope of the ceremony ever ending and had considered simply dumping the old trapper's body and belongings onto the wharf and quickly departing.

Then suddenly a short, stocky man of middle age, garbed in a dark blue uniform with a wide belt of tanned elk hide tightened about his waistline causing him to appear ridiculously fat, stepped out into the open entrance of the fort. Upon his head was a hat of the finest beaver, below which tufts of thick, gray hair escaped, sticking out at the sides like frozen icicles. He was Chief Factor Adam Breen and he had just travelled from Fort McLeod, where the family had wintered, to take up his position as head of the western capital at Fort St. James. Standing with his gloved hands at his belt, his eyes searched out the faces of the five Indians who still squatted beneath their thick robes upon the wharf and who in turn, watched Breen.

With a wave of his arm, Breen signalled to a guard. When a young man, who had been at the fort for nearly two years came forward, Breen enquired, "This, I presume, is the entire Carrier nation which I was warned would be here to meet me! Treacherous and cunning, I'm told they are." Turning to the uniformed guard, he raised an eyebrow in mockery at his own words. "What is your name, young man?"

"Cairns, sir," he replied quickly, careful to remain at attention.

Fort St. James

"Well, Cairns, tell me-- Am I to be watchful of five old men cowering on the wharf beneath hides that must weigh a ton?"

Cairns moved forward. "Sir," he replied, "they are very young men who only appear old because their hair is long and their skin is burnt from many weeks in the glare of bright snow."

Breen smiled, snapping his gloved hands together against the cold. "And?"

"They're waiting for the noise to end and then they'll come into the fort," Cairns explained. "They have three canoes loaded with furs."

Abruptly Breen turned and strode away from the entrance. "Then tell them," he called to Cairns, "to get up off their haunches and bring their furs in here."

With some reluctance, young James Cairns left the main gateway of the fort and walked down to the lakeshore. He was tall and very thin in build, and it was at moments such as this that the more timid side of his nature gripped his imagination. When he strode the length of the dock and finally came face to face with the Carriers who had risen to their feet to meet him, the apprehension which he felt showed itself to the Indians. Cairns did not deeply fear them, but was uncomfortable being outnumbered five to one. He pursed his lips in an authoritative fashion and motioned for them to hook the bales of furs onto the cable which would move them up the bank into the compound of the fort. Then his eyes caught sight of the frozen body beneath the pile of furs. A sudden chill seized Cairns. His glance darted from the dead man to the Indians, then back to the canoe swaying in the shoreline wavelets.

The Indians went about the task of removing their own furs first, leaping in and out of their canoes, all the while tossing the huge bales from one to the other with an ease which made Cairns' muscles ache simply by watching the procedure. Envious of their agility, Cairns turned in a huff and left the scene.

Reporting to Factor Breen at his house that there was the body of a white man in one of the canoes, Cairns elaborated, "It is the old man, McAllister. His son went with him up the river into the Natchutens. But there is only one body in the canoe."

Breen waved an impatient hand toward the rail-straight Cairns who stood before him. "You don't have to stand on ceremony every time you're in my presence, lad."

Cairns relaxed, but remained afoot.

"Now, tell me," said Breen, leaning back against the chair and shifting his booted feet onto a wooden crate before him, "about the McAllisters. And where might we locate the missing one?"

However, Cairns knew nothing of Rayne McAllister's whereabouts and could only presume that, as the Indians had returned the body

17

of the father, they must surely have that of the son captured somewhere in the woods. Such a thought had penetrated his mind so sharply since he first glanced into McAllister's canoe at the wharf, that he now felt considerable relief in getting it out.

"Nonsense!" stormed Breen. "If they delivered his father to us, then they'll get word to his son. We have to trust to that, don't we? After all, they're obviously the only ones who know where he is."

Squirming to get greater comfort from the chair, Breen accepted a tray of tea and biscuits brought in by his wife who had entered the small room so quietly that Cairns had not realized her presence. When his eyes followed her departure from the room, they caught a glimpse of Breen's daughter near the doorway and were held fast by a bold return gaze. In quick assessment, Cairns reckoned her to be about eighteen.

Breen's commanding voice jarred the captured mind of Cairns as he instructed, "Now, go back down to the water and, in whatever language you can speak to them, tell those Indians to get the other McAllister back here to bury the old chap. Be firm with them."

As Cairns disappeared through the doorway, the Chief Factor was immediately converged upon by his young daughter. She had been listening at the door and now wished for all the details of the trapper's disappearance. The fact that none of the Breens were acquainted with the McAllisters mattered nothing at all to her. Having just that afternoon arrived at Fort St. James with barely time enough to arrange the tea tray, any explanation of the Indians' presence on the wharf during their arrival was a welcome interlude in what had been an uneventful morning of travel.

When James Cairns returned to the dock on Stuart Lake, he found that a crowd of men from the post had gathered to view the frozen body of McAllister which had been unceremoniously dumped upon the wharf along with his belongings and several bales of furs. As proof of their trustworthiness, McAllister's gun and knife, powder horn and ammunition had been placed on the planks beside him.

The five Carriers now strode boldly through the gateway of the fort to barter with their season's catch of furs with the storekeeper in charge of the accounts.

In the absence of the younger McAllister, Chief Factor Breen saw to the burial of the old trapper, laying him to rest in a shallow grave which had been difficult to dig in the partly frozen ground.

Seven days later, his canoe heavily laden with furs, Rayne McAllister arrived back at Fort St. James. In his absence, Adam Breen had descended upon the scene. McAllister was accompanied to the Chief Factor's office in one corner of his house by Cairns who, in the past week, had become Breen's right hand man.

Fort St. James

Facing the two, Breen studied their differences. Although Cairns' stiff, military-like presentation was admirable, McAllister's ruggedness was equally commendable. They were both the same age, of the same height and fair-haired. But there the physical resemblance ended. The solid, muscular structure of McAllister's build spoke of his long winters of toil and hardship along the rivers. The tanned contours of his face above the heavy beard showed a confidence that Cairns lacked. Beside him, Cairns appeared pitifully thin. He was an unusually handsome man with a ready smile and an eagerness to please, a spontaneity noticeably absent in the trapper.

Seldom did Breen rely on first impressions, but the Factor realized that with Rayne McAllister, the first one would be the only one. What he read in the trapper's expression as he was told about his father, was instant realization that a way of life full of companionship, reliance and trust had ended and that another, with its path unknown and alone, must begin. Adam Breen saw loneliness seize McAllister for only a moment, then guarded privacy replace it. There is intense independence in the man, he thought, and smiled. Breen instantly liked the trapper.

As he glanced from one to the other of the men before him, he felt bereft of further discussion and could only hope that he and McAllister would become friends. Not that the trapper needed him, Breen decided, but he was the dependable type. Where Cairns might place in their lives Breen could not determine. His glance went past them to where his daughter, who seemed always to be hovering near the doorway, sat at the parlour table, her concentration directed to the repairing of the accounts for the storekeeper who apparently had no idea what he had been doing to date.

Bouncing forward in his chair, for Breen constantly leaned back in it out of habit and not comfort, he rose to his feet and, in a kindly manner, dismissed both the young men from his quarters.

The absence of the old trapper from Rayne McAllister's life lent considerable significance to the decisions which he now faced. Hitherto, Rayne had simply followed the routes which his father had chosen, abiding by the old trapper's will and rarely contemplating what his life might be without him. Now a sudden emptiness tore at his mind and body. Although outwardly McAllister did not dwell in gloom, his mind was not easily rested by sleep or the soothing views of the serene lake and distant mountains which had always afforded him the solace sought in earlier times. There was a new kind of doubt, a self-doubt, a questioning of his worth and abilities. There was a growing awareness of the fact that for the first time in his life he was totally alone in the world. The vast wilderness which had always lent him inspiration was now empty and he silently mourned his loss. He felt, somehow, to be at blame.

Feeling suddenly as though he had been flung out into a great, empty void, McAllister now began to cling to the thin thread of friendship which was developing between himself and Adam Breen. Breen's family consisted only of the man's wife and daughter, but the homey surroundings of their dwelling compared favourably to the cold emptiness of his own small cabin. The friendship which they offered him was received with a fierce eagerness not ordinarily found in McAllister. Although he longed to hear his father's hearty laugh and to sing with him the cheerful songs of the canoemen, McAllister drew strength from the serenity of the Breen family. Of course, the electric presence of Willow Breen had been felt by the trapper and was not to be put aside by any downfall of heart over his father's untimely death.

One evening as they sat in the quietness of their parlour, Breen said to his wife, Emily, "I will offer young McAllister a job here at the fort. Perhaps in the store. If he doesn't accept that, maybe the pack trains will be more to his liking– he is a man of the outdoors." After some thought, he added, "If he takes the offer, he will stay. If he refuses, I know he will leave the north country. He has all the signs of a restless individual and will most certainly move on."

Emily Breen enquired curiously of her husband, "Why do you feel such concern?"

Without looking up from his papers, Adam informed her, "It may be that he will ask for the hand of our daughter." At this statement the handsome features of the dark haired Emily Breen instantly changed expression. Shock registered in her violet eyes, for her daughter had confided nothing of the sort to her.

"Really, really! I always seem so ill informed," she muttered in astonishment and stared reprovingly toward her husband. She felt hurt to have been left out of his thoughts until now. "The way of the west no doubt; secrets, I mean."

An understanding smile curved Breen's lips. "Willow is often in his company of late. And– he's made good friends with me. There's a message in that, as I see it."

"Well," Emily drew in her chin and stubbornly huffed. "I shall have to get it out of her, now won't I? I'll not be left up in the air like this!"

"As you wish," Breen consoled. There would be little gotten out of Willow. Breen knew his daughter well, recognized the stubbornness of her mother's character there, and was willing to bet a silver piece on who would win the round.

When the offer of employment with the Hudson's Bay Company was put to McAllister, Breen immediately sensed a withdrawal in the trapper. Also, to the Factor's great surprise, McAllister did not ask for Willow's hand in marriage. Have I, Breen now wondered, intruded too far into his mind, presumed too much of him? Perhaps I should have let him come to me. But then, that may never have happened, he assured himself. A difficult man to anticipate, Breen decided, as he half-listened to McAllister's explanation and plan.

The two men walked together the length of the long wharf which stretched from the lake up to the warehouse. Inside the enormous log structure were furs of all kinds, barrels of staple foods and wooden crates containing hundreds of trade items. Breen halted at the doorway, glancing into the dark warehouse for any sign of movement. No one was there.

Abruptly he turned to McAllister. "It could be a good life, you know. Conditions are improving all the time and really– a man has to settle down some time, don't you think?"

Inwardly, McAllister smiled. This old man has been leading me on. He's more cunning than I gave him credit for. "I'm going to go north this year," he told Breen. "I've learned something of the dialect of these Indians and, although I don't exactly trust them, I don't altogether distrust them either. Most of the time I feel comfortable enough among them." McAllister shuffled a foot idly against the boards of the walk and stood, hands thrust into the pockets of his tunic. "Maybe I'm not ready to give up the river and its freedom yet. It's a little hard to explain."

Adam Breen did not press for further explanation. "Well, it's not me you must explain it to. You've made sufficient impression upon my daughter to the point where, seeing the two of you together, it was not difficult for me to imagine you as a son-in-law and be pleased about the prospect."

The statement hung on the air long after Breen's departure from the warehouse. As McAllister saw the Factor's house door close in the distance, he made a decision to leave the fort as soon as possible.

Immediately McAllister began the preparation for the coming season of trapping. Although he had been attentive toward Willow Breen and realized feelings deeper than he cared to admit, McAllister did not wish to get married. He wanted to trap and live along the rivers and keep his life as his own as he had always done, free of encumbrances.

Throughout the summer months, he had watched the lovely, young woman move in her lively way over the boardwalks between the buildings. He had caught her strolling dreamily along the lakeshore in the shadows of a setting sun, alone and unafraid, her every move sensuous and commanding of his attention. Had he not followed her, talked to her, held her hand tight in his with a deep sense of longing and desire? With his decision, a sadness crept through him, leaving a new feeling of empty longing. The forces of his restless nature and his youth were at work inside him.

Sometimes Willow sat on the outside step of his cabin as he checked his canoe for cracks, oiled the leather straps of his pack boards, and mended the wide thonged snowshoes which hung on the wall near the doorway. Her soft voice and light chatter came to him as a soothing tonic to his frustrated mind, a mind which he now wondered at for having turned down the Factor's generous offer of employment.

In quiet moments, when little was said, McAllister studied Willow Breen. She presented a gentle beauty that he had never known. She had lovely, fine features and a flawless smooth complexion framed by softly curled locks of dark hair. Wide, gray, curious eyes watched his expressions, causing a strange uneasiness and an impulsiveness during which time he admitted his feelings for her.

"You're the only young woman in the fort and the Chief Factor's daughter at that," he said to her one evening. "And– your father seems to have taken a liking to me."

"That he has," she replied pertly. She sat before him, perched upon the top step of his cabin and seldom took her eyes from him.

There was something different about Willow this day, McAllister decided. Looking up from his leather work, he saw the confidence in her smile. Her dress was new. The full skirt billowed out about her ankles and lay in soft folds over the wooden steps, falling just inches away from his arm. The lovely scent of a lavender sachet tucked somewhere in the lace of the bodice came to him and was welcome relief from the odour of leather soap and hide grease.

He turned his attention again to his work. "Did you know that your father expects us to marry?" he asked cautiously, lest the remark sound suggestive.

"He is not the only one," she laughed merrily. "My mother is at the point of demanding it!"

He was surprised. "Because you spend so much time alone with me?"

"It does leave room for speculation, don't you think?"

McAllister looked up. "And you?"

Leaning over her knees, she searched his eyes and teased. "I cannot marry you if you do not ask me."

McAllister glanced away, unable to meet her gaze directly. Willow had gained control of their conversation and he resented that. "We've been good friends," he continued carefully. "Better than just friends. Closer, I mean. It bothers me that when the time comes and I do wish to settle down, you may not be here. That sounds a little trite, doesn't it?"

"Yes, and I may not be here," she warned in mischief.

A quiet moment ensued, during which McAllister considered the nearness of the woman. Suddenly, warmly, he confided to her, "I could love you." He turned to reach for her hand.

Willow smiled, confidence reigning, and got to her feet, leaving his confession floating on the air. While darkness descended, outlining shadows of the tall trees and distant mountains in graying beauty, Willow moved off the step and walked quickly along the narrow path toward her parents' house. The smooth, flowing movement of her small body and the slight swing of her full skirt soon became lost to McAllister's sight. What had he said wrong? Slapping his hat angrily against his thigh, he cursed, "Damn! Damn! Damn!"

Throughout the hours of preparation, the woman's presence in his life never left McAllister's mind. He traded with the local Carriers for new leggings, tunic and moccasins, and he filled the tins and waterproof moose hide bags with food supplies of dried berries, tea, salt, sugar and rounds of pressed grain, but Willow Breen remained always in his mind. During the restless sleep of nighttime, her image stayed close, floating across his weary conscience. Although he would leave her behind at the fort, McAllister knew he would someday return and that there came a time in every man's life when loneliness became unbearable and the beauty of a woman's mind and body an absolute necessity.

Realizing that she had placed herself firmly in the trapper's thoughts, Willow remained just out of reach, that even in passing, greetings had to be called out loudly, thereby drawing the attention of others.

McAllister was a big man, six feet and well muscled from a lifetime of paddling and portaging. His skin was deeply tanned from the weather. With his unruly fair hair, full mustache and searching blue eyes, Rayne McAllister, at twenty-five years was certainly a young man to turn any girl's head.

Willow Breen was no exception. Furthermore, she admitted to herself that she had fallen in love with him. To marry Rayne McAllister, for she was certain that he would ask her soon, would mean a lonely life at the post. However, this had been a possibility which she had accepted when she had moved with her parents to Fort St. James.

In Montreal, Willow had trained to be a teacher. Although her plans had been abandoned with the move west, the very fact that she was educated brought her way such employment as the operation of the fort necessitated. She soon took over the books from the storekeeper, whose only reaction was a sigh of relief, and managed all accounts with admirable accuracy. So she knew McAllister's worth, and he was far from poor. He was perhaps the best off on the post. But worth played no part in Willow's deep feelings for the trapper. It was the man himself who had won her heart and love.

At her elbow waited James Cairns. From the moment he had spotted her behind the disappearing back of her mother, James Cairns had decided that she would be his. He knew McAllister as well as anyone had known the man. It was a fact, in Cairns' mind anyway, that McAllister would be on the rivers all his life, as had his father. He had only to wait for McAllister's absence to make itself felt in Willow Breen's life. It would not be long before her eyes would turn to his.

On the eve of his departure from Fort St. James, McAllister walked with Willow along the shore of the moon-dappled waters of Stuart Lake. Keeping her small hand tight between his own, he held her arm looped through his, close against his waist.

After lengthy deliberation, he told her: "I want to spend the winters on the rivers for a while yet. I don't want to have a wife here or at any other trading post who is forced to spend half the year alone wondering if the Indians have my scalp or if I have frozen to death."

"The Indians are friendly," she teased him seriously. "I work with Father LeRoux among them. I do know them." When a moment tense with expectation passed between them, she could no longer bear the silence. Willow added quietly, "It's a harsh life you've chosen, Rayne. You've decided upon it over a comfortable life - as best as can be expected in this country - here at the fort, with me."

McAllister became pensive, a rare moment in his life. "Willow, I wonder if you really understand. Maybe I'm afraid of being trapped by the ordinariness of everyday living here. I think that's how I would come to see it. My whole life has existed out there." He stared toward the forest beyond. "I can't cut that off because your father has offered me a good job here or because I want to be with you. It would be like cutting away that part of me that belongs only to me."

Sliding an arm around her shoulders, McAllister drew Willow closer to him as they walked. "The roots of my feelings go very deep," he added thoughtfully, but doubted that she understood him.

"I'm happy with my choice," she whispered softly. "I don't understand yours." Looking up to the side of his face, she studied the firm set of his jaw and met his eyes when he turned to glance down at her. "I love you, Rayne. That will never change," she told him in a voice full of regret at his leaving.

Her confession succeeded in placing a greater blanket of guilt upon him. He halted, drew her body close to his, and held her there. The warmth of their closeness seeped tantalizingly through him. His blue eyes stared out over her head toward the beckoning wilderness beyond the fort, and the utter strength of its call drew him away from her and into the depths of its unpredictable freedom.

4

Before the sun's first brilliant rays, McAllister started up Stuart Lake, keeping out from the shore while passing along its length. He paddled his canoe into its river to begin the solitary life he had chosen for himself. Perhaps if he survived the dangers and cold of winter, it would be time to think about marriage when he returned to the fort.

The land was wild and forbidding. The evergreen forests which marched from the coast to the Rocky Mountains were inhabited by unpredictable tribes which called the plateaus their home. Winter in these forests caused great difficulty in the hunt for food for solitary trappers. But McAllister had been prepared for this way of life and so paddled steadily, fearless and expert in his occupation.

The river was quiet. The forest grew straight up from the water's edge, assuming a protective custody over the large body of water, forbidding any intruder to steal from its wealth. Occasionally small clearings appeared along the shoreline, giving evidence of seasonal encampments of the Carriers and Tsimshian. In this unfamiliar territory McAllister expected at any moment to hear the hiss of arrows winging toward him from the forest depths.

Upon his seventh day upriver McAllister pulled ashore for the night. The clearing before him was deserted, almost brooding in its abandonment. A row of five expertly carved totem poles reached toward the sky. The snow-spotted grounds appeared larger than other camps he had passed, indicating that a large party usually hunted from there. Cross poles of long dead campfires were still in place as were the several racks which facilitated the smoking and drying of fish.

McAllister struck his fire and carried out his evening chores. He felt now a great kinship with the early explorers who, more than three decades earlier, had travelled into this unknown land and managed to retain their life and sanity. While he admired their sense of adventure, he wondered at a courage which would lead men to venture blindly among Indian tribes whose way of life had for centuries remained unchanged, unchallenged, and almost impenetrable.

In the early morning, with mist rising in puffy, damp clouds from the icy water, McAllister moved into the river that would take him along the vast maze of streams and smaller lakes, deep into the northern canyons of the Carriers. His daring was unbelievable. He was accustomed to moving freely among the tribes through whose areas he travelled. In a rough manner he could get them to understand him. He had learned many of their signs and sounds. McAllister also believed that all Indians wished to live in peace and so could be bartered with if the procedure was conducted in a patient, respectful manner.

The canyons seemed to close around him as he left the more open country of Stuart Lake behind. The forest was dense and dark. He became increasingly aware of approaching winter. He kept in mind that he was now in unfamiliar country even if it was still Carrier territory and that he was probably one of very few white men who had ever ventured this far north for furs.

It was times such as this, when he paddled alone on the river and bore the brunt of seasonal storms, that he questioned the drive that continuously sent a nation of men like him into such hazards as could only befall a lone trapper. More especially this season, when all the comforts, such as they were in the northwest in 1830, could be had by simply remaining at the fort with Willow lodged in his cabin with him. To pit himself against the harshest elements and terrain and to live four or five months of every year in total isolation would drive many men mad, bordering on lunacy, he decided now. However, furs and the hunting of them had been McAllister's entire life. He knew nothing else. McAllister wondered at the spirit in himself, the acceptance of the challenge of such a difficult way of life.

The canyons he traversed opened onto a flat stretch of land surrounded by sparse growth of pine and spruce trees. A portage trail existed which caused McAllister several trips of hard work to get his small dugout and stores across. Beyond it began Babine Lake. Enormous, with a seemingly never-ending view of blue water, McAllister remembered having heard at the fort that its measurement had been determined to be over a hundred miles in length. Located on the southwest shore of Babine Lake was a large village of Carrier Indians. They watched him now, as he pulled his canoe up on the bank of the river. There was no doubt in McAllister's mind that his presence in their land had been charted since he had left the Stuart area two weeks before.

Thick curls of smoke rose from several fires in the village. A camp dog yawned and barked lazily at McAllister's approach. Children squealed as they played in the snow, but upon noticing the trapper, ceased their noise. Few totem poles were evident about the compound. Wood carving was not as well developed among the

Carrier as the Haida and Kwakiutl of the coastal regions, and their work was often only roughly cut memorial columns with poorly carved figures of the clan crest.

The peaked grooves of the Carriers' winter lodges, which extended into the ground, showed the spruce-bough covering used in construction. Fresh fallen snow quickly melted and the heat from the fires within escaped. From the semi-circular door of a dwelling located near the center of the compound, a tall, young Indian emerged. His husky build was emphasized by the bulk of hide and fur clothing he wore against the October cold. He stood with moccasined feet planted apart on the snow-packed ground. His hands rested tightly against his hips as he watched McAllister pull his canoe onto the icy shore.

As the Carrier were very strict in the matter of their traditional hunting grounds and even kept their boundaries at the attention of the Sikani, Babine and Chilcotin, McAllister was careful in his signs of greeting toward them. He knew the Carrier were not a warring people, but preferred to trade in a peaceful manner, so he had come into their land with good metal kitchen utensils, sewing needs, tools, cloth and tobacco should he need to bargain for his trespass or additional furs.

Remaining at the water's edge, the trapper waited for some indication that he should approach the village. None came. So, after several minutes of uneasy silence, McAllister boldly turned his back on the Indians and pushed the dugout back into the water. From the dwellings behind the young man who still watched the trapper, several Indians gathered in small groups. As McAllister paddled past them he saw their expressionless faces, thick lips which refused to smile and dark eyes that seemed not to move. It was as though they had never seen a white man before, but indeed they had. What was different about McAllister was that he was alone. The few white trappers to have passed their camp on the Babine route in previous years had travelled in pairs or in groups of four and five.

McAllister felt in no immediate danger, but a mild irritation as he paddled his canoe along the frozen edges of Babine Lake away from the Carrier village. Although McAllister lifted his arm and waved farewell to them, none returned the gesture.

Conflicting thoughts beset him. Why had they neither welcomed him nor shown aggressiveness toward his intrusion? What did they mean by passively allowing him onto their hunting grounds? Why was he not challenged in some way? The Indians themselves were in preparation of the season's first serious fur hunt, which would be followed by a period of rest during December and January before the big hunt of February, March and April got underway. The soft sounds of the paddle in McAllister's gloved hands were like a rhythmic dipping lullaby and although his mind saw again the firm stance of the tall, young man before the entrance of the door, questions of the Indians' intentions and his own safety in their territory soon vanished from his thoughts.

Keeping to the western side of the lake, McAllister turned his concerns toward the coming fur hunt, the preparation of his winter camp, and the catch of wild game he must store. The lake widened. Soon he could no longer see the eastern shoreline in detail. Only the snow-laden mountains rising sharply above it showed themselves in the early graying dusk. Around him in the dugout upon the water the air was quiet and crisp. As the late afternoon chill played about the thick fur collar pulled up around his neck, the trapper allowed the lovely image of Willow Breen to invade the privacy of his solitude. It was nearly the end of October.

Until the ice compacted and hampered his ability to travel the smaller streams, McAllister trapped along the Babine River and its relating ponds. The few pelts that he was able to catch were not so sleek and thick as in the late winter months of March and April when the ice melted and the animals emerged from hibernation.

In the new year McAllister was camped many miles from the great lake, up the long eastern arm, so far north that he wondered at times if he might become lost in such a wilderness. He had moved his camp twice. The farther away from the lake McAllister travelled, the more numerous were the hutches of the beaver. Small open valleys afforded ponds of such reasonable size as to house several families in one area. Prepared as he was for a freezing season in strange territory with every trick of survival kept in mind, he felt he had never known a winter so fierce. Although he had kept a constant watch for any surprise visits from the Carriers and Babines, McAllister spent the entire season undisturbed.

His shelter was a simple structure of logs and boughs placed at a tilt against a large natural hollow in a high bank. Over the wooden tilt were thick bear hides and deer skins. A low entrance was draped with another bear hide. The fireplace just outside the structure was partially below ground, surrounded by large rocks over which a long, narrow grate was placed to hold his cooking utensils. In this rude fashion McAllister lived out the fur trapping season comfortably, surrounded by the warmth of earth, hides and snow and protected by the fire which burned constantly at his door.

A systematic hunter, McAllister visited his traps regularly with little regard to the discomforts of winter travel on foot. A pelt of poor quality brought little gain in trading, so McAllister was diligent in his care of the pelts emptied from the traps. As soon as an animal was dead and dry he attended to the skinning, carefully scraping away all superfluous flesh and fat without cutting the fibre of the skin.

Beneath a protective shelter he hung the wooden stretchers strung with the prepared skins. Before leaving them to dry further, he methodically clipped the long hairs to turn a fine beaver pelt into a smooth, salable fur.

Not all the skins he took were perfect. Some were scarred, showing hairless spots on the hides. If he missed any days in his inspection of the traps, the skin could become tainted and unsalable. The exceptionally poor skins McAllister kept for himself, as he could make a blanket of them to place beneath his bedding or a rug for the dirt floor of the hut, already covered with bear hides.

As the long months of winter wore on, McAllister often allowed memories of Willow Breen to penetrate his mind and tease his senses. At first her image visited him only during the quiet interval of evening. Then, with recurring frequency the woman became so real to him that sometimes it seemed as though she were at his side, that he could hear her call to him. In his loneliness he would reach out for her in the night and find to his horror that his mind had once again played tricks with him, that Willow had been only a dream.

Was he going mad? Had the time come for him to end this lonely vigil along the ice-crusted river? As he sat in his hut in long hours of contemplation, he wondered if he should have accepted Adam Breen's offer and remain at the post, forsaking his freedom to roam at will. His mind reeled. Were not the soft, warm arms of the man's daughter open to him? And the love that he knew she felt for him, his for the taking?

In May, McAllister assembled his furs in each end of the canoe. The trinkets of trade were also secured. They had remained in their bag untouched during the season for the Carriers had allowed him safe travel without bargaining for their favour. In a small flat bag, McAllister hid the tobacco, placing it carefully along the inside of his shirt within easy reach should he need it for barter. The Indians did not place great value on their pelts in the very early decades of the fur trade. So, often they would trade several excellent pelts for the smallest amount of tobacco.

The trapper moved down out of the northern wilderness, along the river which emptied into the great lake. The Indians were all around him. His return passage through their land provoked much more curiosity than his arrival had seven months before. Possibly they had not expected him to survive the season alone, and his appearance fascinated them. Around his overnight camps they strolled at will, whistling signals to each other.

During the daytime they raced their light bark canoes up and down the lake directly past him, calling and laughing to one another in their language which they believed he did not understand. They even moved in close beside McAllister's own craft and made lengthy inspection of the provisions contained there, laughing and jostling about as though the whole process were a game. Four days of travel on the water and four nights camped along the shore held nothing for McAllister but a continual, though harmless, harassment. He refused to show any irritation.

Finally, as he canoed downstream past their main village, the presence of the Indians decreased, until he was alone again in the forested wilderness which was now basking in the welcome warmth of springtime.

5

McAllister's arrival at the Fort St. James post was hailed with enthusiasm by the other trappers who were just getting into the fort from a season of fur hunting. As he tied his canoe to the pilings of the wharf jutting out into Stuart Lake, McAllister's eyes quickly searched the gathering crowd for sight of Willow. She was not there.

Methodically he unloaded his camp gear, furs, tools and traps onto the thick boards of the wharf. Others came to help him. When all the bundles had been hooked securely onto the cable, the pulleys were set in motion and the entire lot of the trapper's possessions and bales was slowly hauled off the wharf, up the long causeway and into the storage shed within the compound of the fort.

As he worked with the other men, a growing feeling of disappointment settled over McAllister as there remained no sign of Willow's presence about the place. What was even more disconcerting was the lack of James Cairns hovering about the compound. Eventually Adam Breen, dependent lately upon a thick, black cane, left his house, stepped out onto the boardwalk and made his way slowly toward the storage building. The instant Breen's eyes turned to look into McAllister's, the trapper knew the truth about Willow.

He looked away from Breen. For a single moment, very private and desolate for McAllister, he stared unseeing across the vast body of water of Stuart Lake. The handsome countenance of James Cairns passed before his mind into his troubled thoughts and he knew he had only himself to blame for his loss. Certainly something infinitely sweet had slipped away from him.

McAllister pulled off his fur cap and ran his fingers through the long, thick strands of hair which fell to his shoulders. His beard, also lengthy, lay against the heavy tunic and, like his hair, appeared knotted and tangled. The weather was much too warm for the clothes McAllister wore. One by one he removed the articles from his body, tossing them into a heap on the boardwalk beside the warehouse. Clad only in his breeches, moccasins and a cloth shirt, the trapper felt relief from the warm June sun. His clothes reeked of the camp odours of wood smoke and animal hides, and of the months of skinning and cleaning the furs. Now the grime of travel and wilderness living piqued his own sense of smell.

He smiled at Adam Breen and nodded toward the support of the cane held tightly in the Chief Factor's hand. "Was there an accident?" McAllister enquired, choosing to ignore the message in the other man's eyes regarding his daughter.

"No, no. Just rheumatism and the like, getting at me in my old age," Breen replied, returning the smile. "They're mean winters out here in the west and I don't mind telling you I wish for better comforts than this bloody post provides. I think most of all it's the scarcity of food supplies that astonishes me." Nodding toward the load of furs moving past him into the shed, Breen said, "You've done well for yourself, I see."

"A good season, yes. I'm pleased." The conversation was of idle curiosities, an avoidance of the real question which must come from himself, so the trapper asked bluntly, "Where is Willow?"

Breen looked up, squarely at McAllister's troubled face. "Ah yes, our girl– gone with young Cairns, of course. Has a mind of her own, you know. Confided nothing to her mother and me." He attempted a smile. "Just simply announced that she had decided to marry and James was the man she had chosen. Before we knew it the good Father was over here and the thing was done."

McAllister remained sombre, unspeaking.

Seriously, Breen told him, "I'm trying to treat this whole matter as lightly as possible, but I see it's not working. I had hoped, Rayne, that you might be the one. But, in a rare reflective moment, Willow took me into her confidence and told me that you had indicated a desire to be free upon the rivers and in the mountains rather than be tied down to the fort, a wife and eventually a family." The Chief Factor shrugged his round shoulders with a hint of impatience over such choices. "Mind you, the home, the wife and family are all the normal things in life a man should want, but apparently you see things differently." He looked into McAllister's suddenly narrowed eyes. "God alone knows why." There was a hint of bitterness and disappointment in the Factor's voice.

"Differently?" McAllister raised an eyebrow sharply.

"Well, it seems to you that marriage represents a certain kind of captivity not entirely within your plans." Breen looked away to stare across the water of the quiet lake. "You will look back one day–" His voice registered his distress.

"I'm sure," McAllister muttered softly. Reaching down, he gathered up his bundle of clothes and strode off to the small cabin that he and his father had built eleven years before near the Men's House at the back of the Fort St. James compound.

It seemed to McAllister that there was nothing left for him at Fort

St. James. All the reasons he had previously given to himself for remaining at the fort narrowed down to one– the woman. Since Willow was gone, so might he leave. Trapping furs in one territory was much the same as in another in the west.

When McAllister had been at the fort ten days, Adam Breen walked across the grounds to the cabin in the evening.

The trapper met him at the door and Breen asked, "Will you accompany the brigade south with me?" The hope in his gaze revealed itself to the trapper. "I'm trusting that I'll be fit to travel. It may be that my chief trader, Southport, will have to go in my stead."

McAllister's reply was immediate. "Yes, I'll go with you."

"Thank you," said Breen and nodded approval.

"I thank *you*," added McAllister, feeling a sense of great relief that the decision had been spoken aloud.

The readying of the Hudson's Bay fur brigade, which would leave Fort St. James for the long trip south to the Columbia River, began.

Previous to the establishment of the brigade trail southward, furs were transported out of New Caledonia by canoe, east to Montreal. A lengthy, arduous undertaking of over four thousand miles, such journeys were hampered greatly by the extreme and rugged distance. Realizing the advantages of a route south, the Hudson's Bay Company pushed the fur brigade trail through the Okanagan Valley in 1826. Forts built at strategic locations along the route were used as collection depots for furs and stopping places. By the means of canoe travel and horse pack trains, the furs were moved out of the north, down the length of New Caledonia south to Fort Okanogan at the confluence of the great Columbia River and the Okanagan River. There the bales of hides were loaded aboard barges and transported down the Columbia to Fort Vancouver.

Rayne McAllister could not help but be caught up in the excitement and preparation for the brigade's departure. The two month journey along the rivers and through mountains of strange territory appeared as the new challenge he was ready for. Never once did McAllister contemplate a return to Upper Canada from whence he had come. He had adapted to this land, travelled its turbulent northern rivers, roamed its vast wilderness and had lived peacefully among its natives.

On the eve of his departure from Fort St. James, when his packs of traps, tools, bedding, clothes and stores of foodstuffs had been readied in bundles for the long journey, the trapper visited his father's grave. Although a full season of hunting had passed, the young man still missed the old trapper. He had been described by others with admiration as a plainsman, woodsman and mountain man. To his son Rayne, he had been the best kind of friend and guide. The courage which had always been displayed by his father was to remain a constant companion to Rayne. Although the warm, sentimental side of the senior McAllister had not been inherited by Rayne, his father's fine example of proud independence and total self-reliance would be with young McAllister all his life. After all, it had been bred into him. He would be a survivor.

Rayne wondered if he would ever stand at this gravesite again.

In the evening dusk Adam Breen stepped up beside McAllister and leaned on the cane. McAllister knew by now that Breen was unable to travel with the brigade and that George Southport would replace him.

"You know--" he began softly. "I can still see the disbelief in your eyes when I told you that I'd buried the old fellow. It was as though you thought it was someone else I was talking about, that this tough, old fellow would never die." Breen glanced up at the tall, young man beside him. "We all must go. It's the Lord's choice of how and when. And that brings me to my purpose of this invasion into your privacy at this time." He reached into his shirt pocket for the envelope there. "Now that he's gone, Rayne, you've your life to get on with."

McAllister smiled indulgently. "It's not the invasion I resent. I'm glad you came. Now, what've you got there?"

The Chief Factor replied, "A letter for you, if you want to use it. I cannot make the trip with you. As you see my hip is getting worse and soon I'll return to Montreal for care if I don't die here first and be rid of this fort at last. My chief trader is going in my place. If you wish, show this to my friend, Mr. Gordon MacKenzie at Fort Kamloops. He is the factor there and this will secure you a position of employment in his service."

McAllister was astonished. "A letter? But I don't need--"

"Take it, Rayne. And use it at any post. You won't be a trapper all your life, you know." The unspoken trust existent in their friendship showed itself in that moment as the young trapper reached out and took the letter from the Factor's hand.

"Thank you, sir," McAllister said quietly.

Breen smiled, clasping McAllister's hand in his own. "This is a ticket to a new life and may God go with you, son." The handshake was firm and full of meaning.

McAllister watched a little pensively as Chief Factor Adam Breen departed the gravesite. It had grown dark. Only pale lines of light remained veiled around the clouds above the distant mountain ridges. The air was cool and pleasant following a warm day. McAllister's eyes glanced about the compound of the fort engulfed in darkness. Only the few sounds made by restless horses in the nearby corral could be heard. To McAllister this quiet period of evening was the nicest time at the fort.

Before first light of the following day, the trip would begin. The noise of shouting men and the screeching rattle of the pulleys along the wharf loading the canoes for travel would fill the air. A lifeline in the economy of the fur trade from north to south, the brigade not only transported the valuable pelts to the Columbia River depot, but returned loaded with a year's supplies to fill all needs. It played one of the greatest roles in the rich harvest of New Caledonia.

On the eve of departure, McAllister enjoyed the quiet of the nearby forest behind his cabin and the calm waters of Stuart Lake. Shimmering in the light from the moon moving up from the far mountains, the lake lay in quiet wait for the morrow's cavalcade of canoes.

THE COLUMBIA

6

The trip made by the Hudson's Bay Company's fur brigade from Fort St. James south to Fort Okanogan on the Columbia River took seven weeks. There were eighteen people in the party leaving Fort St. James that June. With a warm northern sun at their backs and the lively, inspiring songs of the canoemen riding on the air, they embarked on the routes of the Stuart and Fraser waterways to journey by canoe down to Fort Alexandria.

The country opened out to wide flat plateaus, then delved unexpectedly into deep forested canyons. McAllister felt that he had never seen such natural beauty in all his life, for he had been used to narrow rivers and dark, deep forests surrounding even the largest lakes. Here, in the interior of New Caledonia, small lakes were formed in a spacious setting of meadows and marshes beneath clear blue skies, where an early rising sun glistened upon the still clear waters and filtered through the open spaces of the trees to the forest floor.

At Fort Alexandria the rich cargo was loaded onto pack horses and the brigade formed to follow the trail all the way to the junction of the Columbia and Okanagan rivers. Organization of an almost military nature was the order of each day. At the head of the colourful procession rode the Hudson's Bay Company's Fort St. James chief trader, George Southport; a tall, thin man who rode with his back as ruler-straight as when he walked. Below the curled, waxed ends of his mustache was a mouth which never smiled and opened only to bark an order or reply to questions in a terse, clipped manner. He was not liked among the men and totally avoided by the Indian women in the party, who were there because their menfolk were part of the horse wrangling crew.

Beside George Southport rode the flagbearer who deftly slid the British Ensign into place at his saddle, raising the flag to be caught up with the crisp, morning breeze. The commanding sound of the bugle broke the stillness. A cavalcade of great riches in huge packs upon the horses, the men of the Hudson's Bay Company, their guides, wranglers and those families who chose to travel with them, moved away from the camp onto the valley trail.

From Fort Alexandria to Fort Kamloops the temperatures had been very warm, but now, following the brigade trail down into the narrow Okanagan Valley, it was cooler. Evenings spent resting beside campfires were rewarding following a gruelling day of travel. The Salish Indians of the valley were accustomed to travellers passing through their territory and stood in watchful silence as the brigade passed by.

Sometimes McAllister witnessed communication between the brigade leader and some of the inhabitants of the villages who came to the designated stopping places to leave their furs and trade. When he later questioned George Southport about these conversations he learned that not only did the man understand something of the Salish tongue, but that several of the bands of the Okanagan and Lake could speak a bit of French. The French-Canadian traders who had bargained with them could not help but influence the spoken Salish language.

"Of course," said Southport in his crisp British accent, "sign language is the best. Sort of universal, you might say."

Seated beside Southport near the fire, the trapper pursued the subject. "One of the Indians with us tells me that it's called Chinook. The language, I mean, that you talked to them in."

Without turning his head and looking at McAllister, the Chief Trader sneered, "I don't know how he'd know, since he comes from a northern tribe."

"Well, apparently," McAllister told Southport, "he's been down this trail several times already. Every year. Down and back with the brigade."

"Hmm," was all that Southport replied as he lit his pipe, filling the air with the sweet, pleasant odour of strong tobacco.

Although the topic keenly interested the trapper, he did not carry the conversation further. Having just spent several years in the land of the Carrier and Babine Indians where one did not venture into communication until it was absolutely necessary, McAllister considered how difficult it might be to communicate with the Salish.

It was from the other traders that he learned beaver, muskrat and lynx were plentiful in the valley.

The following day the colourful train of men and horses halted their travel at the Brigade Overnight Camp on the west side of Great Okanagan Lake. It was raining. Although the dampness was welcome relief from the hot sun and dusty travel of the day, it made camping wet and uncomfortable. The handling of the huge packs was a miserable chore even on a dry day and many of the men were irritable from the long weeks of hard work and trouble with difficult, green-broke horses. The brigade had taken on additional bales of furs at Fort Kamloops and exchanged most of the horses. The line of pack horses now stretched to more than three hundred, with several new wranglers to manage them.

Despite the rain, their arrival at the Overnight Camp had been heralded with the customary bugling, accompanied by a loud skirl of bagpipes. Curious, watchful Indians who had come to witness the arrival of the brigade, scattered into the trees at the shrieking sound, then disappeared completely as darkness settled over the camp. The Chief Trader's campfire had been the first to be lit and his tent pitched before any of the others' accommodations could be met. A large cleared area, the camp not only provided plenty of forage for the animals, but ample room for men, equipment and the furs.

At this well chosen site, the brigade rested for three days. The Indians in the valley met with Southport to carry out a brisk business in furs and trade goods. On the return trip, stores would be loaded at Fort Okanogan and the agreements of earlier trade with the Indians, would be honoured.

The round trip could take up to half a year, depending upon weather conditions, hazards of the route, and time spent at the forts. There was also the matter of providing meat for the men and families in the cavalcade. While the horses rested and grazed in the pastures and trade was carried out between Southport and the bands of the Okanagan Salish Indians, the brigade's guides combed the hills for game.

As McAllister sat one rainy evening near the fire in the company of the guides, the question was put to him, "Why didn't you stay at Fort Kamloops? You could have a job there."

After a thoughtful moment, he told the man, "Trapping's been my life. I know no other way." He considered the question an invasion of his privacy and wished not to further the conversation. He rose to his feet to leave the fireside.

"It's a matter of settlin' down," the other man interrupted McAllister. "You gotta stop sometime. You're at the end of the trail at Fort Okanogan, you know."

"I'll stay there awhile then." The trapper wished to be gone from this scene. Such enquiries into his privacy irritated him. But the men seated about the fire drew him back to their conversation.

"The winters here are mild. The furs are plenty. And even better, the Indians are friendly enough." The guide glanced across the flames at the trapper. "You're a hell of a private man, I'll say. A loner."

McAllister wondered aloud, "I can't help but think there must be more whites in this valley than there appears. Yesterday only four trappers showed up with furs. The Indians brought in dozens of bales. If there's plenty of beaver here and other furs, why aren't there more white trappers?" He paused, then added with a raised eyebrow, "If the Indians are friendly, as you say."

Beside him another guide replied quietly, "There will be. Give it time. This trail's only a few years old. Being that the Indians here're friendly and we're breaking trail through, the traders'll be along in due time. Twenty years ago there weren't nobody up north either. This here's 'tween two big forts with a rendezvous at Soi'yus, so the beaver ain't likely to go unmolested for long."

Not entirely convinced, McAllister nevertheless resolved to give the Okanagan Valley serious consideration as to its trapping potential.

The trail south along Great Okanagan Lake touched the water briefly before being forced to climb, ascending sharply onto the benchlands above. But even here deep ravines and outcroppings of solid rock cut through the flat lands, forcing the brigade to turn inland toward the higher mountains. Streams swollen with spring runoff washed deep cuts across the rough trail. Canyons had to be skirted. The party finally made camp near a rapid stream and planned an extra day's rest.

The following morning George Southport, accompanied by a scout, a wrangler leading two pack horses and Rayne McAllister, followed the creek down the canyon toward the southern most shore of Okanagan Lake. Entering from the foothills of Beaver Creek, they touched down onto the flats of the Okanagan Indian village of Penti'ktEn, guiding their horses between the trees toward a second, smaller lake. Here Southport would barter with the Indians for their furs in exchange for large Hudson's Bay blankets, cooking utensils, tools and glass beads and buttons.

While Southport conversed and bargained, McAllister walked along the lakeshore. The sun warmed him. The sounds of waterfowl and their young hidden in the marshland filled the air. The lake was calm. A sense of peace swept over him in this tranquil setting. When the men of the brigade arrived, the Indians appeared pleased over the intrusion into their midst. Although they stared inquisitively at McAllister's mode of dress, for it was the same as their own, none ventured conversation with him.

McAllister was suddenly aware of his attire. He was one of the few men in the train dressed completely in Indian fashion, with tunic, breeches and moccasins of elk and moose hide. His hat was the customary beaver fur and hung at the side of his saddle. The weather was much too warm for the wearing of it. At the back of his saddle he carried with him the old buffalo robe, and because of it, he was the only traveller who did not suffer the damp chill at night.

When the furs had been brought to George Southport and the exchange completed, the small Hudson's Bay party settled themselves for the night.

As McAllister rolled up his pack the following morning and

saddled his horse, a curious young wrangler working beside the trapper asked, "Where did you get the buffalo hide? I never seen one before." He was hardly more than a boy and McAllister's own youth, when he had first arrived at the Fort St. James trading post with his father, was brought sharply to mind.

"My father," said McAllister, "traded with some Cree Indians of the Plains when I was a wee tyke and ended up with two of them."

"What happened to the other one? Sure would like one of them. Crees, you say?"

"My father was buried wrapped in his. You can get a good bear hide and do near as well. Keep an eye out for a grizzly and aim well with your gun," the trapper advised with a smile hinting of tease. "And you'll be warm for life."

"Ain't no grizzly down here."

"They tell me there is. You keep your eyes open." He pulled the saddle cinch tight, looping the strap through the metal ring, and tugged it into firm position.

The young wrangler leaned idly against his horse, doubt clouding his eyes. "You're joshin' me!"

"Like I said, lad, keep your eyes open. They're a big brown bear with a ruff-like collar around the neck--"

"And they're vicious as hell!" came the quick reply.

"Well--" reminded the trapper, "they make a good warm bed to sleep on."

Before the brigade had completely broken camp and departed from the lake area, a significant incident occurred.

An old woman drew close to his horse, reached up and touched an otter skin, the edges of which hung out from McAllister's pack. From her brown, round face, wrinkled and dark with age and many years of working under the blazing sun, her black eyes smiled up into his.

"Mika kumtux Chinook?" she asked softly.

McAllister replied in French, "non," that he did not understand the Chinook language.

A composition of words from the French and English languages and several Indian dialects, the Chinook Jargon served as an international language in the west. Certainly in trading with the Indians of the New Caledonia interior and south, it was the only language spoken with any fluency between parties in trade. The Chinook Jargon had begun as a compromise of the two different languages of the Nootka Indians of the Pacific coast and the Chinook tribe of the Columbia River. McAllister had heard mention of the Jargon while at Fort St. James, but was not even remotely familiar with it. It was not a language of the northern bands in the early years of the nineteenth century.

Beside McAllister, the old woman indicated with her small hands closed and passed by each other before her chest, that she wished to have the otter robe. Although McAllister was smiling at her, he raised his right hand in front of his body, then swept it downward to the right, indicating to her that he did not wish to trade for the robe. He turned then and called to Southport for assistance.

George Southport crossed the ground between them with quick, impatient strides. He was immaculately dressed in a blue suit, white shirt and tall, black hat, which all seemed ridiculous on a stifling hot and dusty trail.

"Here's a chance to use your Chinook," McAllister told Southport.

"And a chance for you to learn it!" snapped the Chief Trader.

McAllister ignored the man's sarcasm. "She wishes to bargain for the otter robe."

"And you don't want to, I take it. I see she has a deerskin waterbag and a fine looking fringed suit there." Southport stared across at the trapper, waiting.

McAllister replied quickly, "I'll trade cloth, beads and sewing needles. Or, if she wants, a silver bracelet, for the waterbag only."

Southport stepped toward the old woman, indicating the deerskin bag. "Le-sak," he said bluntly to her. "Trade klikwallie." He then raised two fingers while circling the other hand around his wrist. "Two," he added sharply.

The old woman shook her head, her long braids swinging from side to side. She touched the otter robe again. "Ne-nam-ooks, nike--" Launching into a lengthy and animated story using her hands to demonstrate basket shapes, neck beads, moccasins and other clothing, the woman told Southport of all that she would trade for the otter skin. She spoke so fast and in such low tones that Southport had to lean down and concentrate fully. The woman's wide grin indicated the end of her story and satisfaction in the belief that she had made a deal with the silent trapper.

However, Southport did not agree. "No," he said, listing McAllister's other trade items to her in place of the otter pelt.

The Indian woman retreated and sat down on a rock near the bank to think.

"Well--" Southport said with an impatient sigh. "She tells me that the tunic and breeches were made by her niece who is a very famous weaver and clothes-maker in the valley. She made the waterbag herself. But her niece, she says, whose name is Nahna - as if it matters - will be very hurt that somebody as handsome as you refuses such a beautiful suit." Southport suddenly drew his handkerchief from a pocket, sneezed loudly into it, cursed the chill he must have gotten during the night and said with further impatience to the trapper, "She'll be back here in five minutes and will take the bracelets. Two, by the way. I hope you have two of them," and he strode off, his back stiff as a board, as if he were on parade.

At the edge of the campground McAllister could hear him directing the last details of loading and preparation for moving out. His crisp, military phrases bounced on the early morning air. Southport seemed as totally oblivious to the harshness of his voice as to the unbearable arrogance and belligerence riding on his stiff commands to the men.

True to the Chief Trader's prediction, the Indian woman was once more at McAllister's side and handed him the deerskin waterbag. Without smiling now or indicating any pleasantries, she quietly accepted the two silver bracelets from the trapper and quickly walked away from him without a word. As McAllister tied his packs firmly over his saddle he could hear again the name, "Nahna–" as the old woman conversed with the other women of her village. The name imprinted itself in the trapper's mind, although it could mean nothing to him. Three more years would pass before he would hear it again.

At a shout and wave from the authoritative Southport, McAllister mounted up and joined the others, now moving slowly out onto the trail which took them back up into the higher levels to rejoin the brigade. Ahead of him rode Southport on a fine looking black horse that danced back and forth across the trail. From polished black boots laced over the legs of his breeches to his knees, to the tall black hat upon his head, the man portrayed the Hudson's Bay Company Factor at his finest. The bugle was blown as Southport galloped to the head of the train of over three hundred horses.

A rise of steep bluffs from shores of deep waters on either side of Lac du Chien, proved to be a great obstacle to the train. A smaller lake to the south amidst a great series of bluffs which walled the narrow passage forced the brigade to remain on the trail along the higher benches of the valley. Passing far west the pack train moved across the flats above the Okanagan Indian village of Sxoxene'tk^u (Shoshen-eetkwa) at the southern end of Lac du Chien.

The country was heavy with tall antelope brush and the lower sagebrush, and dotted with thick stands of Ponderosa Pine. Groves of tall poplar and willow graced the small ravines of open slopes where streams flowed. Small ponds, grassy meadows and high ridges abounded with deer, bear, bobcat and lynx and the occasional cougar. Consistent creeks harboured beaver and muskrat.

Considerably west of Lac du Chien the brigade halted at an old Indian campsite near the junction of their trail and Nipit Lakes. Clear water, open meadows of tall grass for the animals, and shade made the stop most desirable. A feeling of contentment prevailed there.

McAllister took advantage of the remaining daylight hours to explore the territory and came across the remains of substantial Indian encampments. The following day he rode out in search of game, choosing a well trodden trail farther west, down out of the draws, and discovered a wide river swollen with spring runoff, plunging its way southward. Sitting atop his horse, the trapper pondered this sight. Two great rivers almost in the same valley, divided only by a high ridge, meant that surely at a distance to the south the waters met and became part of the powerful Columbia. The area seemed to draw the trapper to it. On impulse, he did not wish to leave.

When he said this to the wrangler named Rawlings, whose horse McAllister rode, the other informed the trapper, "Neither can you stay. Look up. There's nearly always clear skies here, sun in the day, water in the hills year 'round, grass for horses and cattle. But– you need more'n the pack on your saddle right now to stay here."

"I have everything I need and there's obviously plenty of game here. I'll catch you for more supplies on your way back."

Rawlings smiled although his expression was gloomy as he glanced across at the trapper. "If you survive the rattlesnakes and scorpions. 'Course, many a man's cooked them up too, in a tight spot for food." He reached out and clapped a hand on the younger man's shoulder. "No, McAllister, you'd best come with us. Go down to Fort Okanogan and see the big river, watch the barges, meet the folks there. Don't stifle your life with hoar frost on your beard and smelly beaver skins just yet. You're too young. There's only a handful of whites in all the length of this valley and that isn't many for the miles or against the number of natives living near you. Not a hell of a lot's known about the Indians yet. They don't mind us packin' through here, 'cause they need our trade just as much as we need theirs. It saves them travel that lasts a half a year. Tradin' with them when you're passin' through is a different matter to living with them year round. Think about it, then pack up and be with us in the morning."

Approximately seventy-five miles of the brigade trail lay in the Okanagan Valley. When it reached the last lake in the great, long chain of lakes, the trail passed the narrows near Soi'yus, the fur men's rendezvous site close to Nk'Mip (Inkameep), a small village of the Okanagan Salish Indians. It was here at the south end of the lake, that the crossing by the brigade was conducted and from there the men and horses then travelled along the east side of the Okanagan River south to Fort Okanogan on the banks of the Columbia River. Continuing through the narrow McLaughlin's Canyon, the party broke onto lower grades, into a brush country of sandy terrain. This provided easy travelling for the horses and almost restful riding for the men of the enormous fur brigade train.

When the brigade reached the confluence of the Okanagan and

Columbia rivers, McAllister's decision was made.

"I think I'll go back with supplies and trap a season in the Okanagan," he told Rawlings positively. In the summertime I'll go on up to Fort Kamloops, or back down here to Fort Okanogan, to sell my furs and get supplies."

"Now that makes sense," Rawlings told the trapper. "Just remember, don't let anybody tell you that the winters around those lakes up there aren't cold. They can be tough to handle. It's a different cold than up north. I've been there, son, so I can tell you. Dig a good hole in the bank, cover your doorway with a thick bear hide and keep your fire alight all the time."

McAllister contemplated Rawlings a long moment, watching the old traveller strike a match to light up his pipe. He considered the worth of reciting his own experiences, but decided against it and listened in silent attentiveness to the veteran wrangler.

"If you insist on livin' up there, remember, don't trust the natives or you'll find one of their arrows in your back. They accept us as a group, but not one of us alone." He grinned. "Unless of course, you marry one of 'em. Good thought, McAllister? It has its advantages."

Memories of Willow Breen suddenly sprang into the trapper's mind. Her lovely image danced lightly in his brain and he wondered, did she ever think of him as he did of her so often? And James Cairns, was she happy with him? Cairns had been sent north to the fort at McLeod Lake to strengthen trade with the Indians and assist the Chief Factor with the management of the post. Willow had gone with him. Other white women and their families were housed at the post. With the many Indian wives and children of the traders living there the population was now nearly two hundred. Living standards at Fort McLeod were much improved from its earlier days when it had the reputation as the most wretched place anyone could be posted to. McAllister could not blame Willow for relocating with her husband. There was certainly more companionship at Fort McLeod.

McAllister cleared his throat and spoke quietly to the wrangler across the fire from him. "If marriage was something for me, I would have taken the matter seriously before now. There was an opportunity once..."

Rawlings studied McAllister's solemn countenance in the dancing light of the flickering flames before them. When a moment had lain silent between them, Rawlings finally said, "Well, I'd like to tell you– there ain't no comfort like that which a woman gives a man. Life is meaningless without love. It don't sound right coming from an old veteran of mountains and trails like me, I know, but my boy, I've known love and the loss of it and the life before and after it. Don't let it pass you by, McAllister."

Long after Rawlings had crawled beneath the covers of his

bedroll, the trapper stayed alone beside the fire, buried deep in thought.

This night was McAllister's time to know the loss and heartache of his choices. He now craved to hear some word of Willow. What was it that drove him, season upon season into the mountains, along the winding rivers and amongst the Indians in search of the beaver? The answer was that he knew no other way of life and was reluctant to accept change. He had cultivated no other close friendship than that of Adam Breen and now even that had been abandoned.

An empty feeling seized McAllister as his eyes followed the flames about the fireplace. Father was wrong, he now decided. A man cannot live entirely alone without knowing someone who cares about his existence. The trapper saw the difference in his father's life; he had the company of his son. "Of course," McAllister whispered to himself, "he always had me. I have no one."

With that sad and lonesome realization penetrating his mind, McAllister crawled beneath the robes of his bed upon the hard ground. Looking up to the night sky, he located the stars of the Great Dipper and soon fell asleep.

When the fur brigade reached the wide, sweeping Columbia River, several barges were waiting to be loaded. French-Canadians in vivid red caps and wide sashes went about the task in joyful mood, filling the air with their songs of the river. They were the true voyageurs of their time, men employed by the fur companies to work in the transport of furs and supplies by water. Their ability with canoes, rafts and barges seemed as natural to them as breathing.

In short order the barges moored at the Fort Okanogan docks on the Columbia River were loaded with the enormous cargo that had just been transported over a thousand miles by canoe and pack horse. With a call of "Bon voyage!" from the crowd gathered on the shore ringing in their ears, the boisterous voyageurs cast off and the heavy barges swept down the great river on their journey toward the Pacific, to Fort Vancouver.

McAllister watched the departure of the convoy with a touch of envy and emptiness. There seemed meaning to the lives of the men on board and they shouted it to the world. The nostalgia which had seized his thoughts the evening before had not left him. For a long while the trapper stood alone on the low bank of the Columbia and watched the passage of the barges until they were only tiny dots upon a glistening horizon.

7

The Colville and Sanpoil Indians, their lives controlled by the topography of the country, followed timeless patterns of living; fishing, hunting and trapping furs. During the summer they moved into the high mountainous areas of the Wenatchee and Cascade ranges for berries and roots. By winter they had returned to the rivers and low plateaus of the Chelan, Methow and Okanagan Valleys.

Fort Okanogan was situated amongst their villages. On a flat space of land along the wide banks of the Columbia River, the fort consisted of two long rows of buildings just above the water where the annual barges arrived and departed from the long dock. Adjacent to the row of warehouses and stores were several small structures of rough hewn logs, housing men engaged in the trade and transport of supplies and furs. Those who did not live in the Men's House, but who had taken Indian wives, lived apart from the others.

One such individual involved in this commerce was a tough muscled, experience-minded Frenchman. Six years before, Evan Dubrais had come up from Spokane House east of Fort Okanogan. According to him, virtually every bone in his body had been broken or damaged in some way, either by accident, foolishness or torture. When he held court among the small number of residents at the fort, his lengthy stories lent a certain measure of mystery mixed with the authenticity of his scars, and left the listener bereft of any doubt about the truth.

The miracle responsible for his survival, he claimed, was his cold-blooded way with a knife, his accuracy with a gun and his ability to talk his way clear of damaging situations. Also, a good travelling and hunting companion was an advantage. He had, he said, the best of them all with a trader named Conager. Dubrais not only enthralled his two young sons, but completely captivated the imaginations of grown men, hungry for entertainment in any form. Among the gathering crowd on the storefront platform enjoying a warm evening at the Fort, was Rayne McAllister.

Evan Dubrais was quick to spot the newcomer and in no time singled the trapper out. Enormously tall beside the bearded

Frenchman, McAllister walked with him to the Men's House at the river's edge.

Waving his arms through the air in a gesture of impatience, Dubrais informed McAllister, "You can't just come down here and set up camp anywhere you like, you know! Your scalp is at stake and you'd best be keepin' that in mind. Even when you sleep, do it always with one eye open. I know more about your Indians up there than you do about ours down here and I tell you, not much peace lies at our door."

McAllister did not wish to argue. It mattered not whether Dubrais knew of his own experiences with the tribes up north; he doubted the little man would believe him anyway.

He remained with Dubrais in Fort Okanogan, having become so accustomed during the summer weeks to the relaxed comfortable way of life at the post and the congenial atmosphere created by the people there amidst the great bustle of activity with the fur trade, that he was reluctant to exchange it for the quiet loneliness of the river again. The talkative little Frenchman had considerable influence on McAllister's decision to stay, if only by the fact that it was simpler to go along with his ideas than to try to shut him up. And Dubrais, indeed, all but set McAllister up in employment with the Company at the post. The barges which plied the great waterway of the Columbia River always needed tough, rugged men experienced in water transport and in Dubrais' eyes, McAllister fitted in admirably.

However, by mid-August Rayne McAllister had become seriously ill. Suffering excruciating pain, every bone in his body seemed on fire. Delirium constantly muddled his brain. He remained in a weakened condition for four weeks, cared for by Broken Bone, the Nez Pérce wife of the jaunty Dubrais. It was not known what strange malady assailed McAllister and no physician resided at the fort for consultation. Dependent solely upon Broken Bone and the ancient medicinal remedies of her tribe, McAllister's life literally rested in the Indian woman's hands.

Broken Bone was a conscientious woman, compassionate and caring. She labouriously moved her bulk about the small cabin, admirably attending upon the trapper. It was easy to see how she came by her unlovely name. At some point in her life an accident had befallen Broken Bone, leaving her with a terrible limp. Despite her obvious handicap, an uncomplaining Broken Bone kept Dubrais' crowded log house in order, the couple's two lively sons disciplined and everyone well fed and clothed. Now, adding to her mountain of chores, was the care of the young trapper who rested beneath several quilts on her bed. His medicinal needs were never left unattended.

Everyone at the fort thought that the trapper would surely die. His incoherent raving, the lengthy periods of time he lay bathed in sweat, and his features swollen and red with a burning fever, lent a certainty to their prognosis that the trapper must have been bitten by a tick.

Occasionally Dubrais peered through the crack between the door and its casing, into the bedroom which he and Broken Bone had forsaken, to view the ill trapper. He forbade anyone else near, but his wife. He kept his sons completely isolated from the house, residing them temporarily with the storekeeper's family. It was Dubrais' contention that where one Indian could survive a plague such as the trapper seemed to have, ten whites would go to their graves. And for the first time in his life, being not able to recognize the exact cause of such an illness, he retreated from a scourge greater than he could understand.

His acute sense of reasoning told him that it was not the dreaded smallpox. The rash which covered McAllister's ravaged body did not have the ugly, pustule appearance of the smallpox plague. Much less, no one else had fallen ill. Indeed, as the days passed and McAllister refused to expire, Dubrais put his friends at ease as to the contagiousness of the fever.

When not at work the men lingered anxiously along the boardwalk of the company store for news of the trapper. Eventually they decided among themselves that it was the mountain fever known to be caused by the bite of a tick. There was some argument among the men, as the tick's season for feeding is primarily the spring months of March through June. It was now August.

However, insisted Evan Dubrais, it was some kind of mountain fever. He had found Rocky Mountain ticks on himself as late as September, and contended that McAllister's illness was certainly the Spotted Fever carried by those woodticks. He emphasized that during his years of trapping in the mountains he had come across men dying from the Spotted Fever, and now considered the trapper's symptoms to be the same. So that, in the year 1831, without a physician's proper diagnosis and advice, the little Frenchman's decision stood, right or wrong, and Broken Bone turned to the time honoured remedies of the Indians to save the trapper's life.

Each day when he was not at work in the warehouse, Evan Dubrais was dispatched by his wife to the nearby creek to bring back clusters of thin branches from the willow trees. From the dry pine forest he gathered bunches of yarrow, a low growing perennial of the sunflower family. With a small sharp blade held tightly in her hand, Broken Bone peeled the bark from the willow twigs, dropping the pieces into a pot of boiling water. From this she made a bitter tea which she forced past McAllister's swollen lips, in an effort to drop the high temperature of his fever. A nourishing broth brewed from the yarrow plant, dried, boiled and strained, was spooned between his lips to give him strength. With an apothecary's skill, she pounded the dried leaves of mint, comfrey and yarrow plants into a fine mix for another invigorating drink. Soon the trapper's high temperature began to drop and recovery was apparent.

When the fever broke, Broken Bone noticed a decided change in attitude of the fort's residents in her favour. No longer did the men of the post and the young people of her tribe stare at the sight of her, almost with a look of disapproval, as she limped past them. Now she was regarded as something of a phenomenon among them. For wasn't the trapper alive as testimony to her special abilities? Others would have died or become horribly paralysed for life. A miracle worker, perhaps, they wondered quietly; a healer gifted with god-given powers? Had she visited a Medicine Man of the Nez Pérce and received special instructions? No, she insisted to those who spoke to her, she was just another Indian woman who knew the value and the healing powers of Nature's gifts to the Indians. Miracle or not, the recovery of the trapper elevated Broken Bone to the exalted position of nurse in the surrounding area of Fort Okanogan.

With his round, barrelled chest puffed to its fullest with pride, Evan Dubrais now pompously strode the planks of the walkway and docks. An incessant verbiage poured forth on the value of Indian ways with herbs, roots and berries, not to mention the natural powers of healing which, he claimed, was the Indians' by birth.

Dubrais' praise of the Indian was short-lived, however, as he noticed McAllister's slow, but steady preparations for upriver trapping. He began then to expound on the Indians' mastery at torture and killing. Following McAllister about the compound, he bellowed warnings against such immediate adventure alone on the isolated paths of the Spokane, Snake and Clearwater Rivers.

"The Shoshoni will have you, you know. They know a sick fox when they see one, and they get rid of him!" Ceasing his angry pacing, Dubrais snapped, "You are not listening!"

McAllister set aside the packboard to which he had been fitting laces, turned and, facing Dubrais, gave the annoyed Frenchman his complete attention.

"I doubt," Dubrais admonished. "I doubt that you are ready for the rigours of a winter-seized river, young man! Your sick body has hardly healed and here-- here you are fitting the packs to your back! I can see the fever has affected your brain!"

Glancing around at the interfering little man who had become his shadow of late, McAllister asked bluntly, but with a smile creasing his face around his mustache, "Do you want to come with me?"

Dubrais began his pacing once more. "Of course I want to go!" Staring hard into the tall trapper's mirthful face, he growled, "But do

I have a choice? Who is to be here when they drag you back into the camp, stupid friend!" Leaning back, pushing his hands deeper into his baggy pockets, he laughed. "Ha, ha, ha! You need me, eh? Upriver maybe, but here, too. So here I stay and wait and remind you when they bring you back to Broken Bone for care. I have nothing more to say to you." He walked away toward the river to be alone in his frustration.

However, silence for long on any subject was not one of Dubrais' better qualities, and before long, when McAllister had loaded his supply packs into a new canoe, he issued another warning, "It is dangerous land through which you plan to move. You are going hundreds of miles away, when you do not have to."

"I have lived in the territories of the Iroquois, the Huron, Babine and Carrier," McAllister told Dubrais deliberately. "I don't believe the Shoshoni are worse than any of those."

From Dubrais, "You'll see! One season with them and you'll be back with everything lost!"

"There are ways of retrieving one's belongings," McAllister stated flatly, almost disinterested now in the views of the noisy, little Frenchman.

"Don't count on it and expect to keep your hide together!" snapped Evan Dubrais.

Following a lengthy silence, while the trapper mentally took stock of his provisions which were now properly assembled in the canoe, McAllister turned and smiled at the man he had come to know so well, owed so much to and genuinely liked.

"Your warnings do not go unheeded, Evan," he spoke softly. "My father was a trader of your time and I travelled with him all my life, so I know it's an old school I learnt from. I also realize that the situation with all Indians is not a lot different today whether you live in the east or New Caledonia, or here. I value my scalp much more than I let on."

As he stared at the young trapper, Dubrais' black eyes snapped in irritation. He wished the trapper would stay at the fort. The man was helpful about the place and good company for himself. Moreover, he was always thoughtful of Broken Bone. And, he told himself, my boys have much to learn from him. Then suddenly, as if he had tossed aside an unwanted responsibility, he threw back his dark head and laughed boisterously.

"Go then!" he yelled loudly. "Go to the mountains, the rivers, the lakes! I cannot keep you back from them. Go, see if we miss you!"

What strange privacy is it, McAllister questioned, that brings a man to deny the truth of his feelings for another? Of course he will miss me! Broken Bone and their sons will also. I've been under their roof for three months now! But, why doesn't he just say so, the trapper wondered, and wish me godspeed and good trapping, and simply call a farewell to me, "Don't freeze under the snow!" Instead, he carries out this constant badgering of threats, dogging my heels every step these last weeks, and promising me a slow death at the hands of the wily Shoshoni. But then, McAllister remembered, his father was often evasive, sometimes even cruel with his words in the making of the man from the boy, and never once told him that he loved him. Yet, he must have. Will I be the same with my son? McAllister suddenly ceased his contemplation. What son, he mused, sadly.

With a warm smile that reflected his feelings, he told the little Frenchman, "What a crusty old man you are!"

To which Dubrais replied with a hearty laugh, "You are barely half my age. Ah, that I would have had a son such as you to raise when I was young and spent my life following a miserable trap line through the bush! Oh, the things I could've taught you."

Warm rays of an October sun, the last of the season, spread out across the wide, rolling Columbia. Beside McAllister and Dubrais the powerful river flowed its turbulent path toward the blue Pacific, a long, great link in the fabulous western fur trade. It brought to McAllister's mind the river of the Okanagan that he had followed with the fur brigade.

He was now ready to leave Fort Okanogan. With his gun placed across his arm, the trapper stood on the sun-dappled banks of the rolling water and raised a hand to wave in Dubrais' direction.

Dubrais smiled, tugging gently at his gray beard in sudden, deep thought. "Ah, the optimism of youth," he whispered, remembering.

8

For the next three years McAllister trapped in the territory of the Nez Pérce Indians. Their hunting and trapping grounds were the benches and ravines in the plateau region of the Okanogan, Columbia, Snake and Clearwater rivers. It was a country of swift, turbulent streams. At the point where McAllister left the Columbia and entered the Snake River, low birch, juniper and willow thrived in groves along the shores and in the meadows. In the deep ravines and on the higher levels, tall pines reached above all but the mountains. McAllister chose to navigate the more passable Clearwater system.

A main tributary of the Snake, the north and south forks of the Clearwater River flowed west from their headwaters in the Bitteroot mountain range. Bleak granite landscapes rose from the river's edge. On the higher, timbered ridges, Lodgepole pine and spruce trees stood tall and straight. It was now the end of October and past the season for edible vegetation such as wild onion, squaw cabbage, and the rocky mountain bee plant. The leaves and flowers of this bee plant were delicious and nutritious when boiled. The large chinook salmon inhabited the waters of the Columbia and Snake to the Salmon River, south of the Clearwater forks, while the smaller streams abounded with colourful rainbow and silvery brook trout. Cut into strips and dried, the fish fit lightly into a trapper's pack and could last him an entire season. Supplemented with venison, dried berries and dried wild vegetables and rice, a man could live without knowing the near starvation that the northern fur men often endured.

Deer were plentiful in the woods of the plateau and, in the fall season, were in excellent form. During his hunting excursions Rayne McAllister often witnessed the Indians' procedure in bringing these defenceless animals down. They hunted in small parties, their moccasins skimming silently over the early fall snows, circling the herd. When the front line had sealed off the escape of the herd, the hunters rushed in from the opposite direction and brought down the animals in great numbers with their bows. Following a successful hunt, the braves returned to their camp to celebrate their achievement, while the women took pack horses and went out into the woods to bring back the meat.

The first horses of the Nez Pérce tribe had been traded with the Shoshoni Indians of the Rocky Mountains and Missouri River territory. It was the Nez Pérce who improved the quality of the animal, developing the spotted, or piebald horse, called the Appaloosa. In use for travelling, hunting, packing and trading, horses had quickly become the Indians' most valuable commodity.

McAllister hunted on foot, travelling the wooded benchlands in search of the small white-tailed deer which he cleaned and quartered at the site. With no horse to make transport easier, he had to load as much as his back could carry by packboard and, with a thick band of leather fashioned as a harness about his chest and waist and connected to the carcass, he dragged the remainder to his camp. It was tiring and difficult work. Consequently he was careful to hunt in areas clear of windfall and relatively close to his winter quarters at the river. If the snow was crusted, the task of pulling the carcass was made much easier. At his camp he prepared and smoked the meat. Cut into strips, it was hung over a rack constructed above a smudge fire of willow shavings. The pieces were then wrapped in cloth and hung from the branch of a tree close by his dwelling.

During McAllister's first winter along the Clearwater River he made a warm winter camp for himself. Lodgepole pine growing on the steeper hillsides behind his campsite were felled and trimmed. Cut into ten foot lengths, they skidded easily over the snow downhill toward the river. Against a large indentation of the bank, McAllister constructed a tilt of the perfectly round trees, fitting each hand-hewn log snugly together, interlocking them at the corners and chinking them with thick clumps of moss. Over the thin timbers of the slanted roof he tied the several hides of moose and bear reserved for such shelters. Bear hides also hung over the narrow doorway, while just beyond the entrance, a constant fire blazed in its rock pit at the side of a canopy, also of hides.

Occasionally small groups of Indians passed him when he walked his trap line. They rode quietly by on their small spotted ponies, along the shoreline, or crossed the river near his camp, splashing through shallow channels and up the icy banks. They left him undisturbed by visits, but watched his activities from among the trees and from the hilltops. Their surveillance of him did not last long, for by December they had become accustomed to his solitary presence among them and soon bored of this pastime. Contrary to Evan Dubrais' warning about the Shoshoni Indians capturing him, McAllister saw no sign of bands wintering in the area west of the Rocky Mountains. Only groups of Nez Pérce roamed near his camp. Not a particularly friendly nation, the Nez Pérce Indians kept to themselves.

They were first known as the pierced-nose Indians. As the pursuit of furs increased, bringing traders westward into the Columbia region, the tribe's name took on the derivative in the French language. Most of the traders and workmen of the fur companies were Canadians and the French language was the most widely spoken. Les Nez Pérce as they became known, were excellent horsemen. For a trapper to purchase a horse from them might cost nearly all of his working tools. Axes, shovels and adzes were the price of such animals, as were knives, guns, bolts of cloth, cooking utensils tobacco and liquor. McAllister needed all his equipment. In travelling by canoe, a limited amount of trade goods could be carried with his supplies.

Each year McAllister returned to Fort Okanogan in late spring with his bales of furs and met the barges on the Columbia River from the west. Every season when he had purchased a sufficient amount of supplies and prepared to leave the fort he was reminded by Evan Dubrais of the wild and terrible country into which he dared to venture. The tribes were unpredictable, he told the trapper, and should never be trusted. By the hour Dubrais recited such horrendous stories that McAllister marvelled that the Frenchman had been left thus far in life with his tongue unsliced.

However, to a man who knew little fear, these warnings fell on deaf ears. McAllister had never considered any Indian a great threat so long as he left them alone. He had learned from his father that, to get along with the Indian, a trapper or trader must move among the people in peace, not pester or cheat them, nor surprise them. His persistence in entering the same hunting grounds each year and the fearless manner with which he conducted his employ no longer piqued their curiosity.

Occasionally McAllister met other trappers and traders along the river who had with them knives, adzes, pipes, cloth and guns, but who foolishly traded their horses to the Nez Pérce for large and healthy beaver skins. They then were forced to build rafts and transport their bales and equipment downriver. Often they lost everything in the rapids and river eddies, and found portaging extremely difficult in the mountainous terrain.

McAllister seldom traded for furs. In the past he had bargained only when his passage seemed at stake, then dealt generously. He trapped alone, transported his bales of furs by canoe and travelled the rivers for hundreds of miles in relative safety. In the country of the Nez Pérce he had met with no interference, living in peace in their midst.

Nevertheless, during the third year along the Clearwater an incident occurred, giving McAllister serious cause to reconsider his bland acceptance of his safety among the tribe. Two

French-Canadians who had been trapping near the Snake River pulled ashore at his camp in late February. In detail they told him of a murder which had recently taken place barely forty miles downstream from McAllister's winter quarters.

McAllister listened attentively as they talked in both French and English, bouncing from one language to the other, relating their tale in hurried sentences. It was difficult to keep up with them, but instruction in his youth enabled him to feel the import of the Canadians' warning.

It had happened, the Canadians told him, that a party of traders, four in number, were paddling furiously downstream in an anxious attempt to pass quickly through an area of some unrest. While keeping diligently to the middle of the stream as was the custom of the canoeist, they were halted by several Indians who appeared near the water's edge indicating that the men should pull ashore. However, the traders pretended ignorance and paddled their fur laden crafts onward. One mile further they experienced the same beckoning to turn their canoes shoreward. When they did not heed the Indians' suggestion, a hail of arrows hissed across the water and one of the men slumped forward. Said one trader to McAllister, "Blood spurted from his head onto the bottom of the canoe!"

The statement was made with such exclamation that McAllister enquired, "Were you there?"

"Of course not! But hearing it is like seeing it first hand!" He extended his arm toward McAllister with his cup to be refilled with the drink which the trapper had brewed for them. "What is in this anyway?"

"Dried comfrey leaves from the ponds along the Okanagan River," replied McAllister. "It's good for a cough I've developed. What did the Indians want? They just don't kill a man in his canoe for nothing."

"Sacré! The furs of course! The cooking pots and all the tobacco and food and liquor they could find. They're starving now. And they're thieves, you know. Or– you should know by now."

"But they have stolen nothing from me," McAllister told them and became thoughtful for a moment. "Not one Indian has come uninvited into my camp. The first year that I was here no one came. Last year some of them came and traded for cooking pots and things. They had good furs and knew I would want them. This winter is not over yet, but I don't expect trouble."

"We do not have trouble either, but we never doubt for a minute that it's just around the corner from us," the second man spoke up. "It may be that the fight was in retaliation of something."

"I suspect so," McAllister agreed. "I'm sure we'll never know, but it's possible that some furs were stolen from the Indians with nothing left in trade."

The French-Canadians helped themselves thirstily to McAllister's hot tea and to the pot of cooked venison hanging over the fire. They were hungry and bit off large chunks of the meat, savouring the taste, and praising their host's ability to cook as well as they.

McAllister asked, "What happened to the men in the canoes?"

"They were kept sitting on shore in a state of suspense while the Indians held council above them on the bank. They squatted in the snow with their robes pulled over them. Quite a picture, I guess it was!" The trader laughed. "They call themselves braves! Who is braver than us!" At this, he grabbed his toque from off his head, swung it around several times and replaced it, giving it a firm pat upon his bushy, dark hair. "Thieves, they are!" he declared forgetting the possibility of the traders having committed a crime. "They emptied most everything out of the boat, traps and all and picked up one of the men and swung him into the river. The others ran into the water pulling their empty canoe and grabbed the man. Then they dared to go back and pull forth the second canoe right out from under those scalpers' noses! They got to hell out of there, I tell you. The story is real."

McAllister gave careful thought to the story. It probably was true; but what had happened, he wondered, to provoke such harassment. Again, he told his visitors, "There is more to this than what you know."

The two men looked squarely at the trapper. "By the time you go out and we go, they will all be on the move also. Maybe we meet and go together, eh?" suggested one of the men. "That's good advice." He tried to measure the trapper's character when McAllister's eyes met his own. The Canadian pushed his woolen cap down upon his head, waiting for his host's reply.

"I'll see," McAllister muttered. He tipped his cup, idly swirling the tea in the bottom. "I'll see."

The two men rose to their feet. "Think on it trapper. McAllister? Your name? You are known to us all, you know. Everybody says you will never die at the hand of an Indian, that you learned all their tricks and know their games. Maybe you are as smart as we. You are still alive and that is something."

McAllister cared not that they knew of him or wondered at his bravery. He wanted to ask them if they had been up in New Caledonia and what news they had of Adam Breen, but more, of Willow. He stood up and walked around the fireplace to where they were. "Have you been up in Fort Kamloops?"

"Last year," one of the traders replied quickly.

"Have you heard of a James Cairns working up at Fort McLeod with the company?"

"He was gone from there and down to Fort George. I don't know from there."

"He's not there now?"

"Gone long ago."

McAllister held his breath. "Did he have his wife with him there?"

"I do not know of any wife. But he left there."

"To where?"

The trader interrupted the train of questions with a loud sneeze, followed by a short coughing spell.

McAllister hung his head and waited with patience for a reply.

"Who knows who goes off to other places," the other man said. "Just that you are no longer there. Just that nobody misses you when you're gone."

Anticipation of more positive news had filled McAllister's mind. He held his voice steady when he told them, "I was a friend of his wife's family. I wondered about them– Breen, was his name. He was the Chief Factor when I left Fort St. James and not well. Cairns left there before I did, when he married Breen's daughter."

"Well, we do not know what happened to him, to any of them," the traders told McAllister, and the trapper sensed an end to the conversation.

As the two men departed McAllister's camp, they reminded him once more, "Think on meeting with us. We are locating above you on this river. We'll do some trapping, but want to trade with the Shoshoni. They are less trouble. There is an old trail through these mountains they call the Rockies, when they traded with the Nez Pérce. But it might be well for us all to leave at the same time. It just takes one arrow to kill you. They have traded for guns, too, and learned how to shoot well with them."

McAllister agreed to meet them in the last week of April if they would be at his camp by then. He watched them push upstream and heard their singing echo across the water of the Clearwater and up into the high mountains. Their red caps in the distance bobbed up and down with the rhythm of the river. They believe, he smiled, that they can scare the Indians with a strange language in a loud song. He could not help but admire the courage of such fearless men.

However, by the end of April the French-Canadian fur traders were nowhere in sight and McAllister left the area without them, presuming they had located the trail they sought.

The snow was now melting, running in rivulets everywhere. The crusted ice was disappearing from the shoreline. Cool winds of springtime blew about him as he dismantled his camp and packed his canoe for the trip. As he guided the craft down the waters of the Clearwater River, he passed the main hunting camp of the local Nez Pérce band.

Their habitations, covered with large mats fixed against sturdy poles filled the space cleared in the trees. Around these dwellings he saw women in long robes move purposefully about their chores. The men of the band languished beneath the canopies of hides, waited on by their women. The robes which the men wore were not so long as those of the women. Leggings of soft deer hides were fastened with leather thongs to a belt about their waists. Moccasins of thick tanned hides covered their feet. Their season of trapping and hunting in the deep drifted snow was finished. It was now time to rest until preparation for transport of the furs to Fort Okanogan was necessary. Like McAllister, they too, would trade at the fort for supplies.

It was the first week of May in 1834 when Rayne McAllister returned to Fort Okanogan. Having travelled from the snow-melting temperatures of the high Bitteroot Mountains to greater springtime warmth in the lower elevations of the Columbia River, he found it necessary to remove some of his heavier outer clothing. When he pulled his canoe ashore at the fort and was greeted with enthusiastic slaps upon his back by Evan Dubrais, McAllister was hatless, shirtless to his underwear, and wore only light moccasins over his feet.

Sizing up the trapper's catch of furs stowed in the canoe, Evan Dubrais grinned approvingly. "When the total worth of these furs is on the books you will be a rich man, no?" he pried. "Not that you are not rich now!"

Beneath the warm noonday sun, he assisted McAllister with the unloading of his stores and furs. "Soon you will be able to give it all up – the frozen rivers and rusty traps."

McAllister was quiet. He was tired. It had been a long, hard journey back to the fort. He wanted to be unloaded, to bath and get his beard and hair cut. So, tossing his personal packs over his shoulder, McAllister walked across the fort yard to the Men's House.

The weather grew warmer. By the end of June the heat had become excessive without a cloud or drop of rain to cool the air. The vegetation began to show the results of drought. McAllister's thoughts turned to the Okanagan Valley and although he longed to head up into that valley soon, he made plans to first visit Spokane House with his friend, Dubrais.

It had been years since he had been in any settlement larger than Fort Kamloops. It struck him again that a good deal of ordinary living had been missed by isolating himself. As he watched Dubrais and Broken Bone in their life with their two sons, he became acutely aware of his own future, of others around him, of employment other than trapping, and odours more appealing than wood smoke in the forest, deerskins and the steamy smell of freshly killed animals. Here at the fort he was able to relax his mind and body and to drop the need for continual watchfulness.

He observed Broken Bone carry out her daily tasks about the cabin and enjoyed the taste of the woman's cooking when Dubrais invited him in. McAllister silently recalled life during the summers at Fort St. James and Willow Breen. Nostalgia gripped him. Where had she and Cairns gone? Did they have children? Was Willow happy with him? When he questioned Dubrais, the man had heard nothing of them. He pushed Willow from his immediate thoughts, stowing memories once more into the secret corners of his mind.

One July night as he and Dubrais walked across the dry flats above the river in the warm evening, the old trader asked bluntly, "You have lots of credit with the company now. And money, no? Rich man, I think. Where do you leave it all? You don't keep it; the Indians would have it by now."

"Why would the Indians have it by now?" McAllister asked curtly.

"Because they are thieves!" Dubrais replied hotly.

"That is only your narrow opinion. I have travelled all my life among them, as you have," McAllister reminded his friend, "and never once have I been directly confronted with the threat of murder or thievery."

Dubrais snorted contemptuously. "That's the passive thinking of a true Canadian," he answered, not looking at the trapper's watchful eyes. "The situation is different down here."

"I think not," replied McAllister, walking ahead.

But Evan Dubrais, in his effort to have his young friend settle nearby, was persistent. "Why don't you invest your money. Here, of course. Land."

"And why would I want to buy land? And who from? If I wanted to stay here I could just go out and declare myself a piece of land with four corner stakes and that would be it."

Dubrais frowned a warning. "You cannot trap all your life," he advised. "The beaver are getting scarce now and–"

"Here, they are getting scarce, but not everywhere else," McAllister reminded him quickly.

"Still," cautioned Dubrais, "you must think of when you are an old man. You have no family. You better start one."

McAllister remained non-committal.

"Well," Dubrais continued as though the silence between them had not ensued, "we go to Spokane!" His voice was full of anticipation and enthusiasm over the prospect. "You can spend some of your credit there. Maybe buy some decent new clothes out of their warehouse, get yourself a good woman, even stay in a fine room and bath in a tub with hot, soapy water, eh? Better than a cold river, no?" He thought deeply for a moment. "Or, maybe I get us a boarding house to stay at. I have a good friend there at whose place

I stay most of the time. This time should be no different." Glancing up at the tall trapper, he grinned. "Good food, good company, and intelligent conversation. Conversation! Now, that is something you are not used to, I know-- unless the trees have learned to talk!" Dubrais nodded his head, very pleased with himself and his decision. "Yes, yes, that's it!"

His enthusiasm for the trip failed to catch hold of McAllister completely. "Sounds alright," he muttered quietly.

"Sounds alright, he says! A hell of a lot better than those smelly skins you're living in, or the empty hides you sleep under. You should live like a man is supposed to live. How old are you now?"

McAllister did not reply.

Dubrais sighed impatiently. "Well, no matter. But I tell you, a man is not really alive without a woman to keep him content and warm under the covers and well fed in the kitchen. Look at Broken Bone. She may not walk so well, but she is a good woman. Two good sons she give me also." A pensive moment gripped Dubrais. "Still-- sometimes I like to have a shapely little white woman in my bed who knows what a Frenchman really needs. So, to Spokane we go! The wagons moving west have left the odd good woman behind. You may meet someone."

The decision was made and, at the break of the following day, Evan Dubrais and the trapper departed Fort Okanogan on horseback for the excitement and entertainment of Spokane House.

9

Spokane House was located on a point of land at the juncture of the Spokane and Little Spokane rivers. A twelve foot high stockade had been built. Square bastions armed with guns flanked the large stockade and provided protection for the main trade building. This building was cut by passageways and counters, and had a separate storage room for the furs until their removal by the pack trains. However, the protection provided by the mounted pieces of artillery was never needed as no hostile natives ever attacked the fort. Many of the Spokane Indians kept peace with the white man here, pitching their teepees just outside the compound walls. Aside from the main trading area there were many handsome log buildings.

Spokane House was much larger than McAllister had expected. It was also livelier. The company store did a brisk business. Smithies worked overtime. Men of all walks of life poured in and out of the gates of Spokane House. Coupons, silver, trade goods and documents of all order changed hands many times in a night and whiskey flowed freely. While men gambled in back rooms, young ruffians prowled the dark corners of the courtyard waiting to rob them of whatever they could.

The only rooming house, which Dubrais referred to as the hotel, was always filled. In the large ballroom, which was a strange and awesome sight in the far west, Indian girls danced the evenings away, their dresses a dazzling combination of eastern cloth and style and their own designs of intricate Indian fringes and beads. They twirled to the waltz and swung in the lively two-step. Then, in the late night, the clatter of horses hooves echoed across the stonework of the courtyard as lovers met in secret rendezvous.

It was the social centre of the inland fur empire and all who could flocked to Spokane House. Its very air was seized by the freedom and adventure of the west. The rugged features of the compound and surrounding buildings held the appealing sensation of being on the brink of awakening and discovery, even though it was now over twenty years old and talk of a recent decline in furs threatened to bring about its abandonment. The merriment contained within its walls encompassed young and old alike.

New immigrants were beginning to straggle in, their trains of covered wagons, cattle and horses all passing by the main gate. They often set up camps on the outskirts to rest awhile before continuing their hazardous journey westward. Some remained, though, drawn by the possibilities of flat benchlands of tall grass and rich soil. They built their log homes and barns and took up farming.

Life at Spokane House was an exciting interlude for any visitor and Evan Dubrais always made the best of it. It was all pleasure, no talk of business ever came from his lips. Business was at home with the furs, the barges, and the dock, or with the traders coming down from New Caledonia's northern forts.

McAllister's first day at Spokane House was spent outfitting himself and soaking in a deep tub of hot water, a rare experience for any man of the woods. He allowed the luxury of a shave and hair cut shorter to collar length. When he viewed himself in the long mirror in his room at the boarding house, he was satisfied with the handsome reflection he presented. In his twenty-nine years his eyes had never looked upon his frame in length. Now McAllister noticed that his fair hair had darkened, and was sprinkled with pre-mature graying at the temples. His skin seemed of a perpetual tan with weather-wrinkles creasing the corners of his blue eyes. Even his full mustache had become darker. He was tall with massive shoulders, a body of firm muscles and straight back. McAllister could not help but be satisfied with the reflection he saw.

McAllister's purchases were not extravagant, only the necessary articles of trade which he took with him annually up the rivers, and gifts for Broken Bone and her sons.

Two days were spent at the race track where betting was heavy on some of the finest horses in the land. McAllister, no judge of horseflesh, was divested of a considerable amount of his assets early in the proceedings, primarily because of Dubrais' poor choices. Also Dubrais was borrowing heavily from him, having lost most of his resources early on in one of the back rooms of the boarding house and saloon.

When the trapper mentioned this distressing fact to him, Dubrais puffed his reddened cheeks and chortled, "I'll have it back in a week. You have no confidence. I know all their tricks!"

Finally McAllister told him, "Enough is enough!" and dragged the drunk little gambler back to his room where he left Dubrais to contemplate his irresponsible ways. McAllister went out to eat his supper.

When he returned to the rooming house, McAllister found the lusty Frenchman frolicking beneath the bedcovers with a young woman with a cascade of the reddest hair he had ever seen. Dubrais attempted to talk to the trapper, calling him back into the room, but

McAllister quietly closed the door on them.

Instantly it was snapped open and the woman, wrapped in a sheet, called to him. "You're moving to Mrs. White's house tonight. That's Evan's friend. Your things have already been sent." Teasingly, she twisted the ends of her red curls over her smooth, white shoulder and smiled into McAllister's eyes.

"Moving?" McAllister stared in disbelief at her words. "What about Evan?"

"Evan says he will be along later." The girl giggled, and flounced back into the room, slamming the door behind her.

Rayne McAllister stepped out onto the walk. The evening air was almost oppressive with the summer heat. A feeling of desolation swept over him. His belongings had been removed to another place he knew not where. And Evan Dubrais, who had been a demanding, constant shadow until now, had seemingly abandoned him.

The clip-clop of horse hooves rounded the building and drew a carriage to a stop before him. The driver called from above and motioned McAllister to get inside. Stepping across to the door, McAllister peered doubtfully into the darkness of the interior.

"Mr. McAllister, I presume," a woman's voice came to him from the far side of the carriage. "I am Mrs. White, a close friend of Evan Dubrais. Is Evan with you? You are to be my guests for awhile."

McAllister coughed in self-consciousness and glanced up at the room occupied by Dubrais and the woman. "He apparently will be along later." McAllister opened the door.

Mrs. White shrugged her slight shoulders and smiled in an understanding way. "Please get in. We'll not wait then."

As McAllister stepped into the carriage, his eyes met those of the woman seated there. Instantly he thought, she is incredibly beautiful. In fact, she is the most beautiful woman I have ever seen! She smiled and he seated himself beside her as the carriage jolted forward.

Above them, Dubrais watched their departure and smiled. Dropping the curtain back over the windowpane, he looked across the darkening room at the enticing picture of youth which lay across his bed. Gently, he reached out and touched the soft curls of her brilliant hair, allowing the silk to flow through his fingers. This was what he needed, this interlude in his otherwise channelled life. He had all the devotion of a wife necessary to him with Broken Bone, but this– ah, this sweet frolic with a lively young woman made an old man return to his youth. Dubrais smiled and banished the trapper from his mind.

In the carriage McAllister studied the woman's profile, made all the more lovely by the upsweep of golden curls and the tilt of her small white hat. He wondered where Evan Dubrais could possibly have met her. "Have you known Dubrais for long?" he queried cautiously.

Her light blue eyes narrowed and measured his for a brief moment. "A very long time," she replied without smiling. "I understand you will be here for awhile and Evan always stays–"

"Only as long as he is here."

"He will be here for a long while," she emphasized with a quick glance heavenward, remembering earlier visits to Spokane House by Evan Dubrais. Her now unsmiling eyes met his once more, and saw there the contemplation of this moment and his acute sense of awareness of her presence beside him, which he did nothing to hide from her.

"My name is Denise White," she spoke softly. "I hope you will find my home to your liking– comfortable, while you stay at the fort."

Formalities, she thought. I am speaking silly formalities while my heart races as uncontrollably in his presence as I know his does in mine. Suddenly the carriage seemed too close, too dark and intimate.

"Comfortable?" she heard him say. "I'm sure– comfortable." It was difficult to concentrate on his words.

"Mind you," Denise continued as though McAllister had not uttered a word. "The choices are very limited, but you could try to talk your way into one of the caravans west of here, or a teepee, but you'd need to wear your deerskins for that and hire on as a guide to boot. As it turns out, your belongings are now at my place along with Evan's." She looked squarely at his astonished face. "The door is always open to Evan, and any friend of his is also welcome."

"You do know where I come from?" he muttered, now lost in her steady gaze. It was a statement more than a question. McAllister looked down at the black boots on his feet. If these were moccasins, he thought, I would know my ground in this matter. And, if my body was clothed in deer hides instead of this uncomfortable cloth suit I would have my feelings under control. McAllister turned his head to stare through the small window beside him.

It was mid-evening and the summer light was quickly fading to darkness. Oxen and carts moved about the courtyard. Several horsemen galloped past their carriage, reining to a quick halt before the saloon. Boisterous voices were heard everywhere and from far down the compound lane the sound of a violin sent soft strains into the night air.

The carriage stopped at Denise White's gate. McAllister pushed the door open, stepped out and reached for her hand. Small and warm, it lingered, clasped there in his for a moment. Standing beside him, Denise looked up.

"My home," she offered. "My husband built it. He passed away five years ago. Come." She was decisive, having now gotten herself away from his immediate disquieting presence. Her swaying skirts billowed and dragged across the rough boards as she moved with positive steps onto the walk and led the way to her door.

Throughout his stay at Spokane House, Rayne McAllister remained a guest, with Evan Dubrais, in Denise White's large log-structured house located at the edge of the enormous compound. The strained silence, which their acute awareness of each other caused, was eased somewhat in the following days by the interference of Dubrais' presence. They moved through the events of each day, more often apart, all the while trying to be together.

The weather was extraordinary. The days, while very warm, often ushered in cooler evenings when the sun disappeared behind the low mountains. Time could be spent strolling the paths of the woods beyond the town, enjoying a buggy ride or a picnic in the quiet countryside. At night they could party the hours away at the homes of merchants and well-to-do traders. Denise White was known to give the best small dinner parties and, of course, had become a most sought after hostess at soirees in wifeless homes where a beautiful woman's presence was the finishing touch.

Evan Dubrais was acquainted with everyone at Spokane House, or so it seemed. He accepted every invitation that came their way and insisted on those which did not, and saw to it that McAllister enjoyed all the available entertainments and was introduced to anyone of any importance. Perhaps, McAllister considered, it was all through Mrs. White? Who was she? And Dubrais? Where did he fit into her life?

One morning as they rested their horses during an early outing, McAllister asked his new friend, "How is it that you know everyone here? Did you live here?"

"Ah, I see. You think this old man in his dirty worn clothes with an Indian woman for a wife-- how can he possibly fit into this life with these people!"

"Not exactly, but close. More particularly Mrs. White. Where did you meet her?" McAllister stretched back on the warm grass, allowing the sun to tan his face and arms, and waited for a lengthy explanation as was Dubrais' way.

Instead the Frenchman simply stated, "Her husband was my sister's son, my nephew."

"And?"

"He became a physician. Denise was a little girl I saved from a burning wagon and refused to let the Pawnee have," he stated proudly.

"What did you do?"

Dubrais laughed. "I could talk fast in those days, and bribed the

Pawnee. I gave them everything I had but the canoe and promised to kill everyone with my bare hands if they followed me and they took me seriously. I travelled and trapped with a man named Conager in those days, and he and I put her in the canoe and took her to St. Louis to the home of my sister."

"And you?"

Dubrais looked over at the younger man. "Me? Well, Conager and I traded our way west until he got hurt with a horse and I went to live with Broken Bone... and you want to know too much."

McAllister rose to his feet and reached for the reins on his horse.

Dubrais stepped into the stirrup and pulled himself clumsily into his saddle. "And you? What about you, Rayne McAllister? No home? No woman?"

McAllister swung up onto his horse. "I'm going back up the river to the rendezvous spot in the Okanagan and decide if I want to live there for the rest of my life."

"Where did you come from? In the beginning–"

"Upper Canada." The words suddenly sounded foreign to McAllister's ears, a life long past, barely remembered. He glanced across at Dubrais, smiling. "No woman," he spoke softly and felt a twinge of sadness at the empty sound of the words. He shook the reins to urge his horse forward.

Dubrais rode up beside the trapper. "You are a stupid man, my friend, McAllister. You confuse my mind– I don't know why I bother with you!"

The trapper tried to ignore what he knew Dubrais would say next.

"Everyday I see you and Denise together and I see the glances you think you hide, the eyes that meet, the hands that touch, and I know– good God, how well I know what's going on inside both of you!" He stared, almost angrily, across at the trapper's stern countenance. "My God man, you deny yourself everything! How were you raised? By the nuns?"

McAllister snapped, "When the time is right–"

"When what time is right? Lord– Lord–" Dubrais waved his hand helplessly. "The time has been right for the two weeks you have been under her roof." Raising his eyes to view the cloudless sky, he muttered solemnly, "Why do I care about you?" He glanced back at the trapper.

The two measured each other for a tense moment.

Suddenly McAllister's emotions became jumbled, threatening his control over the conversation. "You are a meddling old fool!" he snapped impulsively at Dubrais once more, sinking his heels against the horse and leaping out ahead of the other man.

Now the Frenchman bounced and fought to remain in his saddle as his horse attempted to keep pace with the trapper's.

"There's no doubt about it, you're a better rider than me," he called angrily to McAllister. "But do you have to prove it?"

The trapper failed to hear him. He had galloped down over the hill and was now nearly out of Dubrais' sight.

That evening Evan Dubrais was conspicuously absent from Denise White's dinner table. McAllister recognized that the scene had deliberately been set, if not by Denise, certainly by Dubrais.

"Where did he disappear to?" the trapper asked outright.

He had caught Denise off guard as she idly pushed her food about the plate. "Hmm?" she questioned. "I'm sorry, I–"

"Evan– where is he hiding himself tonight?"

"Well, we have a mutual friend here, a Mr. Conager. Evan has gone to visit him. He's very ill at the moment, suffering from old battle wounds no doubt." Her gaze fell upon his and held. "Are you uncomfortable about this? We've hardly had a minute alone to be used to it." Suddenly her heart seemed to leap to her throat. The fork leaned away from her hand, falling against the plate's edge. The room, as in many times during the past two weeks, again seemed too close and intimate.

The longing in McAllister's eyes was there for her to see. Their reflection spoke for him the words he could not say. It had been so very long, too long, since he had held Willow in his arms. Because of the restraints Willow had placed upon their relationship, he was unfamiliar with the depth of intense longing which now surged through him. Slowly McAllister pushed back his chair. "Denise–" His voice faded.

Emotion clouded her eyes, burned in her beautiful face. As he came around the table toward her, she whispered faintly, "I know what you are feeling, Rayne. I have wanted–"

With his hand cupping her fine chin, a finger over her lips stilled the rush of words. As he bent his head to kiss her, it all seemed very natural to him, as if he had known every day that she would raise her mouth to meet his, to encircle his shoulders with her warm arms, and allow his broad hands to move along her back and down over her full, yielding hips. Denise moved her lips gently along his neck and as she undid the buttons of his shirt, pressed her mouth softly against his chest, kissing his skin with a tenderness until now unknown to him. His hands flew up to her cascading hair, tangling, pressing her face against him, cradling her there. In this savouring moment, with the precious feel of her hands, her mouth on his body, and caresses which he had never known, Rayne McAllister closed his eyes tightly against the hard and often cruel life he had chosen which denied him such infinitely sweet pleasures. With a soft murmur against the silk of her hair, he swept Denise up into his strong arms and carried her into the privacy of her bedroom.

The Columbia

Then McAllister closed the door against the world and the sounds outside of the house and the falling evening darkness as he and the woman turned to each other and the teasing sensations of exploration.

In the morning Denise slept late. McAllister had left the house early to collect his stores from the warehouse and make ready for the trip back to Fort Okanogan. While the woman languished in her bed which still carried the tantalizing and warm odours of his presence there, and relived the tender moments of their lovemaking, the trapper fought to control his unravelled mind and to make sensible decisions concerning his life. He had torn himself from the warmth of Denise White's enclosing arms and her bed for no other reason than not to be suddenly come upon by Dubrais. Just why the Frenchman nagged at his conscience baffled him. Perhaps, he considered now, it was because Dubrais thought of Denise as something near a daughter and that, if he could, he would have them married before the week was out.

But not once had marriage crossed McAllister's mind and he was certain that it had not entered Denise's thoughts. Theirs was an attraction of hungry passion, born of their individual need for the act itself. While they had fulfilled a long denied desire in each other they had also created a new one. McAllister knew that a repetition of the night before would happen again. He could not now turn off the longing to saturate himself with the pleasure and sweet sensation of her soft, yielding body and to give to the woman the caress which she craved and which she had given him.

10

On the eve of their departure from Spokane House, McAllister, at Dubrais' insistence, went with the Frenchman to visit his old friend who now lay at death's door.

"His name is Conager. That's all we ever called him," Dubrais chatted as they stepped into the black carriage and were off. "We trapped and traded, legal and otherwise, on every river across the continent out to the Pacific Ocean and back. But for him, my dear fellow-- I would have had ravens picking the eyes out of my scalpless head back on the Missouri. Merciless lot!"

"Who?"

"The Cheyenne."

McAllister did not know whether to believe the old storyteller or not, but many gruesome tales had filtered the channels of the fur trade through the decades so as to leave one wondering over the dangers of the American west.

Smiling, remembering another way of life than the present, Dubrais told McAllister, "He was better at survival than you and I. Much better. He knew it all! And now we, who opened up this great land are old and dying. Yes-- I too am getting old; thirty-two years more than my wife, old enough to be my sons' grandfather."

In the dull light of the interior of the carriage, Dubrais' small eyes, now misty with nostalgia, stared across at the Canadian trapper.

"I think what I am trying to say and why I bring you here to see Conager is-- don't give it up, Rayne, don't lose what us old men have gained for you in the west. The rest of our country and eastern Canada, too, needs the west. There is always unrest in this country of ours and it may get worse." Dubrais' hand touched McAllister's sleeve briefly to keep the other's attention. "I don't agree with you most of the time about the Indians, but it is men with your beliefs and trusts that will help to keep the west and bring a nation and people together."

McAllister looked down at his big hands which had so often clasped the knife kept at his side when strange noises of the night in the woods were heard. "I've never said I trust the Indians. But I'm sure they don't want aggravation any more than us. We have just as many renegades in our race as they have in theirs, and it's a toss-up which side starts the skirmish first."

Dubrais sighed. "Well, I think your day with the Indians is yet to come. You can't spend your life in unsettled territories without the knock of fear at that bear-hide door of yours." To this remark, McAllister raised a brow in mild amusement.

The carriage came to a stop. Dubrais smiled across the interior at McAllister. "Let's go in now and see Conager, the Indian fighter!"

Several hours passed and the sky darkened with the night.

As they were leaving the old trader's home and stood in the dark street, the carriage arrived. Dubrais climbed in first.

As McAllister stepped up there was a hurried scuffle behind him; a knife flashed, and another. He was stabbed viciously twice in the back, then once more in the shoulder. McAllister fell hard against the carriage door.

Dubrais was calling, "Come, we'll be late for our coffee with Denise." Then, in shock, Dubrais' dark eyes widened as he saw the glint of the knives in the lamplight of the carriage and heard the sickening thud of intrusion again and again into muscle and bone.

McAllister slid slowly down against the steps, crumpling upon the ground. A faint moan escaped his lips. Astonishment registered in his eyes as, in a great blur, he saw the hoodlums loom over him, heard them argue, felt them grab at his clothes and hunt for a money belt.

Dubrais leapt from the carriage, swearing in great loud yelps and throwing his thick body upon them, kicking, smashing their skulls together as if possessed of the urge to kill. The driver called out for help.

As he listened to the escaping footsteps, McAllister whispered to Dubrais, "They will be fooled– there's no money there–" and he sank into unconsciousness.

Suddenly the lane came alive. In the night people ran to him, reached for him, placed blankets over him and heeded Dubrais' sharp commands. Once his bloodied body was hauled into the carriage, Dubrais barked, "To Mrs. White's, on the double! The double, you hear!" The reins slapped sharply.

The team leaped in their harness, plunging down the bumpy roadway. Dubrais held McAllister still, close to him and felt the sticky warmth of blood running over his hands, soaking through the blanket into the fabric of his suit, finally settling in a pool on the floor of the bouncing carriage.

The man is dying, Dubrais thought in disbelief. This man is dying, and for what reason? He wanted to cry for the waste. McAllister of the western wilderness who surely has saved his own life countless times over by a careful word or presentation of a shiny trade piece; he who fought the elements through winters so harsh he was driven into his hut for days and weeks at a time; he who could run the rapids so expertly as to never dump his canoe, or could pack over a hundred skins strapped on his back for unheard of distances. Dubrais shivered now with worry. This clever trapper had learned all the tricks of survival, now to end like this? He raised a shaking hand to wipe the perspiration from his brow and to cover his tear-filled eyes and hide his emotions.

McAllister was taken to Mrs. White's house and the carriage quickly dispatched to fetch the physician. "And I'll hold you responsible, even if he's out in those wagons delivering babies!" Dubrais screamed at the shaken driver. Turning to Mrs. White, he began, "Now, Denise, he is to be–"

"Evan," Denise said, her blue eyes staring sternly into his. "I know what to do. You're coming apart, you know. Also, you forget that I was a physician's wife. I know more than you do."

"He may die."

"He will not." She moved to put her arms around him for comfort. "You are too emotional, Evan. Calm yourself. I know that he has become a good friend, but–"

"Hush!" Dubrais whispered into her shoulder. "I am wondering at this moment what you feel." Leaning back, he raised her delicate chin and stared squarely into her light eyes. "I know you will keep him alive, because you need him, too."

Indeed, McAllister did survive the horrible knife wounds which had laid wide two long fleshy strips down his back and punctured a deep hole in the left shoulder. Flesh and muscle had been severely damaged and McAllister would feel the results of such mutilation the rest of his life. He remained in Denise White's constant care. She seldom left his side.

Dubrais told her, "Denise, you have saved him! You are a miracle worker and a saint." His tremendous admiration for her showed itself in his expressive dark eyes.

"Saints! Saints! Only the idle have time to talk of Saints," she rushed at him. "Rayne has nearly bled to death, but– by the Grace of God, or something, the blood has finally coagulated."

Dubrais contemplated the hurried tone of his niece. "Everyone owes their life to somebody else," he pondered quietly, idly. "I owe mine to Conager, you owe yours to me, and now he owes his to you. Lord knows how many owe theirs to him." He stared down at McAllister, who rested quite still upon the bed.

Then suddenly, he bent to peer closely at the trapper's pale face. "He's awake! By God, he is awake!" he declared and instantly sank to his knees beside the bed, crossing himself. "The worst is over."

"Evan, get up, you fool!" snapped Denise. "You're late with your prayers! You should have had your chat with God long before now. Instead you sat around with your memories, whining, while I did all the work. Now go see if the authorities– if we have any at this post, have found out anything about the ruffians who assaulted your friend.

"The strain of the past week was beginning to show. "Help me turn him, then go. I'll manage from now on. Come and get him when summer's over." Denise White stared directly, purposefully into Dubrais' questioning eyes. "If he still wants to leave, that is–"

Dubrais smiled knowingly. "Why Denise, my dear–"

Denise quickly interrupted and ordered, "Out with you!" And, turning her back to him, she smiled smugly and gazed intently down at the injured trapper.

Before Evan Dubrais took his leave of Spokane House four days later, McAllister gave him the gifts for Broken Bone and their sons. "Don't come back for me," he told Dubrais. "I'll get there when I'm ready. Go now or the others will leave without you."

Dubrais bade McAllister a reluctant farewell, handed the belt of silver currency and vouchers belonging to the trapper to Denise White. "This is what those scoundrels were after. The man never carries this with him. He hides it, but nobody knows that."

"I don't want this," she told him flatly.

"He owes you much more than what's here." Dubrais smiled smugly. "He who never owed anyone a thing, is now greatly indebted to you and me." Kissing Denise tenderly on the forehead, Dubrais whispered to her, "I cannot believe how well the Lord has played into your hands, my dear."

Her eyes frowned a warning to him. "It is my contention," she replied tersely, "that the good Lord had nothing to do with it. Goodbye Evan. Take care of yourself."

With considerable fuss, Evan Dubrais settled himself into his saddle, waved, and rode off to join the pack train travelling north to Fort Okanogan.

Rayne McAllister's recovery was rapid. Once the danger of infection was over, the physician no longer came by to see him.

The weather turned hot during August.

Denise's house, although it was a large home, seemed to hold the heat, so that at times McAllister felt uncomfortable in the tight bandages which covered his back and shoulder. He knew Denise was hardly more comfortable than he, so he suggested that they begin walking in the early evening when it was cooler outside.

After one such stroll, he told her, "I'd like to be going to the Okanagan."

"Not yet. When you feel strong," she told him with concern.

"That, I do now. I need to be outside– all the time," he said as he paced the room endlessly, restlessly, never quite meeting her eyes.

"Oh yes, I've forgotten!" She giggled lightly. "You're a wilderness dweller, aren't you? You've spent more time in caves than ever between four wooden walls."

McAllister felt stung and smarted from the sarcasm of her words, though he recognized they were only meant to tease. Suddenly the bandages on his back and the strapping over his shoulder seemed too tight, restricting his movements, confining him to this good woman's house and care.

For the second time since he was a young boy, McAllister was dependent upon someone other than himself. He felt trapped. It was time that he got himself back up the river, he decided, to– caves? Had she actually called him a wilderness dweller? He was becoming pessimistic and morbid, and he did not like it.

The trapper realized that it was time for him to leave Spokane House. It was nearly the end of August and he had much to do. His shoulder was going to be a problem, but he would manage well enough. He had become impatient of late and, as the days slipped by, increased the exercising of his shoulder and finally removed the bandages from his back. It was good to feel the freedom of a shirt against his skin again.

"Aren't you rushing things?" Denise enquired. "You can't use a paddle yet and you know it."

"By October I will. But the rivers in the Okanagan are not so navigable as here or up north, so I'll get some horses." He could not look at her.

Her breath momentarily halted. "Rayne, I'll be honest. I don't want you to leave."

For a few moments McAllister could not speak. A feeling of strangulation engulfed him. Denise stood resolutely before him, her eyes searching his, her delicate bottom lip quivering with stifled emotion. He saw, too, the hope in the pleading expression of her face. He did not deny his desire for this woman and he owed her his life, but if he was ever going to pull away from her, it must be now. He turned away to stare through the window. "Denise–"

She moved to stand close to him and the moment became tense. "Rayne, I know you want to leave. You want to go back to the mountains and the rivers. That is your life. But I could be here for you. Besides," she tried to smile. "You've got a lot of muscle to build in your shoulder before you can carry packs on your back."

McAllister looked down at her, saw the sunlight through the window dance over the golden curls clustered upon her head. "Denise, do you realize the company might abandon this post? There is nothing here for me. And there will be little left for you if the company closes Spokane House."

"There's talk it will be relocated, and I will move with it," she spoke with determination. "There is always a need for someone with medical experience and I am the closest there is to a physician we have when our sometime doctors leave us for farther horizons. I have chosen to make this country my home and I shall not now leave it."

McAllister reached out, drawing her near to him. "My dear Denise, you are very brave and determined for a young woman of twenty-five. Strong women are needed on these posts."

Denise huffed. "I am not interested in how bad I am needed here or anywhere else, just concerned with your complete recovery." She moved away from him.

"There is nothing wrong anymore with my shoulder or my back, and I'll prove it to you." Swiftly he reached out, swung her close to him once more and led her toward her bedroom.

As she lay back upon the quilts, he leaned over her and looked deeply into her wide, light eyes. "Now lovely lady, please listen to me," he spoke softly. "I am not going to stay and nor are you going to wait here for me. It's now that matters, just that. It hurts me to say that this bed is all it's been from the beginning. I know that you know it, too."

Denise reached up, placing a finger over his lips. "Shhh–" She could not hide the anguish and disappointment in her eyes. She knew his words to be the truth.

"I have some deep feelings for you, many feelings," he confessed. "And one of them is not to hurt you more. If I stay that's what will happen." McAllister watched her face, peering into the depths of her eyes for several moments, then he bent and touched her lips with his, gently, waiting for her response. Slowly her lips moved to return the kiss, opening against his, stirring again an empty ache, a longing so many times in the past denied. Sinking down beside her, he drew Denise's slim body close to him and heard a soft sigh escape her.

Before he left her at dawn he told her, "I'm going to the Okanagan and I will not be back." But Denise White closed her mind against the harshness and loneliness of his words.

McAllister departed Spokane House with an additional horse and full packs. By this means he was able to carry extra ropes, blankets, utensils and clothes.

At Fort Okanogan, when Dubrais saw him riding toward the cabin he threw back his dark head and called out.

"Aha! So the fair Mrs. White was not able to hold you after all. And now you go up to the Okanagan, eh? Well, there as here, I suppose. But now you go in style. You have good horses. How is the shoulder? Just as well you bought an extra horse, for packing your furs will be harder for you now."

McAllister waited with patience as Dubrais' questioning persisted. He affectionately patted the tousled heads of the two boys, who were excited to see him. They inspected his bulging saddle bags for gifts and were delighted when they finally found them.

Broken Bone stood by calmly, her hands shading her face from the bright sun. She was pleased to see him return, but judging by the size of his packs and the extra horse, knew his stay would not be a long one. She smiled broadly as her sons chattered at the trapper.

"I'll let you keep my canoe. It's for the boys." McAllister told Broken Bone, "Be sure he teaches them about the rapids properly."

Broken Bone flashed a wide grin. "He's too old man now. You stay. They learn plenty from you." Clearly, Broken Bone was sorry to see the trapper leave.

"How many canoes have you left behind?" Dubrais was curious. "Three, four?"

"Two."

"Ah well, you make another up there. So what else? When do you leave us?" And shaking his head sadly, he predicted, "You'll be dead in your youth yet, and leave no sons behind you."

"We will miss you, trapper," Broken Bone said softly, pulling her two sons near her.

Three more days elapsed before McAllister left for New Caledonia. He joined a small supply train packing upland to Fort Kamloops. Clothed in fringed deerskins, the new tunic made by Broken Bone, breeches and cap, McAllister rode up into the great valley atop a tall bay horse, leading a thick muscled Appaloosa mare loaded with his gear.

It was early September when McAllister reached the fur traders' campsite about one hundred miles north of Fort Okanogan and Dubrais' cabin. He was impatient to be settled for the winter, although time was in his favour for such industry. Often an autumn in the Okanagan was an experience of beauty and warmth.

Several other trappers had gathered at the site near the lake at Soi'yus. Across the water the glow of the fires of the Nk'Mip (Inkameep) campgrounds could be seen.

A voice beside McAllister returned the trapper's mind to the present, for a pensive moment had taken his thoughts back to Denise White and the awful hurt in her eyes upon his leavetaking. He now turned his attention to the man beside him. A long, gray beard rested against his throat at the open neck of his tunic. His voice was serious.

"Wasn't always so quiet 'n peaceful like this," McAllister was told.

"When they weren't takin' time out for makin' their tomahawks 'n knives 'n arrows, them redskins wore out their moccasins chasin' down the She-whaps and anythin' else what got in their way. Run 'em clear outa this valley, they did! Nearly killed 'em all off. Ain't been bothered since." McAllister's knowledge of the Indians in the southern part of New Caledonia was limited, so that his companion's words were almost foreign to him.

McAllister warmed his hands around a tin cup filled with a steaming brew from the Labrador tea plant. The night air was becoming crisp and the heat from the campfire coals was welcome. He could smell fall in the air.

As he watched the other man with curiosity, he thought about the relationship between the Indians of this valley and the white men. The trader across the campfire was entertaining, to say the least and, McAllister considered, there might be some merit to his stories.

In constant motion between the fire and where he had located his bedroll and supplies, the bearded trader seemed unrelaxed, wary, suspicious of every sound, and the more he talked about the Okanagan and She-whap wars, the more nervous he became.

"What happened to the white men?" McAllister asked.

"Weren't none here then. If there were they weren't to be seen, or got themselves killed, 'cause them Indians meant business. One thing about the Okanagans, they's good sneakers. A man can't fool 'em on where you are. They know everythin's goin' on. Mostly they just leave you to yourself these days, if you leave them alone."

McAllister smiled and said, "That's true, isn't it, of all Indians if they're left in peace?"

"Oh hell, no it ain't. No sir, it sure ain't. There's the odd good one aroun'. I been aroun' better than sixty years 'n I got plenty scars to prove you can't trust most of 'em one minute." From beneath a thick crop of graying hair, the dark eyes of the old trader stared out at McAllister. "You– you'll never know what it means to fear for your life; honest to God cold fear. You're just a youngster yet 'n livin' in different times, more peaceable times."

McAllister was inclined to disagree with the old man, but held his tongue. It was generally his contention that the natives of any area were little different than the white man. They hunted and trapped for the same reasons. They set aside their winter stores, made their clothing and did their cooking as any white people might. They loved, laughed, felt emotion and suffered pain and disappointment as any other race and, to McAllister's knowledge, only went to war when provoked.

The chill of nighttime sent the fur seekers beneath their thick robes for warmth and rest to await the dawn of another day which would not likely prove more interesting than the one just past.

Feeling now a deep sense of peace with his surroundings, Rayne McAllister realized that perhaps here, at last, was the crossroad in his life. He was glad to have finally arrived.

LAC DU CHIEN

11

The Indian village Sxoxene'tk^u (Shoshen-eetkwa), was located on a flat stretch of land surrounded by benchlands abundant with high bunchgrass. The waters of Lac du Chien lapped gently upon the beach of the village site. The Okanagan River flowed to the west of the flats over a high rocky ledge, separated in the middle by a solitary sentinel which caused a twin waterfall. The low hills above the benchlands were rich with game and wild berries, herbs and roots of all kind.

Young Two Way, whose given name was Toohey, a French name his mother had simply heard and liked but held no Indian meaning, became the fastest of foot among the boys of his age in his village. It was not easy for a young Okanagan boy to become an excellent provider and astute trader. It was even more challenging for the son of the chief. Not only were there long periods of body conditioning, but there were seemingly endless hours spent listening to the elders share legends and stories. Part of the arduous training to increase strength and litheness of the body was running up and down hills, day after day, mile after mile to become as swift as the horses they were expected to catch. At thirteen years, and with great expectations placed upon the boy, there was none to catch Two Way. Not even the ponies, it seemed, could keep away from him.

Living with Two Way's family was his uncle, Koti'leko', who was named for a large, bright star in the sky on the night of his birth. However, the name did not suit his Okanagan family and by the time Two Way was becoming a young man, Koti'leko' had become Rattler, for his daring mastery in the capture of deadly rattlesnakes prolific in the valley.

Rattler had put himself in charge of his nephew's training in the making of a man, and therefore unceremoniously booted Two Way off his pallet every morning, onto the boughs of fir and mats of tulle which covered the dirt floor, ordering the youngster upon his feet and out into the hills.

Although they conversed always in their native Salishan, Rattler bribed his nephew with, "I promise to teach you the white man's tongue. Now get going!"

Rattler's deep, booming voice was capable of sending fear through young Two Way, and clad only in breeches, the lad's tough bare feet padded swiftly off into the woods and along the time-worn trails.

Like his older brother, Kelauna, who was Two Way's father, Rattler was tall and slender, and below their thick mats of black hair were facial features of tanned rugged handsomeness. Dark eyes, aquiline nose and straight mouth were set in a structure of high cheek bones. Their appearances were almost identical, although Kelauna was taller than his brother, standing well over six feet in height which accounted for the reason he had been named for the grizzly bear. In his youth, Kelauna had demonstrated determination and leadership. He had passed these admirable qualities down to his son. Because he was a chief, and therefore a busy man, Kelauna found little time to spend with his young son. So, as Two Way grew older, the chief depended on his brother, Rattler, to train and prepare his son.

Possessed of a natural skill with the bow and knife, Rattler quickly drew the admiration of young Two Way. Not only was he an excellent hunter, bringing home the largest number of deer each season, he also made the largest catch of salmon taken from the river below the twin waterfalls near the village.

Rattler roamed far outside the territory of the Okanagan, hunting and trading with the Chinook Indians of the Pacific coast, the Shewhaps near Fort Kamloops, the Kootenai of the Rocky Mountains, and the Colville and Spokane tribes in the south. Because of his travels, Rattler had picked up a considerable bit of the languages of other western tribes of the Athapascans. These were lands through which the white man frequently moved and lived in greater numbers.

The esteem in which Two Way held his uncle did not in any way alter his love and respect for his father. He was, indeed, a devoted son and wished only to be an admired combination of both his father and his uncle. He did not desire to be better than Rattler in all the skills, but simply not to bring shame upon his family for failing to become a brave with fine skills in the toughest feats. Such expertise could only be accomplished through patience and endurance. Two Way had been gifted with the body and mind for it. Tall like his father, Two Way was, though slight of build, a strong, muscular boy. The fine features of his wide brown face showed the promise of intelligence.

Two Way knew every corner of the local Okanagan's territory. Travelling with his uncle through the length of the south valley, he had trod many trails along both sides of Lac du Chien and into the higher mountains where traps were placed for furs in meandering streams and quiet meadows. Much of the time that Two Way travelled with his uncle was spent on the trap line instead of the more interesting pursuits such as hunting, fishing and visiting.

Sometimes Two Way roamed the hills alone and, as he lay hidden in the high grass, he watched the bands of wild horses graze with contentment. The beauty of the horse and the freedom in which the horse lived captured the imagination of the young Indian boy. When he moved, startling them, they bolted into a fierce gallop, their proud heads high, mane and tails fanning out with the wind of their movement as they pounded away from him into the deeper mountain passages. In watching their flight, excitement flooded Two Way. Theirs was a freedom to be envied. Their strength was a power to be desired.

Certainly no young boy knows his destination, the road which his life will take, and Two Way was no exception. His wish for greatness as he grew older was as natural as the private envy of his uncle that he silently harboured. All the boys of Shoshen-eetkwa and surrounding encampments aspired to become the Rattler of their generation.

Sometimes Two Way confided in his sister, Nahna, of his youthful longings. She always understood him and never laughed at his wishing and dreaming. Unlike their two older sisters, they shared the gentle, sentimental side of their father. Two Way and Nahna spent a good deal of time together in the hills. While she helped him find colourful rocks and constructive formations of wood for the making of tools, Two Way helped her pick the slender reeds she needed for basket weaving, rushes for mats and colourful flowers used for dyes. Three years older than her brother and four years younger than her nearest sister, Nahna often felt lonely and Two Way filled this empty spot in her young life.

In his company, Nahna would sit for many hours at a time doing beadwork or sewing deer hides and moccasins. She was expert at her crafts. She had been taught well by her mother and the other women of the village. Her beaded bracelets, intricately woven baskets, and fringed door and ground mats brought a high price in silver and glass buttons from the traders. Trappers who knew of her sewing would haul small bolts of manufactured coloured cloth hundreds of miles to the rendezvous site, in exchange for a tastefully decorated and embroidered tunic and breeches of tanned deer hide.

Two Way was very proud of his sister. "I tell everybody about you, Nahna. When I learn English from Rattler I will teach it to you, too. And when I grow older I will tell everybody that it is you who makes the finest baskets and weaves the toughest mats and sews the best clothes in the village."

Nahna read the affection and pride in her brother's eyes. Resisting his impulsive praise, she admonished lightly, "No, no, Two Way, you are a silly boy yet! When you are grown up you will see that

I am no better at things than anyone else."

Standing before her and looking down upon her dark hair lying in soft braids over her small shoulders, he insisted, "You are the prettiest then."

"Hush!" Nahna whispered quickly, though smiling and keeping her head bowed over her work.

It was not just Two Way's contention that his sister, Nahna, was the loveliest girl in their village. The teasing flash of her black eyes held a hint of impulsiveness and drew the admiring glances of many young men who visited and stayed at Shoshen-eetkwa. Her child's body had blossomed gracefully into early womanhood. All of her dresses, shawls and beaded moccasins were fashioned by her own hand and, at sixteen years of age, Nahna wore these clothes appealingly and carried herself in a straight and graceful manner. She could not help but cause envy among the other young girls of her village.

In his compliments of her beauty, Two Way wished for his sister a husband of equal attributes and talents. Often he told her that she should raise her eyes from her sewing more often and pay careful attention to the visitors from neighbouring tribes.

To this Nahna would retort stubbornly, "You bother your head with much nonsense, my brother! I see and do more than you think I do!" Still Two Way wondered in silence.

Sometimes he would hasten away from her rebuff, setting off to cross the river aboard his small raft and climb up the face of the huge bluff that towered above the tumbling waterfalls. Here he could monitor the movements of the people of the village and escape the calls of his elders for assistance with chores when he was tired of work. From this point he could also watch for the white fur traders, whom he never saw up close, to pass by; for all travellers through the valley followed the Okanagan River.

12

McAllister was comfortable with the surroundings of the valley through which he rode. He felt not the threat of a knife at his throat, nor an arrow in his back. In fact, negotiation for safe passage was not even necessary, for the bands of the Okanagan were so familiar with the sight of horses passing through their territory, they all but ignored any intruders until it was time to take up bargaining with them.

At the head of the lake at Soi'yus, McAllister had set up a temporary camp. The area was open, broken only by narrow groves of birch and willow, and he was afforded clear view in all directions. It also lent the Indians identical advantage. However, they did not acknowledge his presence and, McAllister decided, most likely expected him to soon move on. The low slope of the terrain was dotted with antelope bush, or "greasewood" as the traders referred to it, and sagebrush. Enormous clumps of spiny cacti spread over the lowland sands leaving no traveller to doubt that he was, indeed, crossing a desert-like area foreign to other New Caledonia landscapes.

The rendezvous spot for the fur brigades was a short distance south of his temporary camp. Because of constant contact and bartering between the white man and Indian, some Chinook was spoken locally, although most of the traders spoke fluent French. McAllister had no difficulty understanding the few Okanagans with whom he had come in contact. At the end of September when the Hudson's Bay brigade of one hundred and eighty horses bound for Fort Kamloops had left, McAllister loaded his gear aboard his two horses. On a crisp, bright morning he departed the Soi'yus lakeside.

Astride the tall bay gelding and leading his pack horse behind him, McAllister crossed the river at the upper end of the lake and followed the brigade route northward. The horses hooves splashed into the water, crossing the channel easily, and clattered up over the small rocks to the opposite bank.

Throughout the day he followed the river until, turning west, he climbed away from the water up into the rolling hills. Although there were open grassy pastures which provided ample feed for his horses and deep creeks from which to catch small trout, there was little evidence of beaver. And when he had climbed so high as to see the river far below him, he was dismayed to find that he had strayed far too many miles toward the mountains, taking him further than he wished to be from the water. The weather was still very warm during the daytime, but at night its dipping temperatures sent him beneath the buffalo hide. It seemed to him that he had carried this robe with him forever, seldom having spent a night without its protection.

The following morning McAllister packed his saddles once more and, leaving the flat fields of wild grass above the canyon, made his way down into the gullies which he hoped would ultimately return him to the river. At the end of the day the horses slid uneasily along a trail over loose shale onto a flat, clear area directly opposite two rolling waterfalls spilling out from both sides of an island to a single pool which, from out of the turbulent white mist, flowed the Okanagan River.

McAllister's eyes scanned the opposite bank and followed the shoreline across the tumbling water. When he turned and looked up to the darkening sky and the treeless face of the cliff above him, his searching eyes suddenly narrowed. He peered harder against the fading light. Staring boldly down at him from a small perch on a ledge, a young boy sat completely immobile, watching every move of the man and the horses. It was several moments before the boy made any move; then, it was not to dart away, but simply settle himself more comfortably upon the ledge as though alerting the trapper to the presence of his people near the river.

McAllister slipped the reins over his arms, leading the animals to water. Then he stretched out, his back to the young Indian and drank heartily of the cool, clear liquid. Removing his hat, he splashed water up to his dusty face and over his head, wiping away the grime of travel with his hand as he rose from the ground to set up a temporary camp.

Although the grass was high and abundant near the river, the clearing was not a large space and McAllister realized that he would have to search for better pasture if he intended to remain at this site. Another look at the falls showed solid rock on the west and to the north, while behind him the sheer face of it led to where the boy sat, still watching the trapper. Across the river there were treeless areas, but McAllister had the feeling that just beyond the outcroppings of rocks was the camp of the Indians represented by the boy's presence. He could hear nothing but the constant splash of the tumbling falls and, because it was dusk, neither could he see much past the opposite shore.

He began to unburden his horses of their heavy packs. When a moment later he glanced up to the clifftop, the boy had disappeared, as McAllister had expected. As he prepared for sleep, McAllister placed his gun and his razor-sharp knife close by, just in case, he told himself, a wayward Indian roamed his way.

McAllister allowed several hours to pass before he rose from his bed, stuffed his blankets into a heap and covered the top with his hat. Creeping between the trees, he waited near his horses. It was not long before the boy appeared. It was so insignificant that McAllister could hardly believe that he was alone. From his position against a tree, he watched the circle of firelight at his camp and the slow movements of the youngster of the ledge. Believing the trapper to be asleep, the young Indian crept in, squatted and studied McAllister's belongings about the place and the gun beside the bedroll.

Beside McAllister his horses rested quietly. In the night stillness only the waterfalls could be heard. After a time the boy rose, watching the blankets suspiciously for any movement beneath them. He was totally unaware of McAllister's presence as he crept among the horses, looking them over, patting their necks and combing their manes with his short, brown fingers. Suddenly, a few feet away, he spotted the trapper watching him. Now face to face, the young intruder's expression registered surprise and astonishment, but not fright.

They remained so for several moments.

In English the trapper said, "My name is McAllister, but you can call me Many Rains. What is your name?" He waited a moment. "Do you speak any English?"

The boy continued to stare at the trapper, who now stepped forward.

McAllister added, "When I was your age, all the Indian boys I knew called me Many Rains." In the dark he smiled across at the boy. "How old are you? About twelve? Thirteen?"

Two Way stared at McAllister and nodded.

"Now, what do I call you?"

Understanding the trapper, for he had listened to his uncle's teachings, the Indian boy replied hurriedly, "Two Way," and darted off into the night.

McAllister walked down to the shoreline. In the pale light upon the water, he saw young Two Way's small raft bobbing as it angled across the smooth river to the opposite bank. The trapper knew the boy's village was located on the flats. He decided then, that he must search farther south for a suitable place to build a good winter camp. The impassable rocky outcroppings to the north and the impediment of the falls added considerable weight to his decision; but, he really did not care to locate so close to the village.

As the sun rose over the landscape the following morning,

McAllister located a wide, grassy flat south along the river. It was protected by a high bank where he could hollow-out and build a comfortable sod hut and a shelter for his horses. Pleased with the spot, he moved his camp immediately and began cutting the sod squares needed for a warm, winter dwelling.

In the ensuing days young Two Way all but moved in with the trapper, becoming so friendly and constantly underfoot, full of curiosity, that McAllister wondered if he might never be rid of him. He found the persistence unusual, but nonetheless accepted it. Then one day Two Way disappeared and the trapper was once again alone in his preparations for the advancing winter.

October was well upon him and, although there had been only light skiffs of snow during the nights which disappeared with the day's intermittent sunshine, McAllister paid careful heed to the warnings he had received from traders he had met who knew the valley well. Stories of temperatures that could freeze a man to death increased his caution. Tales of flooding ice flows, old hungry cougars, and prowling bears just out of hibernation had been told across the campfire at Soi'yus. The added threat of the swift death strike of the rattlesnake, or burrowing woodticks hiding on the sagebrush all remained in the trapper's mind as he packed the thick sods tightly into place against a hollow in the bank. From small saplings he tied together a frame which stood two feet off the ground on which he spread the buffalo robe and blankets of his bedding. Outside the enclosure he constructed a fireplace with smooth, flat rocks.

By mid November McAllister was well prepared, as he had always been, for the deep snow and cold of winter. His traps were set the customary four inches below the surface of the water and camouflaged with thin dead branches. On a stick hanging above it, he put the horrible smelling castoreum to attract the male beaver. Each day he went out to check them, emptying his catch into a pack. As he carried the bounty home, slung over his shoulders, he thought often of the good canoe he had left behind with Dubrais at Fort Okanogan. Struggling through the snow along the riverbank, his back bearing the burden of the heavy skins, he pondered the value of a canoe upon this river.

During the weeks he had been camped near the river, McAllister had seen only one dugout pass his camp. It appeared small and shallow, hardly practical for hauling furs upriver. For the most part rafts were used on the Okanagan waterways as choice wood and solid bark for building canoes was scarce. Evidence of considerable use of horses lay in the number of trails packed into the snow along the shoreline. During the fall hunting season he noticed bands of Indians riding along the ridge above his camp, outlined against the skyline. They did not bother him, only paused a moment to observe his dwelling beside the river.

Only Two Way visited the trapper's sod house. Crossing the lake on the ice well above the waterfalls meant half a morning's travel on foot through the deep snow to reach the trapper's location. For, once he had left the lakeshore, he must climb up the hill and follow the flat ridge above the lake southward around the high bluff above the waterfalls, and down to where McAllister's camp was located beside the river. Having arrived, Two Way would then remain the day. From him McAllister learned much about the village located on the flats between the river and the lake which earlier French Canadian fur traders had named Lac du Chien. Two Way had mastered enough of the English language to converse with the trapper without struggle, and he was very proud of his acquired knowledge.

One day as he helped McAllister skin a catch of beaver and muskrat, then fasten the fresh hides to the stretchers, they talked about Lac du Chien.

McAllister asked, "What do you call it?"

"Skaxa" (Ska-haw)

Glancing across at the boy where they knelt at their cleaning, the trapper raised a quizzical brow.

Grinning, the young Indian explained, "When the She-whaps were here, they called it Ska-haw. It means dog. But it is horse to us." As he worked with the trapper, Two Way glanced occasionally toward McAllister's two horses who pawed beneath the snow for the sparse grass left from their earlier grazing. Impulsively, proudly, he informed the trapper, "I have a horse, too."

McAllister raised his eyes, quickly searching the surrounding area for sign of the animal. "Did you ride it here?"

Two Way nodded. "Yes."

"Where did you hide it? Go get it," he ordered, whereupon Two Way darted among the huge snow-banked boulders near the river and led forth a small pony.

McAllister rose to his feet and ran a hand approvingly over the pony's mane and neck and patted its shoulders. "Where did you get him? I've never seen you on a horse. You're always on your raft on the river, or on foot. And how did you get him over here? Ah– the ice." He smiled. "That was daring of you."

Two Way's round, brown face broke into a bright smile reflecting his pride at owning such a fine little pony of his own. McAllister peered into the boy's face, half hidden between the fur of his cap and thick fur collar sewn onto his winter tunic.

Two Way said, "My uncle, Rattler, got him for me yesterday. He brought some other horses home from somewhere."

"He traded something for them? With who?" McAllister was surprised to learn that perhaps other trappers were located near him. He walked around the pony showing his interest in the condition of its feet, the well muscled legs and straight back.

Two Way laughed impulsively. "Maybe he stole them! I don't think so. But– sometimes Rattler steals things."

McAllister's eyes swung around to meet those of the boy's. "Steals things?" He was curious now.

"Maybe from another tribe. He has a horse of his own. There aren't many horses in our village. He was gone for eight days once and when he came home he had a lot of horses with him." The smile left Two Way's face and, his dark eyes clouding, he tilted his head in thought. "But it is something that he does, that's all. Stealing. Nobody else in our village steals," he added proudly.

"Well," consoled McAllister. "There are people who steal among us, too. They want more than they need."

Although the conversation with the Indian boy did not unnerve McAllister, he did heed a warning from Two Way's impromptu remarks. While the trapper always kept a sharp eye for wanderers about his camp, his sense of protection of his property became just a little keener. Thereafter, each night he tethered his own two horses closer to his sod house against the bank.

The winter season grew bitter and harsh. Snow fell steadily so that, without a thaw, it was soon piled high around his house. Since the day he had ridden his pony into the trapper's camp, young Two Way had not visited again. The snow had become too deep for easy travel. The new paths which McAllister made each day when setting his traps in the river were quickly covered by a fresh snowfall throughout the night. However, McAllister travelled with the use of snowshoes, whereas he had noticed that Two Way did not.

13

One day McAllister saddled the bay and climbed the hill west of the falls, where he had first observed the Indian boy, and viewed the village below. It was comprised of many kekuli, the Salish winter dwelling. Built over a thirty foot pit, three feet in depth, the kekuli was constructed of four sturdy poles set within the pit and placed at outward angles. These main poles supported the rafters and adjoining poles which formed the conical shape of the kekuli. Lashed securely in place, the outer shell was then covered with thick pieces of bark, dry grass and earth sods. Over the rushes drawn from the marshes and bogs of the river used to cover the dirt floor, the women placed large, thick mats of woven reeds for comfort.

McAllister counted fourteen kekuli, around which were scattered six raised caches made of poles, for storage of meat and fish. Because the soil of the valley bottomland was sandy and dry, several large storage pits had been dug to keep the roots and wild vegetables gathered by the band for winter use.

Smoke spiralled upward from within the houses. On the outer structure of the houses, McAllister could spot no outlet other than the hole in the top. Surely, he wondered, they don't climb in and out through all that smoke, past the sods which must loosen the dirt down upon their fires. However, as he stood in observance of the village, he saw a resident do just that. As the man returned to the dwelling, McAllister noticed that he leaned forward over the hole as if calling a warning of his return. The trapper smiled as he watched the man disappear.

In travel along the river to harvest and reset his traps, it became apparent to McAllister that he was the only white man in the midst of three villages of Salish Indians: Shoshen-eetkwa, Kwak-ne-ta and Soi'yus. The villages were located between Lac du Chien and the smaller Vaseux Lake at the entrance of a narrow passageway between two high bluffs beyond, and Inkameep, near the long lake at Soi'yus. McAllister's trapline extended from a mile below the waterfalls nearly to Soi'yus.

Realizing his close proximity to the Indians' camps and his encroachment upon the Okanagan's seasonal hunting grounds, the trapper wondered often, throughout the winter months, why he had never been approached by anyone from the villages or run clear out of the territory. He knew there were certain courtesies to be upheld between himself and residents of the villages and laws to abide while in their presence. Permission to hunt in their territory had never been requested by McAllister so it was on tenuous ground he walked amongst them. He noticed that young Two Way had always arrived at his camp during the morning hours and never left until evening; an unusual tolerance by the band.

In February the huge snow drifts about McAllister's camp slowly began to sink. The thick sheet of ice over Lac du Chien rumbled and cracked and divided itself into enormous plates. Along the river, a lesser flow of ice pushed up onto the banks, causing the trapper to be concerned about protection of his camp against its constant push in his direction.

During late February and March he spent the daylight hours hauling in his bounty. Most of the pelts were sleek and smooth, and thick from the months of winter hibernation. Throughout his labours the damaged muscles in his shoulder protested furiously under the strain. The slow melting of the snow made transport of the hides with the use of his horses too dangerous, for beneath the deep drifts a sheet of solid ice covered the ground. With the drifting chunks of ice, not even a raft on the river would have been of any use to him. The enormous plates from the lake flowed downstream, crashing and tumbling over the falls, sometimes forming a dangerous dam if the pieces did not break up for several days and move away with the flow. The river was narrow in places and although it held the normal flow of water, it could not contain the bulk of ice movement.

McAllister became increasingly frustrated. He had never been dependent upon a river so inconsistent in its thawing. While the daytime temperatures were well above freezing with the snow melting steadily during the days, the isolating cold of nighttime sealed a new coat of ice over the old. In setting his traps each time, McAllister slipped continually on the icy shoreline, sometimes losing the trap into the water. It could be retrieved of course but not without great difficulty in dealing with the rising river and the hazardous blades of ice.

The warm south winds of late March finally melted the last of the ice along the shores. By the first of April the ground was dry with new grass quickly beginning to cover it. McAllister breathed a sigh of relief and welcomed the springtime, which seemed to have at last arrived in the Okanagan. His horses had fared well during the winter months, pawing through the snow for what little dry grass there was beneath, supplemented by wild bunchgrass which grew along the ridge above his camp that McAllister had earlier been able to harvest. When he took stock of the season's catch, he was disappointed to find that the number of pelts fell short of his expectations. It was usual for him to take a bounty in excess of one hundred furs from a river in a single season.

One day when the snow had disappeared and ice no longer clogged the river, Two Way arrived at McAllister's camp riding his horse. On this day an exchange took place which was to alter the isolation of the trapper from the people of Shoshen-eetkwa and significantly change the course of the nomadic pattern of his life.

Two Way helped McAllister bundle the dried and stretched hides of beaver, muskrat and mink into bales for transport. When he had finished, he dashed off to his horse and pulled a set of deer hide bags from over its withers and ran back to where the trapper stood tying his traps together through one long thong. He hastily handed McAllister the last trap with a hint of impatience, then drew two bundles of clothing from the bags.

"These are for you, Many Rains," he quickly told McAllister. Two Way's round, brown face registered his pride in the offer. "I want to trade for them," he added proudly.

McAllister sat down on the log near his fireplace. Two Way immediately seated himself beside him. The trapper smiled over the boy's obvious friendliness and was genuinely pleased to have the company. He had missed Two Way's constant chatter and the assistance of an extra pair of hands at his trapping chores.

As he untied the thin thongs binding the clothes, he said to Two Way, "It is a long winter alone without company. Were you ill, that you didn't come to see me?"

"I was needed to help my mother and father. And the snow was very deep," Two Way told him.

"Haven't you got snowshoes?"

"Yes, but I don't like wearing them. I can't run fast in them, and I fall lots." Two Way's eyes watched McAllister unroll the pieces of clothing.

"You'll grow out of your awkwardness soon," said McAllister to the boy. "We're all clumsy when we're growing up."

Two Way saw the smile which creased the trapper's face above the thick beard as McAllister turned his head to look at him. He raised the new tunic before them for a better look.

"These are fine clothes, Two Way. They have been very well made and decorated and are worth a good price." His blue eyes stared into the young Indian's. He waited for a response.

Two Way hesitated, then quickly rose to his feet and stood before the trapper. "When I first came here I saw a roll of cloth in your house. You had a box with needles, too, and some thread so thin I could hardly see it. I noticed them one day when you were moving

95

your things around. I want all those things," he stated boldly, not wavering in the steady gaze in which McAllister held him.

McAllister looked down at the tunic as he laid it upon the leggings and moccasins across his knees. Indeed, the work was of the finest craft he had seen. The stitches were even and perfect. Every fringe was of an identical cut. And the moccasins were designed wide to fit over the bulky length of the breeches and high enough to keep out the wetness of the snow. They had heavy laces of elk hide to wrap about the calves of his legs.

"Did your mother make these? Or an aunt, perhaps?" he asked of Two Way.

"No, my mother is too busy making clothes for my father and my uncle. Rattler has no wife of his own yet, so he lives with us and my mother has to sew for him." Two Way was relaxed and returned to his place on the log beside McAllister. "My two older sisters are now married and have moved to the great lake north from here."

McAllister laughed quickly. "Well, I know you didn't make them and you don't want the cloth and sewing needles for yourself. Why then?"

"For my other sister who still lives with us and makes all of my clothes," Two Way told him. "Nahna is her name."

McAllister stilled. Nahna, he silently queried. He had heard that name, but where? Not from Two Way, he decided. "Well," he said casually, rolling the clothes together. "Come on, then. I'll trade you the cloth and the needles and thread. These are good clothes and I am glad to have them."

They entered McAllister's small sod house and the bolt of bright cloth was handed to the boy, along with the small box containing the needles and coloured thread noticed earlier by Two Way's sharp eyes. The trapper appeared pleased, and Two Way smiled happily.

"Nahna's sewing always brings the best trades," he boasted.

As McAllister tidied up what was left of his trade goods, he pondered the name. "Nahna. What does that name mean?"

Two Way smiled. "She is called Pana'llks– it is like a crossed dress," he explained, laying his right arm carefully over his left.

"Folded?"

Two Way nodded. "My aunt from Nicola gave her that name. But my next older sister could not say it right, so she was Nahna to us. My aunt told my mother that she had beautiful hands that would make her famous as the best dressmaker."

"Indeed!" exclaimed McAllister. "And she is the best, it seems."

The two returned to the outdoors. "Tell me," McAllister began carefully. "Why is it that no one from your village has visited my camp in all these months, but you?"

"We do not care that you are here," Two Way informed him

bluntly, with a slight shrug of his shoulders. "One man does not take enough beaver to harm our trade. And look--" he said nodding proudly to the cloth he held tight against his chest. "I have made a good trade with you. Nahna will now wear the best dress of all the girls in the village."

McAllister frowned. Again, he tried to draw on his memory to tell him where and when the name had come to his ears. "You have not mentioned her to me before now."

"No. She did not want me to." Two Way shrugged and kept talking. "The only one in the village who cares that you live so near is my uncle."

McAllister's brows shot up. "And what does he say about it?"

"That we have never allowed that before. He told my father that you should pay for all the hides you take away from here when you leave and there should be a limit to what you are allowed. There are limits on everything, you know. Everything belongs to us." Two Way leaned over the set of bags in which he had brought the clothes for McAllister. Awkwardly he stuffed the end of the bolt of cloth into one bag and finally got it tied with a leather thong, so he could safely get it across the river to Nahna. "I have to go back now," he said quickly.

Leading his pony alongside the log which McAllister used for his bench near the fireplace, Two Way steadied the unstable bundles and climbed upon the patient animal. With one hand holding the rope from the pony's halter and the thong around the cloth, and the other waving in farewell to the trapper, Two Way booted his pony into action. Soon he had disappeared along the river trail, splashing his way across and climbing up the opposite bank to the flats of his home.

In May McAllister prepared to abandon his camp along the Okanagan River. With a sad look clouding his round face, Two Way helped him on the last day.

"Where are you going?" he wanted to know.

"To Fort Kamloops."

"Is it closer than Fort Okanogan?"

"No. In fact, it's almost a hundred miles farther." Confessing to a yearning for even the slightest news about Willow, McAllister added, "I expect to learn something of old friends there." Emptying his packs of all his trade goods, he told Two Way, "Tell your uncle that with these, I have paid twice over for the few pelts I'm taking out of here."

Two Way's eyes widened at the sight upon the ground. Before him was spread a collection of coloured beads, glass buttons, pieces of silver cutlery and three cooking pots. Beside them the trapper placed his shovel and axe and the small deerskin bag in which he carried tobacco. Two Way raised his dark eyes to meet McAllister's.

"My father will be pleased with your gifts. I'm sorry that you are going."

McAllister nodded approvingly.

Two Way gathered the articles of trade together and stuffed what he could into the bags which he carried over the withers of his pony. About his waist he tied the pots and bag of tobacco, looping them with his belt. He held the handles of the shovel and axe close to his side and stood quietly before the tall, rugged looking trapper. He had indeed made a good trade that day and felt proud of himself.

"I will miss you, Two Way," McAllister told him gently. "You've been good company. You've helped me many times with my traps and I've not yet repaid you." He reached into the pocket of his saddlebags and drew out a small knife. Slowly he unfolded it, pulling open the blades, one at each end of the small ivory handle.

Two Way leaned closer to view it.

"It's yours," McAllister said and handed it to him. "It's called a pocket knife. I bought it at Spokane House."

Two Way pushed the blades together, then opened them again, practising. Turning the little knife in his hands, he gave it careful inspection. His pleasure at receiving such an unusual gift showed brightly in his eyes.

"I have one more thing for you," Two Way heard the trapper say. When he turned he saw McAllister folding a large Hudson Bay blanket with red stripes on its ends. Two Way reached out. The softness of it startled him. He had known only furs and hides upon his bed, and although they held out the cold better than anything else he could imagine, they did not have the warm, soft feel as this new blanket did against his skin. He could say nothing to the trapper. His voice seemed to have deserted him.

McAllister grinned, "You have earned it well." Reaching out to touch the boy's shoulder lightly, he ordered kindly, "Now, off you go with all your treasures."

His horses now packed with the bales of furs and necessary provisions to see him through to Fort Kamloops, McAllister placed a foot into the stirrup of his saddle and swung himself onto the gelding. His knife was held in its clasp at his waist. The gun rested in its scabbard attached to the saddle. He could feel the reassuring bulk of it beside his knee. McAllister quickly bade Two Way good-bye, took up the reins of the bridle and began the arduous climb up the bank from the river, leading the Appaloosa mare. They slid in the shale, finally reaching the top of the hill where the Hudson's Bay Fur Brigade trail passed on the west side. It was a warm, sunny day as he turned, waved to the boy who remained beside the river, then reined his horse north-west.

Only Two Way witnessed the trapper's departure from the valley.

14

Fort Kamloops was the heart of the inland fur trade. From its gates the large brigades transported supplies to the northern extremes of the Hudson's Bay Company fur trading posts in New Caledonia. They returned with many thousands of dollars worth of furs bound for the pacific fur capital, Fort Vancouver. Within its boundaries a small town flourished. Businessmen and traders, as well as horsemen required to man the pack trains, contributed to the pulsation of life at Fort Kamloops during the 1830's.

Fort Kamloops had developed as a main horse depot. The plateaus of the surrounding area were abundant with tall bunchgrass, sufficient for grazing the hundreds of horses exchanged when the brigades passed through. Fort Kamloops also became the western defence headquarters as harassment from the local Indians increased.

The Indians of the area were known as the Shuswaps (She-whaps), part of the Salish nation. Their territory was vast, reaching from the Okanagan and Nicola valleys northeast into the Rocky Mountains. The most war-like of all the tribes in the interior of New Caledonia, the Shuswaps carried out attacks upon neighbouring bands of the Okanagan, the Similkameen and Nicola, as well as conducting sporadic raids on the white settlers, fur trappers and traders who moved throughout the valley. By 1833, it had become necessary to station about twenty-five men at the Kamloops post for protection lest lives were lost through continued aggravation.

Because the main Shuswap Indian village was located on the same side of the Thompson River as the fort, life at Fort Kamloops became so intolerable at times that each new incident gave further rise to talk of moving the fort across the river.

In May of 1835 Rayne McAllister rode into the perimeters of Fort Kamloops. Having passed through the country of the violent Shuswaps alone was perceived by some as nearly miraculous. He was greeted by a look of astonishment on the round face of the Englishman who managed the company store and who was the first to meet the trapper.

Staring with amused wonderment at the dust-covered, trail-weary trapper, he said, "How the hell you rode in here alone is a bloody miracle! The way these Indians are getting toward the whites, every year more trappers are found dead than alive, trying to get here. And their pelts are brought in by the very ones who kill 'em. They've nerve, they 'ave." A short, round man, he stood across the counter from McAllister, his thumbs hooked behind his suspenders, and peered inquisitively at the trapper.

Returning the storekeeper's stare, McAllister was starkly reminded of Adam Breen. He asked quietly, "What is your name?"

"Walker," came the quick reply.

"Nothing else?" McAllister's voice was friendly.

"Just Walker. It's really Ellis Walker, but everyone just calls me Walker." Reaching up, he smoothed his bushy mustache with finger and thumb while contemplating the man across the counter from him. "It sounds impressive when they're dickering with me and feel the need to shout at me," he added with a quick laugh which shook his barrelled body. "And yours?"

"McAllister," replied the trapper. Setting his saddle bags against the wall, he removed his deer hide gloves and vest. "Do you hear news from the northern forts?"

"Some. Which one?" Walker raised a curious brow. "Anybody in particular?

"Adam Breen of Fort St. James," McAllister replied soberly. His eyes peered through the dust-covered panes of the narrow window in Walker's store, to the open compound which had suddenly become noisy with men and horses of the fur brigade. He frowned.

Behind him, Walker hastened around the counter toward the door. "Aha!" he cried in a jubilant voice. "They're arrivin'!"

McAllister could indeed see that the fur brigade from Fort Alexandria was just getting in. As Walker stepped through the doorway into the sunlight, a loud skirl of bagpipes could be heard from the distance, accompanied by the anxious voices of the wranglers who kept the long line of heavily laden horses under control. In minutes, George Southport of the Hudson's Bay Company rode into the compound, followed by a company man who was obviously second-in-command. They were followed by the bugler, the flag bearer and sundry travellers, trappers and hunters. Finally, the wranglers led in the one hundred and thirty pack horses.

The compound quickly filled with milling men and animals. Dust rose in thick spirals. The noise of barking dogs running beside the few children who darted about the place calling to the riders, charged the warm May air with excitement. Such a stir and racket always greeted the arrival of a Hudson's Bay Fur Brigade on its pack trip from Fort Alexandria to Fort Okanogan, and again when it returned loaded with the winter's supplies. Little else happened during the balance of the year.

McAllister turned away from the window, gathered up his gloves and saddlebags and joined Walker outside where the storekeeper stood beside the trapper's horses.

"You know," Walker breathed excitedly. "The sight of a brigade arriving is damned good for the eyes, but every time it leaves I think of fellows like yourself who spend their entire life in the mountains gathering those thousands of pelts every year. You walk hand in hand with death every step. As I see it, you got all elements against you, the hand of the Indian at your throat and starvation gnawing at your belly most of the time." He glanced up at McAllister. "A man's crazy or he'd stay the hell off the rivers and let those in old England come and get the hides themselves if they want hats."

McAllister smiled. "It's the whole industry that the furs have created that counts. Some men are meant to wear them, and others are meant to trap them. How're you going to get the furs in if you don't have men on the rivers?"

"Well, I s'pose that's why the Lord made men like you, all guts and no mind for your own safety." Walker smiled broadly and slapped McAllister's shoulder soundly. "And others like me who sit in the middle of the industry and keep you supplied with the necessities of life and off the edge of starvation. Come," he urged. "Let's get those bundles off your horse into the warehouse. The stables are full, but the field is wide open for grazing your horses."

McAllister took up the reins of his horses and led them toward the warehouse. "I've been through here before."

"Well, then–" said Walker. "You've stayed at Mrs. Ross's boardin' house. Costs plenty, but everythin's good." Scratching his chin in thought, he frowned. "I don't remember you passin' through."

"You weren't here."

"Yes, well never mind. My wife's havin' a dinner tonight. With the brigade in and all, we celebrate a bit, you know. Maybe you'd like to sit in with us. I'd like to hear about your travels."

McAllister looked down, squarely into Walker's brown eyes and nodded. "I'll be 'round," he said quietly and moved away from Ellis Walker as they neared the warehouse, where he would unload his packs.

"Seven then," he heard Walker call out to him.

As McAllister led his horses around the corner of the building, Ellis Walker watched with interest. A great surge of envy engulfed him. There had ridden into the fort the man that he had longed to become himself and regretted never having been. There's a certain reckless danger to his life but he's a confident bugger, Walker decided, in admiration of the trapper. Dressed in his deerskins and moccasins, passing defiantly through hostile territories, McAllister was master of his own defence. Ah, sighed the storekeeper, for the power of that knife at his side and the gun in its scabbard beneath his knee when he rides. With the success of his season in the mountains loaded on his pack horse, the man must surely know satisfaction and contentment with his life, Walker felt, making a man like me wish he were somebody else just for a little while.

Walker sighed heavily and snapped the tight suspenders with his thumbs against his round chest and stomach, returning to his own world. He watched McAllister unload his packs. An indomitable man in an indomitable land, who rides tall and straight and fearless in his saddle. But then, he decided, they need the likes of me to provide their stores, look after their credit and ask them in for a tasty home-cooked meal.

Alone in his room in the log home of Mrs. Ross, Rayne McAllister viewed the compound from his window. Few men and horses remained there now. The afternoon had waned and the sun disappeared. The men of the Hudson's Bay Company and the wranglers were indoors. Walker had not replied to him about Adam Breen, McAllister remembered. The excitement and confusion caused by the brigade's arrival preceded any news he might have learned of the family. He resolved to enquire again and press for news while at the Walker home that evening.

Mrs. Walker met him at the door of their home. Behind her stood her husband, thumbs hooked into the pockets of his vest which hid the suspenders of his earlier attire. Taller than her husband, and slender, Mary Walker conducted herself with all the elegance and grace of her New England rearing. When greetings had been exchanged, the two men followed Mrs. Walker into the dining room where other guests waited.

"Now, we have three other guests--" she was saying to him. "You must meet Willard Bromley and his step--"

Suddenly McAllister was aware of only one presence in the room as his eyes looked into those of Willow Breen Cairns. The room became still. For a brief, heightened moment his gaze searched hers and found recognition there, and more? Pleasure at meeting him again? Had she flushed slightly? Yes, her smile told him everything. Then, as if from a great distance, he could hear his hostess' voice reach him and he somehow managed to acknowledge her introductions. But as Mary Walker talked, McAllister continued to see only Willow, whose shocked gray eyes stared back into his own. She was lovelier than he had remembered her.

From beside them Walker observed this unexpected meeting with unrestrained interest. He felt the electricity in the room and saw the careful reserve return to McAllister. The magnificent moment passed. Walker cleared his throat.

"You asked about Adam Breen earlier," he said to the trapper.

McAllister looked around at Walker and waited. He felt Mary Walker's eyes upon him, taking in the fine deerskin suit he wore, which young Two Way had traded. McAllister turned and looked directly at Mary Walker. She dropped her gaze and spoke then, to her other guests.

Turning away from the men, Willow fought to control the excitement fluttering in her chest. She knew her face was flushed. It was impossible for her to hide from her hosts the shock she had felt upon meeting Rayne, and the immediate recognition of the feelings which had rushed through her. The Walkers had watched her reaction at the sight of the trapper. Had this been planned? Most likely not, she decided. It was just coincidence that he and she should be in the same room together, here at Fort Kamloops, after a lapse of five years.

When she felt the flush disappear from her cheeks and neck, and the wildness of her heartbeat begin to subside, Willow turned and glanced at Rayne McAllister once more. I have never stopped loving him, she admitted, and I never shall. This is God's will that we meet again. As she watched McAllister and Ellis Walker talk, she felt again the surge of excitement upon meeting Rayne and the anticipation of what might be from this moment on. She sensed the stare of Mary Walker's querying eyes upon her.

Standing beside McAllister, Walker said, "I wanted to say today that Breen died last year and that his widow is living here. Of course, as you see–" he added with a glance across the room in Willow's direction, "his daughter lives here as well."

McAllister watched as everyone seated themselves around a table which was sumptuously dressed with a variety of foods. Platters of venison and pheasant, spiced and browned to a delicious crispness, browned salmon in sauce and bowls of thick gravy were set upon a fine linen cloth. Covered dishes contained turnips and squash sprinkled with thyme. Completing the meal was a large salad made with wild lettuce, onions and dried berries, and currents from England. A grand meal by any trapper's standards and McAllister relished the change from his own meagre fare.

"Willow's husband–" Walker began, but was interrupted by his wife. He frowned. He wanted to tell McAllister about James Cairns.

"Ellis," Mary instructed gently. "Please seat your friend and say Grace before it all gets too cold to eat."

McAllister glanced across the table at Willow. Her dark head was bowed and he saw that a light frown creased her brow. At the end of the table Ellis Walker mumbled the blessing, but not a word penetrated McAllister's thoughts. His mind was filled with the presence of the lovely woman across from him. He had despaired of ever seeing her again.

The clinking of cutlery, passing of the platters and the humming sound of dinner talk surrounded the guests at their meal. Walker watched McAllister. The trapper glanced often in Willow Cairns' direction. And Mary Walker took notice of her husband's interest in them both.

"Tell me," said Walker to McAllister beside him. "Do you always travel alone?"

"I prefer it," the trapper replied bluntly, looking about him at the young man who was the company clerk at the fort, and who was seated beside Willow. The lack of James Cairns' presence in the Walker home told McAllister that he was either away at another post, or dead.

Walker continued to demand his attention. "You've been in the Columbia area. I hear the Indians there are not as annoying as the ones we have on our doorstep. Were you at Spokane House?"

"Last summer."

"A lively place, I'm told. I was at Fort Spokane only once, on my way up here. My wife and I travelled with a group of missionaries, overland to the Snake River and Spokane House." And, smiling indulgently down the length of the table toward Mary, he wondered aloud to the others, "How I ever talked her into it I'll never know! It must have been the challenge of the west which drew her along with me. It caught everyone up, but many never finished. It was a difficult trip. I needn't tell you about difficulties, I'm sure!" Walker cleared his throat, washed his meal down with a cup of cold water, then refilled the cup from the metal pitcher and drank thirstily again. "Tell me about the horse races at Spokane House, McAllister. They're on the verge of abandoning that post, you know."

McAllister could not immediately reply. Thoughts of Denise White assailed his conscience suddenly and he refrained from looking directly at Willow when she urged, "Yes, do tell us about the entertainment, Rayne."

Mary Walker saved the moment for him. "I hear there are dances in the great ballroom and many more immigrants living nearby the post now. There is even a small classroom set up for schooling, I've learned. How can they abandon a post with so much to offer the people there. Many missionaries have located near there–"

"Mary, my dear–" Walker interjected. "They are nevertheless going to let it go. News has it as fact now. A new location is being considered directly along the Columbia River. Where it is now, it is over fifty miles off the mainstream of the traffic in furs."

On McAllister's left sat a man as tall as the trapper, with a nature of quiet reserve. He had been introduced to McAllister as Willard Bromley, and had remained silent, eating his meal with a steadiness that brought him to a finish when the others were barely half done. He was in his seventy-first year, most of them spent on the western frontier with the fur trade. He had been with the Pacific Fur Company at old Fort Astoria at the Pacific, then with the Hudson's Bay Company as Chief Factor at Fort Vancouver, Fort Kamloops, and last at Fort St. James upon the passing of Chief Factor Adam Breen. He had, of late, retired to Fort Kamloops. Willard Bromley was also the husband of Chief Factor Breen's widow. Emily Bromley was absent from the Walker table only because she had contracted a severe chest cold which had sent her to her bed.

Bromley now cleared his throat, commanding the immediate attention of everyone present. "You came down from the north a few years ago," he stated all knowing to McAllister. "I seem to remember you, because you bought a lot of supplies for a man travelling with the fur brigade and you talked of wintering in the Okanagan. Did you?"

McAllister glanced around at Bromley seated beside him. He had not been paying attention.

"Did you remain in the Okanagan?" Bromley repeated.

"I did not," he replied quickly. "I went along with the brigade to Fort Okanogan where I stayed with a Frenchman named Evan Dubrais and his family."

Bromley's brows shot upward. He smiled. "Well, yes— I know Evan Dubrais. He has been there for quite a while. He's married to a Nez Pérce woman. A brilliant individual, she is, but much suppressed by her know-it-all husband." He chuckled, obviously drawing on a memory or two.

McAllister, too, smiled. He considered that he would not have called Broken Bone brilliant, but perhaps special, more gifted than others, certainly in the healing arts of her tribe as his presence at this table attested.

"Where did you trap?" he heard Bromley ask.

"Babine Lake area and Fort St. James." McAllister glanced across at Willow, meeting her eyes directly. She had been watching him, and now he saw registered in the depths of her gray eyes, what might have been between them long ago. But there is something else, he thought. Something she wants me to know, but cannot at this time say. Silently, McAllister cursed the table full of guests between them. Where is Cairns? He said to Bromley, "That is where I knew Mrs. Cairns and her husband."

Bromley leaned back in his chair. "Ah, yes," he muttered thoughtfully, "yes, yes," - words which told McAllister exactly nothing.

Instantly, Mary sprang out of her chair. "Well, we are all done with this table, I see!" she said cheerily. "Willow? Let us leave the men to their discussions of God knows what and their brandy, and we will do the cleaning up as all frontier wives must."

Obediently Willow got to her feet and, loading her arms with platters and bowls, moved out of the dining room and therefore, out of McAllister's sight.

The conversation between himself, Ellis Walker, Willard Bromley and the company clerk John Spikes, held little interest for the trapper. He felt stifled and wished only for this evening at the Walkers to end so that he might seek out Willow. What had caused her father's death? Where was her mother living? Might he visit her? And James? There was so much to ask, and Walker had hardly been given the opportunity to finish half the conversations he had begun about the Breens.

However, John Spikes had finally found his tongue that evening and McAllister heard him asking, "Tell me, what takes a man like you out on the rivers among the natives and keeps you there year after year through the most abominable patterns of weather? It can't be for riches alone. You now have credit with the company which amounts to more than you'll ever need in your lifetime. Is it to prove something to the world, or perhaps to yourself? Do you feel out of place in other societies maybe?"

When Spikes had ceased his questioning, the room seemed oppressively still. He leaned against the door casing with hands in his pockets, a short, thin man whose raised head displayed a sharp, prominent nose and receding chin, waiting for the trapper's reply.

McAllister glanced across at the clerk. Insolent! he decided and replied stiffly, "I've known no other way of life. And I am aware that you know my worth." He judged Spikes to be about his own age and felt some resentment that in the course of employment, the man would know everything about him. He knew Walker only looked after the store inventory. Spikes took care of everything else for the Company.

The Hudson's Bay man continued in a pessimistic tone as if he were baiting McAllister's temperament. "You know, you'll either drown one day, get an arrow in your back or–"

"Or die of old age," McAllister finished impatiently. "Which, in every case, the Company is my beneficiary. Do you have alternate employment for me?" He felt as though he was being challenged to defend– what? He watched Spikes carefully now. The man obviously wanted something from him.

Walker spoke up and saved Spikes the trouble of trying to deal with a reply to this already defensive trapper. "Actually McAllister, we do have a grave problem with our Indians in this region. Several years ago a young man posted here was killed and the threat of more of the same has hung over our heads ever since. A new location across the river is a possibility and will likely be necessary before long. Now if you plan to remain with us–" Here, Walker contemplated the electric moment which had fastened itself between the trapper and Willow earlier in the evening. "There is need," he said quietly, "for your experience with Indians. You could render some valuable service to the Company. We have at the moment, eighteen men on staff in the capacity of defending our fort, but there is a lack of positive leadership." He delivered McAllister a wide, convincing smile and, meeting the trapper's light blue eyes directly, raised a brow and suggested, "Life on this post could prove quite comfortable for you."

"I notice that there's not a chief factor in charge at this post right now," McAllister stated.

"We're waiting for him to return," Walker informed him. "George Southport will be taking over when he comes back from the Columbia."

McAllister's blue eyes swung around to meet Bromley's. "Southport?"

"Yes, and God help us all! It'll be run like a military post," Bromley replied. Then, considering the matter a moment, added, "But perhaps that's what's needed after all."

"Agreed," spoke John Spikes curtly. "Absolutely what we need here."

Bromley smiled, amused. "Finances and war," he muttered. "In the east it was the French and the British. Out here, trappers and Indians!" Pushing back his chair, he rose to his feet and suggested, "Let us join the ladies in the sitting room. I'm sure they have their dishes back in the cupboards by now." To McAllister he added, with a wink of an eye, "An old man like me enjoys the presence of beauty during my yawning years and wonders at the isolation of men such as you in your youth!"

McAllister smiled in return and got to his feet. He rather liked Bromley. The man was straight forward with a sense of reality and humour. "You have an unarguable point there, sir."

Spikes followed McAllister toward the dining room doorway. "The offer is worth considering," he remarked idly, looking up at the tall trapper.

"My plans are centred on the Okanagan," McAllister stated clearly. "Keep a good account of my credit, Mr. Spikes, for I may be needing all of it soon."

Walker ushered Bromley, Spikes and McAllister into the small sitting room. Comfortable benches with soft cushions and several chairs had been placed at angles In the room for cozy conversation. Mary Walker had planned a room which radiated a welcome and friendliness much needed in the isolated posts of the west.

Willow stood near the door at the entrance of the house. Over her arm was draped a knitted wrap. McAllister's eyes sought hers. Willow was not looking at him, but rather toward Willard Bromley. Is she leaving? How truly lovely she is! The length of her skirt draped softly to the floor in a graceful manner which enhanced her slim waist. The narrow ruffles of the bodice only added to the mystery of her femininity. McAllister ached to reach out and hold her to him.

Mary Walker announced, "Willow is leaving, gentlemen. She must see to her mother who, as you know, was stricken with a dreadful chill."

Near McAllister, Bromley set aside the small glass of brandy which Walker had just handed to him. "I'll go along with you, my dear. Since your mother is also my wife, the responsibility for her well-being rests on my shoulders, too. And-- you should not walk about here alone."

McAllister's startled eyes swung quickly around to Bromley, then once more to Willow. Damn, so much I don't know, he cursed silently. Willow smiled and its warmth reached across the room to him, captivating his senses and spurring him into action. "Please," he blurted hurriedly. "Let me walk with you, Mrs. Cairns."

Bromley raised a quizzical brow. "Indeed!" To Willow, he nodded and remarked, "You couldn't be better protected, Willow, than by the man who may lead our defence department here if we can be convincing enough."

Walker watched Willow and the trapper leave his house. A private envy encased him once more. A perfect match, of course! He had clearly been caught up in the romanticism of the idea. Walker crossed the room to his wife. Although he did not listen to her conversation with Bromley and Spikes, he nevertheless remained close to Mary. His eyes strained into the grayness of the evening outside the long window of the room. He watched McAllister and Willow until they were completely out of his sight.

Mary Walker tugged at her husband's sleeve. "Really, dear," she admonished gently, "do you have to be so obviously interested in them? We could all see that they were more than just acquaintances at Fort St. James, but does your friend know that James is dead?"

"No," replied Ellis Walker and, frowning as to his oversight in not getting it said to the trapper, crossed the room for another brandy.

In the evening shadows a rising moon cast eerie shapes across their path as Willow and McAllister walked toward the Bromley residence. In the close quietness which surrounded them, McAllister told her, "It's good to see you again, Willow," then asked as gently as he could, "Where is he?"

Willow looked up to the side of his face, surprised that he did not know about James Cairns.

He turned his head to stare into her eyes. "James-- where is he?" Even to him, his words sounded bitter and cold, so he knew they pierced her heart. He regretted his show of jealousy and impatience, but could not control it. By her stillness, suddenly he knew that what he had suspected was true. "Willow, I'm sorry," McAllister offered lamely. He thought of reaching for her hand, of touching her elbow, but Willow had now stepped slightly away from him.

"He's dead," McAllister heard her whisper, and he remembered Walker's attempts to get information out to him. "I think Ellis tried to tell me, but kept getting interrupted." Reaching for her arm, he attempted to be comforting, even close to her. Her elbow was unyielding to his touch.

"He drowned," Willow told him, speaking so softly he could hardly hear her. "In the river. Here. His boat got swept away with the current and floodwaters. He was never good in dealing with the outdoors in any way-- like you are. They found him caught in some logs at the lake."

"How long ago?"

"Two years."

"Two years!" McAllister did not believe his ears. Not a word of it had filtered through brigade channels to him. "And you couldn't let me know?" Her elbow slid out of his grasp.

Willow abruptly halted her steps. Standing resolutely before him, she crossed her arms beneath the shoulder wrap she wore as if fending off a sudden chill. "How, pray tell? The rivers have you also," she replied bitterly. "That will never change." She turned her face away from him.

In the darkness it was difficult to read her eyes, but he had heard in her voice, the anger, disappointment, and even some resentment toward this latest intrusion into her life. The hurt filled the space between them.

Impulsively he reached out, touched the smooth skin of her chin, turning her face to his. Softly he told Willow, "I love you, you know. My Lord, how I love you, Willow," and saw the tears spring to her eyes.

Only the rustle of their clothing, as they reached out to each other, broke the evening stillness around them. Gently he reached up, holding her head tightly to his shoulder, his arms encircling her. "I have wasted so much time," he whispered into the soft curls of her hair. "I've wondered a thousand nights where you were and if you even remembered me, if you were happy with your choice." The blessed relief of the moment engulfed McAllister. To have found her again now seemed a miracle to him. So he held her close and still, and pinched his eyes closed to savour the pleasure of this unexpected moment.

"Oh Rayne, it seems so many years," she cried against the

smoothness of his tunic. "A lifetime-- even when James was here, I still remembered--"

Her small body was warm and soft against his own. His desire for her had never died, and he sensed, as he knew she did, what this moment meant and where it would lead them.

"Hush," McAllister whispered. He felt the tears of joy, damp upon her face, and gently kissed them away. She stirred in the circle of his arms, bringing herself closer to him and lifted her mouth to meet his.

The kiss was gentle, searching, finding and deepening. Willow was swept away momentarily in a rush of quick desire for this man whose love for her had never died. The sensation of his kiss, the soft gentleness of his lips along her neck and the strength of his hands as he held her, told her of his deep longing. When McAllister looked into her face, the depth of feeling showed itself in the teary sparkle of her gray eyes, the slight tremble of her mouth, and the lovely flush upon her cheeks.

Willow's small hand slipped down over the sleeve of his tunic until it was clasped tightly, reassuringly in his. "I must check on Mama," she reminded him.

"I'll wait--"

"Come in with me. Mama will be glad--"

"Where do you live? With them?"

"No," Willow smiled. "There-- beside them."

"That's where I'll wait." His voice was decisive. As the moon dipped behind a cloud, Willow hurried into the Bromley house.

Her mother rested, sleeping beneath the quilts. The room was stifling hot from the day's warm sunshine. Willow slipped quietly past the bed to open the small window only enough to allow a bit of fresh air into the room. As she tiptoed about the house replacing the pitcher of water and setting out clean linen so that Willard could bathe his wife's face when she awoke in the night, Willow could still feel the warmth of Rayne's arms around her. A light touch to her mother's forehead told Willow that the fever had broke during the day. Satisfied that all was in order, she turned and quietly left the house.

McAllister waited on the veranda of Willow's house for her. Watching her hurry across the yard and up the boardwalk to the steps, he moved out of the shadow to catch her as she gathered up her full skirt and ran up the steps to him; and, as the moon once more dipped behind a thick cloud, they moved together through the doorway and across the darkened room. Caught up in the engulfing surge of their need for each other, they kissed in hurried moments. He touched her hair, held her beautiful face between his hands and allowed his lips tender pleasures.

As McAllister undid the buttons of her bodice, he watched her eyes. They became smooth gray pools, mirroring his own. Willow's dress slid away to the floor, and McAllister quickly lifted her to the bed. Instantly his tunic was tossed upon her dress, and next his breeches fell beside them. Beneath the linens of her bed, Willow and the trapper locked away the outside world.

15

The arrival of the horse brigade from Fort Alexandria always brought excitement to life at Fort Kamloops. While the men lingered no longer than three or four days to exchange horses and ready the pack train for travel, there nonetheless was a certain amount of revelry between themselves and old friends living at the fort. The daylight hours were filled with gathering the brigade stock and preparing the bundles for loading. McAllister settled himself comfortably upon a thick post at the corrals to watch this procedure.

As the horses were herded in from distant pastures, his own two were with them. The air soon filled with a thick cloud of dust. Departure seemed to be coming too quickly for McAllister. While he knew he must leave, and indeed wanted to, he nevertheless felt a certain reluctance. In the early morning sun, he observed the wranglers at work, sometimes leaping down into the melee of men and horses to lend a helping hand. Unbroken horses were caught, held, saddled and bucked-out by the tough, experienced wranglers of the brigade.

He led his own two animals away from the action, across the yard to the huge, log barn where he tied them to the nearest rail. As he brushed out the dust and any ticks which might have hid in their hair, the yearning to return to the Okanagan Valley with this brigade could not be denied.

Instantly he drew on memories and images of Willow as she had been when he had first seen her at Fort St. James, and her passion through the wonderful hours of the night just past. He felt drained of his senses, but content. Soon the horses of the brigade would be rigged and packed for the four week journey south to the Columbia River. Several thousand pelts would be loaded on the backs of over three hundred horses, in eighty pound bales, packed two bales to the horse. The men would mount up, the flag would be raised and the bugle sounded.

A tug of adventure washed over McAllister. Many times he had assessed himself and his life. As he listened to the sounds of the wranglers in nearby corrals, McAllister had never felt more nostalgic than now. While the fur brigade itself was a colourful parade, the life of men travelling with it was a series of hard, arduous journeys through a vast wilderness. There was little comfort left at day's end, for the men had only the hard, damp ground for a mattress.

There was little difference to his own lifestyle, he now reminded himself. The loneliness of isolation through long, bitter winter months was relieved only by the anticipation of springtime. Then the quiet river, starlit nights and awakening sounds of the countryside pushed aside the harshness of the freezing days of digging traps from under the ice and miles of travel by snowshoe.

McAllister was now forced to contemplate his choices more seriously than ever. Willow had come back into his life and there was no longer room for foolish decisions.

McAllister had been able to bring in only sixty-seven pelts as compared to the enormous bounties of the Stuart Lake area and the Clearwater River. It was not an encouraging factor in any decision to return to the Okanagan Valley for another year. He knew many traders around Fort Okanogan and Spokane House had turned to farming as the quantity and quality of their annual hunt diminished. They planted crops, erected log homes and barns near substantial creeks, while continuing to trap for furs. The Okanagan had much to offer with its rich soil, open slopes, wild grass, and warm climate during the spring and summer months.

The passive nature of the Salish Indians was at its best, it seemed to McAllister, in the Okanagans. Their behaviour had not caused concern over his safety among them. It seemed their preference was trading, rather than warring.

The trapper allowed the image of Willow to play about his mind once more. He saw again her dark hair lying across the pillow, her soft, white shoulders cradled in his arms. He closed his eyes momentarily against the heat and dust and sounds of activity in the corral across the yard from him.

Impulsively, McAllister threw the brush and curry comb into the corner of the barn where his saddle and other tack was stored. This time he would ask her to travel with him. He would use his credit with the company to purchase tools, household utensils, bolts of fine cloth and whatever else it took to convince Willow to go with him. A warm, log house could be built for them. With his new tools he could fashion comfortable furniture for the rooms. He would gather wide, flat, solid rocks and construct the very best fireplace for her to hang the new pots in. No longer was a life with Willow to be set aside.

McAllister strode quickly toward the warehouse and Walker's store. He had become anxious now to get on with the new life which Willow represented. His mind raced with all that he must do to make the trip south with the brigade comfortable for her and prepare for

113

their home in the Okanagan. It did not occur to McAllister that Willow might refuse him.

With careful determination McAllister chose his stores for the pending season of hunting furs. A large sign, a little faded from constant exposure, nailed against the outside of Ellis Walker's store, informed traders of the cost of the basic supplies necessary to the hunter. Although one beaver pelt meant as much as four dollars on the China market, only forty cents was added to a trapper's account. A pitiful amount by comparison, McAllister felt. However, he had plenty of credit to cover his supplies. He studied the sign, aware that Ellis Walker watched from beyond the dusty windowpanes.

Blankets	6 beaver
Cloth per fathom	8 beaver
Scissors	1 beaver
Beads	8 beaver
Thread, buttons	1 beaver
Files 6 inch/1 dozen	14 beaver
Awls/1 dozen	2 beaver
Musket balls/1 lb.	12 beaver
Gun flints/1 dozen	1 beaver
Gun powder/1 lb.	4 beaver
1 Horse	3 beaver
American rifle	32 beaver
Gun/British made	20 beaver

Also available all foodstuffs and other incidentals.
CREDIT YOUR PELTS WITH US

For a reasonable season's supplies, it would require a trapper to bring in nothing less than eighty skins, preferably beaver, which held the highest value in trade.

That day McAllister bought new ropes, a broad axe, shovel and ground pick. His order for more blankets, a pair of scissors, buttons and cloth, cookware, dishes and other utensils caused Ellis Walker to raise an eyebrow in the trapper's direction.

He said, "For a man who should be considering the offer made to him at dinner last night, you're buyin' a lot of unnecessary articles." His face registered his perception of the purchases, and his unhappiness. "The offer is a good one and you're the right man to head our defence."

McAllister told him, "I'm going back to the Okanagan. Life's a little simpler there."

"And the girl?" queried Walker, stroking his mustache in thought. "What does she say?"

McAllister stored his smaller purchases in the deer hide bags he used for packing. Wordlessly he hoisted the bags across his shoulders and abruptly left the store. Proceeding to the livery barn, he purchased another horse.

Walker waited. When the trapper did not return he dipped a hand into the glass candy container, crossed the floor to the door and called to one of the young boys racing about the compound. Placing the handful of candies in the youngster's dusty palm, the storekeeper sent him scurrying away with a message to McAllister.

The boy squatted comfortably beside the open livery doorway and began to eat the sweets.

Walker glared at him from across the street.

McAllister led his newly acquired horse from the barn and tied it with his other two. As he lifted one of the animal's front feet to inspect it, he heard the boy tell him, "If yer name be McAllister, yer supposed to be over at Mr. Walker's for supper, uh–dinner, tonight. They got music and such goin' on there."

McAllister grinned and glanced across at the boy. "And do you need to take an answer back to Walker?"

"No." Quickly, the boy finished off the sweets, got to his feet and dashed around the corner of the livery and out of sight.

The evening held the promise of a warm spring night. From the parlour of the Walker's large house the sound of a fiddle, a guitar and harmonica floated on the air as McAllister and Willow crossed the yard. Above the music the laughter of guests having already arrived could be heard.

When they reached the veranda McAllister took Willow by the hand and led her to the end of it. She was beautiful in the moon's glow and McAllister loved her deeply. He leaned down and kissed her tenderly on the mouth. The impulsiveness of his action touched Willow. Smiling warmly, she took his arm as they entered the house. They danced easily together to the music provided by the fort's combined talents. Their eyes never left each other.

Ellis Walker watched them. Damned if they didn't make a handsome couple, he decided; she in her billowing satin skirt and ruffled blouse, her dark hair piled high upon her head in a mass of curls, and the trapper in the new fringed tunic and breeches traditional for the man and his lifestyle. Willow was enticingly feminine and lovely. McAllister was handsome in his rugged appearance.

Interest gripped Walker now, as it had before, while he watched the drama being carried out between the man and Willow. He recognized, of course, that the two were in love. He considered that this fact alone, out here in the far west of Canada, should be incentive enough for the man to remain at the fort. The time for damned formalities had come to an end! He would speak his piece seriously to McAllister that night about the necessity and advantages of a well-trained defence force under dependable, knowledgeable leadership.

At the first opportunity Walker led McAllister into the small sitting alcove aside of the dining room and reached into a nearby cupboard. "A drink? Brandy?" he offered the trapper. McAllister accepted. They touched their glasses and drank.

McAllister smiled. He knew why he had been brought to this corner.

Walker cleared his throat officiously. "I've decided to speak my mind," he said to the trapper bluntly. "I think you should marry that girl out there. It's evident that you've known her for some time. At Fort St. James, I heard you say the other night."

McAllister opened his mouth to speak, but Walker raised a hand against any words. "No, let me finish, Rayne." He looked squarely across at McAllister. "I'm going to call you Rayne from now on, and I'm Ellis to you. Now you realize of course, that things aren't going to get better for you if you continue trapping. The beaver are on the decline. Pelts are a little more scarce than a decade ago. Everyone knows that!" Walker drained his glass. "And–" he predicted superiorly, "eventually the market will drop off and an end to trapping will begin."

McAllister interrupted. "You're talking in circles, Ellis."

Walker refilled his glass, then offered the decanter to the trapper who refused.

"One day you're goin' to lose your damned scalp despite what you think, or drown, or die in the snow. I hear of it all the time. And, what will you have had for it all?"

"Ellis–" McAllister began. "I've heard all that before. From Adam Breen, from Evan Dubrais, from old traders and wranglers along the route who've lived it before me."

"And it's evident that you've not listened to one word," Walker sighed wearily. "The defence of this post against the troublesome Shuswaps is of the utmost importance! There'll come a time yet, when we have to move away from them."

McAllister set his empty glass aside and stepped toward the window. Peering out into the darkened night, he leaned a shoulder against the wall and felt suddenly overwhelmed by everything. How we have unknowingly insulated ourselves against the rest of the world, he considered. The small troubles which plague us become so magnified that they cause us to give it all up, to move. He dropped the curtain over the window and turned to look at Walker. "We have brought about our own isolation here in the west, you know," he stated sadly. "And every time we move we do nothing more than encourage it further." He closed his eyes a moment and thought aloud, "We don't even know what's happening in other parts of our own country, let alone any other country."

Walker scoffed. "Brilliant thinking, indeed! So why are you planning on moving away from us, when we need you most?"

"Ellis– you know, and I know, that all George Southport needs to do is to notify company headquarters out there in the east, and he'll have the troops he needs soon enough."

"It takes months!" Walker stared hard at the trapper. "I don't believe you are refusing us."

McAllister was blunt. "I'm going back to the Okanagan. And with that move I'll be insulating myself some more. I seem no more able to curb that process than you are."

"My God! Here–" Walker waved the decanter anxiously in McAllister's direction. "Have another shot of brandy. If I am not depressing you with my offer, I'm certainly depressing myself," whereupon he poured himself a third shot and the conversation was brought to an abrupt end.

When McAllister walked with Willow to her house in the late hours of the evening, he saw that the lamps in the Bromley home had been put out. All about them the place was in darkness. When he glanced down at Willow and thought of what he must ask her, his chest tightened unexpectedly. Was it, he wondered, a slight twinge of fear that she might not wish to go with him? I don't believe so, he reassured himself, after what they now shared.

Willow's small hand was warm against his palm, her fingers clasped tightly through his. They ascended the wooden steps to the veranda together. He held the door open for her. When it was closed, she was in his arms, close and seeking, a silent telling of her happiness and her need to have him near. The room was quiet, save for the sound of their quickened breathing and Willow's soft whispers of love against his neck.

He must wait no longer, McAllister knew, so he murmured hopefully against the smoothness of her hair as he loosened the combs which held the curls fast. "We must talk, Willow–"

"Mmm–"

"Willow? About leaving here." He felt her body stiffen and he gripped her shoulders to keep her close. "Leaving here for the Okanagan." There, he sighed, it was out. She had heard him and she had not moved away from him yet.

Against his tunic, Willow pinched her eyes shut. She could feel the quick sting of tears, the flush which crept along her neck. Had she understood him correctly? Was he asking her to go with him to places unknown? She had not heard of one white person residing in the Okanagan except two Roman Catholic Priests. Now, did he expect her to leave the security of a company post and go away into the unknown and expose her life to all sorts of treachery? Surely not! Willow pulled away from him.

McAllister's heart fell.

"Please think--" he began.

"I cannot bring myself to do that, to leave here. All that I have, that I've known is here." Tears filled her wide, gray eyes and Willow could not look at him. "Once again you have been offered good employment."

McAllister's mouth pinched stubbornly. "And James is buried here," he said coldly.

Willow spun about to stare at him, dashing a hand against the tears that had fallen upon her face. "How dare you! After what we have found together, Rayne, how dare you!" In the dull light of the room she saw that his eyes were full of remorse; he was sorry for the words and she knew it.

McAllister could not recall the hurt he had caused. In a voice thick with decision, he told Willow, "I offer no guarantees to you about my life, or our life together, or even apart. I cannot stay here! I'm not made for a uniform and military kind of life and that's what it will be. You know that better than anyone, Willow."

She closed her eyes against his choice. "So you will go to the Okanagan without me? Alone? Despite all that has happened between us?"

"Yes. But I'll come back for you, Willow, when I've built a house and have it all ready for you." Although McAllister was pleading silently for her understanding, he cursed himself for telling her this. Once more he was placing the hurt of losing her at that vulnerable door of his heart. He knew he could remain there if he had to.

Willow stood beside the window, silhouetted in a narrow shaft of moonlight. The room became heavy and electric. Acute awareness of each other gripped them with a new anticipation. "I know you will come back, Rayne. You always come back safely."

"But not sane, it seems," he smiled in the darkness. "I offer you that promise," he heard himself whisper beside her. "That, and I never stopped loving you from the beginning and I never shall."

McAllister watched her face as she turned slightly toward him. "And how I love you!" she whispered fiercely. Reaching up to her throat, Willow undid the buttons of her blouse, as McAllister's arms reached out for her.

Her lips upon his told him of her heartache, the agony of waiting, the intensity of her love for him. Holding her close against his side, in his strong, encircling arms, McAllister led her through the shadows of the house to the privacy of her bedroom.

When the dawn signalled a new day, McAllister left her briefly to go to his room in Mrs. Ross's boarding house. When he had attended to his horses and later returned to her, the day turned into night once more.

They closed their minds to the life which pulsed outside the door of the cottage. To be lost in the wonderful senses of their passion for each other, reigned. So that, when it was night once more and McAllister stayed with her, Willow took him to her bed again, reluctant to let him go, praying that he would forget his plans.

But even as Willow lay with him, revelling in the perfection of their intimacy, she knew it would not last. The time would come and he would go. In the darkness and the quiet which surrounded them in her bed, Willow could almost hear the bugle of the brigade train, calling the men into the wilderness, pulling McAllister away from her, beyond her. Her ears pounded with imaginative sounds of thumping, impatient horses as, amid the tinkling music of harness and buckles, they pawed at the ground, anxious, like her lover, to be away and on the trail.

Willow held him close, a tear stealing its way over her face to be absorbed by the pillow. Knowing that her time now with him would be short, she treasured those precious moments and stored them carefully into the secret corners of her mind. Later, when in moments of intolerable loneliness, she would have them there to draw upon and ease the heartache and worry over her future.

Beside her, McAllister stirred. Willow leaned over and kissed his brow. Oh, never to lose this, she breathed. She held him close, as he held her, and knew while she waited for the dawn, that when he came back for her, she would be ready to leave with him.

When the first ray of sun broke over the far horizon, casting its early light upon the fort, the bugle sounded. Its retort was carried on the air across the wide flats along the Thompson River.

McAllister rose and left the woman. There were no hurried words of parting, no sad tears, no idle promises. It was no longer necessary between them to speak of all that had passed or of what might be. They had finally met again and did not now need sad words to darken their last moments together.

Willow watched from her window as he passed down the path from her home, placed the latch over the gate and strode across the compound toward the livery.

McAllister did not wave or look back. Although his heart was heavy and he knew he left disappointment behind, maybe even sorrow, he nevertheless packed his three horses and departed Fort Kamloops with the Hudson's Bay Brigade bound for Lac du Chien.

16

More than three hundred horses left the post that spring of 1835, laden with rich furs of all kinds, bound for Fort Okanogan. Excitement gripped McAllister as he became caught up in the activity. It gave him cause to wonder if he would ever be able to give up this way of life totally and turn to the soil for his livelihood. When it was time to move out, the trapper was among the first to swing into his saddle, take up the lead lines of his two pack horses and follow the commanding call of the brigade bugle.

When two weeks later the party passed along the plateau west of the Indian village Shoshen-eetkwa, the trapper took his leave. Leading his two pack horses, McAllister disappeared into the narrow draws and gullies which would access him to the crest above the twin falls of Lac du Chien. As he descended the shale slide and saw again his riverside camp, he smiled with pleasure. This was his home and for a brief moment, a tremendous sense of belonging surged through him. He knew then that he would never be able to leave the valley permanently and he realized that he would find it impossible to explain his feelings to Willow.

With one exception, McAllister's camp seemed to have remained unmolested. Only his raft was missing. The open, stone fireplace and the drying poles used for hanging the loaded pelt stretchers, were still in place. There was not even a crumbled sod from his tilt lying upon the ground.

However, a quick glance at the river, now swollen with the floodwaters of spring mountain run-off, reminded the trapper what an impractical campsite it really was. McAllister unsaddled his horse and removed the large packs from the other two. A search must be made, he decided, for better camping grounds and pasture land. Hauling his supplies into the crowded quarters of the tilt built against the bank and walled with thick sods against the weather, McAllister glanced up to the hillcrest above him. The junction of the main brigade trail through the Okanagan Valley and the route used by the Indians between Nipit Lakes and Shoshen-eetkwa, where he had departed from the fur brigade train, seemed now to command his attention as a future homesite. With plans in mind, McAllister set out the following morning, retracing the time-worn Indian path over the hill west toward Nipit Lakes.

Emerging from the narrow ravines sloped with thick timber and bottomed in ponds well dammed by beaver, McAllister topped the crest above the wide valley. To the west in the distance, the brigade trail passed beyond the far shore of a lake. Sloping up from the rich green pastures were low, grassy hillsides patched with fields of wild flowers. He knew this body of water was not one of Nipit Lakes. Those lakes, broken by a narrow spit, were farther to the west. Having hunted in these hills while travelling with the brigade, McAllister recognized where he was. He had entered the small valley which led to that of Nipit Lakes.

Jigging the reins to his horse, McAllister trotted down the hill to the lakeshore. As he rode, visions of a comfortable, practical homestead nestled in this valley marched across his mind. It was to be here, he decided now, where he would build a home for Willow. Beside the creek was where he would locate his house and barn. Later as their farm flourished, a granary would be added to the landscape. McAllister rested his arms upon the saddle horn, contemplating the open country. Such abundant pastures must be filled with cattle, he decided. A trip to Spokane House would have to be made to bring a small herd north to this valley. A team of sturdy draft stock was needed and, if he could locate them, several laying hens should be added to his farm.

The trapper smiled. What had seized his mind? Had he temporarily forgotten his traps, stretchers and bales, or the brigade and the rendezvous site at Soi'yus? No, he decided realistically, he needed the beaver, the muskrat and marten yet, if only to provide for the cattle, horses and seed. Having now planned his future and succumbed to inspiration, McAllister reined his mount around and rode out of the wide valley and into the hills.

To the north and south of the lake of whitish water which told of the presence of alkali, the valley allowed plenty of room for grazing as many cattle and horses as he chose. Without having to cut and clear the land immediate to the lake, building would proceed quickly. The nearby ravines would provide the materials, the creek would supply the water and the fields of natural grass would be adequate forage for his animals.

McAllister rode down out of the hills onto a flat bench above Lac du Chien. Below on the smooth waters of the lake, several rafts floated near a small island on its eastern side. The Indians of Two Way's band were fishing for trout. Thin spirals of smoke curled upward from fire pits within the village at the edge of the lake. Lac du Chien was calm and smooth. Perfect reflections of the high cliffs on its east side played across the water.

McAllister dismounted and allowed his horse to graze. Below the hillcrest where he stood, the lake narrowed to swirl against the steep rock faces of its western border before entering the channel above the twin falls. Large clumps of cacti spread out among the thick sagebrush and low rabbit bush. Yellow sunflowers, blue lupin and the brilliant red Indian paintbrush dotted the landscape of Ponderosa pine and thin white birch. Contentment flowed through McAllister as he stood that day in June beneath the blue, cloudless sky and viewed the land which he now called home.

Returning to the river, a sudden sense of caution prevented McAllister from riding directly into his camp. What he could not see, he could feel. He knew somebody had been at his camp. His other two horses were gone from the small corral. He waited awhile and watched. Finally, he rode in, removed his gun from its scabbard, unsaddled the bay and sent it trotting through the gate into the enclosure. Then, taking up his gun, he moved quietly through the trees away from his camp to the riverbank crossing which Two Way used. There he found tracks in the mud. In contemplation, the trapper thought, I should have known this would happen. I placed too much trust in their avoidance of my camp last year. I was left alone, as were my horses, furs and everything else. For an entire day I would be gone and my camp would remain unmolested.

He moved back into the shadows of the trees. What did this invasion mean? That Two Way's uncle, Rattler, was on the move?

McAllister stayed in the shadows from where he could watch his camp, but after a long wait, nothing happened. There was no movement nearby, no evidence of further intrusion. He turned toward his sod house against the bank.

When he entered his dwelling he saw instantly that a shovel, pick and axe were missing. The canvasses which he had purchased in Fort Kamloops were gone and his clothing had been riffled. Setting his gun aside, the trapper removed a square sod near the back of the hut and checked his cache of ammunition. It was all there. He stepped out into the sunlight and stared across the rolling river. Rattler, he decided, whom Two Way tells me steals and speaks in five tongues. Well now, the time had come, the trapper told himself, to outwit the misguided Indian and do it on the Indian's own ground.

Two Way had not been to see the trapper yet. McAllister had only been back at his camp one day. The swollen river was too dangerous for his little pony and too swift for the raft. But Rattler had crossed successfully and so then could the trapper. The game of pitted wits began between the resourceful, experienced trapper and the cunning Indian, the brave Rattler of Shoshen-eetkwa.

One evening, following the theft of his two horses, McAllister left two traps and several stretchers in plain view beside his house. On a rope line strung between the trees, he hung two new Hudson's Bay blankets. Leaving his camp, he settled in a position among the trees near his corral to watch and wait. Evening quietude prevailed along the river. Although he wished for rest, McAllister did not doze.

Half the night passed before a faint sound reached his ears. McAllister's keen eyes narrowed, searching the shadows, but he could detect nothing. Then, another shuffling sound. McAllister stiffened in stillness against the bark of the tree.

Presently a man's shadow was cast across the yard where McAllister's horse remained tied. As the Indian reached for the rope, McAllister's arm quickly encircled the intruder's thick neck from behind. Instantly, the trapper's knife lay at the other's throat.

"You're careless, Rattler. And you make too much noise," McAllister said close to the Indian's ear. "I know you are Rattler."

The Indian shoved his weight backward, attempting to twist out of the iron grasp which held him tight against the tree. He felt the knife's edge press into the skin at his throat. He grunted, attempting to see the one who held him.

McAllister jerked his arm tighter and pressed the knife deeper. "You are not dead yet, Rattler, but trust it-- you will be! Now, you listen! By the dawn's first light I'll see my two horses back in this corral. You understand also, Rattler, that you do not scare me, for I know all about you and your thieving ways." His arm began to ache, but he held the Indian fast.

"My people will kill you!" Rattler groaned, afraid to swallow against the pressure of the knife. "You do not belong here! You do not obey our laws! You use what is ours and take too many beaver!"

"Your people know me now. They leave me alone. And I do obey what I believe are your laws— I don't take too many beaver, or salmon, or deer, or anything else." Speaking through clenched teeth, McAllister angrily reminded Rattler, "You have my axe and my shovel and pick. I intend to make a deal with you. Do you want to talk some business?"

Rattler remained still.

McAllister tightened his arm and the Indian gasped. "I need help to build a house and a barn, and you're the one who's going to do it with me. I've been thinking about you for awhile, Rattler, and we do not have to be enemies when we can be friends."

Rattler's dark eyes rolled downward to McAllister's sleeve and the hand that held the knife. "You can't stay here or build anything here, but we will make a deal for something," he gasped.

"I am going to build a house." The trapper's grip lessened, but remained. He said, "You may think you are the cleverest one in your village and just as smart as me, Rattler, but, you will never be smarter at the game of survival than I am." Removing his knife from

Rattler's throat, he warned, "My horses by dawn." He moved slightly to stare hard into the black eyes of the angry Indian. Finally he relaxed his grip, removed the knife completely and stood before Rattler, unflinching in his stare and stance. "By dawn," he repeated quietly.

Rattler coughed and rubbed his throat. "We deal. You pay–"

"By dawn, Rattler."

Before the morning sun rose over the trapper's campsite beside the river, his horses had been returned to the corral. Immediately he packed them with the few working tools he had left, swung aboard the saddle of his bay, and departed the riverside leaving his trapper's abode exposed once more in trust of the Indians who lived nearby.

Travelling west to the lake of white water, McAllister hummed a cheerful tune learnt from his father. A feeling of well-being coursed through his veins. Eventually he could expect Rattler to show up at his camp beside the river or perhaps follow him to the flats ahead. Curiosity would bring him, for making deals and trading was the main vein of the Indian's life.

However, it was not Rattler who showed himself at McAllister's campfire while he cooked his noon meal and drank freshly brewed tea, but rather Two Way. Having grown into a fine looking, tall brave, the young Indian arrived, galloping his pony across the flats toward the shore of the lake where McAllister had located himself. Their greeting was warm and the affection which had developed between them during the year just past now showed itself. Their four hands clasped tightly together a moment in friendship.

"I have another gift for you, Many Rains," Two Way called as he reached up and pulled loose the thong that held the parcel on his flat, hornless saddle made from tough moose hide.

McAllister laughed gently. "I do not need gifts every time you come to visit me, Two Way."

"But you need clothes. You have no woman to make them for you. So– I work for my sister and she made this for me to give to you. It is my welcome back to our land, for you." Two Way's eyes shone with his honest joy at having the trapper return to the valley.

As McAllister looked down at the expertly sewn suit which he laid upon the short grass away from the dusty area of the fire, he felt humbled. Embroidered with the precious shells of the Pacific and painted with the brightest dyes, the tunic was held at the neck with fine, braided thongs and fringed only at its length. Tiny bone chips had been deftly sewn into the outside seams of the leggings. Beside the suit he set a pair of plain, thick soled moccasins.

Resting back against his heels, McAllister looked across at Two Way. They were beautiful gifts. But what of their meaning? This was the second suit the boy had asked his sister to sew for him. Pleased as he was to wear such fine clothes made especially for him, there crept a feeling of obligation.

McAllister rose to his feet. Across from him Two Way stood up also. The articles sewn by the Indian girl of Shoshen-eetkwa remained spread upon the grass between them.

Two Way smiled though he sensed uneasiness in the trapper's manner.

McAllister stepped toward the boy and, placing an arm across Two Way's thin shoulders, led him toward the log near the fire. "Come, sit down with me a moment. I want to explain something to you and I want you to do something for me."

"Yes?"

"Next year I'm going to bring a woman to the valley with me. She will be my wife. I need help to build my house and barn. After that I must make a long trip south to Spokane House and try to buy some cattle and horses."

Two Way's eyes never left the trapper's face. To be taken into this man's confidence and friendship was something he had hoped for. He listened carefully to every word. "Yes," he replied softly.

"It will be necessary for me to have some help to do all this. And my wife, too, will need assistance." McAllister looked squarely into the young Indian's dark eyes. "Is that possible? There will be a fair exchange for your labour." Glancing across at the deerskin suit upon the ground, he added, "Perhaps your sister could help us also."

Two Way grinned. "I am glad to help you, Many Rains. Nahna will come if I ask her to."

"Good! Then it's settled." He cleared his throat, reached for his cup and drank. In another moment he had filled a cup for Two Way. "Now," he said more seriously. "I have met your uncle. He has borrowed some tools of mine which I will soon need."

Two Way laughed. The sound was infectious and McAllister, too, smiled broadly. Two Way told him, "A shovel and a pick and axe."

McAllister's brow shot up. "That is correct. I want you to tell him that when he comes to work for me, he can return the tools then. He will need them here to work with. That way he can work and earn the things that he wants, and not have to go out and steal them. Tell him also, that I'll bring him a good American rifle from Fort Kamloops next year and teach him to use it properly. He'll be the best hunter in the village then."

Soberly Two Way informed the trapper, "He is the best hunter now."

"He'll be better than best. Now go– and remember, my thanks to your sister for this fine suit. Tell her that I have never worn clothes made so well, upon my back."

Two Way did not leave immediately and McAllister looked across

125

at him. "Is there something else?"

"Many Rains, my father feels that you should come to our village and present yourself to him. You have lived here a long time now. He needs to see who you are."

McAllister remained silent.

"He says that you are welcome to live in the valley, to live beside us and hunt in our territory because you have done us no harm and not taken much from us."

"That's not what Rattler thinks."

Two Way shrugged, dismissing the remark. "You must come and speak with him." He stood up, waiting for the trapper's reply.

"I will come," McAllister told him.

"When?"

"I will come," he repeated and left the conversation thus.

Two Way turned and picked up the reins on his pony. Springing quickly into the saddle, the young Indian disappeared in a great swirl of dust.

Each day McAllister rose before dawn, ate his breakfast and saddled his horse for the ride over the old Indian trail to the white lake where he had chosen to build his house. Every evening he returned just at dusk. As he sat at his campfire eating his supper, he waited for a visit from Rattler. However, the days passed and still the Indian did not come to see him. I have patience, McAllister reminded himself, and nothing but time. Rattler must come to me before I go into the village. I shall outwait him.

McAllister had been at work with his remaining tools, preparing the logs for his house, when ten days later Rattler made an appearance. With him rode three other men from Shoshen- eetkwa, arriving at his campfire in a great stampede of hoofs and dust. When the air had cleared and Rattler had leapt from his horse, McAllister nodded a greeting.

Rattler said to him, "I bring my friends to help you. We can sit down and make a deal now."

"I think not," the trapper replied coldly. "I will make a deal with you. I do not need your whole camp on my doorstep. There is only enough work for you." Lifting a brow in the others' direction, he instructed Rattler, "Tell them. They do not owe me for three large tools. They did not take them. You did. So it is just you who owes me."

Rattler's black eyes narrowed. He stared against the sunlight to see into the determined expression on the trapper's face. Then he spun on his heel and in Salish, barked McAllister's message at his companions. As their horses pranced about in the white dust of the shoreline, the Indians raised their arms and their laughter filled the still, summer air.

McAllister waited beside the fire. Dipping his cup into the open kettle hanging above the flame, he filled it with steaming venison soup.

Rattler spun around, glaring furiously at him. He had been made a fool in front of his friends. "I give you nothing! You do nothing but cause them to laugh at me!"

McAllister sipped the liquid from his cup. "Do you want some?" he asked raising the cup and indicating the kettle over the fire.

"I want nothing! I do nothing now!"

"It is your fault they laugh, Rattler," McAllister pointed out with an even voice. "You borrowed my tools without permission. If you want to keep them you have to pay me, and I offer you work to do that. You did not have to tell them. They would not have known it from me."

Rattler's fiery eyes were held tensely by the trapper's stiff gaze.

"It's your choice how you deal with me," McAllister told him, "but– we deal. There are better things in store for you than stealing, Rattler. Think about it. Come to my place by the river and we'll talk together." McAllister turned his back and tossed the tin cup into a pail of water. Behind him he heard the movements of Rattler and his horse.

Argument between the four Indians broke out. Their horses stomped impatiently at the ground. Then, realizing that the trapper was quit of them, they turned their mounts, quickly breaking into a galloping thunder across the wide flats.

17

The advantages of both worlds, Indian and white, were clear to Rattler. Not only would the greedy side of his nature be satisfied by all the supplies that could be had, but there was a certain sanctuary in an association with the trapper. Other whites moving into the valley might not find it so easy to blame him for petty thefts which he continued to carry out. Having thought matters over, he felt it necessary to keep McAllister in the area. Moreover, the trapper seemed to have the sanction of his brother, Kelauna. With Two Way, Rattler knew, McAllister kept communication, and would know any gossip within the village about his activities. He decided to help McAllister.

His decision made, Rattler showed himself once more at the day camp on the flats of the white lake. Thereafter, each morning he rode with the trapper over the hill from the river, following the trail of his ancestors to the place of McAllister's homestead. Logs were cut and trimmed and hauled to the building site by their horses. Often young Two Way accompanied the men, helping wherever he could.

One day in early August as the three rode over the hill together, Two Way impulsively blurted, "Today we will see our people arrive at the flats by the lake."

McAllister's head swung around to stare at his young friend. "Arrive? At the white lake?"

Two Way smiled proudly. "Our village moves up there for the berry picking and root digging season. The women do that and the men hunt for deer and small game. Ask Uncle."

McAllister glanced quickly across at Rattler who rode silently beside him. "You said nothing of this to me."

Rattler shrugged his shoulders. "It is our land, don't forget," and trotted his horse ahead to avoid further questioning.

But McAllister caught up to him. "If the men are hunting, and you are the best hunter in your village, why are you not with them?"

Rattler grinned, "Because you are paying me to work here, Trapper. I will hunt when autumn comes around."

McAllister stared from Rattler to Two Way. "Well, I refuse to budge off this ground. They can hunt and dig roots all they want, but

I will not move. I'm not here to cause any disturbance in their way of life, and I don't want any in mine."

As they crested the hill above the white lake flats, Rattler murmured, "It is still our land you are on and you have already disturbed us."

McAllister ignored the Indian's final remark and trotted his horse down the slope toward his unfinished log house.

By the end of the long, hot summer, the house was finished and roofed. The barn was begun, with the thinner poles piled aside for corrals. In a nearby draw a well-house was built around a spring which trickled toward the lake.

As autumn approached, Rattler left to join the band members for their annual hunt. Two Way hunted with McAllister one day only, for deer, then left to join his family. Once brought down, the animal was cleaned, skinned and hung. Cut in strips, it was dried and packed away for food during the winter months. Fish and berries were also dried and stored away.

Two Way was criticized for spending too much time with the trapper and was soon ordered to remain in the village. It was brought to his attention that the trapper whom the band allowed in their midst had not yet complied with the request made by their Chief and therefore, Two Way should not give any more time to the well-being of such an unsociable individual.

Two Way did not agree with his family and when he could, escaped across the river to remain with McAllister. In their employment together, tales of his tribe were repeated by the young Indian boy. McAllister listened attentively. They were not exaggerated stories of a youthful, imaginative mind, but rather true tales of old wars with other tribes, during which his family lost many members.

As McAllister listened, he doubted not the ability of the Okanagan, Lake and Sanpoil to wage war on any white men in their vicinity if they felt provocation. Although he could not imagine Two Way rising against him, it was not difficult to picture Rattler with a hatchet in one hand and a knife in the other. In a moment of serious contemplation, McAllister questioned his selfishness in asking Willow to follow him to the Okanagan, away from the protection of a Company post. It was, in reality, something of an insecure world she must share with him. Soon, McAllister decided, he would go across the river and present himself to Two Way's father.

At Shoshen-eetkwa a hunting party returned. Several deer were skinned, cut in strips and the meat hung from racks in the drying process. Geese and ducks from marshlands south of Kwak-ne-ta were stuffed with dried thornberries and served in a delicious feast.

Preparations for the annual fishing festival got underway in the village. People from many tribes inhabiting the Similkameen and

Nicola valleys, Kamloops Lake and Thompson River, as well as members from all the local bands were gathering at the famous fishing spot, the twin falls. The flats across the river from the high bluffs were soon dotted with the campfires of visitors. The celebrating of the fishing season sometimes lasted through the night. Bone games, stick games, ring and spear games, dancing and drumming were accompanied by laughter and singing. The festivities would continue until the first salmon appeared in the river.

As he rode home from the white lake along the bench above Lac du Chien, McAllister smiled when he saw the gathering of men, women and children along the riverbank and on the hill above the rolling falls. Shouts of cheer echoed across the flats, signalling the arrival of the huge salmon. They leapt up, out of the tumbling water, to fall back exhausted in their attempt to throw themselves above the falls. Everyone waved their arms excitedly, calling to others who had not yet come to see.

Before the traps and weirs could be put in place, each man entered his sweat lodge to cleanse himself. It was believed that the salmon and water spirits would not be pleased if they entered the water with dirty bodies. Rattler was chosen to manage the fishing.

At dawn the following day Rattler prepared his quil'sten (sweat lodge). Several smooth round stones were heated outside the dome-shaped structure of willow stems, reeds, hides and sod, then lifted carefully by huge forks and placed into the small area within the house which had been scooped out to hold them. Then removing all of his clothes, Rattler crawled into the quil'sten which had been built near the creek that flowed from the eastern mountains. As he sat alone inside the house Rattler sprinkled the hot rocks regularly with water, causing the dome to fill with hot steam. When sufficient time had elapsed that his body glistened with perspiration, Rattler crawled from the quil'sten and threw himself into the cold water of the creek. Having cleansed himself, he rested upon a mat of pine boughs covered with a soft, tanned deer hide, to dry his body by the warmth of the early autumn sun. As he dried, he meditated. Clean in body and mind, Rattler was then ready to lead the fishing party into the river to set the weirs and traps.

Throughout the day following the setting of the weirs, the salmon were brought in by the men. Other male members and visitors cleaned, cut in strips and roasted the large salmon for the first day feast. The women remained away from the scene of activity, out of sight, while the men ate until all of the fish caught that day were gone. On the second day the women and children were allowed to cook and eat.

At his camp, McAllister conducted his own fish catch. Like the

Indians up the river from him, he cleaned and cut the salmon in strips. Hanging them from a rack made of saplings, he smoked them to a delicious tenderness with added flavour from willow chips. His preparations for the winter season were much the same as those of the Indians. Wild raspberries, currents, saskatoons and chokecherries were pounded and rolled into small, round cakes and dried. Rosehips and leaves from the Labrador tea plant (sometimes called Hudson's Bay tea, for it had become popular with traders in the area), were dried and stored in a deerskin bag, as were dandelion leaves, wild onions and garlic, mushrooms and fiddleheads for use in soups and stews.

Daily hunting brought him the large geese and smaller mallards which remained in the marshes of the lake south of his camp. Rabbits and grouse were plentiful in the area. As well, there was always deer. The bounty of the Okanagan Valley was unbelievable to him, and taking great care to lay aside plenty of provisions, he knew he would never have to eat beaver meat again.

Two Way did not cross the river to McAllister's camp for several weeks. During the months of September and October there was too much to do in the village to prepare for the winter months. It was time, his mother told him impatiently, that he paid more heed to his own responsibilities within his family circle and the life they shared with other members of the village. This did not upset Two Way for these were exciting times at Shoshen-eetkwa and he did not wish to miss anything.

Five weeks passed before Two Way appeared at the trapper's camp. It was nearly the end of October and a light snowfall had settled upon the ground. When he arrived he leapt from his pony and looped the deer hide reins over its neck and let it graze on what remained of the half frozen grass.

The trapper was glad to see the young Indian and had walked out to meet him when he had spotted the approaching pony. He had missed the company of Two Way and his uncle.

Wiping the dampness of snowflakes from his hair and face, and smiling warmly, McAllister enquired, "What news from your village do you have for me?"

Two Way informed him that the big fishing feast and salmon catch was over. "And now," he told McAllister, "My uncle and many of the other men are away hunting for deer and bear."

"And you? What're you doing in your village at this time?"

The young Indian laughed half-heartedly. "Trying to grow up! Nobody believes I am old enough to do more than help my mother and sister, and I am very unhappy about that! But, it is my fault."

"How is that?"

Two Way fell quiet a moment. "Because-- I keep coming over

here. They are calling me the wayward one. My mother is unhappy with me. My father is disappointed. He says I defy all our traditions. Nahna says I am lazy."

McAllister smiled encouragingly. "Well, Two Way, I want to go to your village and meet your father now. Will you tell him that I'll be there tomorrow?"

A wide grin broke over Two Way's face. His dark eyes looked into those of the trapper for a long moment. "Will you tell my father," he asked seriously, "that you wish me to go and work with you when the winter is over; that there is men's work to be done and that I can do it?"

"That you are tired of doing women's work?" He smiled, understanding Two Way's request. "Ah, that you want to prove to them that you are a builder and that I'll teach you how to make the land provide better than what it already does for them."

"The land already gives us everything we need, but we could have more. That is what I want. Tell him about the cattle and horses you will get from Spokane House." With eyes full of hope, he added, "And that you might want me to travel there with you to bring them back."

McAllister's brow shot up. "And who then," he asked quickly, "will I leave with my wife to protect and help her?"

Two Way's chest fell. "Woman's work then," he muttered, shifting his eyes away from the trapper's.

"No," McAllister corrected gently. "My work." Resting a hand firmly upon Two Way's shoulder, he repeated, "My work. And– because I can trust you to do it. I will take Rattler with me if he will go."

"Rattler?"

"Yes. Then I know where he is when I'm not here."

Two Way turned away to think about the offer. The moment of contemplation was swift. Glancing back toward McAllister, he nodded his approval of the idea and with it, his consent to remain behind when the time came.

Reaching for the rope on his pony, Two Way leapt onto the blanket strapped over its back. He wished now to be alone with his thoughts, for he felt the excitement and challenge rising within him of a life outside the village. If I stay here longer, he told himself, I will be nothing more than a little boy and show my silly feelings of gladness; it is more manly to remain calm about such exciting things, I think! So, lifting the reins, he urged his pony forward. "I'll see you at Shoshen-eetkwa tomorrow," he called out to McAllister. "I'll tell my father of your visit to us." In a moment he had departed the trapper's camp and disappeared across the river.

18

While he saddled his bay the following morning, McAllister thought about the Indian boy. Could it be that a valuable and lasting friendship was developing between them? A kinship? Indeed, did he not smile with pleasure whenever the boy arrived at his camp and miss his presence upon each departure? It was more than an alliance formed solely for the trapper's own gain, to have assistance with the construction of the buildings at the white lake, and to serve as protection for himself and Willow from any uprising against white residents which might occur in the future. No, McAllister decided, the boy was enjoying a way of life much broader than that which he was familiar with. Two Way was an inquisitive lad, he knew, eager to learn more of what lay beyond the boundaries of his valley. McAllister realized what a unique association it was and that a lasting bond was being established.

McAllister urged his horse into the river at the crossing point below his camp.

Atop the hillock beside the waterfalls, where he waited in anticipation, Two Way spotted the trapper riding along the riverbank toward Shoshen-eetkwa. Hurriedly he ran down over the rise onto the flat and raced to meet McAllister.

"Hello, hello!" he called, finding it difficult to restrain his enthusiasm.

The trapper waved and returned the call. When he was abreast of Two Way, he dismounted and walked with him. Two Way reached around McAllister, taking the reins from him to lead the bay himself.

McAllister smiled in response to Two Way's obvious joy at his presence in the village. "Now, have you been sitting up there long, watching for me?"

Two Way grinned. "All morning!" he replied quickly, keeping stride with the tall man beside him.

"And your father?"

"He waits. He is pleased to receive you in our village. He has many questions."

"Your mother? Is she there, too?"

"Yes, yes, and my sister," He laughed merrily. "We are all waiting for you! There," he pointed, "in the meeting house."

McAllister cast a quick glance across at Two Way, who was now growing quite tall. "You are getting longer in the legs every day, young man. Soon you will be as tall as me or taller because you are young yet with lots of time to grow."

Although he appeared not to have heard the trapper's words, Two Way felt a surge of pride in himself. Looking ahead, he saw his father step out of the house into the mid-morning rays of a late October sun. The snowfall of the day before had long since melted, leaving the ground damp and frosty.

Two Way tied the horse to the sturdy rail between the trees behind the kekuli, the conical-shaped house of his family, and he and McAllister went to meet Kelauna.

Just outside the doorway Kelauna waited. He was a tall man and stood now very straight and rigid, his arms crossed over his chest and his expression unsmiling.

"If you like, we will show you around our village later," Two Way told McAllister. "This is our meeting house. There are other places to see."

McAllister nodded recognition toward Kelauna, and Kelauna nodded his head in return. Two Way went to stand beside his father.

In Salish he said proudly, "Father, this man is Many Rains. I have told him of your message that he come to present himself to you and now he does that." Two Way smiled brilliantly, and in English continued, "Many Rains, this is my father. He is the head of our band. He is happy to greet you and welcome you to our village."

The Indian Chief and the white trapper nodded once more in each other's direction. The introductions were over. Two Way raised the decorated hide which covered the doorway and Kelauna led the way into the long house. McAllister followed.

Despite his age, which McAllister reckoned to be nearly seventy, Kelauna was an impressive figure. His attire was of the finest tanned hides elaborately decorated with tiny discs of silver, dyed porcupine quills and many claws of the great grizzly bear. Each fringe along the sides of his leggings was marked with a large coloured bead. Over the long braids of his black hair he wore a fine plumage of eagle feathers.

McAllister allowed his eyes to adjust to the dull light of the interior of the house. When Kelauna had seated himself upon a robe folded several times and placed near the fire pit, the trapper lowered himself to the floor on crossed legs. The large room was warm from the heat of the open flame. Two Way remained standing.

It was several minutes before McAllister noticed the two women seated at the farthest end of the long house. The boy's mother, McAllister decided, and the sister who sews my clothes.

"My father welcomes you to Shoshen-eetkwa, Many Rains," Two Way said in English. "He is pleased at last to meet the one who takes me away from him so often."

McAllister complimented Kelauna then. "Tell him that he has a fine son, one who is a smart trader and who is becoming my good friend. Also, that I wear with great pride, the fine clothes his daughter has made for me."

While Two Way spoke to his father, McAllister's eyes scanned the room once more, resting briefly on the two women seated in the corner. They talked in low tones, careful not to disturb the men. Although the older woman glanced often toward the trapper, the girl did not. Her eyes remained focussed on weaving the basket in her lap.

Two Way was speaking to McAllister again. His father, he told the trapper, wished to know what he was building at the white lake and why he kept returning to the valley to hunt.

So McAllister cleared his throat and began the story in English, for his Salish was limited. The conversation, with Two Way's interpretation, reached the women. Although they understood, they gave no sign of it.

Following the long visit between Kelauna and the trapper, Two Way turned toward the women and motioned them to move forward. McAllister got to his feet. When they had been introduced to the visitor, Kelauna indicated to his wife to bring them food and drink, that they should show their guest proper hospitality. His daughter remained standing, slightly behind him, keeping her eyes lowered.

McAllister watched her face and saw that she was indeed, as pretty as her brother had told him. She appeared very shy. Humble? Coy? No, he decided quickly, she was none of those. Beneath her evenly proportioned features there more likely harboured a strong determination and staunch independence. Most Indian girls of her age were married. McAllister recalled Two Way explaining to him that his sister had not yet met the man most suitable for her. What kind of man would that be? No doubt she had many suitors.

The food was placed before Kelauna and Two Way indicated to McAllister to sit down once more and eat. Then by invitation from his father, Two Way happily joined them, taking the gesture to mean acceptance once more; for of late, he had fallen a little out of favour with his father.

It was a personal moment between father and son. Clearly, Two Way was very proud of this time shared with his important father and his new friend, Many Rains. Equally thrilling was that McAllister should meet his sister Nahna, for Two Way was proud of her, too. He remembered that Nahna had been invited, as he had been, to be friends when the trapper brought his wife to the white lake.

Nahna moved about the room assisting her mother with the meal for the men. When it was finished, Kelauna, McAllister and Two Way returned to the outdoors. This time they were followed by the women. McAllister breathed the fresh air gratefully. It had been too warm in the house and the visit had gone on for several hours more than he had anticipated. He had answered all of Kelauna's questions about his continued presence in the valley, given several promises, and had been made abundantly aware of the band's generosity in their allowance of his hunting and building.

The fall sun was now casting long shadows across the village grounds and the air had taken on the chill of late afternoon.

Two Way brought McAllisters's horse to him. When the reins were handed to him, McAllister's eyes turned to meet Two Way's. He saw that across the back of his saddle were strapped the canvasses which had been stolen by Rattler. They were now returned by Kelauna.

"This is a significant offer of friendship," he told Two Way in English. "Please tell your father that I understand this and I'm grateful to have them back. Tell him that I respect his honesty, and that of his people."

As McAllister bid Kelauna and his family farewell, Nahna raised her eyes to look at him. In her brown, round face, the wide, dark eyes held his gaze for several moments. Loosely plaited black hair hung over the bright poncho around her shoulders. Beneath her dress of smooth tanned hide, Nahna appeared small and delicate. Indeed, he reminded himself, the girl is fairly pretty, but there is something different about her. Strength? Yes, perhaps, he decided, and determination. On impulse, McAllister nodded acknowledgement and smiled appreciatively at Nahna. Turning then, he placed a moccasined foot into the stirrup of the saddle and swung himself up onto the bay.

For a short distance Two Way walked alongside the trapper and his horse. When they parted McAllister thanked him again for the hospitality of his family and invited him to visit his camp more often so that they could make plans together.

"When you come I'll give you my snowshoes to use in the wintertime," he promised the young Indian. "I'll have lots of time to make myself another pair."

Two Way smiled and waved, and the trapper rode toward the river and out of sight.

19

During November the snow fell steadily. When it ceased, the wind howled in chilling gusts about the sod house beside the river, causing thick drifts to bank against the sides. The snow lent warmth to McAllister's dwelling. For his horses, McAllister had built a shelter of heavy fir boughs tied with thick thongs to a frame between the trees. Against this he had fastened the large, heavy canvasses used to cover his packs while travelling, and which Kelauna had returned to him. Throughout the day he tethered them in the field along the river where they pawed through the snow for what little grass that was left. As well, he had harvested some of the tall grass for supplement, and stacked it against the shelter.

The winter lingered, bitter in its freezing coldness. The ice which covered Lac du Chien became a thick, frozen sheet extending across the narrow end toward the falls. From beneath the ice, the water moved smoothly over the edge to tumble in cascades of spray which formed frosty patterns along the walls of rock which channelled it. Below the falls the Okanagan River spread out to flow smoothly once more between its crusted shores.

The weather seldom kept McAllister inside. He worked along the river from his camp, across the meadows to the hutches of the beaver and muskrat. With hands nearly numb from the icy water, he emptied his traps and reset them regularly. Neither Two Way nor Rattler visited his camp during the coldest months of December and January. As the days wore into weeks and stretched into months, McAllister admitted to himself that he was lonely. It was no longer enough to have the company of others for just part of the year.

During the third week of February two traders arrived at McAllister's camp. They were travelling north to Fort Kamloops where they planned to remain. Their horses were loaded with supplies, but no furs.

"We traded all our furs," one of them said, "at Fort Okanogan. They've closed Spokane House, you know."

McAllister looked across at them quickly. "And where did everyone go?" He wished to know of Denise White and her welfare.

The traders ate McAllister's stew and drank the tea he offered.

"Most everyone moved to the new site. It's better, closer to everything."

"Do you know of a Mrs. White?"

"Oh yes. She's still there. She runs a hospital in her home. The company built it for her."

A sense of relief flooded McAllister with the news that at least Denise was safe and comfortable. "What of Evan Dubrais in Fort Okanogan?"

"Oh, there's news of him," replied one of the men. "He's dead, you know." As he spoke the words, he saw McAllister stiffen in disbelief.

"Impossible!" McAllister breathed.

"Oh yes. A barge rammed the dock and Dubrais was there."

"What of Broken Bone?"

"She went back to her people."

McAllister could not move, as if frozen to the spot on the log before the fire. "And their boys? What about them?"

"His wife took them with her. Did you know them well?"

McAllister dropped his gaze to stare into the flames of the fire. "I lived with them briefly," he replied solemnly. "I would say that Dubrais twice saved my life."

The two men stepped away from McAllister's fire. "We'll move on. It's a long way to travel in this snow."

"When you get to Fort Kamloops," McAllister said to them, "tell Walker at the store that you saw me. McAllister is the name."

When the traders had gone, his camp seemed suddenly too quiet. With sad thoughts that plagued his mind, McAllister crawled beneath the warm blankets and buffalo hide, unable to sleep. Outside the night air was still. Perhaps, he wished hopefully, the weather will turn warmer and bring a quick end to this winter. Then I'll leave for Fort Kamloops sooner than usual. With that thought, he closed his eyes.

McAllister awoke to a bright February sun. When he had washed and dressed, he went out into the yard and tethered his three horses to stumps in the meadow. Following his breakfast of roast duck and dried raspberry and currant cakes, he pulled his empty packboard over his shoulders and set off over the snowbanks south along the river to his traps across the meadows. It was late in the afternoon when he started back to his camp.

The pack was very heavy upon his shoulders. Reaching up he adjusted the strap around his forehead to a comfortable pressure and leaned forward as he walked, to balance the load. The snow-packed trail was softened by the day's heat from the sun. Several times McAllister slipped off the trail, but caught his step and proceeded. Then, unexpectedly, from along the river's channel,

McAllister heard the sound of a shrill whistle. Rattler, he smiled, and knew the Indian was near his camp. He was glad to hear the call and quickly returned it. Hurrying along the trail, his shoulder began to pain angrily from the strain of the pack as it swayed back and forth with his stride.

A group of Indians from Inkameep watched McAllister travel and, from across the river, called out to him in Salish which he barely understood. He ignored them. It had now grown late in the day. The trail was soggy with melted snow and he slid often, throwing the heavy pack out of balance.

Presently McAllister heard the Indians' horses splashing through the water as they crossed the river and up the slushy bank, sliding in the wet snow. In a moment they were all around him, circling, prancing their animals about on the trail, thumping in and out of the soggy drifts. They shouted at him about being on their river, taking out their beaver, and wanted to bargain with him regarding the distance of his trap line. It extended, they claimed, into their own territory and they informed him that he no longer could hunt there.

McAllister halted his step, staring hard and impatiently at the Indians blocking the trail before him. Suddenly he flung out his arms, screaming at them in English, cursing them in French, with such fierce frenzy that they quickly backed away. While the trapper continued in this vein, the Indians became convinced that the white man's mind was surely gone. Instantly they broke into a roar of laughter and swung their horses around, plunging them into the icy water of the Okanagan River and forsaking the purpose of their harassment.

McAllister shifted his pack into an easy position once more. As he did so, his feet suddenly slipped from under him. His body was dragged backward by the load of skins. He fought to regain his footing, but it was futile. The bank quickly gave way to its store of water and McAllister was carried with the sliding mass toward the ice-crusted shores of the river. His right leg became twisted and entangled by the mass of rocks and rotten branches which were harboured in the soft snowdrifts. A fierce pain seized his right knee, searing along the muscles of his thigh. The band around his forehead slipped off and the pack pulled furiously at his shoulder. He could do nothing to regain his balance.

The racket of shouting men and McAllister's screeching drew Rattler's attention as he followed the trail close to the river. When he came upon the stricken trapper, all that could be seen of him was an arm protruding out of the snow. A boulder, loosened by the slide's shift, had rolled and fallen against McAllister's neck. A cascade of wet snow all but buried him.

Rattler bent over to view the arm. For a moment the Indian

contemplated McAllister's laden body as it lay buried beneath the slide. An urge to leave him there seized Rattler and he actually squatted on his heels against the wet snow to think about it. He wondered where the trapper's knife was, the double-edged weapon that had once been placed at his throat. This thought now held the Indian in lengthier contemplation of the situation. Beside him the river flowed noisily, choked with large plates of ice gouging at its banks. He could throw him in the water and no one would know the difference, Rattler knew. Trappers were found drowned every year along rivers.

Not this one, he decided. Everyone in his village would suspect something of the incident. Besides, he reminded himself, the trapper had been decent toward him through all that had gone between them. So with a sigh of mild resignation and a faint smile upon his thick lips, Rattler reached out and began to dig away the snow to free McAllister.

The deer hide gloves on his hands were soon soggy with water and the leggings of his breeches were the same. But Rattler dug and scraped at the snowy shield over McAllister's body until he had it free. Finally he was able to brush away the slush from the trapper's face and clothes, and slip the straps of the packboard from a shoulder. When he had pulled McAllister free of the slide, Rattler removed his gloves and patted firmly against McAllister's cheeks to revive him.

"Come on, come on," he urged, wondering if indeed, the man might be dead. "Wake up, Many Rains. Come on!"

The response was slight. Without waiting, Rattler looped his arms through the straps of the packboard and shifted it comfortably upon his back. He pulled McAllister up to lean against him. The trapper was taller than Rattler and the Indian was nearly cast off balance. McAllister was roused. His eyes rolled around to meet the Indian's, but his leg was injured and he slipped back into the snow. Quickly Rattler caught him up once more and held him tightly against him. McAllister groaned with pain.

A smile broke out upon the Indian's brown face. "At least–" he breathed with honest relief, "you're not dead and maybe only have a broken leg." Hoisting McAllister carefully, he pulled the trapper's arm behind his neck. Together they stumbled along the slippery trail toward the camp.

When he had assisted McAllister into his bed of blankets and robes, he raised the coals in the fire bed outside into a quick blaze. Soon the heat could be felt in the hut as it warmed the air beneath the canopy of hides. When he had brewed hot tea and given it to the trapper, he departed for his village to seek help.

When Two Way heard of it, he leapt upon his pony and darted

along the river, splashing furiously across to McAllister's camp. Rattler followed with less enthusiasm.

The trapper was sleeping soundly and failed to hear the Indians arrive. As Two Way looked down at McAllister, he asked of his uncle, "Where is the knife?"

"I don't know," Rattler replied with narrowed brows.

"I know you have an eye for it," Two Way accused. "And you took off his clothes you said, to get him into bed."

"The knife was not on him." Rattler's thick lips were pinched very tight against such interrogation from his nephew. "And you should ask yourself, young boy, just who it is you are now questioning! No one doubts me!"

Which is a bad lie, Two Way thought, everyone doubts you.

"That knife is always with him." Two Way persisted, his eyes darkening with despair. He frowned over Rattler's inclination to steal, knowing the knife had been removed from his friend. "The knife is his, Uncle."

Anger then flashed in Rattler's black eyes. "You are a young, stupid boy!" he snapped in Salish. Spinning on his heels, he left McAllister's dwelling.

Two Way followed. "What did you give him to drink?" he asked curiously. "Many Rains is still fast asleep and does not hear us one bit."

"Only a strong brew of his tea. It will make him sleep well and that's all he needs." At that Rattler laughed at the irony of the situation. "I save his hide and then I get nothing but questions of dishonour!" Lifting McAllister's pack, he pulled the thongs loose which held the freshly skinned hides tightly together. They fell onto the wet ground. "Tonight, Nephew, we're going to look after these. They must go on the stretchers right away."

But Two Way had taken up the reins of his pony. "When I come back with Nahna, then I will help you."

Rattler swung his gaze around to that of Two Way's. "Nahna?"

"She will come and look after Many Rains, because I will ask her to."

"You are wrong to ask that. He can look after himself." He sighed tiredly. "Besides, your father will not allow it anyway."

"I will come back soon with Nahna." Two Way booted his pony in the flanks and trotted toward the river.

With an impatient sigh, Rattler reached for McAllister's hide stretchers. From within his bulky tunic he drew the trapper's knife from its sheath which he had tied around his thick chest. A smug smile spread over his face as he picked up one of the beaver pelts to begin the scraping.

Behind him in the house, McAllister stirred restlessly beneath his blankets. Despite the warmth of the room he shivered with cold while beads of perspiration rolled off his body to soak the bedcovers. His right knee had become swollen and hot, and too painful to move. He tried to get off the low bed, but failed. Darkness swept over him and he fell back.

When in the evening Rattler and Two Way had departed the trapper's camp, Nahna remained. She had brought with her a medicinal bag containing pieces of willow bark, yarrow, mustard seed and tea. Refilling the kettle which hung over the fire with fresh water from the river, she tossed in several handfuls of leaves from the Labrador tea plant. The water quickly boiled and turned green, then dark brown in colour. Using a round, smooth rock from the riverbed, she pounded the dry mustard seed into a fine powder and stored it away in a wooden bowl for later use. Before she rested for the night, a cold compress was placed against McAllister's swollen knee. When she was finished, Nahna sat down upon the hides which covered the dirt floor of McAllister's house, and pulled a soft Hudson's Bay blanket over her. She did not sleep, listening to his restless stirrings.

Two Way returned to the camp early in the morning. Together they woke the trapper, and bathed the perspiration from his body. Nahna continued to change the cold compresses over the swelling. She forced hot tea past his lips to warm him. Outside, working in the warmth of the late February sunshine, Two Way cut sturdy straight poles from young pine and lashed them together to make a useful crutch to assist McAllister when he could get up. Strong saplings were trimmed and wrapped in cloth, to use as a brace for the injured leg. Setting the pieces against the swollen skin, Two Way tied them snugly and wrapped the knee with strips of soft leather.

Two Way explained to McAllister, "As the swelling goes down, Nahna will tighten it some more. Your leg will be kept straight then and will heal properly. I must go back to the village now, but you will be alright."

At no time during her care of him did Nahna look directly into his eyes. She knew he watched her as she cut his long hair to collar length and shaved away the heavy beard of wintertime. This nearness quickly created an awareness between them. Despite the sedative in the teas that she brewed and which he drank thirstily, he remained awake for several hours at a time. She moved quietly about his camp, refueling the fire from the woodpile and bringing fresh water from the river. When he needed to be up she assisted him expertly, so that he would not stumble and fall.

Gradually the swelling about his knee and thigh subsided. The heat that had radiated from the injury and reddened his skin

142

disappeared. Even the rattling sound of congestion in McAllister's chest could no longer be heard when he drew in his breath. It had been drawn out by the thin plasters made from the crushed mustard seed.

When Two Way arrived on the fifth day after the accident, Nahna drew him aside and told him in Salish, "Your friend is better now." She smiled smugly. "And I have found the knife you told me about." Her dark eyes danced with mischief. "Our uncle thinks he could fool me."

Two Way stared at her. "Where was it?"

Nahna reached beneath the heap of blankets that had become her bed on the floor of boughs and hides. "When he went to bring in the last bundle of furs he forgot it. It was left underneath the stretchers. I watched him use it to clean the skins, then he forgot to take it with him. He thought I wasn't looking." She giggled lightly. "Then I take it and hide it in my bed. He cannot ask me about it, but he knows. You see, to ask me is to admit that he had it!"

"Yes, yes!" Two Way and his sister laughed merrily together at having fooled their uncle.

Then, "Hush, hush," Nahna whispered, quickly cupping her mouth with her hands. "We might wake Many Rains and then we must explain ourselves."

Two Way reached out and put his arms around Nahna and hugged her. "You are a good sister and I thank you for caring for him."

"I tell only you these things, Two Way. But there is something else–" She looked hard into her brother's eyes, dark like her own, telling him that she trusted only him to know her secret.

"Well, tell me, my sister!"

"I took away one of the pieces of sods inside his house. It was loose. So I looked into it."

"Yes," he urged impatiently. "And?"

"There are many things," Nahna informed him, and told Two Way of McAllister's arsenal in the cache. There were two smaller knives and a bullet mould and pouch, lead, gunpowder and a powder horn. As she talked she pursed her lips together in thought. "I saw those things at the trading site once– when I went with our aunt. I know what they are."

Two Way sat down on the log near the fireplace to think. "Nahna," he said solemnly. "You must never tell anyone, and never go to that hiding place again. It could mean a lot of trouble if our uncle found out about it." He watched her face a moment to be certain that she understood the implications. "And Nahna," he added quickly, "quit looking everywhere for things."

Nahna shrugged her slight shoulders. "There is nothing more."

Two Way supposed not. No doubt, in her curiosity, she had already combed the place several times over. He wondered what it was with all young girls, that they must know of everything! When he turned once more and looked up to smile at her, his eyes widened in surprise. Behind Nahna in the doorway of the hut, stood the trapper.

Instantly Two Way was upon his feet. "Many Rains!" he exclaimed, blinking his eyes in astonishment. "We were so noisy and woke you! You have been listening to us--"

McAllister reassured him. "No, no, Two Way. I can't understand your jargon anyway. When a man is trying to get on his feet and walk without tripping on the hides, there is no time for listening to another's talk."

But Two Way knew they had been overheard and that McAllister understood more than he was letting on.

"Now," McAllister was saying to them. "Where is your uncle? I know he has kept my traps cleaned out. The stretchers are full." He looked from Two Way to Nahna. "But I never see Rattler, only hear him about the place."

"He did not come today," Two Way told him. "He has gone with my father to visit my married sisters at the end of the big lake. He won't return for one full moon."

As McAllister moved with the support of the crutch to the log near the fire, Nahna slipped through the doorway behind him. Inside the room she pulled the blankets from McAllister's bed and returned to the outdoors. Flinging them over the rope between the trees, she left them to air in the late winter sunshine. Inside once more, she gathered up her own things and bundled them together for her leavetaking. Now that McAllister was up and about without support from either Two Way or herself, she was positive he would not want her there further.

But McAllister saw quickly what the girl was up to. To Two Way he enquired, "Has Nahna been asked to return to your village?"

Two Way glanced at his sister who stood in the sod-framed doorway. "No. But I must leave." Whereupon Two Way rose and strode toward the corral where his pony ran loose.

McAllister struggled to his feet and leaned against the crutch. Ignoring the pain in his knee, he stepped toward Nahna. For the first time since their meeting in the village she raised her dark eyes to meet his, and for a fleeting moment he became lost in their depth.

"Nahna--" he began carefully. "You have taken very good care of me. I owe you much. In fact, I am greatly indebted to you all."

The girl's eyes did not waver under his gaze. He saw that she agreed with him. A secret expression played about her round face and it told the trapper how much she knew of him.

"You did everything-- washed my clothes, fed me and made the medicines it took to help me." His voice was very soft. "And you kept my bed tidy and bathed me, also. My hair is clean and I thank you for cutting it. I watched you when you shaved away my beard". It was an acknowledgement of an intimacy which they had shared.

Nahna nodded her understanding of his words. "I did everything," she agreed in halting English. She could say no more. He might read my mind, she told herself, and know my heart.

McAllister shifted his gaze to where Two Way led his pony from the corral. "I will miss you," he told her with feeling in the words, and brought his eyes back to hers.

When Two Way led his horse nearer, Nahna handed him the bundle of her belongings, and he tied them over the blanket. "You are alright alone?" he asked McAllister, glancing from the trapper to his sister.

McAllister nodded. "I'll manage."

Nahna was silent and stood waiting for him to climb up on the pony, that she might do the same to ride behind him. Once more her eyes looked into those of the trapper. "I will come back," she told him. "This is not finished yet."

Two Way frowned. "Then why do you leave?"

Wrapping her arms about his waist, Nahna booted the horse with her small moccasined foot and it stepped quickly away. How innocent my young brother is yet, she smiled to herself. As they departed, Two Way leaned back and waved to McAllister.

"I'll come and bale the furs for you," he called out. "And then— then you can take me to Fort Kamloops maybe, when you go?"

McAllister smiled and returned the wave. "To Fort Kamloops, it is! That is my promise, good friend!"

He remained standing on his injured leg for several minutes. The place seemed very still. He suddenly felt his aloneness. Then with careful handling of the crutch, McAllister got himself back into his house. In the dwindling February afternoon, the air had cooled and he was grateful for the blazing fire at the entrance.

Once back inside, he found that the girl had laid out his supper. On his small table there were pieces of roasted rabbit, cooked that morning. With them on the tin plate were rounds of Saskatoon berries, strips of smoked salmon between slices of fresh bannock. Nahna had pounded the flour for the bannock herself, using roots of the bullrush pulled from the marshes along the river.

McAllister smiled to himself. Indeed, he was going to miss her! She had done everything for him, caring for him with a knowledge and ability which could not help but draw his attention. Although she had spoken little to him and had seldom looked at him, she had been the company which he needed. Without her presence there, his hut now seemed very empty.

However, late that night Nahna returned to the trapper's home. In the dark he felt her presence in the room before he saw her. The glow of the firelight outside his door cast flickering shadows throughout, outlining Nahna as she stepped over the hides to stand at the side of his bed. She knelt down and laid her head close to his for a tender moment. McAllister raised his hand to touch the soft cascade of hair, loosened now of its braiding. Like silk, he thought, turning slightly to reach over her shoulder. Nahna lifted her face to look at him, and in the faint light of the fire's glow, the trapper and the Indian girl allowed their eyes to speak for them of this moment and her presence at his bed.

Did he know all along that she would come to him in this way? Yes, when her eyes met his today. He had only to wait. She knew he needed this, for he was only human, he conceded, and she has desires of her own, too.

"Nahna–" he whispered in the quiet. She allowed no words, placing a finger over his lips. The softness of her hand as it stroked his face and neck, the sensation of her mouth when she leaned down to kiss his brow, his eyes, his chin, coursed wildly through him. He strove to touch her lips with his own, but she teased with her tongue, along his jaw to his neck, raining tender kisses upon his shoulders. Quickly, McAllister reached up and pulled the ties of her dress. He pushed it back off her shoulders and down, away from her, flinging it upon the hides of the floor. Then forgetting the pain in his knee, he moved to pull her over him so that he could bury his face against the soft skin of her shoulders, feel the smoothness of her round breasts against his chest, and her warm body pressed to his.

In the morning McAllister could not look at Nahna. He could not even look inward, to himself. He could barely believe that he had kept her there, not allowing the night to end. More difficult yet, was admitting his selfishness in their intimacy. He had sought to satisfy his own need, more than to take care in the pleasure he might have offered her.

Eventually, as McAllister had known it would, his mind forced him to think of Willow. As if Nahna had known the other woman had crept into his troubled thoughts, she stirred beside him in the bed and rose from its comfort and warmth. Without looking at him, she slipped her dress over her head and flung her long, black hair out over her shoulders. He watched her tie the thin thongs of her bodice with the same deftness of her hands which had brought to him wonderful pleasure in the night. He pinched his eyes momentarily shut against the memory of it all. When he opened them again, the girl was gone.

While McAllister helped Two Way bale the pelts, with twenty skins tied in each bale, no mention was made of Nahna's disappearance from the village the previous night. Perhaps, he decided, they might never know. Certainly Two Way did not speak of it. Yet, she must have borrowed his pony to cross the river.

McAllister pulled the ties over the bales as tight as possible, while Two Way held them pressed. Sometimes he sat on the log near the fireplace, with his injured knee held straight by the brace. Or when necessary, he leaned on the crutch for support and took the dried and stretched skins from Two Way as they were handed to him. He was quick to notice that all the long hairs of the beaver skins had been carefully clipped. They were sleek, clean hides which had been attended to with diligence.

"You have many beaver," Two Way pointed out to the trapper. "There are also a lot of muskrat and mink. And still I have traps to empty."

McAllister looked down at the bundles bound and ready for transport. "How many do you have here?"

"I count eighty-seven." Two Way grinned. "I have learned to count in English, you see now."

"Two Way, how do I thank you?" said McAllister. "And Rattler– who I know must have had second thoughts about saving my hide." He deliberately made no mention of Nahna.

"Many Rains, have you forgotten? I am to go north to Fort Kamloops with you!" Two Way swung his dark, questioning eyes around to meet McAllister's. "That's all I want. And for Nahna, too. She says I should go with you. That I need to be away from the village like Rattler does sometimes. I am too much around old women and little children."

"I promised you, Two Way," was McAllister's only reply. This sudden intimacy with Nahna, indeed, her whole family, gnawed at his brain. For the first time McAllister forced himself to consider his weaknesses rather than his strengths, and he discovered that he was just as vulnerable to friendship, to dependency, and togetherness as any other man, and yes, he knew, to the natural yearning in a man for a woman's soft caress.

"I promised you and you shall travel with me this time," he repeated and saw a wide smile break upon Two Way's brown face. "I agree with your sister that you need to be away from old women and children!"

Two Way and McAllister laughed happily and the bond between them grew.

They struck out for Fort Kamloops together. Two Way did not use his little pony, but rode, instead, a sturdy, reliable black mare which was a favourite of his father's. Kelauna seldom rode now and was pleased to give his horse to his young son. When they had tied tight the packs of furs and their bedding and food, McAllister took up the rope of one pack horse and Two Way the line of the other.

As the sun broke over the mountain ridges on that twentieth day of March, the trapper urged his horse along the trail that crossed the steep bank, away from his campsite. He was closely followed by Two Way.

It was the first time that Two Way had been absent from his village. Although his uncle had always promised to take him on trips into faraway territories of other tribes, these journeys had never happened. Now that he was fifteen, Two Way knew that he should be amongst the men of the band, hunting with them and bringing down his own share of deer. He and Nahna were growing older, he felt, and nobody in the village was noticing. At eighteen his sister was still not married, when other girls her age were already mothers. And as for himself, he wondered, if he was nothing more than a boy to the old people, what young girl would look at him as a man worthy of her? To dwell on the matter was depressing.

He booted his horse to catch up with the trapper's. Where the trail widened to allow it, he rode abreast with him. Exhilarated by a new sense of freedom which coursed through his veins, accompanied by genuine affection and respect for the tall trapper, Two Way sought to catch McAllister's glance as they rode.

A strong feeling of kinship prevailed and he called across to the trapper. "Many Rains–" His voice was clear, lilting with his pleasure on this day. "I want to be a brother with you!" Passing the rope of the pack horse to the hand already filled with bridle reins, Two Way reached toward the trapper.

McAllister called back, "We are friends, Two Way. That's what's important."

"Clasp my hand like you white men do, Many Rains. We will be better than friends. We will be brothers!"

McAllister watched Two Way as he pulled on the reins of his horse, drawing the animal to a stand. He, too, stopped his horse. The boy is very serious, he cautioned himself, treat this moment with care. Clasping Two Way's smaller hand, he said softly, "Two Way, I take your request very seriously. I will be proud to be a brother with you."

Eagerly, Two Way leaned forward and held his grasp tight in the other's. McAllister looked across at Two Way and read the promise registered in the depth of his dark eyes. He allowed the Indian to read the same in his own. At that moment the pledge of brotherhood was sealed between the New Caledonian fur trapper and the Okanagan Indian boy.

As McAllister rode once more ahead of Two Way on the trail, he could not possibly know then the full import of that stirring moment between them. Throughout their lives the bond they had sealed that day would be honoured, more especially by Two Way, but also respectfully by the trapper. Even into other generations, the established affection of one for the other would result in relationships which would always know honesty and trust.

20

The landscape of rolling hills over which Two Way and McAllister travelled gave way to open, treeless benches above the wide Thompson River. Fort Kamloops lay below.

The fur post was a welcome sight to McAllister and Two Way. It signalled, for the trapper, seeing Willow again. It also meant enjoying meals of a better variety than his own, and a warm, comfortable bed in a house. As well, it meant a hot bath in a round metal tub, as opposed to quick morning plunges into the cold river! All that was familiar to the trapper would be strange to Two Way, who had never known the luxuries of white men located at a fur post.

Their arrival did not go entirely unheralded. The company storekeeper, Ellis Walker, spotted Rayne McAllister and the Indian riding across the flat bottomland and, dipping his short fingers into the candy jar, bribed a young boy to run across the compound with messages to Mary Walker and Willow Cairns.

Both women instantly emerged from their homes to stand at their yard gates in wait. With arms and hands shielding their eyes against the glare of a bright, late March sun, they anxiously monitored the travellers' progress to within less than a quarter mile of the fort. Then as Mary Walker walked along the path toward the store, Willow gathered up the bulky length of her skirt and dashed back into the depths of her house.

Before a small, framed mirror above the wash stand in her bedroom, she adjusted the curls of her hair, pinched her cheeks to bring the desired flush and, tossing aside her apron, smoothed a hand over the folds of her dress.

Excitement captured her senses. Her heart raced wildly. Rayne had come back for her! Then for a single moment Willow closed her eyes, clasped her hands tightly together over her chest, calming her impulses, and asked herself seriously, was she really ready to go with him to begin an entirely new life? Was she truly prepared to meet the unexpected? She had done it before, she reminded herself.

When Willow opened her eyes and stared at her image, she saw no answers reflected there. In spite of the doubts, she whispered quickly, "Oh yes– yes," and turned toward the doorway.

McAllister and Two Way had reached the company warehouse after nine days of travel. Willow could see them unloading the bales of furs and their travel packs while they talked with Ellis Walker. As much as she wished to rush across the compound to meet McAllister, Willow remained fastened to the floor of the veranda as if nailed there. Her feet simply would not move for her, and her heart seemed suspended. Then, as Two Way walked toward the store with Walker, she saw the trapper step aside and cross the compound toward her house.

Holding still no longer, Willow leapt down the veranda steps, dashed through the gateway and raced out across the dusty ground to meet him. McAllister caught her up in his arms, swung her around, held her close to him and buried his face deep against her shoulder.

At the store, Mary Walker turned away from the open display of their happiness. Glancing toward her husband, she met his eyes and read the query in his raised brow.

"Do I detect just a touch of envy, my dear?" he asked suspiciously.

Mary Walker veiled her displeasure at his suggestion and replied, "Not envy, my husband, for the days of travel and uncertainty are over for me. Who knows where Willow's feelings will lead her and what perils she must face because of her choice." Smiling indulgently, she added, "I'm not disposed to such public display of affection, but then Willow is quite a wilful, impulsive one." Turning, she watched the enraptured couple retreat into Willow's house.

Willow and McAllister held each other close, kissed, touched each other's faces and kissed again. Their pleasure in being together once more could not, it seemed, be curbed. So without further wait, he scooped her up, crossed the floor to her bedroom and kicked the door shut behind him.

Throughout the following days Two Way stayed with the Walkers while McAllister remained with Willow. McAllister learned that her mother had died and Willard Bromley had left the country for Montreal.

The subject of marriage between Willow and the trapper was raised at the Walker's dinner table by Mary, and McAllister replied quickly, "As soon as a fellow can be found to do it."

Willow, who was still fighting with her conscience over the surprise presence of Two Way, could only murmur, "Five days is quite a short time. There is much to be done for a wedding."

Ellis Walker reluctantly raised the matter of religion, for no other reason than that it should be raised by someone. The parties involved, it seemed to him, appeared oblivious to the lack of it in the trapper's life. He said to McAllister, "Willow is of the Catholic faith. Is there a one to which you adhere, that we don't know about?"

Mary Walker smiled approvingly at her husband.

While he ate, McAllister informed Walker, "As I recall my father on the subject, no." He glanced up and across the table at Two Way, suggesting, "If getting married is going to prove a problem in our world, maybe we'll turn to yours."

A gasp escaped the throat of Mary Walker and she quickly dabbed her dinner napkin to her lips. "Do not attempt to shock us, Rayne. I will arrange it. There is a Chaplain from the east lodging with Mrs. Ross at this very moment. You've met him, Rayne, since that is where you normally stay."

Willow's eyes widened and her gaze fell on McAllister. She had not once thought of his faith or the lack of it. She told Rayne, "The chaplain was travelling with his brother who is Chief Factor at Fort St. James, but he's going to go to Spokane House. He doesn't like it up here in New Caledonia. Eventually he'll go back home." Willow sighed, her story over.

Mary watched McAllister scowl as he finished his meal in silence. "He is a Presbyterian," she said, "but Willow, you must overlook that."

Shortly, McAllister left the house, leaving the women to worry about what must or must not be overlooked, and walked with Ellis Walker and Two Way to look after the bundles of furs which had been left in the back room of the store.

They were two months ahead of the Hudson's Bay Brigade and so conducted their business of buying what tools and necessities they could from the store which had become, with the passage of winter months, somewhat depleted of supplies. The shelves would not be restocked until the brigade returned from Fort Okanogan in September. However, as McAllister planned to journey to Spokane House for horses and cattle, he would complete his purchases there.

Two Way had never been near a fur fort in his life. It was an awesome sight. All the buildings were made of wood and each one had a separate use. The warehouse astonished him, with its rows of barrels along the back wall, stacks of Hudson's Bay blankets at one end, and a variety of furs hanging from the ceiling timbers. In Walker's store he found, to his amazement, several hundred tins containing various staples. It was a quantity that surpassed the number to which he was able to count in English. He saw pots and pans, tin plates and cups like those he had traded for with McAllister, long bolts of coloured cloth, and many boxes of beads, silver jewellery, needles and thread. On racks hung articles of clothing much different than that which he and the trapper wore. Everyone he had seen at the fort dressed in those clothes.

Two Way could not comprehend it all.

He tried to remain with the trapper as often as possible, leaving

McAllister's company only when the man's attentions were diverted by the women, and to sleep in his bedroll on the floor at the Walker residence.

The women kept Two Way at a distance, but Ellis Walker accepted the boy readily, regardless of his thoughts toward the race, because he was so obviously attached to the trapper. There was, Walker contended, no Indian to be trusted. However, this one, he decided, might be the exception. One could not go along with McAllister's generosity toward Indians, for he seemed to trust them all. "Probably," Walker told his wife, "because he lives so easily among them and most times looks like one."

"Perhaps that theory is the secret to staying alive–trusting," Mary replied quietly. "I hope it is anyway, for Willow's sake!" she added, unable to hide her concern over her friend's safety in the Okanagan.

Rayne McAllister and Willow Cairns were married on a warm late May afternoon in the parlour of the Walker house. For McAllister, this time of promise could not come too soon. He wanted Willow with him. He had grown tired of lonely winters, lack of companionship and unfulfilled needs. He had also become afraid of losing her. He believed that, had he not returned to Fort Kamloops when he did, in another year she might have left with someone else, as she had with James Cairns; and he would not have blamed her. He had noticed that the company clerk, Spikes, had made himself conspicuous in their presence as if in wait of something.

For Willow, the doubts surrounding a life away from the security of a fort were buried momentarily. She knew they would surface again and again with time, but she resolved to deal with the challenge when it happened.

Mary Walker sighed in disbelief at Willow's leavetaking. She had lately begun to lose patience with McAllister's hurry to leave the fort, and sometimes wished he had not shown up in their lives at all. It was not because she thought Willow incapable of faring well with the trapper, for he would, she conceded, look after her. It was a world without other white women into which Willow travelled. Here at least, Mary considered, there are several of us. Life is pleasant in each other's company and passes nicely, without loneliness.

Only the Indian, Two Way, stood aside from what was happening, his thoughts veiled. The white man's ways baffled him. In his way of life, horses or other gifts were given, a wife was taken, everyone was pleased and the happy couple went off to live together.

McAllister and Two Way prepared to leave Fort Kamloops two days later. Willow, in her reluctance to depart from friends and a familiar place, was slow in her preparations. McAllister had purchased two extra horses to accommodate her belongings and a third, of superior gentleness, for Willow to ride.

In their parting, kept brief by the impatient trapper, Mary Walker and Willow clasped each other tightly. Hurried promises were made to post letters back and forth with the fur brigade as it travelled through the valley, and to visit once a year in the springtime at Fort Kamloops.

As Willow rode away from the spot where the Walkers stood near the store, she whispered to McAllister, "I don't suppose, really, that I shall ever see Mary again."

Her voice seemed to hold a sad portent and McAllister cringed a little. He did not reply, for he knew that in the future he would be inclined to travel in the direction of Fort Okanogan rather than Fort Kamloops.

When the same sentiment was expressed to her husband by Mary, the reply was a definite, "Nonsense!"

However, a reunion was never to be.

MCALLISTER HOMESTEAD

21

When Rayne McAllister returned to the Okanagan Valley with Willow and took up residence at the new house on white lake, he noticed a growing restlessness among the local Indian bands. He learned that several white families were moving into the Okanagan to take up farming.

Resentful of the increasing loss of land and game hunting grounds, Natives began to harass homesteaders such as the McAllisters. Some families were actually assaulted in their homes or cruelly driven into the river where some drowned. Better tools and weapons made the Okanagan Indians more proficient in warfare.

McAllister was dismayed, even shocked, to find himself caught in the middle of the terrible situation that now existed in a land where he had known extraordinarily peaceful times. Two Way and his uncle, Rattler, rode over the hill from their village to the white lake homestead each day to work with McAllister. It was because he lived in the security of their friendship that McAllister had failed to realize the discontent brewing in the villages throughout the valley.

McAllister had not noticed any signs of increasing population during the trip along the brigade trail to Fort Kamloops. Appalled by his acute lack of knowledge, caused no doubt by his own inattention, McAllister now asked of Rattler, "Where are all these white people living, that your family claims are here?"

"In the hills," Rattler replied curtly, skirting the subject as he cleaned and polished the new rifle that McAllister had brought him. Rattler regarded the gun with the same kind of respect he knew McAllister held for his own, and so took care of the weapon with a meticulous perfection. Also, when his total concentration was directed toward such occupation, Rattler could pretend he did not hear the trapper's probing questions.

Willow's acceptance of Two Way and his uncle was rapid once she was established in the house. It was obvious to her that she had no choice in the matter of their friendship. They needed these Indians on their side. The situation appeared, to Willow, far removed from the peaceful existence which her husband had lauded as a benefit to residence near the white lake.

Further, she contended, if there were as many families living in the valley as she was led to believe, they remained fearfully hidden, never leaving their doorstep. She saw no one passing on the brigade trail near her home, so it would appear that only the Indians knew of them.

In all ways, Willow strove to please McAllister, and she succeeded. Her familiarity with frontier life had prepared her well, and she hoped never to disappoint him. McAllister was very proud of her.

In July, he decided to ride to Spokane House and purchase a small herd of cattle as well as a team of good draft horses. Willow was jubilant. She immediately began to prepare the packs for the trip, including one for herself. Her high spirits, however, were soon dampened by McAllister's decision that she must remain behind, for a long cattle drive was no place for a woman under any circumstances.

Weeping inconsolably, she protested, "It's insane to leave me here among all these Indians! Oh, Rayne, look at what you've brought me to, this wilderness, this isolation and uncertainty. Now you want to leave me all the more vulnerable to their whims! I fear for my life without you!"

"You'll be safe with Two Way," he told her, but his voice was not reassuring.

"Rayne– he is but a boy! I feel no protection in that!" Willow cried.

McAllister sighed. It was difficult for him to fully appreciate her concern, for he felt no fear in their existence among the band. Crossing the room to her, he wrapped Willow tightly, securely in his strong arms. "I will ask that Nahna come up and stay with you also."

Willow's head shot up from his shoulder. "Nahna? Who, pray tell, is Nahna?"

McAllister's eyes blinked. Had no one in all this time mentioned Nahna? Obviously not, he concluded sadly, and now he must explain.

McAllister's story of the Indian girl's presence in his life was kept brief. One more strange Indian in her house was no reassurance for Willow, and she tried to the end to win the battle and travel south to Spokane House with him. All her arguments failed, quelled by his promise, "I'll bring back some things for you, cloth and better plates and things. This is the best way." Willow was forced to accept McAllister's reassurance of the strength of young Two Way's protection and Nahna's companionship.

Accompanied by Rattler, for the trapper deemed it prudent to take the Indian with him rather than leave him, McAllister left his homestead in the still dark hours of early morning on July 10th, for Spokane House. The air was calm, a tranquillity that suggested protection.

Two Way had departed the homestead earlier to bring his sister to live at the white lake. He would pack all her belongings on an extra horse, for he knew that once there, Nahna would remain.

Willow McAllister stood, that morning, alone at the kitchen table the trapper had made for them. The wooden window cover had been lifted and secured against the inside wall of the cabin, exposing the mesh which covered the open window on the outside, keeping out the flies and mosquitoes. The sky was orange with the bright glare of the rising sun. In the stillness of the house, Willow watched the horizon and its beautiful changing morning hues.

Tears sprung to her gray eyes. He is gone only an hour now, Willow thought, and already I am lonely and afraid. Closing her eyes against the tears, she whispered reassurance to herself. "Two Way will be back soon. I must believe that I am safe here with only him–" Willow opened her eyes. "And Nahna–" she added. What would the girl be like? How old was she? And how reliable was she? Sorry now that she had not spurred more discussion about the Indian girl, Willow turned away from the window and resolved to take a more positive attitude toward her dilemma and make the best of whatever would be.

When the sun had risen over the distant ridges and Willow again looked out, she saw a long spiral of dust curling up from the ground, across the flats toward her home. As the horses and riders neared, she noticed that there were four of them. "Oh, my–," Willow said aloud, "the Indians are coming now. I pray that Two Way is one of them–" She put her hands together as in prayer and whispered, "Dear Lord, keep me safe!"

Outside, the horses were pulled to a wild, abrupt halt near the corrals. Dust boiled up from beneath their dancing feet. Inside the house, Willow could hear their voices, loud and excited. She saw that Two Way and the girl were not among them. Her heart raced with fear as she watched the Indians goad their mounts as they rode furiously in circles about the yard, clattering into the corral where they chased McAllister's two remaining horses out across the flats to be picked up later. Calling out to each other and looping their ropes about the gate and poles of the corral, they kicked their horses forward, yanking the structure apart, dragging the logs through the dirt of the yard toward the house.

Instantly Willow fled from the open window, hoping that the Indians would believe her absent from the house, with the trapper. She dashed toward the bedroom, throwing herself beneath the wooden planks of the bed and tried desperately to quell the pounding of her heart. The dryness in her throat threatened to choke her. Then the door was kicked open with a violence which caused her to bury her face in her hands and pinch her mouth against the cry that tried to escape. Willow listened as the Indians stomped importantly around the kitchen, throwing her things about the place and kicking the chairs over.

Without thought to further safety in silence, she crawled quickly from beneath the bed, through the mesh-covered window, and raced away from the house and into the trees beyond. Any noise of her impulsive movements was drowned by the racket in the kitchen. Although she could not see them, Willow heard their voices. Their high-pitched laughter was wild now in the excitement of their destruction as the four Indians leapt from the veranda onto their excited horses.

Galloping wildly about the yard, and several times around the house, they rode perilously close to where Willow hid in the bushes and trees, the horse's hooves spewing up dust and twigs against her as she crouched out of sight. When they had gone and only clouds of dust filled the morning air, she sat up and leaned back against a boulder. She lowered her head into her shaking hands and waited for the rush of tears. Although her whole being wept inside, Willow's eyes remained dry.

When a long time had passed and the sun had traversed half way across the sky above her, Willow crawled away from the rock, glancing cautiously around the yard. Finally she rose and moved wearily toward the barn and its inviting sanctuary. There Two Way found her at four o'clock in the afternoon.

Two Way and Nahna had come upon the homestead quietly, without notice to Willow, who lay sleeping in a pile of animal hides and horse blankets. They had followed the tracks of the four horses, saw the open door of the house, the broken logs of the corral and its gate.

While Nahna remained quietly atop her pony, silent in the knowledge of what had happened at this place, her brother slid off his horse and ran into the house.

In a moment he returned. His black eyes blazed fury. Balling his wide hands into tight fists, he spoke through clenched teeth. "She is not here! They must have taken her somewhere." Looking up at Nahna still astride her pony, he admonished, "You took too long to pack your things!"

"I did not want to come," Nahna replied coldly in Salish, seemingly unmoved by the morning's events at this homestead.

Surveying the damaged gate, he murmured, frustrated, "If we had been earlier–"

"It would not have made a difference, my brother. They were probably here when Uncle and Many Rains left, hiding, waiting." She swung her leg across the withers of her pony and jumped to the ground. "You can see how old these tracks are."

160

The sound of their voices woke Willow, but she could not move. It was as if fear had drained her body of all its strength. When Two Way led his horse into the barn, halting in the doorway to peer into its dullness for signs of further destruction, Willow's voice involuntarily cried out to him. He dashed toward the sound. She flew up from the hides as his arms reached out to her, and he clasped her tightly against his chest. A sad, helpless feeling surged through him.

"It's alright now," he murmured soothingly to her, and suddenly her tears fell. Against his face, against his shoulder and into his hands, Willow wept, as Two Way continued to hold her close, pat her shoulder, smooth her hair and reassure her.

Behind them in the doorway Nahna stood watching as he kept his arms around Willow, consoling her. On this day, she decided, my brother has passed into another important place in his life. Too long he has hovered in uncertainty; no longer a boy, not yet a man, not sure where he really wanted to be. His display of tenderness and concern is beautiful and he should show them more often, she thought. To him, in Salish, she whispered in the stillness of the barn, "You will feel things in life differently now, my only brother. Today has changed everything for you."

"It has changed nothing!" he snapped, as he listened to Willow's pitiful crying. He had no time, nor mind at this moment, to assess the meaning of her words.

"Yes, it has. You have grown to be a fine young man. I am proud of you. But I feel, Two Way, that today is the beginning of your drawing away from our people. From now on your heart will always be in conflict with your mind. Sometimes you will wonder who you belong with. I hope you never have to make a choice, my brother."

Nahna left the barn, entered the daylight, and in thoughtful silence during which she contemplated the consequences of their alliance with the McAllisters, she led the horse packed with her belongings toward the house. Her life too, she knew, might be confusing and tangled at times, but not in the same way as her brother's would always be.

Late that night when the house had been returned to decent order and Willow rested in her bed, Nahna slipped out across the yard to the barn where Two Way worked at repairing the furniture. Nearby their horses were tied in the stalls. By a dim wick light, he braced and tied the splintered pieces of the chairs together with thick thongs of elk hide.

"Tell me, my young brother," Nahna began in Salish, "what are you going to tell our father about today?"

"I will think on it, but they were not from our village."

"Don't think too long," she warned. "It may happen soon again."

Two Way glanced suspiciously up at his sister and smiled, "I know you have some ideas. Tell me them."

Nahna moved closer, kneeling and resting back against her heels. "It might be wise to forget what happened, is that what you are thinking? Or to take your time in telling our father? They may have been from our village. You don't know for sure, Two Way. I have heard some of the men talking about their old hunting camp that was here. And the women cannot dig the speet-lum on these flats anymore. The trapper will graze his cattle on this place that was ours."

A long pause ensued. Two Way cleaned up the mess before him, put away his tools, and picked up the bowl containing the grease and wick. Before he extinguished the flame, he looked across at his sister and told her, "I will tell Many Rains." He blew swiftly at the flame, bid Nahna goodnight, and watched her leave the barn to cross the moonlit yard to McAllister's house. Little evidence remained of the terrible episode that had occurred to temporarily shatter Willow's world.

When, in several weeks time, McAllister and Rattler returned, Willow watched from the window as they travelled across the dusty flats. Her smile widened while her heart raced with excitement. She dashed outside, waving her arm, calling to Two Way and Nahna.

The small herd of five cows and a bull of Durham and Shorthorn-breeding ran into the yard, tearing off in all directions. Willow was forced to retreat to the house and watch from the window. They were followed by two draft horses, loaded with bulky packs of stores, one with a square cage made of thin poles containing six black-speckled hens and a noisy rooster. The horses were tied to the replaced rails of the corral and the new gate. McAllister and Rattler raised their eyebrows.

Unloading was commenced immediately by Two Way and Rattler while McAllister and Willow enjoyed a moment of tender greeting, under the watchful gaze of Nahna. When Willow glanced around at the Indian girl a warning flashed which seemed to say "let Two Way tell him". Willow started to tell McAllister, but faltered. She saw that he had other matters on his mind and decided that later would do.

McAllister smiled at her, "I brought you some cloth for dresses. There are other things for you, too."

Willow leaned against him. "Thank you, Rayne. Thank you. I'm so glad that you're home at last." She felt his arms tighten around her shoulders and closed her eyes, willing her mind to forget her hurt at not being allowed to go with him. She just wanted to revel in his safe return and the strength of his presence.

That night lying beside his uncle on their pallets upon the boards of the veranda, Two Way was troubled in thought. He knew that

McAllister could not help but notice the new gate, the fresh logs of the corral and the repaired furniture in his house. He was positive that, at this very moment, Willow was confiding in him all that had gone on that day which seemed long ago. So, too, would Rattler have noticed the repairs. Why, then, hadn't one of them come right out and asked what had happened? They're waiting on me, he decided.

He was right. In the morning, McAllister stepped out onto the veranda and sat down beside the brooding Two Way. Behind them, Nahna passed from the small room at the end of the long veranda which had been cleared for her bedroom, and disappeared quickly into the kitchen.

"You are now going to tell me," the trapper spoke softly, and Two Way did. When he had finished his story, McAllister rose from the steps and went into the house to eat his breakfast. Before he sat down at the table, he called loudly for Two Way and Rattler to join him and Willow and Nahna.

"I believe," he told them, "that even though we sit here together in a family atmosphere, certain events tear at the roots of this friendship. Now, Two Way, I would like it if you went down to Shoshen-eetkwa with Rattler today, and told your father everything that you know. I think you both have your own ideas on who would have done this to Willow. Who the four men were." Preposterous as the thought was that one trapper might control an entire valley of Indians, McAllister nevertheless warned, "I want you, Rattler, to tell your brother that he should pass word along the valley that if any man from any village sets foot uninvited on this soil to make trouble, I will shoot him. On the spot! I will not tolerate harassment and trouble!"

Willow's gasp was ignored. The room fell still. Nahna dropped her gaze to contemplate the plate of food before her and it was several minutes before she stole a glance at her brother.

Two Way ate his breakfast as though the trapper had not spoken. Every word he had heard was what he had expected to hear. Has my brother forgotten, Two Way wondered, that this land belongs to my family? Does he not realize that he is privileged to live here, and is only welcome because we like him? Many Rains' attitude is changing toward us, yet we have done him no harm. "They will be back," he warned quietly, but nobody listened.

It was Rattler who wrestled silently with this warning from the trapper. It raised again the question in the older Indian's mind, of just how involved he wished to remain with these white people. He was uncomfortable in the middle of a conflict that might soon erupt into all out war between the two factions, and unlike his young nephew, Rattler chose sides. Consequently, when Two Way returned to the white lake homestead that evening, he rode into the yard alone.

McAllister, waiting on the step, watched him arrive and, nodding to Two Way, acknowledged Rattler's position by his absence.

"He'll come back," Two Way assured the trapper as he dismounted his horse. "There is lots of talk in the village tonight. Many arguments between my father, my uncle and the others, but those who came here were not from our village."

"So says your father!" snapped the trapper irritably.

Two Way glanced at his sister who hovered near the corral gate, and fell silent for a moment.

"Is that all?" McAllister asked coldly.

"Except that my father was unhappy that I should want to leave his house. And, that Nahna is here."

McAllister closed his eyes and thought a moment. "I'm sure. Yes, I'm sure he was." He picked up the reins of the young Indian's horse, led it into the barn for unsaddling, saying to the other, "Tomorrow, Two Way, we begin building a cabin for you and your sister."

So, once more, as a bright moon sailed above a troubled land, young Two Way rested uneasily on his pallet of hides and colourful Hudson's Bay blankets, trying to banish from his mind the pain of his conflicting loyalties.

22

As the trees were felled and became logs for the cabin, the distant rumble of trouble in the valley went seemingly unnoticed by the four people who worked together on the homestead beside the white lake. The strained moments between the trapper and Two Way soon fell away. As Willow watched the small house for Two Way and Nahna take shape, she could not stop the questions which raced through her mind regarding Nahna. By careful scrutiny of the girl's expressions, Willow perceived that much more had gone on between her and Rayne than the trapper had let on.

In an effort to ferret out the truth, no matter how painful, Willow made provocative remarks such as, "she is a very lovely young girl," or "she sews remarkably well. Her weaving is exquisite!" Once, she grudgingly added, "Anyone who can carry two buckets of water with a clay bowl atop her head has to be a valuable asset to anyone's life!"

McAllister shrank at the suggestion such remarks insinuated, for he could never quite rid himself of his intimate knowledge of Nahna. Her dark eyes followed him everywhere. She was a shadow, haunting him at close range, as if she knew something of the future which he did not. He wondered at his patience in letting her live so close, even to building a house for her! Although there seemed no explanation for circumstances having planted her into his life so permanently, he nonetheless conceded that he perhaps owed her his life.

In a feeble response to his wife's caustic verbiage, McAllister stated flatly, "She could be showing her worth down at the village, if you'd prefer."

Unshaken by what she felt to be a coverup, Willow pointed out, "She's here now and we do need her here, it seems."

"I don't."

"I do. After all, if I'm to be raising a family in this wilderness, I might have call for some medicinal knowledge of which you have none and they have all, I'm told." A secretive smile played about her lips as Willow teased.

When McAllister's silence brought her glance around to his, she saw that he was staring intently at her. "Am I to have a son?" he asked quietly.

"Or a daughter, perhaps."

In a bold leap he was out of his chair, around the long table he and Two Way had rebuilt, scooping his wife to him, holding her close for a moment. It was as if he was willing his enormous strength to her, to help her to live and survive in these rugged, harsh times, and to bear the additional burdens that were often visited upon frontier women.

"I love you," she whispered against his shirt, "I love all of you, David Rayne McAllister, and more especially because of this little one I carry."

In a rush of intense feeling, he was desperate to say much to her, but the words never reached his lips. Instead, they raced wildly about his brain and he thought that the love which he felt for this woman knew no bounds. Instead, he said nothing and held her close until the moment had passed.

After that day they were more as one than before, and what had been with the Indian girl slid further into the background of his life. When he worked in the fields, she came to him with marvellous snacks of biscuits with mountain currents and fruit bread generously portioned with wild blueberries. Cold, fresh raspberry tea quenched his thirst during the long, hot days of late summer. In the evening Willow crossed the ground from the house again to take her husband a flask of fresh water and urge him to go back to the house with her.

"It's growing dark and time you came in," she informed him. "A hot scrub in the tub with me pouring the water over you is what you need!"

"Should you be doing so much walking? What if you fell?" His enquiry was also a warning.

Patting her now swollen body, she told him, "Walking is the best exercise ever." Then to cease his worries, she changed the subject. "Look how green everything is. The fields are so flat and clean once more, now the hay is cut and in. It reminds me of the parks back home."

"Back home?"

"Oh, before I came out west." She smiled pertly at him. "We called them Greens, like in England." Her voice became dreamy and thoughtful. "When I was a little girl and the weather was good, I walked each evening before bedtime with Papa across the Green. And in the springtime I brought handfuls of wild flowers home to Mama." Glancing up at him, she added with teasing eyes, "The highlight of my life, I daresay!"

McAllister was staring at her. He could not imagine his wife ever having been a little girl. She was always, had always been to him, just as she was now, a grown woman, even when he had first met her at Fort St. James and she was only seventeen. Her soft beauty still captured his heart. Her warmth and passion in her love for him amazed him, leaving him wondering at his own worth. As well, her dry humour teased his imagination endlessly.

"Rattler was by the house this afternoon," she informed McAllister one night.

At this news his brow shot up and he asked, "Was there a special reason?"

"He saw you working in the distance and thought he might come by and help you, but he changed his mind."

He felt weary and did not pursue the subject of Rattler's presence at their place that day, but instead sat down to the table, and tasted the soup she had set before him. He ate in silence.

"The soup's not all that good, is it?" Willow asked in a wondering way. "You're too quiet."

"If you made it, it's good."

"Is it hot enough, then?"

"Plenty."

"Am I pestering you?" she began to tease, smiling to herself.

"Yes," he smiled in return.

"Shall you throw me to the natives then?"

"They're waiting for me to do that, alright!"

"Maybe Rattler would catch me!" Willow laughed merrily.

The sheer hint of that curdled McAllister's blood and set murderous thoughts loose in his brain. However, her giggling and sprightly flouncing about the kitchen set him right again, only to be jarred with, "Now, wouldn't that be something! Rattler and me!"

"Willow!"

Little images of Nahna and her husband sailed through Willow's thoughts and to cover up the hurt caused by them, she deliberately teased further, "Yes, that would be a forbidden something!"

The trapper ate in stubborn silence, then rose from his chair to carry the water from the creek for his bath. What could be behind Rattler's appearance here today, McAllister asked himself. Having come to know Rattler better during the trip to Spokane House and back with the cattle and horses, the trapper realized all too well the Indian's sometime fickle temperament. Although Rattler felt a certain alliance with him, McAllister knew that it was not the same as with Two Way. Things must have quieted down in the village, he decided.

On January 11th, 1837, Duncan Rayne McAllister made his appearance, bawling loudly at the cold world into which he had been born. A blizzard of monstrous proportions blew furiously around the McAllister house. Nahna was summoned from the cabin which she shared with her brother, and remained at the bedside of the struggling mother. A difficult birth, it spent Willow completely. As she lie haemorrhaging in her bed, Nahna raced about the house, issuing orders for more water, more cloths, and tea from the inner bark of the thornbush which had been dried and ground and stored away and now steeped in a tin pot set against hot coals in the stone fireplace.

While her baby slept in a spruce basket made by Nahna, Willow bit her lip against the abdominal pains which seized her and wept with fear that the haemorrhaging would not stop. She knew what could happen to frontier women in childbirth.

Two Way left the homestead on his horse, plunging through the thick drifts of snow, over the trail to Shoshen-eetkwa, to seek advice from his mother in aid of the stricken white woman.

McAllister paced the floor beside the bed in worry and impatience, casting suspicious glances in Nahna's direction as the girl insisted that the foot of the bed be propped up with a thick log. Cold packs of ice from the lake were placed alongside Willow's body and the prepared tea was brought for her to drink. Still, the pain tore at Willow and the haemorrhaging, already severe, only worsened. Looking down at his wife, McAllister was agonized by the grayness of her complexion and the drawn lines of pain etched on her face.

Turning away with a heart full of anguish, he wondered, why should this be happening to Willow? He blamed himself for everything, even though he remembered that she had wanted to start a family. Standing before the basket, he stared down at his sleeping son. A life begins-- a chill seized him, for he knew what was happening to his wife. The baby lay content, while behind McAllister, Willow's struggle for life abruptly ended in the night.

During the days that followed Two Way stayed beside the sorrowing trapper, leaving him only to help Rattler dig the grave beside the creek which bore her name. The digging took a long time, for the ground was frozen, necessitating a fire to thaw it, then steady pounding with McAllister's sharp pick to raise the chunks of earth. When it was finished, her body was wrapped in a blanket and thick robes and laid to rest nearby Willow Creek.

She had known her share of sadness and disappointment but, on the farm near the white lake, Willow had been happy. Whereas Rattler had respected her and Nahna had finally accepted her in what she considered her country, Two Way adored her. No other person in his life had been as dependent upon him as Willow since that day in the barn when he had found her terrified, buried amongst the hides. He had, ever since, been her eager servant and friend.

McAllister veiled his grief. No one ever saw it, but all knew it was there, locked inside him. No one mentioned the loss of his wife. Nahna kept his son constantly at her side, taking him to her cabin where she looked after him with great tenderness. When Two Way milked the cow, he brought the warm nourishing liquid to his sister, so that the baby would have what it needed. Nahna strained the milk, added small portions of syrup made from the sku-leep moss from trees, and carefully spooned it into the tiny baby. Duncan flourished.

McAllister trod the snowy paths of his new trapline along the eastern mountain streams in much loneliness and remained absent often for days before returning to the white lake. He had quickly slipped back into the life of a trapper, trusting Nahna in the welfare of his son. When McAllister finally returned to his home and went to Nahna's cabin to see his son, the baby was nearly a month old.

Two Way ventured to tell him, "Many Rains, you are too long in the mountains. We need you here. This is your home, not ours alone."

Nahna dared to add, "Duncan needs you, too," and with her eyes, she silently reminded McAllister of her own presence.

The scowl which passed over the trapper's weather-tanned face silenced them both.

23

Raids upon the few farmers inhabiting the valley increased. Rattler was seen less and less at the farm near the white lake. During the trapper's absences through the winter months, Two Way assumed the responsibility of managing the horses and cattle as well as providing for himself, Nahna and the baby. Two Way had developed into a fine looking, strong, intelligent and capable young man. There were times when he visited the village that his mother would smile proudly up at her handsome son and remind him of his responsibilities to his own people, often pleading with him to return to Shoshen-eetkwa. His father spoke to Rattler, learning of the absence of the trapper during the winter months, and felt obliged to call his son home.

"I wish him here with us," Kelauna told his brother in Salish. "It is where he belongs, where he was before those people came."

"He'll never come now," Rattler informed Kelauna. "He likes his life up there. Better things there with the trapper, than here. A good warm cabin, for one thing."

"And my daughter? Why does she stay?"

"Nahna is needed there. The baby has no mother, I remind you."

"Then bring the baby here. He will not be harmed, but loved."

Rattler spoke carefully, knowing that Nahna remained in her cabin for reasons other than just the care of the baby. "The trapper needs her, too," he added quietly.

Kelauna sighed heavily, lamenting his losses. "We were a family before he came. Maybe I was wrong in letting him alone. Maybe we should have chased him away from the river at the beginning. Nahna should be here. She should be with one of her own people, married and caring for her own baby son." He remembered, with an aching heart, the daughter who fashioned the finest tunics, ponchos and beaded belts and wove strong, beautiful baskets. He looked up to the clear, blue sky of early summer, saying to his brother, "I am growing old and my children leave me in my old age. It is not our way of doing things."

Rattler hunched before Kelauna, where the chief sat beside his conical-shaped house. "Times change now– for all of us, but it is not all bad. Life is easier for us with the things I bring to everyone." He paused to think more about the situation. "I know other white people will come. Where there is one now by the white lake, more will come. Sometimes I think about what will happen to our land. They will want more of it, and then I am afraid of where the change will lead me, so I come back to the village sometimes and live in the old ways. I never really left it anyway, but Two Way has, and he'll stay with Many Rains till one of them dies." He waited a moment to let Kelauna speak, if he wished to. However, Kelauna was quiet, listening, thinking.

Rattler continued, "Nahna will never let the baby go, you know. It has become her own child. She stays with Many Rains, too, and will until something happens to him or he gets tired of her nagging and throws her out!" With these last words, Rattler burst into laughter, but his brother did not find it funny, and reached out and thumped Rattler's knee soundly with his balled fist.

"You know that McAllister isn't going to die yet." Rattler sighed as he ceased his laughing. "He's the best with a gun. And, he carries that knife and it's deadly to all who touch him or his if he catches them, so Nahna is really safer there than here if a war between them and us happens. But, as I see it, that won't happen. Times that are changing are all in his favour. Only a little bit in ours." Rattler rose to his feet and stretched, for he had knelt too long and his knees now ached.

Kelauna remained sitting and looked up against the sun to his brother who was much younger than himself. "Where do you see that times are changing that you speak of?" He did not give Rattler credit for any amount of perception beyond his immediate needs.

"My brother," said Rattler smoothly, "you never leave our village. You no longer go on the hunt or to any of the summer camps. You close your eyes and ears to the raids that are being carried out in other parts of the valley, as well as the increasing numbers of white people moving near us. You do not look much beyond this village."

The old chief pinched his lips together, then spat, "No! It is Two Way who tells you these things!"

Rattler nodded. "Sometimes Two Way talks to me about these things, yes."

Kelauna struggled stiffly to his feet, refusing Rattler's hand in assistance, and stood before the house with crossed arms and his chin defiant. His sorrowing eyes looked into those of Rattler, whose dark depths stared back. "Two Way will only help us to disappear," Kelauna predicted forlornly. "We will cease to live as we have lived and will not be a people to take into account. You are telling me that we will be led by the white man and all our land will become his. You are saying that our people will become their slaves. First Two Way and Nahna, then you, Koti'leko'; then the others– one by one you will

171

all disappear! But I, "he cried, "will die first! I will not go their way! I will go into the mountains and die!"

Rattler had not heard his real name spoken in a very long time. He was surprised to hear it from his brother, and it meant to Rattler that Kelauna's words were in earnest, out of true concern for his family, his village and its people. Rattler contemplated a future of real change and possible trouble.

"Maybe you will not see it happen, my brother," he spoke softly and turned away. He did not believe Kelauna would simply go into the hills and die out of stubbornness, but more likely of old age. He did not have the heart to tell Kelauna that there was talk that he was getting old and a new Chief was needed in his place.

The old Indian's watery eyes stared out across the calm waters of Lac du Chien. For more than seventy years he had lived on these flats in this ancient village of his tribe, fighting the wars of the Okanagans against the Shuswaps or trading with the Kootenai to the east. With his cousins, Kelauna had rafted the lakes of the interior valleys, fishing and hunting the bounty of the forests. As Chief of his village, he had witnessed the arrival of the first white man in the valley, and had allowed the presence of white traders with their shiny trinkets and delicate shells, beads, silver and blankets. Now, he decided, those same trappers and traders had taken out most of the beaver and mink.

He muttered to himself, "This is our land and our hunting grounds." With those worrying thoughts, Kelauna walked toward the long house and went inside. Settled upon the rugs, with his legs crossed and his arms over his chest, the old man closed his eyes in meditation. No one disturbed him.

The old chief was right. The Okanagans did possess their land. The sites of their villages, the camps from which they hunted wild game, the fishing sites and berry picking areas had defined boundaries, recognized by landmarks. There was no doubt where their trapping routes were. All boundaries were respected. Kelauna lamented that he had mistakenly allowed the trapper, McAllister, on his river, and because of that leniency his family was now adopting a new way of life. His sorrow for all that he had lost was real and profound. He could see the changes more readily than his brother credited him for.

He considered the news which had recently reached him, that the Northern Coastal Tlingit Indians were dying in huge numbers from the dreaded Smallpox. "Another scourge," he had despairingly announced at the time, "visits our people from the white man to hasten our decline!"

As Kelauna sat in the meeting house and stared through the open doorway out across the yard and beyond to Lac du Chien, he felt very alone and, for the first time in his life, truly afraid of the future.

McAllister paid little attention to the changes afoot at Shoshen-eetkwa, for he doubted that very much was taking place that was not for the best. He was not uncaring about it, just not overly concerned.

He recognized that Rattler's popularity within the band would increase with the number of horses he brought to the village and gave away. Rattler would also distribute the large Hudson's Bay blankets, thick ropes, shovels, picks and axes to the village, which he earned while living at the white lake and working for the trapper.

Nonetheless, as much as Rattler earned for his people, talk in the village against him began to grow. Like Two Way, he was accused of helping the white man to steal their special hunting grounds.

Some said, "We can no longer dig for speet-lum and gather berries there," and others, "the trapper claims that where his cattle roam belongs to him now." So even though Rattler provided considerably for his people, esteem gained by his generosity was tainted by the loss of their primary hunting and gathering grounds at the white lake where the trapper was expanding his farm. Once more, Rattler decided to move back to Shoshen-eetkwa.

24

Many times during the next several years the trapper would trudge homeward from his traplines through the snow to the white lake homestead, contemplating the time when his son would travel with him. During the lonely days and nights he lodged in his line camp, Rayne McAllister's thoughts would return to happier times and Willow. He could not bear the memories for long. No amount of time, it seemed, could ease the pain of his loss, nor could the willing arms of the Indian woman comfort him completely. To see his son each time he returned home stirred memories which only brought him pain. McAllister knew that Duncan was well attended in Nahna's care, and that knowledge was the only comforting thought which the trapper had to sustain him throughout the empty weeks of his self-imposed isolation.

The task and responsibility of raising the baby had fallen to Nahna. She lavished a tender love upon him, cooing and rocking him to sleep. Eventually his diet of milk was broadened to include nourishing berry juices with syrup melted from the long sku-leep moss from the trees in the forest and gentle teas from raspberries and rose hips.

On warm spring days, Nahna tied the baby securely in a soft tanned buckskin pack against her chest and rode her pony through the hills to her village beside the river. She took him to visit her family, pretending that he was her own, until after a time, indeed, he became hers. Along the way she acquainted Duncan with the sounds of the many birds which flitted through the tall trees. They enjoyed the soft breezes which blew down from the hills and across the flats, and the gentle, caressing feel of new grass as she placed him upon Nature's spring carpet to crawl. Nahna taught Duncan his first words and eased him into his first steps. She dipped his tiny feet in the warm shoreline water of Lac du Chien and thrilled at his squeal of delight. Almost always, Two Way was at her side. Without him watching, Nahna would have taken baby Duncan to live permanently at Shoshen-eetkwa. That the trapper might have protested such a move would not have concerned her.

The small farm on the flats surrounding the lake which McAllister called White Lake became the permanent lodging of the two natives, the trapper and his son. McAllister returned home several times during the trapping season, taking his furs to the Rendezvous Site at Soi'yus on the brigade trail in early June, and meeting the supply train of packhorses again at the end of August as it passed through the valley.

Often Two Way sought moments to talk to the trapper about his son, but just as time became available, it was snatched away by some suggestion of work by McAllister.

"If I didn't know better," Two Way said to his sister one morning, "I would say that he gives me work away from him purposely so that he does not have to hear me. He knows that I wish to remind him of his son."

Nahna, dressing the youngster leaning against her knees in his little breeches and tunic, warned her brother, "Do not speak of things to him that will change our life. He is not himself all these months. You know that he seldom talks to Duncan, and that he leaves the house immediately when there is crying. Do not push him." Pulling the little boy upon her knees to cradle him securely in her arms, Nahna stared directly into her brother's questioning eyes. "He is my son, Two Way!" she whispered passionately. "The trapper does not want him, I think, so I am teaching him our words, our ways. When he grows up, he will be of our family and will take another name for himself. I already call him Greylegs, for he will be as quick and fierce as the gray wolf is, and stand up for himself as the wolf does."

Two Way reeled with the sudden knowledge of what was taking place in his sister's life. It was as if he had been given access to her secret plans. Suddenly his throat became dry and he reached quickly for the dipper which floated against the edge of the water pail. After a long drink, Two Way wiped a hand over his mouth and turned back to face his sister. "Duncan McAllister is his name and he is the trapper's child. Nothing you do will change that!" he informed Nahna firmly.

"Does he look at this child? Does he take him anywhere with him?" Nahna snapped back, her black eyes blazing. "Does he ever talk to him? No! He does not know the boy lives! So– he is mine!" she hissed, clutching the bewildered child to her chest.

Two Way sank into the chair beside them. Nahna's words overwhelmed him. When in a few moments he had collected his thoughts, Two Way reached out and touched his sister's arm in a gentle manner. "Nahna, tell me something. Why have you never been with child, when Many Rains stays in your bed constantly?"

"He is not constantly in my bed! He is in the hills!" she shouted at him, angry at his intrusion. However, the young Indian woman's shoulders sagged suddenly, and she lowered her gaze upon the child who squirmed for freedom from her arms. "Only someone greater than us knows the answer to that. A greater power perhaps, is punishing me for--"

Two Way stopped her. "Don't tell me such nonsense!"

Once more Nahna's eyes flashed. "It is not nonsense! It proves that this child is mine; he has been given to me."

Two Way was still for a moment, mulling over her words. "Ah," he murmured finally, in deep thought, "we have become so cut off from the rest of the country and our people, we see only each other up here, just the two of us at this place that is not even our home. It's almost like we don't belong to our own family anymore. And, a child that is not of us, has become one of us, but will never quite belong to either of us." His voice sounded very sorrowful and full of regret.

Nahna felt sorry for him at that moment. He had come to fully realize the truth of their situation.

A hint of the fall season was in the air as the breeze from the hills became cooler and the late September sun set earlier than it had two weeks before. McAllister prepared for the coming season of trapping in the same manner he had throughout all the years of his life, repairing his equipment and packing his stores.

As he worked, he thought of his son. Some day, he decided, he will walk with me along the river, through the mountains and gather pelts with me. When I am through with all of this, he will see to my ending as I was never able to do for my father.

He failed to see the infant as a baby, as a toddler, or even as a young boy. Instead, all of McAllister's thoughts were centred on Duncan as a young man, able to trap, or to build a good warm cabin in the hills. He would hunt deer, sheep, rabbit and grouse, and know which berries to pick or roots to dig. He would be capable of carrying out the essentials of survival without receiving much instruction.

At the age of seven, Duncan McAllister was removed from Nahna's possession and thrust into life with his father. Trudging along the snowy mountain trails, he tried to follow closely behind the trapper, but was often left several yards behind. Rayne paid scant attention to the fact that the young boy was not the tall, long-legged lad that he had been in his youth.

After a time, McAllister began to respond to Duncan's questions regarding the business of trapping. He took heart in his son's interest and soon became an ardent teacher. Under such instruction Duncan quickly learned to sharpen his own knife to a razor-edged bite, and toss it in the same manner as McAllister had been taught long ago by his father.

When home on the farm, McAllister was amazed at Duncan's ability to catch and ride a pony, as well as throw a rope at full gallop and loop a young calf. While McAllister admired his son's expertise and wanted to bring him through the winter, he realized he could not. He recalled his own youth where, during the spring and the summer, he lived at the forts where there were lots of other youngsters and schooling. Duncan did not have that. With those nostalgic thoughts, McAllister knew he was starving his son of the main essentials in life.

The relationship between father and son was carefully fostered by Two Way, who indirectly encouraged a closer bond, while attempting to lessen Duncan's emotional dependency on Nahna. He occasionally warned McAllister of Nahna's possessiveness. He did so one April morning while they worked on a new rail corral, saying, "Nahna took Duncan to Shoshen-eetkwa again, when he should be here with us."

"I have eyes. I saw that," McAllister snapped. "She is looking after him. That's her job." He wiped at his brow, not looking at Two Way.

"No, Many Rains," Two Way responded, "she assumes too much. When you are here, he should be working with you, because when you leave him behind, all his time is spent with her. Much of it is in our village while you are away. I know she teaches him what is important in life, but don't you think part of that job is yours? Things other than trapping, I mean."

Scowling, McAllister straightened up and stared across the rails at Two Way. The young Indian saw a warning in the trapper's narrowed eyes and resolved not to speak of Duncan again.

The original herd of five cows and one bull brought from Spokane House by McAllister and Rattler in 1836 had been increased to twelve. The first year two of the three calves had died because Two Way knew little of the care of newborns, and McAllister was still in the mountains in February. The following year four survived. Fine looking Durham calves, they kicked and played their way across the flats in the early spring sunshine. Two Way watched with great pride. He guarded them constantly from predators which roamed down from the higher regions and prowled about the farm.

He told McAllister, "Soon you will have enough beef to trade with the fur brigade."

McAllister replied with a grunt, "If your sister doesn't pack it all down to your relatives. I know what she's up to. "

In June the work team bore a fine looking filly. While McAllister smiled with moderate satisfaction, Two Way openly beamed with pride.

The cattle and horses were not the only increases on the farm. The six hens had produced large hatches. Eggs and roasting chickens were in abundance. Some were taken by Nahna to her family in the village.

No ridicule had been hurled at Nahna when she returned to the village, and no attempts had been made to steal the child for a slave. No burning of buildings had taken place. The shared homestead at the white lake was left safe, while rumours continued of terrible raids being carried out wherever new settlers dared to stop.

Throughout the summer Nahna gathered roots and berries, wild onions, clover and the young shoots of the salmon berry to add to the winter supply of food she stored. She found leaves of the Labrador tea plant, raspberries, rose hips, tall reeds from meadows of the river, bark from the birch trees and flowers from which she could extract the dyes necessary to her sewing. Small animal bones, porcupine quills and bear claws were collected and utilized in jewellery, and sewn on tunics and moccasins.

Two Way hunted in the higher regions for deer. Both white tail and mule deer ranged the benches and, with the musket given to him by the trapper, Two Way brought home meat which Nahna prepared for winter. During the fishing season he returned from the twin falls with a fine rack of salmon for drying. Added to this storage was a steer from McAllister's herd. Such industry served to keep Two Way, Nahna, McAllister and his son well clothed and fed.

Three days before McAllister was to leave for the rendezvous at Soi'yus, Two Way saddled the horses and invited him to ride away from the White Lake flats, over the hills to the benchland which stretched above the western shore of Lac du Chien.

Two Way threw away resolve and said to the trapper, "Many Rains, did you know that your son is fast becoming an Indian. He wears the clothes of our people, speaks the language of our people and has learned to shoot an arrow as straight as any young boy in the village. He also knows the best angle to throw a hatchet and could kill with it."

McAllister stiffened as he rode beside Two Way. "Well, I have worn the clothes of your people all my life. You're trying to tell me something again."

"I did not want to speak of this again, but Duncan has now become more Indian than he is white," he said quietly. "It is not that he is so skilled that makes him dangerous or brings danger to himself, just that he will be caught between two worlds – where he should not be."

McAllister was stubborn. He sat straight in his saddle, his muscles taut. He was mildly irritated by the heat of the day against his cloth shirt. "He has learned to look after himself, that's all. That's what is important."

Two Way was not to be put aside by simple reasoning. He brought his horse to a halt. "But he learns nothing of his mother. He knows he is white. He knows Nahna is not his real mother, but that does not bother him. To him, Nahna is his mother."

McAllister stilled and slowly turned to meet Two Way's dark, unwavering gaze. Two Way realized that in eight years no one had mentioned a word to the trapper about Willow. They often talked about her among themselves, but not a word had been spoken in the trapper's presence. The moment between McAllister and Two Way was very tense.

Two Way's eyes did not waver under the strain. In fact, he was relieved that his concerns were finally out in the open. "She was his mother," he dared to say further. "Nahna is not."

For a second a nerve twitched at the corner of McAllister's mouth. It was unseen by Two Way, hidden by the beard of winter months which had not yet been clipped off. Through clenched teeth, McAllister replied stiffly, "I do not forget."

"Then tell him about her! What stops you?"

"I see no reason to mention it. If he knows he's white, then he knows the difference. I did not know my own mother either," McAllister confided. "I never learned a thing about her. I only knew Indian and Metis women who looked after me."

Two Way felt sympathy for the trapper. "Do not deprive your son in the same way," he advised cautiously.

"Don't tell me–"

"Many Rains– I am your friend, your brother. I'm not a boy anymore. You haven't noticed, but I have grown up. In growing up– living with you all these years, I accepted your ways, as Duncan has become used to ours. They are not so different. But, it is necessary to know about a family."

The trapper fell silent, thinking, wondering about the consequence of such a talk with his young son. Two Way is right, he told himself, the boy must know everything about his mother.

"I speak the truth, Many Rains. She was a special woman. Tell him all there is about her before he loses sight of who he is."

"Nahna is not to be hurt over it." McAllister truly meant what he said, for he had developed a genuine fondness for the Indian woman.

"I know that," Two Way replied quickly. "She looked after you by the river and now she cares for your son– and you. Many Rains, you are not an old man. My father is, but not you, so you can understand the future, that the way you live now, is not the way Duncan will live."

Two Way dismounted and, holding the reins loosely so his horse could graze, looked toward the eastern horizon. "Everything is changing - for my people and for you. The raids that we hear of will not stop, but will flare with tempers over the land. There will be more stealing and burning, maybe even killing. One day Duncan will have to choose. Will he go to our village and our people? Or will he choose the path of his own people?" Two Way waited for a response from McAllister, but the trapper only stared at him with a frowning brow.

"The white man will swallow us in time," Two Way continued. "It is starting already. Bits and pieces of our hunting grounds and food gathering areas are being taken from us by trappers like you who have chosen to become farmers. Do you want Duncan to be beaten by his brother, the white man, who does not know there is not a drop of Okanagan blood in him?"

Without taking his gaze from Two Way's brown face, McAllister stepped down from his horse and faced the young Indian. "Where did you learn to speak of all this? Did I teach you to think like you do?"

Two Way smiled slowly. "Yes, Many Rains. And to think for myself. To be truthful. You tell Duncan about her, or I will." Two Way fell quiet, remembering. He saw Willow again, as he had found her in the barn, frightened and alone. He had cradled her in his arms and wiped away her tears. She was beautiful and brave and gentle, and he had felt a great affection for her.

McAllister looked away toward the distant mountains, to Lac du Chien glistening beneath a warm June sun below them, and to the river cascading over the rocks of the twin falls. Suddenly he began to laugh.

Two Way frowned.

"When I first came here I looked up in the dusk that day and there you were, watching me. From over there. Why?"

"I had never before seen a white skinned person close up."

"Did I look so different? I'm shaped the same."

"Not different. Your clothes are the same. You rode your horse, you made your camp and did everything the same, and you were even as smart and quick– no, better at it all than Rattler." Two Way paused, sensing a shift in the conversation. "But after a while I saw inside you, that you were different."

"How? When?"

"When you would take the poncho and breeches and fine tunic I brought from Nahna, but waited a very long time to come to our village and meet her and thank her."

McAllister cleared his throat conspicuously. "She lives with us now."

"Not of your choice, Many Rains. Only because she has made Duncan her own son. All these years you have left us your work while you trapped in the hills without much thought of us, because you know we are certain to manage well enough. You take us for granted, perhaps because we are Indians, but it proves–"

"It proves nothing!" Suddenly McAllister's raised voice grated against Two Way's ears. "Nothing! I lived by the laws of your band

and traded generously with your people. There has been nothing taken for granted! I have provided well for you both in return for what you do for me. I also took you to heart and now I wonder why I did. You grew up all of a sudden and now you tell me what to do in my life and how to raise my son!"

Two Way fought to remain calm. He stood proud, eyes unwavering, before the trapper. He was nearly as tall as the other man. His long black hair flowed back from his forehead and dropped softly against his broad shoulders. Dark eyes that could show his deepest emotions were also adept at hiding hurt and disappointment. The temper inside him rose, but he quelled it. Inwardly angry, Two Way dropped the reins of his horse for the trapper to retrieve, turned away and strode down the path that led to the river and the village of his family at the end of Lac du Chien.

25

Annually, McAllister made the trip to Soi'yus with his bales of beaver, marten, muskrat and lynx. In June 1845, Duncan's eighth year, the trapper was accompanied by his son, whose responsibility was to look after the horses. Although the McAllister homestead was located a mere half mile off the fur brigade trail, where his bales could be picked up, McAllister chose to make the trip to the rendezvous held on the lake near Soi'yus each summer. There he met with other trappers, traders and men of the Hudson's Bay Company where he got news from the northern fur forts and learned of events happening in other parts of the country.

The rendezvous site in the Okanagan had been established in the same year the Hudson's Bay Company's first fur brigade travelled through the valley to the Columbia River. Although its purpose of trade was the same as the rendezvous held in the Oregon country, its primary objective was to pick up furs along the way, keep a strict record of all transactions and distribute supplies on its return journey.

McAllister looked forward to the trip each year to Soi'yus and so made necessary preparations to be away the last part of June.

They left the homestead at dawn on Wednesday, the third week of June. The early morning sun was warm at their backs and the countryside peaceful as they rode southward. McAllister enjoyed the quietness in the hills, broken only by the hollow sound of their horses tramping softly upon the grassy ground. Following the Indian trail which wound through the valley from White Lake, McAllister and young Duncan remained on the higher plateau above the Okanagan River until turning south to emerge upon the bench overlooking the river. Below them was a panoramic view of the bottomland as it lay still beneath the hot, midday sun. The Okanagan River meandered smoothly toward the long lake at Soi'yus. Its oxbows were lined with rushes and low growing willows, a haven for migrating waterfowl.

Riding steadily, they reached the rendezvous site at dusk, entering the camp slowly without creating a swirl of dust from the desert floor. McAllister stepped down from his saddle, dropping the reins of both his horse and the mare loaded with the bales of furs.

They did not move; they were well trained.

McAllister immediately strode across the ground toward a man whom he met each year at the site. "Hello, McNarr," he nodded with a smile. "What news of the Walkers have you this year?"

"Good news for ye, I think," McNarr replied quickly, with a wide smile showing from within his bushy auburn beard. His blue eyes twinkled at McAllister's obvious surprise.

"And how is that?"

When McNarr hesitated, looking upon the tousled head of the young boy who had come to stand beside them, McAllister smiled and urged, "Well, I'm anxious to hear. Tell me now."

"Wheel, they ar' 'ere. They're a-waitin' for ye!" Turning to Duncan, he stated, "Ye must surely be the laddie yer father speaks so proudly of each time we meet!"

Duncan looked up at the big, bushy-haired man with the broad grin who spoke with a sound starkly different from his father. He nodded and said quietly, "My name's Duncan." He watched his father's eyes scan the crowd for several minutes, finally coming to rest upon a couple seated on a thick log near the main campfire. "Who are they, father?" A long silence ensued, during which Duncan noticed that his father never lifted his gaze from the man and woman across the crowd from them.

"Walker." McAllister's thoughts tumbled. It has been a long time, he reminded himself. An overwhelming sense of guilt regarding his loss of Willow descended upon him. He could not banish it. Did they blame him for her death? He had sent word to them with McNarr on the return trip of the brigade train, but McAllister recalled that no message had ever come from them in the succeeding years. Why were they at this camp? Travelling to Spokane House, perhaps?

Turning to the old trader, McNarr, he enquired bluntly, "Where are they going?"

"Ask them. Ellis is ailin' of somethin', he dinna say, and wants to get 'is wife to a more civilized land."

"Civilized?"

"The Indians ar' too much for 'im! He dreams of a scalpin' and becomes afraid."

McAllister rested a hand upon Duncan's shoulder. "Come. We'll make a camp and clean up." Moving his concentrated gaze from the Walkers toward McNarr, he nodded. "Thank you. We'll see them."

Duncan unbridled the horses as his father removed the packs of furs and their camp supplies from the packboards. Within half an hour their camp was settled, they had washed away the day's travel grime at the lakeshore, pounded the dust from their clothes and were prepared to meet the Walkers.

Each were struck by the aging of the other. It was clearly visible to McAllister that Ellis Walker was, indeed, failing from some ailment. Mary appeared well, although lines of worry creased her brow. Much handshaking and backslapping took place, talk and boisterous laughter in quick reminiscence.

Duncan stood apart from them, waiting to be recognized, but that did not happen for several bewildering minutes. He shuffled his moccasins in the desert dust and watched idly as the flames of a nearby campfire flickered high. Finally, when he had almost given up of any notice, his father surprised him and reached out, took a firm hold on his arm and presented him to the Walkers.

Instantly he was captivated by Mary Walker's eyes as they stared openly, admiringly into his own. Barely audible, the words, "You look so like your mother, child", reached his ears. The grip of his father's hand upon his thin arm tightened and held, until Duncan was forced to wriggle free. They moved to be seated upon the log.

"What ails you, Ellis?" asked McAllister in his blunt fashion.

"Old age! What else!" The storekeeper laughed at himself. "The time has come for me to move on to safer camping grounds. I'm too afraid of the wild west and Indians, even though the fort has been moved across the river. I wish for the safety of compound gates and more peaceful tribes since the Indians must live nearby us."

"Come live with me at White Lake," McAllister offered with sincerity. At this, Duncan's head swung around to look directly at his father and he felt, immediately, the motherly gaze of Mary Walker upon him once more.

"No– A good offer, I know, an honest one." Walker conceded. "But, look at me! I am sixty years old now, with a gut full of pain and a beautiful wife who should not be left to live alone in the wilderness."

Mary Walker stood tall and straight, dignified beside her husband. "Last year we sent word that we would be along now at this time to Spokane House," she informed McAllister. "It has grown and developed into quite a good post, we hear, and I really wish to move there. I'll take up teaching. Lord knows," she added with a smile, "such talents are sorely needed in the west."

"Indeed," Rayne McAllister replied with thoughtful interest. "Teaching– I may have need of your assistance with my boy."

Mary's eyes turned toward Duncan once more, and he cringed. An unexplained sadness swept over the boy. He closed his eyes tightly against the scene before him, turning his face into the trapper's soft tunic. Who were these people, he questioned silently, and where is this Spokane House they speak of? Without being told, young Duncan sensed that during that impromptu conversation, his destiny for a few years at least, seemed to have been decided.

Behind them on the flat land which swept away from the

lakeshore, the Hudson's Bay men had made their camp and were conducting trade with trappers and Indians. McAllister noticed that Chief Factor Southport was not travelling with the brigade and questioned Walker.

"He was hurt by his horse. It rolled on 'im in the mountains last year and he died from haemorrhaging inside." Walker snorted. "He was a pompous ass, but a good Factor. Knew his stuff, he did, but nobody misses 'im!"

By nightfall the noise of singing by whiskey-drinking men, whose laughter and loud talk echoed across the lake, had taken on an increased pitch. Mary and Ellis Walker retired to their tent, for the trip had weakened the storekeeper, whose abdominal pains assailed him with particular strength that evening.

McAllister and his son moved away to their camp. McNarr had thrown out his bedroll nearby. A steady fire blazed in the small pit dug into the sand and soon the hiss of boiling water began. McAllister dropped in a generous measure of pounded coffee beans. The odour of the boiling coffee surrounded them and even Duncan could hardly wait for it to be ready for sipping. Coffee was a treat. McAllister hoarded the few pounds of beans purchased from the Company each year in August, doling them out only when the drink would be especially appreciated, such as now, when resting beside a campfire following a long day of travel.

"I've not been back to Fort Kamloops in nine years," he told McNarr, with whom he shared the coffee. "It was good to see the Walkers again."

"It's a different place, the new fort, growin' fast," McNarr told him. "Many new people, but the Indians don' leave them alone."

Again, Duncan listened intently to McNarr's voice, thrilling to the rolling brogue and its musical sound.

"I brought out a pack load of tools and supplies right at the beginning," McAllister said. "Then I drove my cattle and horses up from Spokane House where I bought them from settlers living there."

Beneath a darkening summer sky the men drank their coffee, while young Duncan sipped slowly at his, savouring every tasty drop. In the lateness of night they listened to the yip-yipping of a pack of coyotes that had taken a position upon the hill behind the fur traders' campsite.

"It's no' like travellin' in the ol' days," said McNarr sentimentally. "No canoes an' rivers. We 'ave horses and trails now. No Indians in the dark ta send a chill down yer spine with their secret calls."

"Not the same challenge," McAllister added, remembering.

"Aye, McAllister, ye're right! The challenge 'as disappeared."

When McNarr rolled himself into his blankets and McAllister and Duncan were alone at last, the boy moved closer to his father.

Looking up at the clenched jaw and serious, unsmiling countenance, Duncan was perceptive enough to realize that his father had known many hardships and dreary years of loneliness. The few winters spent trapping with him had shown young Duncan a far different nature in his father than that displayed at home. Along the rivers and here at the rendezvous, his father was in complete control. At the farm Two Way seemed to be in charge.

McAllister scanned the sky for sign of continuing good weather, but its pattern had changed during the evening hours. "It's going to rain," he told his son, "and that makes my old bones ache. So if you're hoping for something on this trip, hope for the sun again tomorrow."

Duncan had not been hoping for anything on this trip. He was barely able to understand all that was, at the moment, going on around him at the rendezvous site. "The sky is black," Duncan remarked, looking up at the dark clouds, attempting to feel at one with his father as he had while trapping in the mountains.

"Very black."

"Nahna says that's a sign that the white man is going to make war on us."

McAllister was astonished. He had never heard such nonsense and doubted its truth. "Us? We are the white man," he stated flatly, perturbed.

For a moment Duncan sat quietly. He thought briefly of Nahna and Shoshen-eetkwa, and how much he felt a part of the happy life that pulsed there. He told his father, "You are."

"What? So are you!" McAllister was stunned. "You are never to become otherwise just because you like it down at that village!" Two Way was right, he told himself. He must be told about his mother now, or the time will be lost. "The black sky indicates only bad weather," he said, "not war. Nahna is full of crazy superstitions." With his mind dwelling on Duncan's closeness with Nahna, he enquired further, "What else does she teach you besides which side starts a war?"

"That all our land belongs to her tribe. That we only have permission to stay on our farm because her and Two Way live with us."

"And?"

"The white man calls it wild country, but it was only wild after the white man came. It was always tame to the Indians."

"She is quite a teacher," he remarked unhappily.

"Two Way says I should be living somewhere else where there is a school. Like a fort, he says. I'm glad all the forts are many miles away from us." Duncan sighed as though relieved of a burden. Remembering the intenseness of Mary Walker's gaze upon him earlier and her mention of teaching, he was certain he had now put to rest any question of his schooling away from home.

A tense silence prevailed between them.

"Two Way's right," McAllister said at last and told his son decisively, "Come the fall when the fields are clean and the place is in order again, I'll take you to Spokane where there is a school. You can stay with the Walkers, who are going there now."

A coldness swept over the boy as he turned pleading eyes toward the man beside him. "I don't want to leave, Father! I just want to go with you. I like the fields. I like the river and the mountains, and all the things you do. I want to be like you."

"You want to be like yourself, Duncan, what you really are," he told the boy. McAllister could not bring himself to glance down at his son, whom he knew sat stricken in fear of the unknown.

He heard Duncan whisper, near tears, "I promise not to go to Shoshen-eetkwa again if you don't like it."

"It is not that, Duncan. I believe you that you want to be like me, but you need to be more. I'm giving you that chance. It'll be the only chance you'll ever have." McAllister looked into the cup between his hands, drained of its contents, its metal reflecting the orange and red colours of the firelight before him. He said solemnly to Duncan, "You should know more about your mother. Listen now–"

The strands of auburn hair which fell over Duncan's brow hid the fear of what lay before him, as he tried to listen attentively to his father. The flickering fire danced sombre shadows across Duncan Rayne McAllister's fine features which revealed nothing of his heartfelt sadness or sudden withdrawal from his father's presence beside him.

26

Whenever McAllister viewed the landscape from the porch of his house, he saw a sea of wild grass stretching from the corrals across the wide flats of White Lake, sweeping gracefully up into the lower hills. The cattle, under Two Way's care, had more than doubled in numbers, and a second foal had, that season, been safely delivered. Fields along Willow Creek were cleared. Behind the barn additional rail fencing was added.

The years seemed to have slipped by unreasonably fast for McAllister. Duncan was growing up quickly. He became painfully aware of their isolation from the nearest fur fort and contact with other white people. Seeing Ellis and Mary Walker again reminded him that he must consider his son's schooling.

One day while working with Two Way, scything the tall wild grass near the barn, the young Indian told him, "If a trail could be cut through the mountains from the ocean, past here to the big mountains of many glaciers, I think we could end up located in the middle."

"What do you know of the mountains of many glaciers?" McAllister asked with a smile of amusement, and swung his scythe wide against the grass.

"They divide us from the land of the Plains people and the buffalo. I've listened to Rattler, who travels everywhere. My father has also told me." Two Way lowered the blade of his scythe against the ground and leaned on the handle. "I think that we could build us a stopping place and everyone who goes to the rendezvous would come and do their trading here. What I mean is, that everyone would pay us something for good food to eat and a house to sleep in."

McAllister, too, now leaned over the handle of his scythe and stared with curiosity at Two Way. "Whatever gave you that idea? The rendezvous happens only once a year. What would you do with the building the rest of the year?"

Undaunted by McAllister's skepticism, Two Way replied, "Rattler tells me that there are more people coming into the valley, moving through to other areas. They need some place to rest."

McAllister was astonished, for here was Two Way thinking,

talking, like a white man. "I'll never get rich depending upon other people," he said. "Folks don't give up their vouchers easily." Suddenly realizing the strategic location of his farm, McAllister marvelled that he had not conjured up the idea himself. "But– Two Way, I think it's a good idea."

Construction of the new building began on a site a short distance from the McAllister home. The intent was to establish a halfway point between Fort Kamloops and Fort Okanogan, providing comfort for those travelling with the fur brigades as well as settlers moving through the valley.

As the logs were hewn and notched, Two Way felt a special pride in seeing the structure built. A great sense of change and ambition prevailed, catching Duncan up in the excitement of it all.

Often, Indians riding by on their way along the valley would stop, watching in stony silence from a distance, thinking this development meant a further encroachment upon their hunting grounds. Rattler, too, made an unexpected, rare appearance at the farm, riding up to White Lake atop a great white stallion, galloping to a dusty halt before the half finished house. Seeing him, McAllister was amused at the Indian's way in which attention was commanded.

"It's been a long time since you came to my place, Rattler," the trapper said, as he watched Rattler dismount from a new saddle. When no comment was made by the Indian, McAllister added, "Welcome back. Where did you get the saddle? It must have cost you a lot in trade."

Stroking the cantle of the saddle smoothly, Rattler replied, "It is Mexican. I traded three good horses for it." He walked toward the intended doorway of the new building and heard McAllister say behind him, "Amazing that it found its way all along the coastline to you. Came up the Columbia River no doubt, to Fort Okanogan. A very good trade, considering horses are easy for you to locate."

Rattler had lost interest in the saddle, and allowed his white stallion to roam out into McAllister's fields. "There are some white people moving through our valley. I saw them south of here. They say they will stop when they find a good place for a home." He turned and stared into McAllister's deep blue eyes. "Their name is Carmichael. You started something here, you know, which doesn't make us very happy. Soon there will be nothing left for us; no place to hunt and no berry patches to gather from. And white people everywhere."

McAllister cleared his throat. "I can see that you're not pleased, alright, but there's more room here than your band will ever need or use. I don't want to argue with you about it. Go home and think about it– this whole big valley for a few bands of your people to share with a half dozen white families." Aware that the number of white families entering the valley would increase, McAllister dropped the subject and walked away. Behind the trapper's back, the Indian spat into the footprints left in the dust, then strode importantly around the building in assessment of it.

With grudging admiration, he observed Two Way's skills with the broad axe upon the logs. Each corner notch was carved perfectly to allow the log above it to rest securely. Then, whistling shrilly toward his horse, he watched the animal spin about and trot quickly to him. As suddenly as he had arrived, Rattler was gone.

On the last day of building, Two Way, McAllister and Duncan stood together and admired the size and appearance of the house. Nahna prepared a feast, as McAllister had asked her to, in celebration of its completion. In August, when the fur brigade once more journeyed through the valley, word was left with the Indians at Soi'yus to meet at White Lake where supplies could be left by the Company and subsequently picked up by those in need. Thus, the planned expansion on the McAllister homestead had begun. Two Way felt a special, deserved pride, although recognition that it was his idea went relatively unnoticed.

In the last week of September McAllister spoke to his son of the schooling available at Spokane House. News travelling with the Chief Factor of the brigade had told him that Mary Walker was arranging daily classes in a small building there. Duncan's limbs shuddered unhappily with such news.

It was very exciting to live at White Lake now with the "Lodge" in business. Duncan had not known that so many people moved through the valley, travelling both north and south, on their way from one fur post to another. Until now they had simply followed the brigade trail or stayed close to the river below in the valley, unaware that a very good farm existed on the nearby flats of White Lake. Word of McAllister's stopping place raced along the fur trade route. Soon it would become a well known place in which to lay over a few days during the long journey from the Oregon country.

Exercising continued silence through the days following McAllister's mention of Spokane House, Duncan hoped the matter of his education would be dropped. Such luck was not with the youngster and with an unexpected abruptness, Duncan was told to make ready for the long journey south.

"Life," his father told him, "will be different for you there. No deerskin clothes; good wool suits and ruffled white shirts with stiff collars are worn instead. Boots, not moccasins. And no more of Nahna's horrible rabbit stew! You'll be turned out as a young white man ought to be when Mrs. Walker's through with you!"

Duncan failed to be impressed. Tears filled his eyes, which he tried to hide, but he knew his father had not noticed anyway. He never minded Nahna's rabbit stew, especially when he had become adept at snaring the thing for her to cook. Suddenly the matter of his future seemed firmly decided. Duncan felt shut away from the paternal heart. There was no longer room for him in his home. At night he lay in his bed of Hudson's Bay blankets and remembered, with a smile, the round shaped house of Nahna's family in the village; the fun he had climbing the ladder to the entrance, calling his signal that he was arriving, then descending on the inside ladder to the floor covered with reeds and soft hides. The games he had played with the other children-- would they remember him when he would be gone so long? He openly wept over all that he would leave behind and miss so much.

When he mentioned his dilemma to Two Way, the Indian tried to ease his anxiety with words like, "He loves you very deeply. You're all he has. He loved your mother completely and you are part of her. He wants the best for you, it's what she wanted, too."

Whenever Duncan thought of the mother whom he had never known, he wondered why Two Way and his father made so much of it. He had not been cheated of a mother in his life, for he had always had Nahna. It hardly mattered to Duncan whether his skin was white or brown, for at nearly nine years old he was perceptive enough to realize that he enjoyed the best of what both worlds had to offer.

On a sultry August afternoon while he and Two Way gathered dandelion leaves and roots together, Two Way talked of Spokane House and the need for learning. Looking up at Two Way, Duncan quickly put his hands over his ears to shut out the flow of words. "I can learn everything from Father!" he announced. "Who taught you to speak our language and do the things you know how to do? It was him!"

"But not to write things down on paper, or read a book, or how to talk to other smarter people. I am only smarter than some of the people of my village, not smarter than white men." Patting the youngster in a consoling manner, Two Way told him seriously, "Many Rains is getting older and having more to do each year. He needs you to come home and take over for him when he is an old man and should rest. Our times will change. They're beginning to change now, and you'll need to be taught to deal with how it will be later."

It was true. McAllister was getting busier as he got older. The summer's labours had been increased by the building of the Lodge. A new and wider trail had been cut through the trees beyond the flats to join the brigade trail.

As well, a log and earthen dam had been created upon Willow Creek, far up into the mountains, where it originated from a small spring, so that when the water level dropped during the hot summer months, the dam could be lowered by lifting a large, wooden plate to allow the desired increase in flow. From a point on the creek close to McAllister's fields the water was then diverted into a deep trench which ran along the top of the fields, then into many smaller ditches. As a result of the extra moisture in the ground, the wild grass grew thicker and higher.

On the day of departure for Spokane House, Two Way and Nahna stood in the yard, waiting to say good-bye.

As McAllister checked his pack, he warned Two Way, "I'll not hear of Rattler packing off with my traps and tools while I'm gone! When he borrows things, he deliberately forgets to return them. And when I get back I don't want to have to sweep other uncles and cousins out the door. Remember whose house this is and guard it carefully." Two Way and Nahna knew McAllister was remembering the raid upon the place when the trapper had gone to the Columbia to drive his cattle to the homestead.

McAllister took up the reins of his horse and turned to look into Nahna's dark eyes. In their silent pools he saw the reflection of affection for himself as well as for his son. With his smile, warm and understanding, he acknowledged the hurt he knew she suffered at young Duncan's departure. She had cared for the boy from his first breath and taught him most of what he knew. In the tender moments of her good-bye to Duncan, McAllister witnessed a far gentler, maternal side of Nahna's nature than he had ever imagined. Indeed, he realized now, this parting was more heart-wrenching than he had expected for both of them.

Glancing at his son, who waited patiently atop his horse, McAllister saw that Duncan did not look back at Two Way and Nahna. Instead, the boy hid his unhappiness and stared toward the rolling hills beyond White Lake, while he contemplated the unknown into which he was travelling.

Upon their arrival at the new Spokane fort, the McAllisters immediately learned that Ellis Walker had lived only long enough to make the journey and see his wife comfortably settled.

"It was a dreadful, malignant thing that took him," Mary Walker told McAllister. "It wasted him, totally, down to a bundle of bones beneath the blanket, begging for death to come. A young woman came each day to help me for awhile, but she moved away with her husband and I was alone with him at the end."

It was difficult for McAllister to express his feelings, so he simply said, "He was a good man, you know. I liked Ellis." He remembered his own hurt in the loss of Willow.

Mary Walker received young Duncan McAllister into her heart as well as her home. She had a special feeling for him, as he was

Willow's son, and she praised Rayne for wanting the best possible education and social training for him.

"Oh, I'm so happy that you have brought Duncan to me," she told McAllister in a soft voice. "Life is very empty, living it alone. Of course, you know all about that. I needn't ramble on."

McAllister abruptly turned the conversation to a name which had plagued his mind since his decision to bring Duncan to Spokane House. "Can you tell me if you have met a Mrs. White? Denise White," he enquired.

Mary Walker looked up and, meeting his eyes, saw hope registered in them. "No. It was a Denise Merchant who assisted me with Ellis. She moved away." Searching his eyes, for she understood the enquiry without being told the story, she added, "Spokane House is a small place. There would in all probability, be only one Denise living here. Quite likely the same person, wouldn't you think?"

"Most likely," McAllister replied quietly and turned away to watch Duncan romp about the yard with a dog.

Mary stood beside him. "She moved to St.–"

"It's of no concern," McAllister said swiftly, stepping out onto the veranda and into the fresh air.

Mary smiled, suddenly understanding more than McAllister would have thought. She remembered that he had stayed at old Spokane House where she knew Denise Merchant had lived as a widow. Obviously, she decided, there had been something between them, or he would not have made the inquiry. He hurts still, Mary thought.

"Come, Rayne," she said quickly. "Let's plan your visit with me and settle some questions about Duncan." Her smile was bright in her attempt to cheer him.

McAllister was not in a mood for cheering, insisting that he must depart immediately for the Okanagan. Within a day he had packed his horses with supplies and left. It was an abrupt departure, which left Duncan hiding tears of apprehension and lingering doubts in Mary's mind about McAllister's paternal heart. As she watched him ride away from the fort, she wondered that he could feel so little for his son as to just shake his hand with few words of goodbye!

Reaching out, she drew young Duncan close to her side, leaned down and whispered gently, "You can cry now, for there's only you and me." He drew away from Mary and she let him go across the yard and into the nearby trees. To herself she said, "No sense to warn him of the Indians hereabouts. He fears them naught!"

Duncan did not cry. Nor did he talk about his father. He kept his tears hidden. Already he missed Nahna, her happy laughter and affectionate teasing, and remembered Two Way's comfortable companionship.

SKAHA CROSSING

27

The construction of the Lodge at the Crossing was well timed, for McAllister was beginning to feel the need of extra income. Although he continued to trap for furs, the length of his territorial lines was decreasing due to a decline in beaver, and so the numbers of his catch. He needed to extend his trapline. To do this, he would have to move into higher ranges, necessitating longer periods of travel. He would also have to build another winter cabin. It meant more time away from home. He decided to enlist Rattler's help.

He began to miss his son and the little bit of life they had shared, but refused to give in and bring Duncan home. The boy was safely lodged with Mary Walker in Spokane and there he would remain.

The Crossing quickly became known along the trail as men flocked northward. Some remained, bringing their families with them. Ian Carmichael was the first to linger at the homestead.

The Carmichaels arrived in the South Okanagan, having spent two years in travel from Independence, Missouri along the North Platte River, crossing the Great Plains and over the Rocky Mountains. Leaving their companions at Spokane House in February 1846, they moved northward into the New Caledonia region and stopped in the Okanagan Valley. The trip had not been an easy one. It was early in the year. Snow still lay upon the ground and often vicious winds from the north had plagued their temporary camps. They longed for a solid, warm house before another winter was upon them.

McAllister and Two Way met them in the yard. Carmichael, who McAllister reckoned to be about thirty-five years, presented his wife, Alida. Standing beside her, Carmichael was broad-shouldered, tough-muscled and, for the most part, unsmiling.

They waited for the trapper's wife to appear. Nahna conspicuously hove into view.

Carmichael glanced toward the doorway of McAllister's house. "Your woman?" he enquired, not entirely surprised. A humorous twinkle showed in his eyes beneath dark, bushy brows, as he glanced at his wife who stood beside him clutching her Bible close to her chest.

McAllister cleared his throat. "You might say," he replied curtly. "Light down and settle in. This is Two Way, and his sister's name is Nahna. They live here and promise not to scalp you in your sleep." A mischievous smile accompanied the humour which creased the trapper's weather-brown face as he winked an eye in Two Way's direction. "But don't turn your back on the one called Rattler. He'll show up sometime. He helps me on my trap lines when he's in the right mood."

Two Way took up the reins of Carmichael's pack horse. "Nahna," he called to his sister, "make extra for supper tonight. They will eat with us."

McAllister followed Two Way and Ian Carmichael toward the Lodge where the horses were unpacked. Boxes containing flour, beans, bacon, salt, sugar and coffee were taken inside. Large bags of quilts, clothing and kitchenware were emptied and distributed about the room for the comfort of the couple.

Alida Carmichael, it was obvious, was with child, and this had been the deciding factor in stopping at the Crossing. Nahna could not take her eyes from the tall, full-bellied woman with long flowing brown hair and large brown eyes. She followed Alida everywhere, insisting that she be allowed to help. Alida Carmichael showed her irritation with such company, in deep frowns and curt speech, which she doubted the Indian girl understood. Finally after several days of the silent harassment, McAllister felt compelled to speak to Nahna on the matter of the woman's privacy.

"You'll not take over that baby when it comes, like you did Duncan," he informed her pointedly. "It already has a mother. Duncan did not. And I know you're thinking that the only woman who can have a baby in this wilderness and live to raise it, is an Indian woman. Well, you're wrong. White women live too, and this one will."

The bitterness of the loss of Willow showed in his face and Nahna felt it in his words. She did not cringe before the bite of the moment, but stood resolutely before him, straining to look into his eyes which would not meet hers. During those tense moments between them, Nahna made her decision to tighten the bond between the trapper and herself.

Thereafter she remained in McAllister's house, moving her belongings across the yard and giving her cabin to Two Way. She asked no one's permission, just stared boldly across the supper table into the trapper's questioning eyes and offered no explanation. Without being told by the trapper, she knew this was what he had wanted all along. Following her establishment in McAllister's house, Nahna gave Alida Carmichael scant time of day.

One evening when the Carmichaels had been at the Crossing a week, Rattler arrived at McAllister's house and slowly lowered the heavy pack from his shoulders onto the step. The ground was white with a fresh snowfall. The temperature was dropping fast. Rattler was in an irritable mood, for his left arm was tightly bound in a rough sling. He suffered excruciating pain and, in a weakened state, wished only to be rid of his cumbersome burden of pelts.

McAllister did not enquire about the arm, believing that later Rattler would come to him with his story. Lifting the bales of furs onto his own back, he thanked Rattler in a grateful tone and strode off toward the shed where he stored his stretchers and traps. Rattler was left to Nahna's care.

While McAllister untied the bales and inspected the beaver and muskrat hides, the thin shadow of Two Way cast itself across the floor in the half light of the large shed. Two Way's expression was pale and drawn, registering the shock and loss he felt.

In the dark from the doorway, he spoke quietly to McAllister. "A white man shot him. Rattler is dead."

McAllister stilled. The darkness between him and the young Indian was heavy with anticipation. The trapper moved toward the open doorway. "From an arm wound, he's dead?" he asked incredulously.

"Through the back," Two Way replied stiffly. A dreadful, solemn moment engulfed them. "He carried the bales over it to stifle the bleeding. There was nothing for us to see until he went into the house. He told us the man was wild, crazy like a bad animal, then he coughed and he died— in my arms."

Reaching out, McAllister gently took Two Way's elbow and steered him through the doorway. They stepped out into the light of the night created by a full moon and the snow. From the house across the yard, Nahna's voice rose in the soaring wail of mourning, lowering to a soft, low moan. The sound of her cry hung on the still, winter air as though it was a forecast of impending danger and involuntarily, Rayne McAllister shivered from the cold and the warning.

Looking away, up to the bright moon, McAllister's eyes swept the sky. A man could turn crazy in the wilderness, he knew, remembering long, lonely months, year after year along the rivers of New Caledonia and south on the Clearwater. He glanced across the yard to the house, then down at his thick moccasins pressing his footprints into the soft snow.

"I did not ask him," he murmured, thinking aloud. "I thought he would tell me later, on his own time. I thought it was only a broken arm, that he had fallen." He clasped a hand over his chin, hung his fingers around his beard in deep consideration of the dreadful, barely believable incident which had occurred that day. In the pale light he looked across at Two Way. "Am I to expect the worst now,

Two Way?"

"Perhaps, Many Rains. I do not know. I do not live in the village anymore." His voice was thick with sadness and hurt.

"And Nahna?"

"She will never leave you. Until you tell her to go."

Pinching his tired eyes in thought, McAllister told him, "Rattler must be returned to your village. I will go down with you."

"Many Rains– you've not been there, but only once!"

"I'll go with you! It's settled."

The passing of Rattler had a profound effect on McAllister's trust of the white man. Until this time the trapper had thought little on the matter, believing that the question of how much trust could be placed in the Indian was of greater concern. However, it loomed now as a matter which could not be ignored, for more often than not a shot could be fired in haste, or when someone was drunk on whiskey.

A sense of emptiness and loss settled over McAllister. Although he had been at odds with Rattler for most of their friendship, he had come to like him and, to a larger degree lately, trust him and depend on him. All of the choices in their friendship had been Rattler's. However, as Nahna and Two Way, in an obliging way, had become his family, so had Rattler. His regrets must be paid to Kelauna of Shoshen-eetkwa. So with Rattler's body strapped upon one of his horses, the trapper rode with Two Way out across the flats from White Lake, through the ravines to the bench above Lac du Chien, where below stretched the snow-dappled ground of the Indian village.

As they halted in contemplation of their descent down the bank toward the river, McAllister saw Kelauna standing in wait upon their arrival. He knows, McAllister told himself; he already knows the sad news I bring him this day. Urging his horse forward, McAllister took Rattler home.

The Okanagans of the Lac du Chien village received Rattler's body with seemingly calm acceptance. Dark eyes peering from unsmiling faces, watched in veiled silence as McAllister rode into their presence, passed by them and stopped before Kelauna. McAllister dismounted and greeted the chief. Kelauna nodded acknowledgment as he crossed his arms over his chest, as was his habit, but did not speak to the trapper. McAllister reckoned the absolute silence in the village to be normal at a time of death. He did not sense animosity, nor feel threatened in any way.

Two Way stepped down from his horse and greeted his father. He spoke softly to Kelauna, offering an explanation of the death. "Koti'leko' was come upon by–" he began, but Kelauna nodded and waved a hand toward the door of the village meeting house. Rattler's body was removed from the horse and taken inside. Presently Two Way's mother crossed the yard and disappeared inside the house, dropping the door flap behind her.

On the return ride to the Crossing, McAllister attempted to recall any hint of retaliation which he might have read in the expressions of the Okanagans. Their eyes had followed his every move amongst them in the village. Two Way had told him there would be no trouble from his band, but Two Way had remained behind.

Nonetheless, Ian Carmichael was afraid. At the Lodge door he kept a loaded gun and Alida lived in fear of giving birth with only the Indian woman, Nahna, in attendance. She had hoped that when they decided to settle, it would be where other white women resided and she could expect assistance from one of her own people when her time came. A tall, raw-boned, thin woman, she had made the trip west with stoic determination, standing proudly beside her husband in all his decisions.

Alida Carmichael lived by "The Good Book" as she called the Bible. She kept the rooms of the Lodge in immaculate condition, scouring and scrubbing the walls, cupboards and floor with an energy that astonished McAllister, but which her husband took as a daily ritual in the course of their lives. Silently she cheered as she watched the logs being skidded down through the drifts of snow, over the hill by the teams to a spot near Willow Creek where, in the springtime, the Carmichael's house would be built.

As the winter months wore on, a gnawing uneasiness crept through McAllister. He rode his horse eastward over the hill and along the river, spending several days at a time inspecting his traps located along the waterway and its meadows, camping overnight in his old abandoned sod hut against the bank. The pelts which Rattler had brought to him were not of top value, for they had been taken much earlier in the season when the animals' fur had not yet thickened. In his travels he noted little movement of the local bands, and wondered at this. In former seasons the Indians had ridden along the benchland above his hut at least three to four times in a week, hunting, or perhaps watching his progress out of curiosity.

At White Lake they were often in evidence atop the knolls surrounding McAllister's farm and sometimes he would comment to Two Way, "They contemplate the number and fatness of my cattle! I know how their taste runs these days!"

Two Way only smiled and shook his head. "I don't think you know much then."

Then one day McAllister suddenly realized that the Shosheneetkwa riders were no longer around his homestead. Their absence gave rise to a belief that reprisal might not be long in coming.

The first incident occurred in the higher mountains on the east side of the valley with the robbing and murder of a lone trapper who was wintering near one of the many small lakes inhabited by beaver and muskrat. Word of it reached the farm the middle of March. Although Carmichael worried and his anxious wife fell into constant prayer, the incident was not considered to be unexpected. Many reasons could bring about discontent on both sides. From time to time in the past, news of this sort had reached McAllister. However, real apprehension settled disconsolately over the little group when a week later, the bodies of two prospectors were found dead in their small cabin twenty miles south of the Crossing.

Carmichael felt compelled to speak to McAllister regarding his tolerance of the local band and crossed the yard to the trapper's house. "Those savages are gettin' closer and they're gettin' bolder and meaner!" His robust body shook with anger at McAllister's patience.

"They're not savages."

"Oh? What d'you call what's happening all around you then, if it isn't butchery? I stopped here because of the safety I heard about."

"You are safe here."

"There's no guarantee!" Carmichael was furious. His face was red and he stared hard at the trapper while pacing the floor.

McAllister stretched his legs out from his comfortable chair near the fireplace and reminded Carmichael calmly, "There's no guarantee of that sort anywhere in the west."

Carmichael ceased his pacing and considered the situation a moment. "How is it you've never been bothered? Because of them?" He waved a finger in the direction of Two Way and Nahna.

"I had Rattler on my side," McAllister joked half-heartedly.

"You haven't now!" retorted Carmichael, hotly.

Two Way informed him, "Many Rains has his knife," with an exaggerated gesture of clapping a hand to his right hip, in an effort to lighten the discussion.

"What knife? What does that mean?"

With a smile playing about his mouth, Two Way told Carmichael, "You may see it someday if he ever has to use it."

Looking up at Two Way, McAllister chortled, "It'll never hold an Indian nation at bay, I remind you."

In anger and confusion, Carmichael turned and stomped out of McAllister's house, strode angrily across the yard to the Lodge and slammed the door behind him. He was frustrated beyond explanation and refused to speak to anyone the remainder of the day, contending that he had been undeservedly ridiculed.

At the end of March two wranglers travelling from Fort Kamloops to Fort Okanogan lodged overnight at the Crossing and brought a story of more tragic proportions. In his tack shed, McAllister sat on a bench mending a piece of harness and did not glance up as he heard the men out.

"Shot the man in his own doorway, they did. The buggers got guns now," said one man.

"And burned every buildin' to the ground," added the other.

"Someone seen his woman half crazy runnin' 'round the place. It was still smokin' two days later, but she disappeared."

"Lit for the mountains, she did. Some buck'll get her!"

McAllister looked up. "A woman?"

"Yah, well– keep a squaw 'n yer safe. Bring a white one 'n yer dead, I always say."

A thin veil of warning registered in the trapper's blue eyes as he fixed a cold stare upon the men. "Do you want to sleep by the fire tonight, or outside in the snow? With your head and neck together, or apart?" he asked evenly.

The wrangler quickly raised his hands against the warning. "I meant nothin' personal," then glanced toward Nahna, who walked across the yard, and offered again, "No offense meant."

Long into the night McAllister remained slouched deep in his special chair beside the fireplace. It was a large chair constructed of fir poles bound tightly together with thongs and padded with large pillows of soft tanned hide stuffed with feathers from the geese caught on the meadows. Its comfort afforded deep thought, and when McAllister wished to be alone to think, he sank into that chair.

Two Way, upon noticing the flickering light at the window, went inside and squatted down, turning his hands to the warmth of the flames. His expression was sombre. The long black strands of his hair lay loosely upon the tunic over his husky shoulders, hiding his face from the trapper's scrutiny.

"What's happening, Two Way? What do you know that I don't?"

"I know nothing, Many Rains."

"You wouldn't lie to me? You Indians know everything that's going on."

"Not everything," Two Way assured him.

"And Nahna? She lives in this house and never opens her mouth to speak anymore. She knows something."

"Nahna has grown away from me. We do not talk as much as we used to."

McAllister looked across at Two Way. His voice was very serious. "I'm going up there and look for that woman. I'll be gone awhile. It's about twenty miles in the mountains from half way up the big lake," he explained, referring to Okanagan Lake and the higher ranges between the Okanagan and Nicola valleys. Leaning forward, he warned the young Indian sternly, "Lord help all your hides if I come back and there's a single thing burnt or anyone's been harmed."

"I'm not to blame for what my people do, or do not do." Two Way felt compelled to defend himself and his particular band, even though no offense had yet been committed by any in his village. "There's a reason for all this—"

"I'll hold you responsible for what happens on this place!"

"I'm not an outcast because I live here. I can leave anytime and go back to my village," Two Way informed the trapper.

McAllister nodded. He sighed wearily. "You can, but you won't," he said softly and held up his hand. "I'm part of you and you of me. Do you remember? You were about fifteen then and we clasped hands on our life together. You're twenty-six now. That's a lot of years, Two Way, that we've been friends."

"Brothers," Two Way reminded. "I'll go with you to find the woman. It should not take too long. She won't be into the higher mountains yet."

"And leave the Carmichaels?" McAllister rose from the chair. "While we're up there, the Indians'll sweep in here and kill them off, too." He sighed softly. "And more's the pity; all for the likes of Rattler." McAllister stared into the flames of the fireplace. "The smartest one in his village, he told me once. Smart or not, I liked the stubborn bugger, and I miss him and our awkward kind of friendship." Abruptly he moved toward the door, stepping out into the cold night air.

Two Way rose to his feet. He smiled wanly. "I'll stay. I'll see to them," he murmured in resignation.

"I know you will." Turning, looking directly at the young Indian, McAllister added warmly with concern, "And Two Way, don't let anything happen to yourself."

28

As was usual with McAllister, he was atop his horse and away at dawn's first light. A cool early April breeze threatened to become a bitter wind before nightfall. Crusted patches of snow lay about the countryside, but the trails were clear, facilitating easy travel. Within the first day McAllister reached the charred buildings of the farm. No cows were anywhere to be seen. Only a few chickens scratched about the empty yard. The horses had been confiscated by the Indians. The place was dead.

It took McAllister all of the evening hours to bury the charred remains of the homesteader. The ground was still partly frozen, so rocks had to be gathered to finish building a mound over the body. He made his camp at the edge of a small pond, keeping a sharp eye for intruders. He hoped the activity would draw the woman out of hiding.

There was no doubt in his mind that the Okanagans and perhaps some of the Nicola bands, whose territory lay to the west, knew of his presence in their midst. McAllister stuffed his bedroll with his poncho, picked up his rifle and moved into the shadows of the woods near his horse. With his gun beside him against a tree and his hand resting on the butt of the knife at his side, he waited.

McAllister lingered there through much of the night before he sensed another's presence. It was a lone brave who did nothing more than inspect the camp briefly before disappearing into the darkness.

The following day McAllister rode deeper into the mountains, holding close to the creeks and ponds. If nothing else, he reckoned, the woman could survive awhile on water if she had not been captured by now. A light rain fell throughout the night, but McAllister remained dry beneath a roof of boughs and canvas. The trickling sound of water and tumbling rocks gave rise to suspicion that the sudden change in the weather might hamper his search and send the woman into places where he may never find her. The country to the west, he knew, was deep, dense and wild.

However, the following morning dawned from a clear sky. In the crisp, damp mountain air the trapper broke camp. Good trails were becoming harder to find, but he could still pick up animal paths through the brush. Horrendous rock cliffs made his passage arduous. His eyes scanned the canyon landscape for an encouraging sign of life. None existed. The world around him was quiet. McAllister was about to give up when, on the fourth day, he glimpsed a small piece of cloth caught on a pine snag.

The following day he knew he had found her, for a single day-old footprint in the mud of the trail led him to a small slide. Quickly, he dismounted. His heart leaped with hope when he discovered what appeared to be a cave behind the slide. He knelt down and crawled forward, pushing the debris away.

Crouched at the back of the narrow cave, her eyes protruding with fear and appearing ghostly luminous in the gray light from the opening was the woman. Spring thaws had brought down logs and rocks, filling in most of the entrance and almost completely trapping her in its cramped interior. The air was very damp and musty inside. A pool of water had formed in the middle of the floor. She did not move as McAllister broke through the debris and crawled into the cramped space.

He stared in disbelief at the pitiful, ragged, frightened creature. In the nine days since her tragic loss, her body had wasted considerably. Her hair was matted and her eyes held a vacant gaze. He did not speak, but simply smiled and extended a protective arm toward her. She remained curled against the rock wall, as though awaiting some final, horrible fate.

After several moments crouching before her, McAllister touched her arm and whispered, "I won't hurt you. I've come to help you." Drawing her gently to him, he held her thin body to his own and rocked her in a comforting manner. "I'll not harm you. I'll take you to my farm where there's help for you." His legs began to cramp beneath him and he was forced to move.

Holding her hand tightly in his, McAllister led the woman out into the evening shadows. Neither spoke. Conversation was not necessary, he decided; it could even prove disastrous. Apprehension showed in every glance she gave him. With water from his canteen, he washed most of the grime from her face and arms, then held his cup to her swollen, cracked lips as she took little sips of the cool water.

When he had wrapped a warm Hudson's Bay blanket around her, he took up the reins of his horse and, holding her hand tightly, led them down the hillside to a strong stream on the valley floor.

Camp was set up quickly. It was several minutes before McAllister could coax the woman into the circle of firelight, nearer to him and the warmth of the flames. The evening mountain air was cool and he placed a thick hide upon the ground to keep out the dampness. Warm at last, huddled in the blankets, the woman ate some of Nahna's biscuits and sipped water. Later, McAllister offered hot tea to warm her.

The long hours of the night remained light with a bright moon, affording McAllister much time for thought as he kept careful vigil. Sounds of owls in the night and the scurry of small animals in the brush floated on the cool, still air. The hours passed without incident and McAllister dozed lightly.

In the morning he gave the woman a fringed dress from Nahna and a pair of Two Way's breeches, which would make riding behind him on the horse more comfortable. Wordlessly scooping up the clothing and moccasins in her arms, she took McAllister's drying towel and disappeared along the creek. Once scrubbed and dressed, she returned and, without expression, tossed the rags of her dress and damaged shoes into the fire.

As McAllister watched, he determined that with this gesture she had bid goodbye to the past. When she turned to look at him, he saw for the first time how young she was. She can be no older than Two Way, he decided with astonishment. Of course, the gauntness from hunger had added age to her features. Her long hair, having been rinsed in the creek, clung in damp curls around her face and neck. When it's dry, he concluded, it'll be light and, without a doubt, she's probably quite pretty. She did not speak to him and he did not insist. Placing his poncho over her shoulders, McAllister pulled the woman up behind him onto the horse and they rode out from the canyon walls.

On that cool, clear April morning, they made their way directly east toward the Great Lake. Once there, they stopped on the crest of a hill above the valley. The water was calm and reflective. The quiet beauty of their surroundings reminded McAllister again why he had chosen to make his home in the Okanagan. So must the reason have been for the woman and her husband. He kneed his horse forward and rode down into a gully.

Deciding on a favourable spot beside a small stream for their night camp, McAllister immediately built a rock firebed in which he kept a low flame. Below them wound the trail of the Hudson's Bay Fur Brigade, which they would reach early the next morning. When he had set the water to boil for their tea, he emptied his saddle bag of dried berries and salmon. He took his knife and sliced the boiled deer meat and bannock Nahna had packed for him.

As McAllister knelt before the fire, the sound of snorting reached his ears. It had not come from the direction of his own horse. He tensed, but continued slicing the meat. A keen sense of danger warned the trapper that someone was closer to his camp than the horse was. In the darkness it was difficult to determine the Indian's outline at first; it melded into the shadows of the trees. The Indian was only observing. The horse snorted again. The man turned to move away. Instantly McAllister's thick moccasins carried him soundlessly away from the fire and into the shadows. With absolute quietness, McAllister moved in behind the Indian, clamped a hand firmly over the mass of thick, long hair and slipped the knife against his throat.

In what Salish he knew, he said with a warning edge to his voice, "My name is McAllister. I'm known to all your bands and I live in peace with them, and some of them live with me. I am brother to an Okanagan. You go back to your band and tell them you saw me and that I have the woman." He heard the Indian's horse wandering in the dark toward them. "Tell them this killing and burnin' has to stop. The woman goes with me near Shoshen-eetkwa." Then reaching for the rope that dangled from the Indian's horse, McAllister told him, "She rides, you walk."

When the surprised Indian had disappeared into the dark, he led the horse out of the trees and presented it to the young woman. "You are safe. He's gone. The horse is yours now."

She stared at McAllister and the horse for several moments, then took the rope from his hand and tied it to a tree near McAllister's. She pulled off some of the short dry grass exposed from the melting snow along the creekside, and fed the animal and patted its neck.

McAllister lowered himself upon a stump near the fire and watched her at the edge of the firelight. "I'd like you to talk to me," he ventured gently. "Just a word or two, that's all." When she did not reply, he turned to stare into the flames of the fire, contemplating the silent world in which she continued to live. "You're safe now, you know." He hoped his words would create confidence and encourage some communication. If he failed to get her to speak before they reached the Crossing, he knew that the sight of Two Way and Nahna could have a devastating effect on her.

The woman stepped closer to the fire and stared at him.

"My name is McAllister. Rayne McAllister," he persisted gently. "The Indians where I live call me Many Rains. I'm a fur trapper." He looked up at her and saw that her back stiffened as she pinched her lips together, but she did not move away.

"They're good Indians. They're my friends. Will you tell me who you are? Just a name, so that I know what to call you." He smiled at her. "We'll be together for awhile."

She remained silent. After a moment, McAllister rose from the stump, stretched his legs, then sat down upon the robe he had laid before the fire. Reaching a hand toward her, he motioned for her to sit beside him. She did, and he wrapped his poncho and a blanket around her, saying, "The Indian will not come back. Lay down and go to sleep." Assembling his gun and knife beside him, he assured her further, "I'll be right here beside you."

McAllister knew the Indians would not give up. Unrest in the valley had brought about the death of her husband, the burning of her home and theft of the horses. He knew they would return for the horse he had kept and most likely try to take the woman and his own horse. Certainly he could expect that they would monitor his travel down the valley to White Lake.

In the morning while he broke camp, McAllister saw a party of them at the crest from which they had ridden the evening before. Throughout the day the party broke into groups, making themselves known at various intervals by calls. It caused McAllister no uneasiness. All his life he had lived among Indians of one nation or another. He knew of their games of sounds, harassment and threats, so was not surprised when, in the afternoon he topped a hillock above Lac du Chien to find three of them blocking the trail.

The centre rider raised his hand in peace and indicated the confiscated pony upon which rode the young woman.

McAllister shook his head. "Your people," he said in halting Salish, "stole her horses. You owe her this one. Now we pass." He urged his horse forward and leading the other, snubbed closely to his own, forced his way between the Indians. From the corner of his eye he saw the leader incline a hand toward the woman. In passing, McAllister warned in Salish, "I would not touch her if you want to live."

From nowhere it seemed, the trapper's rifle was raised in careful aim at them. Instantly, the Indians wheeled their horses about and clattered away, their taunting laughter echoing through the mountains.

Glancing across at the frightened woman beside him, he was astonished to see tears stealing over her cheeks. Smiling at her, he nodded his satisfaction at this show of emotion, as he slipped his gun into its scabbard and slackened the rope of her horse.

That night the Indians were upon him in the dark before he hardly had a chance to be settled with his camp. The woman knew of them first. When one seized her arms, a small noise from her throat warned McAllister of their presence. As he turned and rose from the fireside, his eyes caught the glint of a knife. Then a searing pain raced along his thigh as one of them leapt at him and drove the knife deep into the flesh. As the Indian struggled to raise the knife once more, the trapper caught him, and tossed him into the blazing fire. Screams filled the night air as the burnt man ran into the creek. McAllister's gun blazed from his shoulder and another man fell to the ground, freeing the woman. The last one fled from where he had untied the horses, running off into the trees, leaving his partner splashing along the creek.

A terrible stillness settled over the camp. The scuffle had ended as quickly as it had begun. In the distance the splashing faded. The freed horses could be heard snorting and neighing in the meadow nearby. The dead man lay at the edge of the firelight. In the circle of light, the woman crept across the ground toward where McAllister stood. For the first time he became aware of the blood on his leg. Reaching down he pulled the torn material of his breeches back, exposing the gaping wound. Ignoring the pain, he crouched down and pulled the woman toward him. Above her head his eyes searched the darkness for movement. He listened carefully to every sound around them. Then suddenly he felt hot tears drop against his neck and the woman's body shake with her weeping. The agony of her suffering and terrible loss seemed uncontrollable.

As he held her and felt the warmth of her near him, a sudden turmoil swelled in McAllister's mind, and the many years since his wife's death, fell away. He closed his eyes, and for a single moment it seemed as though he held Willow there. He allowed the peace of the moment to envelope him. Then, against her hair, he whispered softly, "Tell me your name."

"Catherine," she murmured into his tunic. "Matthews."

McAllister smiled, leaning back to look down into her face. "Well, Catherine," he said gently, "we'll be home tomorrow. Now help me patch up my leg, then I'll drag that fellow out of sight and we'll go out and fetch the horses back."

In the morning Catherine Matthews helped him saddle and pack their horses. They moved away from their empty camp, out onto the brigade trail once more and followed it without stopping until they arrived at the Crossing.

Late afternoon shadows were cast upon the ground as they rode across the yard to McAllister's log house. Carmichael met them, taking the reins of the trapper's horse and tossing them over the hitching rail.

"Had a scuffle, did you?" he enquired in noticing McAllister's bound leg. Turning, Carmichael reached up to assist Catherine, but she had already leapt to the ground. Alida Carmichael arrived and led Catherine Matthews away toward the Lodge. From the window of the house Nahna watched and McAllister saw that her head turned to follow the steps of the new woman wearing her fringed dress.

Two Way called and waved as he walked from the corrals. "Welcome back. I want to hear every detail!" Then he glanced, with a questioning expression, from the trapper's bandaged leg to his eyes and back to the injured leg.

McAllister nodded. "It's good to be home," he said with relief in his voice and hobbled toward his house. The door was opened by Nahna and he disappeared inside.

Late that evening Two Way and McAllister sat together before the open fireplace as they had on the eve of the trapper's departure. Two Way told McAllister, "My father is very ill. He has caught a bad chill and breathes with great strain and coughs up much blood now. I don't think he'll live very long."

"Are you moving back to the village, then?" McAllister enquired, unhappily sensing changes to come.

"Only for a little while. He needs me there. A lot of things are happening now."

"I'm very sorry about what's going on."

After a moment, Two Way said, "Many Rains, Nahna is going with me. We waited until you came back. I had a promise to keep, but that is over now and I can leave." Two Way paused, feeling that the trapper would say a word about Nahna, but the room remained silent. "Tomorrow, Many Rains. We'll go to the village tomorrow."

"I'll ride down with you."

"When your leg heals, not right now." Two Way rose from the chair, bid McAllister goodnight and left the house.

McAllister remained in his large, comfortable chair through most of the night. While the flames played among the logs, he enjoyed the warmth of the fire and allowed his thoughts to turn to Nahna. She had spoken nothing of her leavetaking to him when he had entered the house. He had held her close to him for a moment in greeting, then she had turned his attention to the blood-soaked bandage around his thigh. Carefully she had soaked and removed the caked rags, bathing and wrapping the torn flesh with a gentleness that had always been a part of her nature. McAllister appreciated such a quality. He had grown very fond of her and it saddened him that she would be leaving, even for a short while, for she had been a part of his life for many years.

In the morning Two Way told McAllister, "I think Nahna will stay in the village now," as he helped pack his sister's bundles on the horse. "Our father is old and frail and wishes her home with him."

The tall trapper turned from Two Way to watch Nahna walk toward them from the house. "It seems like Nahna has just always lived here– from the first weeks after I brought Willow here. She can look after your father and then come back here."

"No, Many Rains," the young Indian told him. "She will stay. My village welcomes her. That is her home. Now she sees you have another here, a white woman who does not have a man. She knows that your eyes will turn from her to the new woman."

McAllister spun around to level with Two Way's dark eyes. "Mrs. Matthews is not my woman."

"She will be," Two Way replied softly.

McAllister clenched his teeth against Two Way's prediction. "Do you know already that I shot one of your people and wounded, burnt another?"

"I heard. They were Lakes strayed over from the east, not Okanagans. Maybe they were looking for a place to set up camp, I cannot guess. You had good reason, Many Rains?"

"I did," McAllister replied, nodding toward his injured leg. He was glad to have steered the subject away from Nahna, as the Indian woman had reached the corrals where they stood.

Inclining his head in thought, Two Way mused, "They might have killed you just because you are who you are among us, because you are well known to us."

"Yes, well, I think they couldn't give a damn for who I am among you," McAllister replied with a slight grin.

He turned to Nahna, giving her an assist onto the horse as Two Way led his own off a distance to leave them alone.

"Now, don't be long away, Nahna," the trapper spoke softly and reached for her hand. But as he looked up into the deep pools of her wide, dark eyes, McAllister realized that her brother had been right. It was unlikely that she would return to him. He felt a deep sense of loss as memories flooded his mind. Their hands touched and held. He asked, "Does Mrs. Matthews really make such a difference?"

Nahna nodded. "Yes," and predicted, "She will become your woman."

"I think not." He tried to smile, feeling crestfallen, even a little abandoned by her. He was not happy about all this.

Nahna leaned down from the horse to lay her cheek gently against his face for a moment. "I am right and you are wrong this time, Many Rains," she whispered near his ear. "I know some things about women that you do not."

McAllister suddenly felt his control of their conversation slip away from him. "I will miss you," he sighed sadly.

"Goodbye." Touching a finger gently, warmly to his mouth for a moment, Nahna added hopefully, "Maybe I will see you sometime when you come to the village." Then she reined her horse away from him.

"You must come back," she heard him say, but did not glance around to see his upraised arm.

Nahna's heart was heavy. It pounded inside her chest as though insisting that she reassure the trapper of her return. It was heartbreaking to leave behind the comfortable, happy life which she had enjoyed for so long, and to give up the trapper's care and attentiveness to her. She loved him, but she had always known that love would not be enough. Against the strongest longing to stay and, if necessary, compete for McAllister's affections, Nahna bid him farewell with a slight wave of her trembling hand and rode away. She motioned to Two Way to escort her as she turned the Appaloosa mare McAllister had given her toward the hills between the Crossing and Lac du Chien.

29

Catherine Matthews slipped into life at the Crossing with amazing speed, taking charge of McAllister's housekeeping and cooking. She carried out such chores as looking after the chickens and milking the cow. During May she turned the soil of a small plot in which she planned to start a vegetable garden, something neither Willow nor Nahna had done as seed stock was not available to them. Catherine had persuaded Two Way to bring back from the June rendezvous at Soi'yus, whatever possible could be grown. Two Way had complied with her request and obtained some potatoes, a bag of corn, and a package of turnip seeds.

McAllister recalled that in his youth he had attempted a rough form of gardening at Fort St. James, but as the growing season was too short and the ground already leached of the necessary nutrients in earlier attempts, he had given up and concentrated on canoes and furs. In the Okanagan, Catherine's labours would pay. The seasonal length of sunshine was ample. Water from Willow Creek was soon channelled into an irrigation system of little ditches running between the rows, allowing adequate soaking of the young plants.

Regularly Catherine worked in her garden, her blue bonnet warding off the hot sun from her face. Sometimes she was aided by Alida Carmichael; however, as her baby, Heather, was barely one month old, Alida preferred to remain inside the Lodge. There she happily tended to the baby's every need, studied her Bible as time permitted and cooked and baked, rapidly using up all the extras purchased by Two Way at Soi'yus. This depletion of stock only increased McAllister's already lengthy list of supplies to be brought back from Fort Okanogan.

The small ranch at the Crossing had been expanded to accommodate the men and horses of the Hudson's Bay Fur Brigade in their travel through the valley. Word of supplies and horse exchange was passed along the route. Soon the ranch became known as the Brigade Horse Exchange Crossing. When Two Way heard of that, he quickly changed it to Ska-haw Crossing, explaining to McAllister, "It means horse and sounds a whole lot better than that other big long name!"

"Horse? It means dog, I heard."

"Dog to some, to others, horse. Depends on where you come from, Fort Kamloops, or here."

McAllister shortened it still, to Skaha.

In July of 1847 McAllister and Carmichael left for Fort Okanogan. They planned to bring back as many head of cattle as they could gather, including a new bull. It was important to ensure that the herd was continually increased for an abundant supply of beef. Also, McAllister wanted to buy several more horses. Once more Two Way was left in charge of the settlement.

As McAllister and Carmichael neared the large fort located on the sunny banks of the great Columbia, they could hear strains of the boisterous boat songs of the French Canadians. A joyous and busy lot of men in billowing white shirts wrapped at the waist with bright sashes, they moved rapidly about the narrow wharfs and enormous rafts, unloading the crates and barrels of goods.

The hot afternoon sun beat down upon a land barren of trees along the great river. The many horses of the fur brigade pawed at the dirt in the large corrals, impatient to be let out to pasture. Screeching sounds of pulleys pierced the humid air as hundreds of bales of furs were moved from the warehouse down the long ramp to the loading wharf. Voices of men, calling orders, echoed across the water. The entire scene was one of intense activity.

Life here is much the same, McAllister decided. "In the twelve years since I first arrived here," he said to Carmichael, "nothing much has changed. It's a busy place."

They made their way to the main trade building, an oblong structure built of peeled logs, faded and scored by weather. Rough-hewn timbers fitted with wooden pegs framed the door and small windows of the store. Bare chested Indians in fringed deerhide breeches and moccasins grouped on the boardwalks and passageways, visiting. McAllister made enquiries of Evan Dubrais' family, only to learn again that Broken Bone remained with her people somewhere along the Columbia River.

McAllister was astonished to see several white women located at the fort, but then, he recalled, Alida Carmichael had passed through here not long ago. Mary Walker had travelled before her when the hazards were much greater.

"Most of them are in missionary work," the storekeeper informed him. What hardships they must know, McAllister thought, forgetting that he had asked the same courage from Willow ten years before. "There's a few missions between the Willamette Valley and the western forts now," he heard the man add.

At the end of the week McAllister left Ian Carmichael at Fort

215

Okanogan and rode southeast to Spokane House. There, three days later, he was met by Mary Walker and young Duncan. The greeting between McAllister and his son was, for the trapper, more emotional than he had expected it would be. He suddenly realized how much he had missed Duncan.

Duncan, at ten years, had grown taller than McAllister had thought he might find him. From beneath a mop of auburn hair, the boy's eyes showed his happiness as he smiled up at his father, his face displaying the finer features of his mother. Looking upon him then, McAllister's heart seemed to pause for a moment as a vision of Willow swept before him. Then jovially, he said, "How tall you are now! Turn around, let me see you. Still pretty thin!"

With tremendous satisfaction, Mary Walker saw McAllister unconsciously place an arm around his son's slight shoulders and walk close beside him. Rayne has changed, she decided; he is much more relaxed and friendly. "I'm very proud of your young man," she said, catching up to them, telling McAllister of Duncan's studies and good horsemanship.

Duncan no longer skipped and romped about as he had before, but walked with assurance in his step as they crossed the compound of the new fort. He showed his father the warehouse and the huge barn where horses used for racing were stabled. That night, at the dinner table in Mary's house, McAllister took note that his son did not gulp at his food, nor use his fingers, but rather chose certain pieces of the polished cutlery to cut and fork the food. Little had he realized how far they had strayed in the past ten years from the good habits of daily living.

McAllister felt pleased and very proud of Duncan. Watching and talking with him, he was reminded of how few were the refinements he had been taught as a boy, and how narrow his life had been through the years spent in solitude.

When the visit ended four days later, the parting was less strained than before. While Duncan gave the appearance of being completely happy at Spokane House, he felt a lingering sadness at his father's leavetaking. There was disappointment, too. When he asked to be taken back to the Okanagan, he was refused. Later, he talked to Mary about his sadness that Two Way was not along with his father, and the news that Nahna no longer lived at Skaha Crossing. Mary's comforting arms and words eased his homesick heart, and he resolved to think no more of home until the time arrived to return.

At Fort Okanogan, Ian Carmichael had gathered twenty-five head of cattle and twenty horses to be trailed to the Okanagan. He and McAllister set off on their journey at the beginning of August. The sun beat mercilessly upon them. Dust rose in great, gray clouds around them. Four pack horses were loaded with crates, sacks and small barrels.

At their first overnight camp, as the two men rested in the cool night breeze, they were hailed from a distance by a lone rider trailing three pack horses.

"Light down!" they told him. The rider did. McAllister invited the stranger to their fire, served him a tin bowl of hot stew, then helped him unpack his horses.

"Name's Holinger," the man said as he yanked at the wide straps over the packing crates. "That's how I prefer it."

With a smile, Rayne said to Holinger, "McAllister."

"Carmichael," Ian added.

"As you can see," Holinger began, "I ain't no spring chicken, but I got me a forge on top these here horses. I know, in bits and pieces, but it's all here."

Indeed, the others could see the huge, heavy metal rods, iron firepit and wide bellows strapped atop the horses.

"Got no particular place to go," Holinger continued. "Just stoppin' when I see the need." Glancing quickly at the twenty new horses in one rope corral and McAllister's other six in another, Holinger grinned. "Use me, could you?" he asked, and so a deal was struck.

Holinger would stop at Skaha Crossing and set up his blacksmith shop. Thereafter, every horse that needed a shoe, every rim and repair of a wagon, the iron hooks in fireplaces, and all the metal hinges and handles bolted onto windows and doors, would come from the heat and hammer of Holinger's forge.

The more residential Skaha Crossing became, the better Carmichael liked it. There was greater safety in numbers he felt, and although their numbers were few in 1847, they seemed to be protected, by some divine right, from sporadic attacks that sometimes plagued other regions. He considered that possibly Two Way's presence on the place held sway. He had no reason to believe that the bands of the Okanagans were essentially a peaceful lot, for ever since his arrival at Skaha Crossing he had heard nothing but the opposite.

In the fall McAllister left the ranch and retreated into the mountains to set his traps and build new tilts along the creeks. He had moved away from the Okanagan River, into the eastern slopes across the valley. He liked it higher up. The mountain streams ran more abundant with beaver than did the river. His absence from the settlement was to be expected. Rattler had done most of the trapping for him while McAllister completed the construction projects at White Lake. There was still considerable wealth in furs and McAllister was quick to realize that in the pelts lay the financial support of Skaha Crossing.

At times Two Way grew anxious over the trapper's long absences and contemplated the consequences should McAllister some day fail to return. Of course Carmichael would hasten to take charge, Two Way knew, and with that takeover, he realized he would soon be back in his village. All he had worked for with the trapper would be lost.

To Catherine Matthews, he lamented, "One day he will not return and we won't find him till the snow is gone." His concern was real and she recognized the depth of the Indian's bond with the trapper.

When he sat before the fire of his meagre winter camps, alone, growing older, McAllister often wondered about his son. The presence of the Carmichael's baby at the Crossing increased his awareness of Duncan.

As well, his thoughts strayed constantly, almost longingly, to Catherine. Although she kept his house clean, cooked the food for his table each day and took care of his laundry when he was at home, the young woman remained housed in the Lodge under the careful scrutiny of Alida Carmichael. At times he had caught glimpses of her watching him. Then, her eyes were soft and inviting. Whenever he heard her laugh, the merriment of the sound tugged at his heart. Occasionally he wished that she would remain at his table when she brought his meal, but she never had. He realized his fault; she had waited for him to ask and he had not spoken.

Silently, in the far reaches of the mountains in the middle of winter, McAllister cursed his lack of initiative. Although his life was extremely busy and full of employment, it was also empty since Nahna's departure. So was his house. The wind howled around his tilt and the snow banked heavily against the poles and hides in the storm as he resolved that when he got home, he would snatch the young woman out from under Alida Carmichael's eyes, away from her lengthy Bible readings, and make a proposal of some sort to her. Would she live in his house with him? Would she want to marry him? It was a fact, he decided, as snow blew furiously around his tilt, reminding him of his lonely existence, that the situation must change. He was once again admitting to the need of a woman in his life and the permanency of one in his home.

Two Way was the first to see the change in McAllister upon his return. He brewed fresh coffee for them while McAllister splashed warm water over himself in a large round metal tub. Two Way waited for an explanation, for once more the long beard had been cut and shaved away, leaving only a neatly trimmed full mustache. McAllister's graying hair was cut to collar length by Carmichael. Two

Way had watched this process before when the trapper had gone to Fort Kamloops to bring Willow to the Okanagan, and again after Nahna had moved into his house. When he cuts away all the hair, Two Way smiled knowingly, it means a woman will soon move in with him.

A stiff March wind howled around the corners of the house and tugged at the hides and heavy board flaps fastened over the windows. The only light in the room was given from the fireplace and a thick wick in oil.

McAllister rose out of the tub, water splashing off his tall, muscular frame.

Tossing the trapper a large drying sheet, Two Way broke some news of his own. "I am to be married soon, Many Rains," he said calmly. He set the empty pail aside and tossed more wood into the flames of the open fireplace.

McAllister wrapped the sheet around him. "Married? What is this!" He hunted for clean clothes.

"I went with my father once to visit my sister at the long lake and met her there." Two Way turned, facing the trapper, his expression serious.

"You've kept it a secret until now? To who?"

"Her name is Waneta. She is from a Lake family near Tselo'tsus. They have been visiting there for many months. Her family paid my family the highest of honours by approaching me about a marriage with her." He laughed lightly, "They knew I had an eye for her."

He felt a great deal of pride in attracting such a lovely girl as Waneta. Several trips had been made between Tselo'tsus and Shoshen-eetkwa by members of Waneta's family and his. Some small gifts had been exchanged. As well, Two Way had presented her family with four horses, a legacy of Rattler. But as yet, the betrothal was not regarded as settled. He had kept his secret well and was pleased at having surprised the trapper.

"Ah yes, the Lakes," McAllister murmured, remembering, while vigorously drying himself. He reached for his breeches. "With my strange luck, it was probably her brother I shot!"

"Many Rains, that was two years ago! I would like you to welcome Waneta to your place. We would like to live here, in Nahna's cabin where I am now. I have fixed it up, you know."

The mention of Nahna's name sent a twinge of guilt through McAllister, but he quickly shrugged it off. It had, indeed, been nearly two years since the Indian woman had left his house, yet there were still moments when he thought of her and missed her presence.

"Yes, yes, the cabin's yours. I gave it to you long ago. You've certainly earned it. Do what you want with it. Is there a special ceremony for marriage among your people?"

"No," Two Way replied. "Just family consent and presentation of gifts. It will be settled soon."

"Bring your young woman– wife, here. She's very welcome." McAllister was frowning as he talked and pulled a cloth shirt over his head. Other matters now raced around in his brain.

Two Way sensed this. "What's wrong, Many Rains?"

"I've heard some news that may doom this settlement to nothing more than a big farm. News I should have heard last year, but for the fact that we are more or less isolated here."

"What is it?"

"There's going to be the establishment of a border, dividing this territory into two countries."

Two Way stared at the trapper, not comprehending the consequences of such a division. "Where?"

"At Soi'yus."

Two Way was stunned.

"Do you know what that means?" McAllister asked. His brow furrowed deeper with a frown. Distress showed itself in the pools of his blue eyes. "It means, first, that the fur brigade may change its route in order to get its goods to Fort Vancouver. Or maybe build another fort on our side. Secondly, eventually we'll be restricted in bringing cattle and horses and everything else up here. There'll be a borderline to cross!"

McAllister was clearly upset and Two Way suddenly felt at a loss for words. Restrictions of any sort had never been a part of McAllister's life, much less Two Way's. The whole idea of not being free to move about the country at will was appalling to both men.

Dressed now, McAllister lifted one end of the tub and Two Way the other, and in one great swoop, the bath water was heaved away from the step of the house. As McAllister hung the tub over a peg on the outside wall and ducked back in out of the wind, he heard Two Way saying, "Everything is changing and will change even more. I am afraid."

"Perhaps I should be wary, too, but I'm not."

Two Way looked across into the trapper's eyes and said, sadly, "The changes will not stop now," as if predicting a gloomy future, "and they will not be the same for you as for my people."

Seeing into the deep pools of the Indian's dark eyes, McAllister felt the truth of the words. "Goodnight, my friend," said the trapper.

Two Way pulled a warm poncho, given him by McAllister long ago, over his broad shoulders. Feeling despondent, he replied, "Goodnight, my brother," and stepped out toward his cabin, walking bent against the wind.

Catherine Matthews, with the long gathered skirt of her gingham dress billowing about her ankles, stepped briskly away from the walkway of the Lodge the morning after McAllister's return. She had let her long hair lay curled over her shoulders, a soft change from binding it into a knot. She had pinched her cheeks to bring colour to her face and her smile was bright and happy. She looked very feminine and pretty.

The air was still, with a bright rising sun. It was as if the wind of the night before had not blown at all. Large patches of icy snow remained upon the ground. What snow was left would soon disappear with the customary warmth of April.

Springtime was Catherine's favourite time of year. Soon the countryside would blossom with new life, would quickly be covered in a yellow profusion of sunflowers, buttercups and daisies. Above her a large formation of Canada geese passed overhead. In the distant meadows the melodic sounds of robins, meadow larks and wrens reached her ears as they flitted amongst the bushes in search of twigs and fluffy down with which to build their nests. She wanted to sing aloud, romance is in the air!

Romance! The word caused her step to slow, as thoughts of the tall trapper entered her mind. A mixture of longing and resentment fused within her, leaving her emotions muddled. Would he never see her there? Really see her, she wondered. "It has been nearly two years," she whispered aloud. Mind you, she considered, he has been away a good part of that time. Catherine stepped up to the door of his house, saw it open and peered cautiously into the darkened interior.

"Come in," McAllister's deep voice from a corner reached her.

"Oh!" Catherine gasped in surprise. "I thought you might have left. Gone with Two Way somewhere."

"Not yet. Come in." McAllister moved out of the shadows of the corner into the light cast by an open window. The hides had been rolled up and the wooden flaps lifted, allowing the bright rays of the morning sun to drench the middle of the room.

"Here, I've brought you some fresh biscuits." As he reached out to take them from her, Catherine said boldly, looking up into his face, "I hoped you would be here. Bringing these gave me reason to see you."

"And me to talk to you," he added. His smile was warm. His blue eyes mirrored his feelings of affection for her. Looking up at him, Catherine saw that his beard was gone. She noticed his hair was shorter and his forehead appeared very tanned from months of winter's reflection against the snow. Really, she thought, he is such a tall, handsome man! I've never seen him so trimmed!

"Catherine," McAllister began softly but without hesitation, and Catherine's heart sang at the sound of her name from his lips. As if from a lovely dream, his words reached her. "...been here a long time now... I'm not sure, but I think you feel..." Oh yes! she wanted to cry out. "...I've thought about us for many months and I think we might..." she heard his voice, gentle, as it had been in the cave so long ago. Without a second's thought, without any hesitation, Catherine stepped impulsively toward McAllister, raising her arms to his broad shoulders. In one quick sweep he caught her to his chest, holding her there, burying his face in the soft waves of her hair, and whispered, "Thank God, thank God!" against the smooth, silky skin of her neck.

That evening as Ian and Alida Carmichael strolled away from the Lodge, across the meadow and through the fields with their little daughter, Heather, perched on her father's shoulders, Catherine Matthews quickly gathered her personal items together with her clothes and pushed them into a large bag. Then, as if carting the trapper's laundry, she strode purposefully across the snow-dappled yard to his log house. Catherine's light, hazel eyes twinkled with merriment over what she had done to fool Alida. As darkness fell, McAllister dropped the hides over the windows. An impish grin played about the corners of her full mouth as Catherine clasped McAllister's big hand in the warmth of her own and led him toward the smaller room and his bed. She rejoiced in her determination to reach for, and grasp, a new happiness.

30

When the Oregon Boundary Treaty was signed by the British and the Americans on June 15, 1846, the Hudson's Bay Company obtained a promise that its property south of the Boundary would be retained and that easy movement on the Columbia River would be allowed to continue. However, as if foreseeing the future, the Company made preparations to establish a new route to the Fraser Valley where, in 1827, its chief post, Fort Langley, had been erected. Of three different routes explored from Fort Kamloops to Fort Langley, none could compare with the ease of travel that the terrain of the Okanagan Valley provided. Until the new route over the Cascade Mountains to the Tulameen Valley, through the Nicola Valley to Fort Kamloops went into use, the old familiar brigade trail of the Okanagan would be used. For a while, it appeared, Skaha Crossing was saved.

In celebration of that reprieve and to honour the arrival of Two Way's wife at the Crossing, a special supper was arranged by Catherine to be held in the Lodge. A large beef roast, turned regularly until it was browned and deliciously tender, cooked slowly in its iron container set on a grate inside McAllister's fireplace. Potatoes and turnips roasted in the juice from the browned beef. Two Way and Catherine gathered wild onions and lettuce. With fresh watercress from the creek, the small leaves and delicate stems of the Indian lettuce plant, combined with chopped onion and sprinkled with tiny cubes of chicken breast made a delicious salad.

As they worked together cutting pastry for pies and preparing the saskatoon fillings, Catherine waited for Alida Carmichael to mention her absence from the Lodge. Instead, Alida muttered through clenched teeth, "Such a fuss over an Indian whose brats may someday burn us out of here."

Catherine was mildly shocked. "Hush! No such a thing as burning us out will happen here."

"Much as I hate to remind you, it's happened to you once. You'd think your opinion of them–"

"Alida, don't pick on Two Way and Waneta." It was almost an order. "What you really want to talk about is me, isn't it?"

Alida Carmichael's thin mouth pulled tight as she pursed her lips. "What you're doing is sinful, and I find I cannot abide it."

"Then ignore it!" Catherine snapped impulsively. "It's not happening to you, so it really isn't your concern, Alida." She felt as though she had drawn a battle line between them. She knew that if she was ever to live beside the Carmichaels with any shred of peace, her feelings and full intentions must be made clear. So she braced herself against further tirade, and said, "I will live with Rayne as though I were his wife until someone comes along who can marry us. If it takes forever, that is the way it will be, and only you and Ian and Two Way will know."

Alida spun around to face the younger woman. "And what if you get in the family way? The child will be without–"

"Its father's name?" Catherine finished for her. "Well, Alida, getting in the family way has so far eluded me."

Stunned and feeling suddenly bereft of adequate words, Alida Carmichael dropped the subject. The Lord does have His ways, she reminded herself, of making the sinner pay! This woman will never know the joy of holding one's own flesh and blood. Coveting that pious thought, Alida decided, smugly, some atonement at least would be made!

The supper was a splendid affair. Catherine was pleased to see such obvious happiness between Two Way and his wife. Ian Carmichael dug into a pack which held the few non-essentials of his life and brought out a small harmonica. With a foot perched against a chair, elbow upon his knee, he placed the instrument to his mouth and blew the sounds of a fast tune which no one recognized, but to which they could dance.

Immediately the women, setting aside their moral differences, crossed their arms and joined hands to swing about the room in circles. Their full skirts flipped around their slender ankles and their high buttoned shoes tapped rhythmically against the rough board floor.

As he watched, Holinger leaned back against the wall, lit his pipe and grinned broadly.

Delighted, Waneta clapped her hands with glee in her excitement. She had never seen such happy dancing. Most of the dances she had grown up with were spiritual and war dances. Never had she seen an instrument as that which Carmichael blew into among the goods obtained in trade, nor heard such melodic sounds. Turning her round face, creased with a bright smile, toward Two Way, she spoke to him with expressive dark eyes, telling him of her joy at being there. Her shining black hair hung nearly to her waist in even plaits. A narrow band of soft, thin leather onto which coloured beads had been stitched, circled her forehead and complemented her

224

elaborately fringed and ornamented white dress. The dress was made of many rows of evenly cut fringes. Her moccasins were decorated with porcupine quills and tiny silver circles.

Waneta was of a small build, delicately boned. Watching her, McAllister was painfully reminded of Nahna.

It had been a long time since McAllister had heard music. Memories flooded his mind– the large ballroom at old Spokane House; Denise White's dinner parties, which included the boisterous little Frenchman Evan Dubrais; Willow dancing with him in the house of Ellis Walker. He covered his eyes a moment, willing the visions to disappear, but they did not. McAllister looked up, meeting Catherine's eyes as she danced by him. They sparkled with a new happiness. In that brief, intense glance, McAllister saw how much she had come to love him.

Exhausted, the women fell onto the bench along the wall. Their laughter peeled forth. Little beads of perspiration from their exertions glistened against their foreheads, for the June evening was very warm.

"Oh my, oh my–" Catherine gasped, "that was just wonderful! It has been so long since I danced, I'd almost forgotten how."

When the remaining food had been covered and stored away, and the party over, Two Way and Waneta left the building to cross the yard to their cabin. Holinger retreated to his room in the Lodge. McAllister bid the Carmichaels goodnight. Unashamed, Catherine took hold of his hand and left with him. Alida turned her back, pretending not to witness sin so openly flaunted.

If Skaha Crossing was to survive, his credit with the Company must be built up. Tools and household articles had drained his credit and there were still many more things needed. McAllister waited anxiously for the brigade to return from the Columbia on its trip north.

It arrived on the twentieth of August, remained for a three day rest, during which trade goods promised to the local bands who had bartered in June were distributed. Supplies for the long winter ahead were unloaded at the Lodge. Of special significance were the two crates into which pane glass windows had been carefully packed and securely lashed onto the steadiest horse in the brigade. As well, glass lamps with wicks that could be turned up, were encased in wooden crates. Articles such as butter churns, paddles and moulds, cutlery and baking utensils made in England, were opened amid cries of excitement from the women. There were even supplies for Holinger's blacksmith shop.

Several of the horses were exchanged. Plagued by deer flies and bots, the animals bucked and kicked against the process of saddling and readying for travel three days later. Impatient wranglers cussed and pulled the thick straps tight despite the antics of the horses. Quantities of beef, potatoes and butter were strapped aboard the wide saddles, and the brigade once more moved out onto the worn trail across the flats, along the draw and into the trees. When the long train of men and horses was gone and the excitement had dwindled to a mere hum, Two Way noticed that a man and woman remained.

"This raises our population to nine," McAllister said quietly to Two Way. "Well, let's find out who they are, although I'm sure the women know everything about them already. Three hours is ample time, never mind three days!"

Lenny Parr was the man's name. With him was his wife, Clarissa. "I'm a storekeeper, 'cept you ain't got a store to keep." His smile was compelling, but friendly. "We'd like to throw in with you. Heard about you down at Spokane. Seems the Indians are easier to live with here than down there. Getting restless and up in arms over so many settlers moving in. T'aint no place for a woman with all the threats and fuss."

A short, stocky man willing to work, Lenny Parr soon fit into life at Skaha Crossing. Powerfully muscled, he wasted no time in cutting and hauling trees from the hills to build a small store next to the Lodge, with living quarters attached. It seemed not to occur to him that the cutting and building he now carried out in the Okanagan, was the very thing that was inciting riot with the Indians of the Columbia region.

Often, from beneath a furrowed, questioning brow, he contemplated Two Way, as the Indian worked with him, and wondered at his presence in the settlement. Perhaps, he reckoned, this Indian recognizes that things are going to change in the west whether he likes it or not, and has decided to go along with it. Like others before him, he believed that benefits could be reaped by the natives, although he could not say exactly what those benefits would be.

Skaha Crossing suddenly seemed charged with new activity, despite the imminent loss of the fur brigade trade. Although the store was not completed before winter, it hardly mattered for there was no stock to put in it and no credit established by anyone to purchase from it. The living quarters were soon ready and the Parrs moved in as the first heavy snow of the season fell. Beneath its blanket the settlement lay still and quiet. Faint lights from the tall glass lamps flickered behind the new pane windows.

By the winter of 1848, the flats at White Lake contained the house and tack shed of McAllister, Two Way's cabin, Parr's store and home, the Lodge where the Carmichael's and Holinger continued to reside, and the large barn in which Holinger's equipment had been set up.

To the Indians of the Okanagan it was an awesome and fearsome sight. They saw it as a definite threat to their existence. The bands could hardly ignore the fact that some of their own had lived among the whites, and one was still there, helping to further the unwanted encroachment.

As the winter months wore on, McAllister roamed the mountains and its streams in pursuit of furs. Two Way and Holinger hauled sleigh loads of wild grass scythed from the fields during the summertime, across the snow-drifted pasture for the cattle and horses. Carmichael and Lenny Parr skidded more logs down the mountainsides and across the flats to complete Carmichael's house. Viewing it, Two Way thought it might never get finished and the family would remain in the Lodge forever.

When spring arrived, and the land was once again bathed in warm sunlight and the hillsides blanketed by a yellow carpet of wild flowers, McAllister methodically baled his furs for transport. Two Way watched with obvious paternal instinct, over a fine crop of new calves.

From the blacksmith shop rang the steady clang of hammer against iron as Holinger set shoes for the horses. As well, he built a new blade and handles for the plow, a seeder and rake. A new set of harness hung on the wall of the shop beside several pairs of riding chaps.

At his store in the front part of his house, Parr carefully drafted his order of supplies, impatient for the empty shelves to be filled.

"The push northward by settlers from Oregon is bound to happen soon," he told the others, "and I will be prepared."

Carmichael peeled, notched and trimmed the logs for his house and agreed with Parr. Alida watched, impatient to be in her own home.

Despite the air of anticipation and spring activity which prevailed at Skaha Crossing, a feeling of doom plagued McAllister's mind. From the Chief Factor travelling with the fur brigade to the Crossing in June, he heard of the possible closing of Fort Okanogan. The Hudson's Bay Company would, it was contended, build new posts in the Okanagan, as well as in the Similkameen Valley to the west.

"In all likelihood," the Factor told McAllister, "the first one will be at the rendezvous spot, that meeting place we now call Sooyoos." he smiled, remembering. "Those were the best years, you know."

Despite the Factor's enthusiastic reminiscences, McAllister could not help but feel dismay. The grand era of the enormous colourful fur brigades was drawing to a close, at least in his part of the country. Like a nagging hurt, it had bothered his mind throughout the past year. The route through the Okanagan Valley would be abandoned. There were rumours of a new trail from Fort Kamloops to the new post of Fort Hope through a valley called Tulameen, with which he was totally unfamiliar.

The Chief Factor entered the Lodge and he and McAllister sat down to the supper table opposite each other. "Where will it go?" McAllister asked bluntly, not in a good mood.

"From Fort Kamloops through the Tulameen country," the Factor told him, nodding his satisfaction, while hungrily forking the food to his mouth. "To Fort Hope and to Fort Langley. This is the last year for the Okanagan. Our supplies will come from our own ports and depots. Oh, there'll no doubt be the traffic of furs by individual traders through here, but times really are changing!"

For a brief moment McAllister thought he detected the excitement of change and new adventure in the Factor's voice, but decided that it was only his own gloom looking for it.

The Hudson's Bay official continued between mouthfuls, "Even though we no longer take our furs to the Columbia– the border ended that– I wonder if it'll halt the flow of settlers moving into our country."

"Lenny Parr thinks not," McAllister said. "In fact, he's looking forward to a steady influx in the area and is preparing for a booming business."

"It'll happen," decided the Factor, pushing his empty plate away. "And you?"

McAllister swatted angrily at the flies and mosquitos which had found their way indoors. "Originally, we set up this lodge to accommodate the brigade twice a year, nothing more. Now there are four families and a blacksmith living here, so maybe Lenny's right."

"Not only here. Up the lake near Tselo'tsus, there's a place along the shoreline called L'Anse au Sable," the Factor told McAllister, "and a Scottish-Indian from the north is living there with his wife and sons. He traps and fishes. And Chief Nkwala, or Nicholas as we call him, is gardening, for Lord's sake! At the head of the lake, they're all cultivating corn and potatoes among other vegetables."

McAllister sat back in his chair to consider all the news. "Well, so do we cultivate corn and potatoes."

The Chief Factor stood up, pulling his shirt from his skin, which was drenched with sweat caused by the intense muggy summer heat. "So you see– some of the Indians are adapting, slowly."

"That is how the Okanagan has changed, I guess," McAllister stated. "The word from the south of us is not so cheering. There is much antagonism and unrest among those pressured by the missionaries moving in. White settlers are not entirely welcomed."

The Factor mused, "True, true," and stepped through the doorway into a hoard of thirsty mosquitoes. Furiously swatting his face and neck, he snapped impatiently, "Good Lord! Are these things always this thick?"

Indeed, not only did McAllister spend long hours of the summer nights in contemplation of the future, but Two Way lost as many hours of sleep as well. To him, the dilemma appeared even more scary than it did to the others. Lately the thought constantly plagued Two Way. Had he chosen wisely? Should he have listened to the warnings of his elders, voiced at the appearance of the first white man? Should he have taken the advice of his father and returned to Shoshen-eetkwa long ago? He had been young and enthused by a new and different activity. No one, Two Way considered now, had envisioned more than a dozen white families in the valley. Now, by what he heard, a mass migration of them, undeterred by a border, threatened the livelihood and old ways of his family.

In the morning the men and horses of the brigade pulled away from the Crossing in a much quieter fashion than had been their habit of earlier years. No bugle had been heard signalling their arrival; none sounded their departure. The Chief Factor donned a wide-brimmed hat, leapt agilely into his saddle as if trained in the same arena as the wranglers with whom he rode, and waved an arm in farewell.

The men of Skaha Crossing watched the long line of horses file southward on the dusty trail. With their parting, a sadness crept over McAllister and refused to leave him. The melancholy mood possessed him until Two Way told him, "I remember the brilliance of the past, too." Only then was he rid of it.

31

In the first week of June 1849, a small cavalcade of wagons, trailed by cows, horses, sheep and several dogs left Fort Walla Walla, a settlement south of Spokane House, destined for the Okanagan. Their trip northward was arduous and delayed by breakdowns of some of the more well-used wagons which had weathered the harsh trials of the westward trek across the plains and mountains from Missouri. These repairs to wheels, reaches and tongues, constituted a time loss of several days.

The cavalcade held over at Spokane House to restock their wagons. Watching their activity from the steps of a house across the compound was a boy whose curiosity could not be contained for long. During the three years he had lived at the post, Duncan McAllister had never known a wagon train to pass through going northward. Usually there were several families travelling westward together for safety, or mountain men dealing in furs, and always the men who worked for the Hudson's Bay Company. Those who moved on went only as far as a sizable piece of farmland might be found or to sites already established by the missionaries. The mountain men were as nomadic as the Indians, so few remained to make Spokane House their home.

Unable to contain his curiosity, young Duncan dashed off the steps of Mary Walker's house, crossed the compound and came to what, he hoped, was a casual halt in front of the store. He did not wish to appear anxious simply because rumour had it that these people were moving northward into a new country. By quick reckoning, Duncan knew the first place past Fort Okanogan they would stop at would be near the Indian village, Soi'yus. Just before the village they would have to cross the Okanagan River, for the sharper slopes of the hill along the east shore and the sandy reaches spreading away from the lake could not be easily negotiated by the immigrant wagons now loading in front of him.

Stuffing his hands deep into his pockets and smiling broadly from beneath his wide-brimmed, flat top hat, Duncan announced casually, "I know that place well."

When several of the muscular, bearded men glanced at him in

doubt, he informed them further, "It's the fur traders' rendezvous spot. There's a big lake there, and there's an Indian village on one side of the lake and the fur camp on the other. I went there with my father."

"What is the name of it?"

"Who is your father?"

"How old are you, lad?"

The rush of questions were left unanswered as Duncan leaned back against the log wall of the building, realizing that no one believed him. He watched the settlers go about their business. He glanced occasionally at a young Negro boy about his own age, who took curious glances at Duncan as well. When another hour had passed during which the remainder of supplies were loaded and the youngsters of the group were called together, one man stepped away from the others and drew Duncan aside. His curiosity had been piqued.

Getting himself together by tucking in the tails of his shirt, which had pulled loose with the activity of loading, and tugging his starched collar up for buttoning, the tall, dark haired man in his late thirties questioned Duncan with "If what you say is true, please inform me further of this country. My name is Hackett and I am a missionary travelling north to Canada."

Duncan looked up. The smile he saw belied the harshness of the command and he relaxed, feeling a trust toward the man. Into his heart crept a homesickness he had been unaware of for a long time.

Linas Hackett saw this. "You may call me Preacher, if you want, for that is what I am," he said gently. "I believe your story." He stood tall and straight before Duncan, looking down upon a mop of auburn hair and wondering eyes. "Now, tell me about this place, and when we get there I shall say to your father that I saw his fine young son and he is worthy of my friendship. We know not our true destination, and nothing much of the Indians to the north of us." He waited.

When no comment was offered, Hackett, who appeared to Duncan to be the leader of the group, suggested, "If you have some news to enlighten us, I think we should hear it. We leave in the morning, and if it is to your home, then by the Lord's will, I wish I could take you with me. You look like a fine, well brought-up young lad who is very homesick right now."

Something happened inside Duncan then. Tears that had not threatened to surface since the day of his arrival at Spokane House, now rose like flooding pools behind his eyes. Emotion choked his throat. Was it the Preacher's understanding words or the simple longing to see his father and Nahna again that now caused havoc to play inside him.

From across the compound Duncan heard Mary Walker's melodic

voice calling him. He turned his back for the first time against her and began telling the tall man in the white shirt, black trousers and high black boots about the Indian woman who had raised him; that she called him Greylegs and he spoke some of the Salish language. Also that he had stayed in their village and they were good people. Duncan told him all about the Okanagan Valley, the Crossing and his father.

"Well," Hackett sighed after listening to Duncan and glanced up at the clear July sky. "It sounds like your Indians are more peaceful than those down here. The Cayuse are becoming resentful about intruders. That is how they see us, invaders! They're unpredictable and becoming more warlike with each passing week, it seems." He looked across at young Duncan where they sat on a bench beside the store. "I'm glad I had this little talk with you, Duncan. You're a very grown-up young fellow. In time I shall meet your father, no doubt. I'll be proud to tell him I saw you."

It was the end of July when the wagon train reached the lake at Soi'yus. The travellers struggled with their wagons, whipping their teams into the river at the crossing below the lake. Young boys and girls yelled and chased the cows and sheep into the water behind the wagons. The camp dogs barked and nipped at the animals' legs to keep them swimming. At this point the width of the Okanagan River posed no real danger. The banks were low enough for an easy haul up from the water. Flooding had passed. There were few holes in the riverbed and no large boulders that the wagons might smash against in the currents. Men on horseback carried the children across. The women rode with their wagons, clinging tightly to the wooden sides as the cumbersome wagons lurched across the river. There was a great deal of noise, orders called by the men, the bawl of cattle and sheep, whinny of horses and barking of dogs bounding about the shorelines.

The racket quickly drew the attention of the Indians, who carried out annual berry picking amongst the bushes along the river. While not totally unmindful of the raucous, the women continued their search for food. Presently, several young men on horseback appeared, galloping across the flats, and halting in a cloud of dust. They watched the activity with avid curiosity until the cavalcade formed up once more and pulled away from the riverbank.

Later that day a rider from Shoshen-eetkwa galloped into the centre of Skaha Crossing. Leaping to the ground, he allowed the animal to graze at will. He strode directly to Two Way's cabin. When he emerged from the house with Two Way, the yard had filled with Catherine, Holinger, the Carmichaels and Parrs.

"It's not every day that one of you folks from down there gallops in here and runs to Two Way's house," Carmichael stated to the Shoshen-eetkwa man.

"Well, it seems," said Two Way, "that there are some wagons and cattle moving up past Soi'yus."

Catherine's eyes widened in surprise. Alida Carmichael clasped her hands together over her chest as though giving thanks for a prayer answered. Lenny Parr shoved his hands deep into his pockets, rocked back on his heals and grinned. At last his store would be needed!

"Glory be!" sang Alida. "I wonder that such news should get here with the speed that it did."

"Smoke signals," smiled Two Way. "It seems you didn't notice them." Alida stared at Two Way, her smile fading.

Carmichael said impatiently, "He's just making some fun, Liddy. You know the Indian brought the news! No doubt they've been following those wagons ever since they left Fort Okanogan. They set up relays you know, for spreading the word, the Indians do."

Glancing across at the rider from Shoshen-eetkwa, Two Way winked an eye in amusement, then looked back to the group standing before him. "No one has been bothered. They're moving in peace," he stated quietly and waved good-bye to his cousin, as the young Indian leapt quickly upon his horse and galloped away.

McAllister met the group a day later at their overnight camp at a base on the fur brigade trail where it left the bottomland and climbed a bench. Here the Okanagan River meandered across the wide flatland which was banked by high benches on both sides, where bunchgrass grew in abundance. Various tall reeds, cattails and rushes crowded the marshlands of the river oxbows, home to mallards, geese and other waterfowl. Sizeable trout flipped up from the river's surface, twirled and splashed, leaving circlets upon the calmer pools below the bends.

"Such a sight almost beckons a man to stop here and make what he can of it," commented one of the wagoners. A short, stocky man, Horace Whiteman, was the oldest of the group and admitted to travel weariness and a desire to be settled.

"Yes," Hackett agreed, "but the boy told us of his father's place and that is where we'll go. There is safety in numbers." He was their leader and no one questioned his wisdom.

The draws to the top of the plateau were steep. The trail was well used and had been hardened by the combination of weather and brigade traffic. Looking toward the bench to which they must make their haul, the men of the wagon train discussed the procedure.

However, a torrential downpour fell upon the valley that night, washing out sections along the trail, sending small slides of sand and brush to the base of the plateau. The world around the camp was white with rain as it fell in great sheets, soaking the valley. Thunder rolled among the black clouds. Lightning flashed in brilliant forks.

When McAllister reached the encampment in the evening, he tied his horse to one of the wagons, loosened the saddle and placed his slicker across it for protection from the rain. He was greeted and got in out of the rain, to the largest of the four wagons where the men had gathered together.

"A typical August storm," he told them, crowding in. "Some years it lasts throughout the month, others-- well, one rain might be all we see for a whole season. It's hellish dry country when it wants to be. Name's McAllister. Welcome to the Okanagan Valley."

Near the front, Hackett looked across the interior. The boy's father, he thought. Leaning awkwardly against a cupboard, he contemplated the trapper. The young Negro boy who sat beside him, whispered, "That's him." On a wooden crate in the middle of the group, a single candle flickered, its light lending outline to the strength of McAllister's regular features and large build.

Linas Hackett said, "This here is Billy Willemeyer, and Francis Bean beside you. Next is Horace Whiteman, and I'm Linas Hackett. This young man beside me is--"

"Mercy Bright!" the young Negro sang out.

"I do believe," Hackett continued, "that behind this wagon train ride two men of undesirable character and that is what this meeting is about. That, and the abominable weather that has descended upon us."

Close to morning, the rain ceased. The air was damp and cool, but still and quiet. A hint of sunshine pierced the gray light of dawn. While the women cleaned up the mess of breakfast and put out their morning fire, the men harnessed the teams.

McAllister, who had remained overnight in the Hackett wagon, explained, "If you retrace your route southwest about four miles, you'll find another trail to the bench. It's a more gradual incline and brings you to the same point. Just takes a little longer. You'll have to double up on the teams to get these wagons over the top, one by one."

When they resumed their journey, Linas Hackett called McAllister aside. "I've news of your boy," he said. "I've talked with him."

McAllister's questioning blue eyes swung around to meet Hackett's. "You did not mention that last night."

"We talked of other matters last night." Hackett's open gaze held the trapper's. "He wants to come home now." That was all. No more need be said about it, decided Hackett, the man knows what he's up to in his life and why the boy remains where he is.

Following McAllister's advice, the cavalcade moved away from the draw, to take a route that would, in less than ten years, be pounded to a hard-packed roadway by other settlers following the hoards of anxious miners that would pour into the valley.

Willemeyer, Whiteman, Hackett and Bean wasted no time in laying claim to certain patches of land that would best further their intended efforts in agriculture. Such planning was done before hardly the first meal was taken, so excited were the settlers to begin their new life. Only Horace Whiteman expressed an interest in trapping for furs.

Mercy Bright, fifteen years old, standing barely five feet tall and always happy and smiling, quickly made it known that he travelled under the protection of Linas Hackett. "The Lord's man," he stated. "He understan's us colo'ed folk; knows what's good in us, n' acceptin' what's not so good. Jus' like any other people, we are."

Linas Hackett elaborated. "He's from South Carolina– a runaway, you can figure that. His mother and father were captured, but somehow Mercy here managed to get away. He was brought to me starving and bleeding from wounds." At times Linas Hackett's drawl seemed much like young Bright's, and although McAllister and the others did not question Hackett's origins, they suspected that he had been a sympathizer to the Negro plight. Perhaps, they reasoned, the Hacketts were being sought as well.

"Killed the dog that trap' me, Ah did!" Bright interjected, and proudly exhibited the thick scars along his arms as proof of the fight.

"It is my strong suspicion," Hackett continued, "that the two men following our wagons are after this young man, and therefore, hunting my hide also." Lifting an eyebrow in McAllister's direction, he added firmly, "I would say it is because of the boy's colour. Nothing else. 'Course, there is a bounty–"

The people of the west, especially those of the New Caledonia west, were hardly aware of America's national problems. They were more concerned over the new boundary at the 49th parallel and its effect on the fur trade, or their personal relations with local Indian bands, but most importantly their ability to get by in the wilderness. The Hudson's Bay Company, who controlled the territory west of the Rocky Mountains, though under British rule, was tight and effective.

Major issues such as the Mexican War or the controversial slave trade in America did nothing more than raise a quizzical eyebrow of most people in the continent's northwest. News of such import only reached the western outposts by way of the immigrant movement and scraps of mail which managed to reach the forts from family members left behind in eastern Canada and the united states.

Therefore, the presence of the young black boy at Skaha Crossing was accepted with little curiosity and no malice toward the colour of his skin. But the arrival at the Crossing of the McLaren cousins aroused immediate suspicion and the strong protective nature in all who abided there.

The two riders galloped into the yard of the barn and Holinger's blacksmith shop eleven days after the settlers had arrived. Staring down from their saddles to McAllister and Hackett, they told of a creek twenty miles south of the Crossing.

"It looked prosperous, but proved not worth our time!" grumbled the taller, heavier man of the two. He had announced his name as Boss McLaren. By McAllister's guess, he was about twenty-four years old. "No beaver hutches or sign o' muskrat in there, an' worst of all it was like a bear's den. More no-good brown bears movin' back and forth, crossin' all over the place, than I need!"

"And rattlesnakes!" added the other, a shorter, thinner and younger man. "Dens of 'em!" Despite the expression of fear on his face as he spoke, there was a hint of excitement and glee in his voice at the danger the reptiles represented. "Used them for target practice, I did. A man gits to be pretty accurate starin' one them stingers down."

Holinger, McAllister and Hackett listened to the McLarens tell of the places they had been and the adventures they had encountered. Braggarts, McAllister told himself; they're not old enough to have done everything they say, although they're right about the rattlesnakes. As they talked, the eyes of both the cousins scanned the yard and corners about the buildings and wagons for sign of Mercy Bright.

We don't need them here, decided Hackett, for it would seem they know of nothing other than stirring up trouble. They are the ones. It's the boy they want! On all accounts, the men of Skaha Crossing who watched them, were accurate in their assessment of the cousins.

"We'll be movin' on," the younger McLaren told McAllister while staring directly, coldly into the defensive expression of Linas Hackett's eyes. "Goin' further up north– more activity there." His voice lifted. "More excitin' times!" His eyes then shifted to fourteen year old Rachel Hackett, who stood half hidden behind her father. With a charming smile, the younger McLaren lifted his hat in a gesture of polite departure. "Name's Happy," he informed her. "You won't forget me now, will you? When yer all growed up and such." Tightly reining his horse around, he called loudly, "See ya all!"

The following morning the McLarens broke their camp near Willow Creek, packed their horses and rode away from Skaha Crossing.

Mercy Bright made his presence more clearly known to Holinger when emerging from hiding in the Hackett wagon once the McLarens had gone. He appeared at the blacksmith's shop ready to work. "Ah kin keep the barn clean. Ah kin haul yo' water an' wood. There's nothin' Ah can't do!"

While Bright dashed in quick steps about the shop, his curiosity prompting a string of questions, Holinger swatted his hands against the thick apron around his sides as if irritated. "I can see the energy stored inside you is just achin' to be turned loose!" he said with a slight edge to his voice. He was getting on in years, he claimed, and the energy exhibited by the young often wore him down. "Now, quit bouncin' about here, 'n go do all those things you say you can."

Mercy Bright's face lit up. "Maybe Ah kin earn some credit at the store," he ventured, "since Ah don' have no money."

"Money's only good in the east. Not much need for it out here. Credit and work's the same thing. Now off with you!" Holinger was inclined to like the young man, but just how he was going to extend Bright credit at the store for his labours when he needed all he had for himself, was beyond him. "I'll find a way," he muttered aloud and meant it.

At the store a week later, Mercy announced to Parr. "Ah kin read 'n write some, Ah sho' kin. Learned it secretly, Ah did."

"I know what you want," Parr replied understandingly. "Some more credit." Looking across at young Bright, for Parr was not much taller than him, he asked, "What're you goin' to do with all that credit?"

Presenting a wide smile, Bright elaborated, "Ah'm goin' to build myself a house, tha's what! An' Ah needs it filled with stuff from this here store-- an' other thin's Ah knows yo' kin git."

"Uh huh," mused Parr. "Well, we'll see you through. There's plenty jobs to be done, mostly wood for the winter and scythin' the hay and such in the summer. And I daresay those folks you came up here with could use some help from you."

"Oh, Ah knows that! Ah'm not forgittin' 'em," and off he ran to begin in earnest, his occupation among the settlers of Skaha Crossing.

Bright could not continue living in the Hackett wagon, nor prolong occupation of a room in the Lodge. For the present, the Lodge was overflowing with residents. Without being told, it was clear to young Bright that he would need his own cabin. To that end, while he laboured at building the homes of others, he set aside for himself, the thinner logs they deemed as poor material. Everybody worked, including the youngsters of the group when they were finished with their morning studies with Mrs. Willemeyer.

As they worked, building one house at a time, the men from Oregon were acutely aware of groups of Indians riding by their construction sites. Sometimes they dismounted and rested back on their heels, watching the activity for hours on end. Sometimes in groups on horseback they would swoop down the hillside inclines, yelping and waving their arms in protest of the invasion, riding so close that the men labouring there would taste the dust from their galloping for several minutes afterward. At other intervals riders sat stiffly astride their ponies on the higher bluffs, as if sending messages of warning to the immigrants below.

The original McAllister homestead had now burgeoned into a small community, thriving on the raising of cattle and sheep, poultry, dairy products, vegetable crops and fur trapping. Some trade with the Hudson's Bay Company was still carried out through the Fort Okanogan centre, although 1849 would be the last of any fur transport through the Okanagan Valley.

The imaginary boundaries of Skaha Crossing were extended against the bluffs to the east and west, up ravines and draws into higher ground where cattle could be summer ranged, south along the brigade trail where the creek flowed, and northward. The settlers cultivated large productive gardens, fields of grain and meadows of wild hay.

To the Indians who watched the transformation upon their land from the ridges of the narrow valley, the fields and new buildings appeared as a horrible blot upon their landscape. They perceived a dramatic threat to their way of life. And, they observed, there appeared no halting the ambition and industry of the white men building on the flats. They could only hope that in the end something good would come of it.

32

David Rayne McAllister and Catherine Matthews were married in September, with only Two Way and Alida Carmichael to witness. Linas Hackett performed the ceremony with an astuteness that lent a sense of dignity to the ceremony. Catherine wore a new blue and white pleated dress that she had made. Rayne put on his newest fringed tunic and breeches made for him by Two Way's wife, Waneta.

The matter was done with hardly a ripple in the course of the day's events at the Crossing. No celebration supper was arranged as there had been for Two Way and Waneta. Although Linas Hackett conducted the regular Sunday Worship from the main room in the Lodge, Catherine and Rayne had chosen to be married quietly in their own house, with no fuss made of it. No one at the Crossing other than those present knew that the marriage had taken place. It was the way to do it, Alida had contended, as all but herself, Ian and Two Way believed them married already.

Outside the McAllister home that evening, a light September rain fell, dampening down the dry, powdery dust in the yard and the freshly scythed and cleaned hay fields. It lent the air a fresh, sweet odour. Rayne turned to his wife and whispered gently, "Mrs. McAllister, you are the dearest person in the world to me."

Catherine believed the truth of what was conveyed to her. "And, you are the dearest person in the world to me," she repeated to him. McAllister held her in his arms and she pressed close to him. "I do love you so," she whispered and remembered the gentleness of his voice in the cave and the protective strength in his presence beside their campfires when she had travelled with him to the Crossing. Although he did not express his feelings for her aloud, Catherine knew he felt a love for her he could not explain. Her own feelings were no less entangled at that moment, for each of them had suffered the heartbreaking loss of their first partner. Each had loved deeply the first time, and perhaps because of that depth, they had more to offer the second union.

Reluctant as he was to leave Catherine alone, McAllister, with Horace Whiteman's assistance, packed the traps, hide stretchers, packboards and other essentials for living at his line camp into the large pack boxes for transport by horse. Marriage to Catherine lent a new dimension to his life and caused him to reconsider his old way of trapping. Whereas when Willow was alive, McAllister's days and nights away from home were only as many as three or four spent along the Okanagan River, his present traplines were set in the creeks high in the eastern ridges of the valley, necessitating several weeks absence. It seemed important now, that his wife's wishes be considered. Still, it was already mid-November, he reminded himself, and he should have been well into the mountains.

Winter thus far had been mild. As McAllister looked out from the window of his house across the snowy pasture where Two Way was spreading the hay from the team-drawn sleigh, he assured Catherine that he would be back at the farm in three weeks, by the mid-December holydays. Horace Whiteman was going with him and did not wish to be away during the festive season.

"The first catch of furs are not the best anyway, but every pelt counts," McAllister told Catherine, and promised, "I will be home soon."

"Well before Christmas, I hope," she smiled with a hint of pleading in her voice, for she knew how time could slip by and delay him in the mountains.

Holding her close beside him, McAllister realized how strange the word Christmas, as Catherine referred to the holydays, sounded to him. Willow had celebrated the birth of Christ in prayer throughout the day, privately, in the two years they had shared together. There had been few times in his life when he had been aware that the festive time actually existed, for he was never at any fort, but always camped near a river somewhere.

Trusting her husband's word, Catherine prepared for a fine Christmas celebration at the Crossing. Together, the women made a dozen plum puddings, a symbol of Christmas to the people of the fur trade. Then, feeling that the children of the Crossing must have something with which to remember Christmas, Catherine convinced Francis Bean that carving a small toy for each child would be ideal, although the exchange of gifts was not a part of the season's traditions.

In three weeks time she viewed the collection. Before her, on the work bench, stood miniature wooden dolls, horses, wagons and a menagerie. It was the finest collection of wild animals and she could hardly believe Bean had produced them. She was astonished to see how accurate and beautiful the polished carvings were. She clasped her hands together beneath her chin and studied the pieces. Looking up at Bean, she exclaimed, "Why, Francis, they're lovely. Goodness, so many children living here– there must be some I haven't noticed."

240

Tall beside her, he smiled down into her bright face, pleased that he had done such worthy work. "There's one for each of 'em. Their names are underneath." He raised one. "See? Heather. That'll always be hers. Nobody can claim it and it stops any fightin' about it. You know how all young'uns are, always wantin' somethin' that ain't their own."

Catherine thought about that statement. "Well, no," she murmured, "I don't know about children, but I'm learning. These are truly beautiful, lovely." Catherine looked into his eyes and smiled. "Francis, how can I thank you for all of these?"

Bean grinned in a teasing way. "An extra good plum puddin' will do just fine!"

Catherine laughed merrily. "That, we have for you!"

Closer to the day, while she fretted that McAllister and Whiteman had still not returned, Catherine prepared berry pies, sweet rolls and bannock, storing them outside the door in a packing box, safe from animals, but where the winter cold would preserve them.

In the late afternoon of December 24, Two Way saw the figures of McAllister and Whiteman on horseback, leading their pack horses through the thick snowfall. Meeting them at the corrals, he noticed only one bale of furs. Although McAllister's mood was dour, his greeting was cordial.

Unsaddling McAllister's horse for him, Two Way mentioned, "Not many furs."

"It's early," the trapper replied, shaking snow from the saddle blankets and carting them into the warm barn. Two Way and Whiteman followed with the saddles and more tack. "It's coming to an end, you know, this trapping."

"How can that be?" The statement surprised Two Way, but before McAllister could answer, he motioned them toward the house. "Come, there are happier things to talk about now. Horace?" But Whiteman left them, waving goodbye and trudging through the snow toward his farm, where his family waited.

Two Way walked beside the trapper. "What took you so long getting home, if the trapping is light?"

"We built a cabin near one of the creeks."

McAllister entered his house, where warmth from the large stone fireplace flooded the rooms. Garlands of coloured beads were strung along the walls, and stars made from yellow soap hung from the ceiling. He smiled as he viewed the decorations. A festive feeling prevailed. McAllister scooped his wife into his arms, holding her close, savouring the pleasure of that intimate moment. He was glad to be home.

It was a grand feast which was laid before everyone at the Lodge on Christmas day. The children thrilled to the carvings. The men clustered together to discuss furs, farming and the weather, while the women filled the table with platters of browned roast beef and venison, a goose stuffed with bread, onions and seasoning, and large bowls of steaming vegetables with baskets of bannock and berry-filled rolls. Linas Hackett delivered a prayer, reminding everyone of friendship, peace and goodwill. He gave thanks for the birth of Christ. He then proceeded to carve the meat.

Waneta, who had been caught up in the preparation for that special day, sat beside Two Way and watched the procedure with unreserved wonderment. She had no idea why everyone had gone to so much trouble to celebrate the birth of a baby who nobody could see or touch. Two Way was of little help, for the whole experience of Christmas was new to him, as well. When the meal was finished, the children were sent outside to play in the snow, or to slide down the hillside on smooth deer hides. The men remained at the cleared table, sipping brandy and toasting each other in friendship.

Two Way and Waneta departed the Lodge and the unfamiliar festivity for the quiet of their small cabin near the frozen creek. There, in the comfortable home they had made together, they drew close and talked happily of the life stirring within Waneta.

"You did not tell him?" she asked of Two Way.

"He was not ready to hear it." he replied solemnly. "He will see for himself soon enough."

"Yes, yes," Waneta laughed merrily. "It will be our secret for as long as we can hide it," and she cuddled close to Two Way beneath the warm Hudson's Bay blankets.

While McAllister and Whiteman fought bitter winds and drifting snow during January and February to pull their traps from the ice covered creeks, Two Way visited his father regularly in the village of Shoshen-eetkwa. From where he lay on his soft pallet in his conical shaped house, Kelauna reached out to clasp his son's hand. Two Way sat on the reed covered floor for several hours at a time and held his father's hand, now small and wrinkled and weakened. No words passed his lips, for he knew his father could no longer hear him. Kelauna's health had failed throughout the winter and he now lay dying. He waited for the end of his fruitful life lived in a truthful way without regrets.

When in March Kelauna passed away, a new leader was chosen from amongst the strongest, bravest and wealthiest young men of the band. Almost instantly when the meeting had ended and the selection made, Two Way was advised by one of his cousins that he should leave his mother's house and return to the white lake.

"There are bad feelings toward you here," one of his cousins told him in Salish. "You have lived too long with the trapper and helped him take everything away from us. You did not come back to the village like Rattler and Nahna did." With his black eyes staring hard into Two Way's, he said stiffly, "You even talk like them!"

"So did Rattler! Everything I have done was my choice, as it was Rattler's," Two Way reminded his cousin, "to decide my own way in life and where I want to live and how I want to live. Those are the freedoms of my family, and yours, of all of us."

His cousin sneered. "But you have helped them up there– the white people, take away all that was ours!" Pausing for a moment, standing tall and straight, he delivered a final blow. "You even have a white man's name. Toohey– what is that? Two Way– what does that mean? It is not Okanagan!"

Two Way was stunned by his cousin's judgement. "I will go," he said hotly, "when I have finished visiting with my mother and Nahna, and not before I am ready! And yes," he added quickly, "My name is Toohey. It has meaning for my mother. That is all that matters about a name."

However, it continued to plague Two Way's conscience that some members of the band had secretly risen against him. "As they see it," he told Waneta once he was home, "I'm the root of their trouble, the cause of their losses. They fail to remember that I'm also the provider of much of their meat and all of their dairy foods."

Of course, he reminded himself silently, in their way of life, no one needed his help. The people had always provided amply for themselves before the trapper came to the valley. Sighing wearily, Two Way turned over in his bed. He felt the warmth of Waneta's body curled behind his, her swollen abdomen pressing against his back. It was comforting to him, and he fell asleep, exhausted by the constant turmoil in his life.

33

In early June Horace Whiteman and Lenny Parr packed several horses with McAllister's bales of furs and left Skaha Crossing for Spokane House to trade for supplies. Whiteman carried a letter from McAllister to Mary Walker. It suggested that Duncan return home and it included a note of credit for Mary to draw as final payment for the boy's care and tuition. So, when trading was completed and the horses packed for the return journey, Duncan McAllister rode with Whiteman and Parr to Skaha Crossing.

On the day of their arrival, McAllister and Linas Hackett were away in the low hills considering a dam on Willow Creek. It was possible, McAllister had decided, that if the creek could be dammed at its higher elevation, a system for irrigation could be devised to provide ample water for the fields and gardens later in the summer when the creek level normally dropped to a mere trickle. As the Crossing developed, there was a greater demand for water. So, Hackett and McAllister investigated the possibility of a more substantial dam on the creek than the old one.

Whiteman, Parr and young Duncan rode into the yard, separating at the steps of the store. There the men unloaded the packs of supplies that would fill Parr's shelves. Duncan drew his horse to a halt before the rail at his father's log house. Catherine stepped out of the dairy, sometimes referred to as the granary for it was not used solely for separating milk, making butter and the collection of eggs, but for storage of grain as well. With a small basket of eggs tucked under her arm, Catherine walked toward the house to greet Duncan. For several moments each contemplated the other. Catherine smiled. Duncan did not.

"I know you are Duncan," Catherine said softly. "Welcome home." Her smile was warm and meant to be cheering, as she led the way through the doorway of the house.

Duncan's expression remained perplexed, and confusion showed in his eyes. "Ma'am, who are you?" he asked with a bluntness which startled Catherine. "This is my father's house, and Nahna's."

Catherine was surprised that he had not learned of her marriage to his father from either Whiteman or Parr. But then, she reminded herself, the newcomers to the Crossing had believed them married long ago. In fact, they might well have assumed that she was Duncan's mother! She replied proudly, "Catherine McAllister."

Duncan did not believe her. Catherine saw this.

Two Way's shadow was cast across the floor as he entered McAllister's house. From behind Duncan, he said softly, "She is your father's wife. They were married last September, Duncan. It's good to see you back with us."

Duncan spun about to stare at Two Way. Oh, how great it was to see his friend again! But where was Nahna? What has happened here? "Did Nahna move away for good?"

"Back to the village," Two Way replied, smiling. "Now how about a good handshake and we'll talk later. Again, I welcome you home, Duncan. Your father is in the hills at this moment, but won't be long."

Catherine had gone to the kitchen, setting a basket of eggs upon the table. Grateful for Two Way's timing, she suggested quickly that they all sit down and enjoy some tea. She could think of nothing else to say.

"That will be good!" Two Way reiterated. "I'll get Waneta." Turning to face Duncan once more, he added proudly, "I've taken a wife myself. It is not intended that any of us live alone, you know. When you meet her, you will see that we are soon to have a little one in our house."

Duncan leaned against a wall and turned his hat nervously between his hands as he watched Two Way's face. "Time," he heard Two Way add, "time changes things, Duncan."

It was late afternoon when McAllister returned to the Crossing. As he looped the reins from his horse over the hitching rail, he heard the voices of Catherine and Duncan as they settled Duncan's belongings in the small bedroom in which he had been raised. From the doorway McAllister watched them for a moment. "It's been a long time, Duncan, that you've been gone," he said in a gentle voice and nodding. "I'm glad that you are back."

Duncan turned and stared into his father's eyes. He was suddenly overwhelmed with emotion and grateful to be home. McAllister reached out and impulsively clasped his son to his chest; an unexpected move which surprised Duncan, but one which had the reassurance that Duncan needed.

Behind them, Catherine quietly stepped toward the doorway. As she heard them talking together, she went outside, away from the oppressive heat in the house. He is not as tall as I believed he might be, she thought, and he doesn't seem to smile at all. Of course, I must have been a shock to him. He expected the Indian woman. She walked across the yard to Willow Creek, where she splashed the cool water to her face and neck. When she glanced back, she noticed that McAllister and his son had come outside to sit on the steps. Smiling, Catherine turned along the path to the house to prepare the evening meal.

Suddenly, screams from Two Way's cabin pierced the air, shattering the afternoon stillness, followed by soft crying and Two Way's comforting murmur.

An hour later Catherine sat alone beside Waneta, who lay weak and sleeping, her ordeal over. Two Way had taken the tiny stillborn girl, wrapped in soft buckskin, from the room. Outside, McAllister led Two Way's horse across the yard. Then he held the small, still bundle while Two Way stepped into his saddle.

"Two Way," McAllister spoke softly. "This child– baby– she can be buried here at the Crossing." His heart ached with sympathy for the young Indian. Several moments passed, with the hot stillness of the day pressing upon them.

Two Way looked sorrowfully down at the trapper. "No, Many Rains," he said firmly. "She is going to our village, to our own people, where my family lies. She is Indian. She should be remembered through the story of my family." Settling himself comfortably in the saddle, he gathered up the reins. Reaching out, he took the small bundle that was his daughter from McAllister's hands. "I will take her home. Please look after my sad wife, who grieves for this little one, until I return."

He nodded to the trapper with whom he had shared a similar time thirteen years before, and booted his horse onto the trail. He could barely comprehend the sadness that had invaded his home that afternoon. It was impossible to shut out the sight which had greeted him when he entered the cabin to take Waneta to meet Duncan, and it seemed he might never cease hearing her screams through the difficult, premature birth. For the first time in his life, his heart was heavy with a sadness different to any other he had known.

In the evening dusk, Two Way reined his horse eastward toward the draws that would take him to Shoshen-eetkwa.

Skaha Crossing had developed considerably since Duncan's departure four years earlier. It was almost unbelievable to him that several new houses and barns dotted the landscape of green pastures and cultivated fields. He was astonished to see the store, with the shelves filled. He investigated the barn from where the sound of Holinger's hammer rang out across the flats. He met again the Preacher, Hackett, whom he had talked to at Spokane House the year before, and recognized the young Negro who he learned was two years older than himself. There were several children, all much younger than him, and Rachel Hackett who was one year older than he. However crowded Skaha Crossing seemed to have become to

Duncan, the one person most important to him was missing.

Duncan rode his horse alongside Two Way's over the hills and along the ravines to Shoshen-eetkwa one week after his return to the Crossing. Anticipation gripped him. To be back on familiar ground, to see the people of the village again and to talk with Nahna once more, totally occupied his thoughts.

Two Way had attempted to explain that different attitudes now prevailed and that four years had made quite a difference to everyone. He could see that Duncan's mind was preoccupied with memories of earlier times, so left it unsaid.

A happy reunion was not to be. Duncan was shocked to find that the kindly old Chief no longer lived. Nahna seemed much older, tired and withdrawn. He noticed the tears she tried to hide at the sight of him and recognized her quiet pleasure in seeing him again, but the warmth and spontaneous joy were missing. Even the other members of the village appeared to stand back from him as though it was he who had changed so much.

Indeed, it was he who had grown up, Two Way told him as they rode back over the hills to home. "You wear different clothes, like those of the new people at the Crossing who came from Oregon. You speak differently, like a well educated young man should. You'll see as time goes by that you think beyond others here and will be able to deal with changing times and situations which arise in the years to come. I hope so anyway. Better perhaps than your father would be able to."

Duncan remained silent. Life as it had become at the Crossing seemed as strange to him as was the pulse of Spokane House when he had first arrived there. As at Spokane House, he knew he would adjust quickly but, he told himself sadly, a wonderful, carefree part of his life was now lost to him.

He remembered Mary Walker's words, when once she lectured him, "Nothing ever remains the same, Duncan. The advantages to you in changing times are of your own making. You must work very hard to make your life worthwhile to yourself, and to others." Was this what Two Way had been trying to tell him? He wondered.

Duncan McAllister and Mercy Bright soon became close friends. Together they finished building Bright's cabin near a spring east of White Lake. Located between Hackett's small farm and the Crossing, it was the only building within the mile between the two. Bright relished the privacy such distance afforded and cherished the freedom he now enjoyed. In all his childhood dreams, he could not possibly have imagined a life so wonderful as his had become, and he placed his salvation at the door of Linas Hackett.

Duncan's expert horsemanship soon became evident at the

Crossing. He began to teach Mercy Bright all he knew about horses and the sport of gymkhana. They challenged each other to contests in the large corral beside the barn and Holinger's blacksmith shop. Throughout the summer and fall Holinger cussed regularly about the dust their cavorting sent into his shop. However, their concern with the old man's discomfort was short lived and the following summer the two were at it again. By that time their games had attracted the attention of many young men of Shoshen-eetkwa and Kwak-ne-ta.

Sitting atop their ponies on the hillsides, the young Indians viewed the scene below them with little amusement at first. Such antics, they contended, when speaking with Two Way, only indicated a greater measure of permanency of the settlers upon their lands. However, in time they took a different view. Had they not raced their own ponies against one another and jumped them over the many log barriers among the trees in the forest? Games of all kinds were a great pastime in their social life. Eventually some of the younger members of the band ventured into the Crossing at Two Way's encouragement.

Soon serious competitions were carried out amongst the white and Indian youth. There was much horse racing back and forth along the trail in front of the Lodge and Parr's store. There were further complaints of dust as well as danger to the younger children who sometimes played there.

The complaints were brought to an abrupt end when Duncan, Bright and Linas Hackett, assisted by Two Way, Waneta and Rachel Hackett, built a large pole-fence arena one quarter mile from the Crossing. With such a grand new facility at their disposal, Bright and Duncan, when not employed in field work, set up a gate from which the horses could break out into an immediate run along the cleared path that circled the new arena and race to a finish line where someone would be posted to note the exact horse first over the line. In the arena, the young colts and fillies needing a "breaking in" were bucked out by Duncan, Bright and a few of Two Way's relatives from the village who were changing their minds about the immigrants in their midst. Cheers from a growing audience, who sat atop the fence posts, or peered between the rails, encouraged the competitors.

Sundays were the best times. It quickly became a pattern that following the morning service in the Lodge, a picnic was held if the weather was decent, followed by gymkhana in the arena, with a race afterward.

Rachel Hackett, now fifteen years old and appealing in appearance, perched as sedately as was possible atop the arena rails and cheered everyone on. In time her cheers ceased to be for every rider and, when one more year had slipped by, became directed singularly toward Duncan McAllister. She was the only girl of her age at the Crossing and as she had grown, Rachel had developed an average prettiness, with dancing eyes that openly flirted from beneath her wide bonnet. Fifteen year old Duncan did not fail to adequately notice her. Although three new families had located near the Crossing, none had daughters to rival Rachel. Nor were there any young men in the group, therefore Rachel's pursuit of Duncan McAllister as a husband took on added strength as she celebrated her sixteenth birthday.

"I could end up an old maid," she tearfully confided to her mother one day, "and be stuck in this dreadful place forever, alone! The only men my age around here are Two Way's cousins and Mercy Bright, excepting Duncan, of course. So that's just what I mean. It has to be him!" Staring wistfully from the doorway of her father's house across the field toward the southward trail over which they had travelled in their wagon four years earlier, Rachel wished aloud, "If only someone would come riding by–"

While Mrs. Hackett sympathized with her young daughter, she felt the situation must be kept in proper perspective. "Dreams and wishes are only just that– dreams and wishes."

No sooner had Rachel Hackett idly wished a rider by her door, than two of them showed up in the distance, their arrival determined by a great funnel of dust which boiled up behind their horses as they galloped along the trail. Rachel blinked her eyes. She declared to her mother, "They're on their way to the Crossing!"

"Indeed!" Mrs. Hackett pointed out, "there is nowhere else to go but the Crossing."

The tranquillity of Skaha Crossing was instantly shattered that September day in 1852. The riders passing by, the sight of which had excited Rachel Hackett that afternoon, were none other than the two McLaren cousins. Galloping into the Crossing, they skidded to a halt at the hitching rail before Holinger's blacksmith shop. Arrogantly, the cousins leaned over their saddlehorns, surveying the new buildings, the recently scythed fields and Lenny Parr's store. They felt very rich as they had spent the last few years in the Williams Creek area of the Cariboo, where gold had been easy to find and life fairly exciting.

Testimony to the kind of excitement the cousins had enjoyed since their earlier arrival at the Crossing, was a long, red scar on Boss McLaren's face from his left eye to chin. "Hey, old man!" he now bellowed into the dark interior of the shop where Holinger continued to round out a metal wheel rim hot from the coals.

Before Holinger bothered himself to reply, knowing full well who lingered at his doorway, a slight movement in the farthest end of the large barn caught Happy McLaren's attention. Without turning his head, he squinted his eyes against the outside sunshine to see more clearly what had caught his glance in the barn. His smile was a knowing one and he hissed from one side of his mouth to his cousin, "It's him, the nigger, 'n thar'."

"Where?"

"Shhh! In the barn, stupid," Happy whispered. "I seen 'im. Now, call out that old man an' pretend we don' know that stinky nigger is in thar'." With that order, he casually dismounted, standing authoritatively before Holinger when the blacksmith finally appeared.

"Be needin' room for our horses in here," Boss McLaren announced, "and a bed for ourselves up there," indicating McAllister's Lodge. "You got a store now and we need some important items from that, too." Dismounting, he tossed the reins of his horse to his cousin. "How about you settlin' in our hosses right away, Hap, while I go rustle some attention up the road."

Holinger, mindful of Mercy Bright's presence in the barn where he had been cleaning the stalls, told the cousins sharply, "Now, you go along together 'n I'll see to both these horses. 'ppears they's a bit lathered. Bin ridin' hard, eh? Don't s'ppose yer a'runnin' from anyone though, so on up you go!"

Saved from exposure to the cousins for the moment by Holinger's stern insistence, Mercy Bright nevertheless fell into their hands the following day. The incident occurred at the stables where the cousins had left their horses and where Bright lingered the following morning to harness one of McAllister's work teams. The McLarens came upon him quietly, purposefully.

"Mornin', Nigger!" chirped Boss McLaren. "See you clean out my horse's stall good 'n brush 'im down, too. See to Hap's horse along with it!" he ordered brusquely, strutting along the seemingly endless row of harness which hung along the wall.

Running the lines through their loops and clipping the straps into place, Mercy replied tensely, "Ah ain't yo' servant, man, but Ah don' 'ject ta doin' with yo' horses. Ah sho' will do th' bes' Ah kin, Ah will."

Instantly Boss' big fist was around the young Negro's throat. Pieces of harness clinked against the barn floor. "Now! You is ma servant, boy. No nigga' is goin' to be anythin' else, so don' let those words pass yer lips again! Now git to it!" With a quick snap of his powerful wrist, Boss sent Mercy Bright flying into a corner against the stall and strode importantly away from the barn, followed by Happy.

After several minutes during which he gathered his thoughts, Mercy rose from the floor. At the water trough outside he cleaned away the blood from the deep scratches and slivers along his arm where he had landed against the rough boards of the stall, then returned to harnessing McAllister's team and to groom the McLaren horses. He spoke nothing of the incident to anyone, covering the wound with a long-sleeved shirt. He decided to stay out of sight until they were gone.

The cousins were not persuaded to depart Skaha Crossing for several days. When they did pack up and ride out, leaving the impression they were off to Fort Okanogan, they moved away only so far as to afford themselves close observance of the Crossing from a safe distance. Hidden in the bushes of the ridges above the small townsite, the McLarens watched the activities with gleaming eyes and scheming minds.

Then for reasons known only to themselves, they swooped down upon young Bright one morning as he hoed in the Hackett's garden while the family was away. When they left the scene fifteen minutes later, galloping furiously southward, Mercy Bright lay sprawled in the dirt, beaten, bleeding and unconscious.

Linas Hackett approached McAllister with the problem of the McLarens' possible return to the Crossing, and while raising his angry eyes heavenward as though seeking Divine permission, suggested they shoot both the cousins on sight and be done with the matter.

"We will live to regret--" he cautioned, peering warningly from beneath bushy brows, "regret that we allow them to ride in and out of our town without showing some positive concern for the heathens that they are!"

Under the care of Mrs. Hackett and Rachel, Mercy Bright recovered and returned to his small cabin beside the spring. Each day Rachel followed the trail from her parents house to Bright's with a basket of fresh baked bread, eggs, milk, cheese, meat and vegetables. She had grown fond of Mercy and showed genuine concern for his well-being. As well, she recognized the opportunity of meeting Duncan occasionally, for she soon discovered that he often rode the trail to the Crossing with Mercy Bright and often remained overnight, should the McLarens unexpectedly once more turn up in the area. But the winter of 1852 passed pleasantly into the new year with no disturbance.

One day when Duncan offered to accompany him to his cabin, Bright replied kindly, "Ya don' have ta do that no more. Ah knows ma own way home! Ain't nothin' gonna git me. They's gon' fer good, Ah thinks now."

"Well, I'm calling on the Hacketts anyway, so I'll ride with you," Duncan insisted, placing a foot firmly in the stirrup of his saddle.

A wide grin broke across Mercy's dark face. "Fine young lady, Miss Rachel Hackett is," he chided honestly. "Ya takin' a likin' ta 'er?"

Duncan swung a playful swat toward his friend, as Mercy leapt into his saddle. "Shut yo' teasin' mouth yo' nosey coon!" he mimicked in good humour, "or I'll break yo' all up worse'n those McLaren varmits did!" Together they trotted their horses down the trail toward

Hackett's farm.

When Duncan spoke to his father of his intentions toward the Hackett girl, McAllister was not surprised.

"I've not been missing what's happening here," he told his son, pacing the kitchen floor. "but you're a bit young for such a load of responsibility."

Duncan was stunned. "Young! I'm sixteen for heaven's sake, and Rachel's seventeen. Who else is there here that compares with her? Have you ever really looked at Rachel? She's beautiful! She knows all about keeping a house, sewing and all those things that count to being a good wife."

"Granted," agreed McAllister, aware that Catherine had slipped unnoticed out of the house to leave father and son alone.

"For the future," Duncan continued heatedly now, "the only good prospect is the Carmichael girl. The others growing up here all look like horses– well not quite that bad, but compared to Rachel, they do. I can tell you Father, I'm not waiting ten years for Heather Carmichael to grow up to marrying age." Storming about the room, he added, as though to settle the matter, "Besides, Father, I love Rachel."

"Love?" McAllister enquired in a thoughtful way. "I wonder what you know about serious love." He did not wish to bruise his son's sensitive nature, nor appear to quell a relationship which might enrich the lives of both young people; but marriage was a lasting thing. Did Duncan realize how lasting it could be?

Duncan remained quiet.

When McAllister looked up from his big arm chair he saw the determination in his son's expression. Duncan stood resolutely before his father and announced, "Come next spring, we talk to her father about marrying us. Mercy and I will build a house. I think over near Mercy's spring would be nice. Rachel will be close to her mother there and she's all they have."

Rising from out of his chair, McAllister stared incredulously at his son. "You've thought about this for a while, I see."

"I've thought about nothing else for nearly two years! Rachel says I can ask her father for her. I haven't yet." Duncan's eyes looked squarely into his father's. "It was important to me that I tell you first."

"I see. I thank you for that."

"I love her, Father. It doesn't matter how I know that, just that I do."

"Well," McAllister sighed in resignation, turning toward the doorway. "Life does have a way of continuing. You'd better get the teams going and start hauling logs for your house." Glancing back a moment, he smiled at his son before leaving the house.

The thick fir logs were dragged down the ravines toward Mercy's spring where they lay exposed to the weather for drying. During the following year, they were peeled and trimmed to size. Stealing moments away from the industry of preparing their new home, Duncan and Rachel took long walks together along the grassy hillsides and among the tall trees which shaded the deer paths. Their moments alone were very few and, therefore, precious.

They planned their future while playing teasing races out of sight among the trees. Duncan would catch Rachel, hold her to him and rain gentle kisses upon her face and neck. Feeling alive and happy, Rachel would dart away, only to be caught up once more against Duncan's strong body and kissed until she was breathless. Each time they stole away from watchful eyes at the Crossing, their games amongst the tall trees became more passionate, until once Rachel fell to the warm, leaf-covered ground with Duncan upon her. They lay together perfectly still, knowing the consequence of moving their limbs together would bring condemnation upon them. Tears stole from the corners of Rachel's eyes, mirroring her longing, and slid over her cheeks to fall into her mass of brown hair spread out upon the ground.

"Oh, Duncan," she murmured softly. "I want it to be right for us."

Duncan's mind reeled with the rush of feeling which coursed through him. A yearning, stronger than he supposed he could now manage to control, to gently pull away Rachel's clothing and clasp her to him, gripped him. Bending his head, he kissed her tenderly, his lips lingering at the corner of her seeking mouth, then moving to her throat. He allowed his legs to fall carefully along both her thighs, placing his body against hers, which she lifted to meet him. Duncan felt exquisite pleasure, while Rachel whispered, "I love you. Oh, how I want you!"

Suddenly the spell was broken by the pawing and snorting of horses near them. Duncan and Rachel flew up from the ground, brushing hastily at their clothes, then stood in absolute silence to determine the direction of the sound. From where they hid in the trees, their eyes searched the ridge above them. Two riders sat astride their horses, their faces shielded by the wide brims of their hats and stared down the hillside to where Rachel and Duncan waited with held breath.

"They know we're here," Rachel whispered against his ear. "Oh Duncan, I feel afraid. Let's hurry back."

"Maybe they didn't see us. I doubt they can-- the trees hide us. I can't make out who they are. The sun's against us," Duncan said quietly, reaching for her hand. With her free hand Rachel gathered the yardage of her skirt together, lifting the bulk slightly for easier stepping and quickly followed Duncan. Hoping that they had not been discovered, Duncan led Rachel along the narrow deer path out of the trees and down the road to Mercy's spring. Holding her hand securely in his, he said, "I couldn't see who they were, but everything'll soon be okay. You go on home now. I'll talk to your father again. Then we'll set a date."

Rachel held tightly to his hand. "Oh Duncan, please don't think of me as–"

"I love you, Rachel." His tone was positive as he searched her worried eyes. "I love you. You have no idea how much I do."

Smiling, finally, reassured that her flirtations which had led to the more serious moments on the forest floor had not been considered passing fancy, Rachel Hackett left Duncan sitting desolately beneath the hot summer sun upon the logs of what would be their new home.

News reached the ears of Lenny Parr at the store that the McLarens were camped in the vicinity of Skaha Crossing. When he told McAllister this, the trapper frowned in concern.

"There's trouble brewin'" Parr warned. "I can feel it in my bones, damn it! Why d'they keep comin' back? They know we're gonna watch that young Bright closer than ever."

McAllister thought aloud, "Young Bright is now nearly twenty years old. Given a gun, he could more than handle the two of them."

"If they don't surprise 'im", added Parr.

"Where are they?"

"On the creek above Willemeyers panning for gold," Parr answered. "Everybody knows there's no gold in that little creek, includin' those two dummies! They're nothin' but a couple of dumbbells!" Clearly, Parr was working himself into an agitated state over the cousins' presence. "Want everythin' for nothin', those two. Let them come in here again, showin' me who's boss, and there'll be lead a-flyin'. I guarantee it!"

McAllister leaned back against the counter in Parr's store, pressing the thumb and fingers of one hand against his temples as if willing an immediate solution to the nuisance of the cousins. "No doubt about it," he muttered. "We have to get rid of them. They've been hanging around here for five years now. They're after Mercy, we all know that."

Parr added, "And they're takin' their time at gettin' 'im; a kind of slow game."

"We'll give Bright a gun," McAllister suggested.

The bold audacity of the McLarens was unbelievable. They moved in and out of the area at will, venturing into Parr's store to legitimately purchase sufficient staples for a hibernation period of two or more months. Throughout the winter Linas Hackett remained close to his home, leaving it only when both his wife and daughter were with him. Duncan moved some of his clothes to Bright's cabin and spent most of the winter sleeping in a second bunk built against the opposite wall to Mercy's bed.

The winter of 1854 was the first during which McAllister had not spent at least some of the weeks trapping in the mountains. Horace Whiteman, now familiar with the terrain, travelled on horseback alone to set and clean out the traps.

Rachel Hackett, feeling dismayed that yet another year had slipped by without a wedding ring circling her finger, pulled back the curtains of her closet occasionally to admire the lovely wedding dress she had made of crisp, white taffeta. It had taken longer than a year for the material to finally reach Spokane House after she ordered it, then another three months until Willemeyer and Parr returned with her precious bundle of taffeta. When at last it had arrived Rachel had set about designing, cutting and stitching the bolt of material into the beautiful gown which hung in her closet that spring.

"I despair of ever having the wedding actually happen," she told Duncan one morning as they walked through the empty rooms of their finished house.

"Oh, it'll happen!" Duncan whispered hotly into her hair, pulling her back against him. In the privacy of their house, he pressed his thighs against her round buttocks and slipped his hand beneath the bodice of her dress, gently cupping her warm breasts. "All I need to do now, is find the ring," he breathed, his lips caressing the back of her smooth neck.

Rachel turned swiftly in his arms, her body melding suggestively against his. "Duncan, you terrible tease," she murmured against his mouth, longing flooding her.

"I've had that ring for so long, I may have lost it now." He moved away from her in an effort to gain control. "The last thing I'll build in this house is the bed, you know." When he turned to look at her, Rachel was smiling boldly. He too, smiled. "If it were there right now, I believe we would accidentally fall into it and not be able to get out. I can tell you, Rachel, I've become very impatient with dips in that cold creek after every time I've been near you!"

Seriousness had replaced the lighter tone of the moment before. "And I've become exhausted from dreaming and not having," Rachel told him. "I've become so bold in my thoughts and dreams, I'm almost ashamed of myself."

Duncan crossed the floor and cradled Rachel against his chest. Looking over her head out to the distant ravines beyond their doorway, he remembered the happy times they had shared among the trees when first they had discovered their love for each other.

"Next month," he told Rachel, his voice hoarse with emotion. "The

255

first day of June. We have nothing more to wait on. Mercy will have the table finished. Old Holinger has all the hinges for the cupboards done. And– I will build the bed." Glancing down into her face, Duncan saw a slow flush move up into her cheeks. Reluctantly they drew apart, left their house to cross the fields and speak once more to Linas Hackett.

The wedding ceremony was performed on the first day of June as planned. The sunshine was bright, warm and cheering. Rachel was beautiful. She repeated her vows before her father who read them, with a clear, resonant voice. Relieved that finally the day had come to pass, Duncan McAllister stood beside his bride with great calmness. When he was advised by Linas Hackett that he could now kiss the bride, he did so with such enthusiasm it raised whispers among the women.

As he lifted his head, Duncan's glance crossed to his father. Impulsively he clasped Rachel closer and thought, as he held his father's gaze, You know what I feel this day. You know the joy, after all the waiting, that comes with being with the woman you love. I know, Father, that it was my mother who gave you the joy that Rachel will give to me tonight. Duncan had no way of knowing that, before Willow, it had been Denise White who had given to Rayne McAllister the infinite pleasure of a woman's wonderful passion.

Rayne McAllister turned away from his son's gaze to walk alone in thought. Only Catherine noticed his mood and let him go. "Here's one over you, Evan Dubrais, you old prophet!" McAllister whispered aloud to himself, smiling as he walked. "No son shall I have? Ha! Now, grandsons, perhaps." Satisfied with his life and the pleasure of having a son, and now a daughter-in-law, McAllister returned to the crowd in the Lodge to join the wedding celebration.

34

By 1856, news of disputes within the united states regarding slavery rumbled westward and, consequently, filled the ears of the McLaren cousins during each trip they made to Spokane House. It reaffirmed, for the McLarens, their purpose in hunting down Mercy Bright. They knew of no law north of the Boundary which protected a slave, and so their relentless pursuit of Mercy Bright knew no limits.

For two weeks in mid October, as they were riding north to the trapping grounds out of the Okanagan, the McLarens lingered near Skaha Crossing to observe, in earnest, the day to day activities of the settlement. They learned that the White Lake valley had become filled with several new houses and small farms since their last visit. They noticed that the Hackett girl now lived with young McAllister in a house between Bright's and her parents. Regularly, they noted, she visited the little cabin beside the spring, taking baskets of food. Together Duncan, Rachel and Mercy worked in their combined fields and garden, unaware of watching eyes.

While observing such activity one day, Boss commented, "I ain't seen no young'uns taggin' along on her skirts. You seen any?"

"Na, probably that dumb young squirt don't know what he's suppos'd to be doin' in that bed!" Happy's instant laughter at his own joke was loud enough to bring a swift, calming swat from Boss.

"You want that they all knowin' we're here a-watchin' 'em, stupid?" Boss snapped, clearly irritated by the waiting game which they were playing. "Soon, soon. When that nigger is next left alone, we move on 'im!"

"Or better yet," suggested Happy McLaren, a lewd smile creasing his round bearded face. "I think I'm gonna git me that woman first." Remembering the day that he had first cast his eyes upon Rachel as she stood beside Rayne McAllister and her father at the Crossing, he whispered low, "I bin waitin' a long time. Too long." Settling his round buttocks more comfortably in his saddle, the younger McLaren leaned contemplatively upon his elbow against the horn as he watched Rachel walk along the path between Bright's cabin and her home. "Maybe they'll blame the nigger if we have a little fun with 'er. I mean," Happy wished to point out, "what does it look like to you?

Her goin' there all the time an' the two of them alone so much."

Glancing across at his cousin, Boss McLaren could clearly see how excited Happy had become at the prospect of such a dalliance. "Ah well, what's the difference!" he finally agreed. "Bin awhile since I enjoyed the finer pleasures o' life anyway. When?"

"Tomorrow, first time she's alone," Happy replied anxiously. "I ain't waitin'." His black eyes flared in anticipation.

Unmindful of the consequences of their actions, uncaring of the unbearable hurt and personal devastation which would result, the unscrupulous McLarens moved toward their goal of abducting Rachel McAllister.

While Mercy Bright worked at cutting wood for Lenny Parr behind the store, and Duncan was away with Two Way to make a final check before winter of the reservoir on Willow Creek, the McLaren cousins rode down upon Rachel as she walked the trail to her mother's house at mid morning. They quickly dragged her into the nearby shrubs, bound her hands to a small stump, and stuffed one of their filthy gloves into her mouth to stifle her cries for help. Impatiently Happy tore at Rachel's clothing, flinging himself upon her in a frenzy that startled his cousin. His besotted mind could not get enough from her bruised, protesting body. After slapping her into silence and inert submission, he heaved himself upon her one more time, slavering over her full, round breasts.

Eventually, Boss reached down and yanked his panting cousin to his feet. "Do up yer pants, you damned little pervert! Go out there an' keep a watch, an' I mean keep yer eyes on the trail an' not me!" Slowly Boss lowered his bulk upon Rachel. The fun of the idea had been spent with Happy's wild rutting. Rachel's body lay limp upon the ground. Cursing his cousin for having taken the sport out of the escapade, he fumbled half-heartedly with his own clothes, then quickly bent toward the unconscious woman beneath him. For a tense second, as his spent body slumped in finishing shudders, Boss McLaren thought that Rachel was dead.

Linas Hackett slapped the reins across the teams of his wagon, anxious to be home before dark with the load of wood. His mongrel followed alongside. He knew his wife and daughter would have a hot meal waiting for him. Later in the evening, when Duncan had returned from the dam, a constructive conversation with his son-in-law would round out the day perfectly before the two would leave for their own home.

The dog sniffed the trail ahead, then, suddenly growling, dashed away to the right of it. Linas pulled the team to a halt. Climbing down from the wooden seat, he buttoned his wool coat against the early evening chill and followed the dog into the darkness of the trees. The sight which assailed his eyes froze his mind and body, but only for a second. He spun into action, cutting the ties that bound his daughter, pulling off his coat and wrapping her gently into its warmth.

Hackett entered his house carrying his daughter's limp body, his eyes blazing with fury. Hatred filled his heart. He could feel no other emotion and did not pause to question reasons for such an invasive allowance in their lives. Together, Linas and his fretting wife bathed and dressed their battered daughter, wrapping her in a warm blanket. All the while the two faces of her assailants remained lodged in his brain, dangling there as though at the end of a hangman's noose; and with every tear that Rachel shed, the noose in Hackett's mind tightened.

Suddenly the door opened and Duncan McAllister stood in its entrance. When after a moment, his eyes took in the scene in the Hackett sitting room, he rushed to the couch where his wife lay. Leaning over her, he raised his eyes to meet those of Hackett, beseeching him of news.

Words between them could not express the horror of the crime. Duncan lowered himself to the floor beside the couch and, reaching out, held Rachel's head against his shoulder, gently rocking her. Love for her, and deep tenderness, flooded him. He looked again toward Hackett, who paced the floor in a furious manner, his cheeks red with anger.

"I don't know what to say-- do--" Duncan murmured forlornly against the tears on Rachel's face. Fury flooded his brain.

Hackett waved an arm through the air. "You can't change it back. It has happened and nothing can--" Overwhelmed, Linas Hackett left his house to walk around the yard in the cold night, in deep sorrowing contemplation.

Duncan gently lifted his wife and carried her to her old bedroom, where her mother raised the cover for him to lay her down. When he had pulled the coverlet over her, tucking it around her shivering body, he lay down beside her and tenderly dried her tears. In time, with the warmth and comfort of him close to her, Rachel McAllister fell asleep.

Steeped in a deep sense of shame, Rachel spent her first days of healing in prayer, huddled close beside her father, who urged her to speak of the incident to them, rather than hide it. Her mother never left her side, encouraging Rachel toward a comfortable return to normal. Linas Hackett departed his house only when Duncan returned each day from work to take her to their own home.

It was difficult for Rachel to be a willing partner with her husband in their bed. She knew anger, frustration and hurt were constant companions to him through the months following the incident. While cradled against him closely in their warm bed at night, reassured that she was completely protected and loved by Duncan, Rachel continued to turn away from further intimate contact.

She could not rid herself of the feel of Happy McLaren's assault upon her. The cruel glint of his steel blue eyes often floated tormentingly in her brain. She would have to press her fingertips hard against her temples to rid herself of the image. When it became evident that she was not with child by the rape, she beseeched, through prayer, freedom from her anguish. She prayed that soon she could accept the love offered by Duncan and be allowed the child that she knew he wanted.

Contrary to the belief held by the McLarens, that the Negro would be blamed for the rape, Mercy Bright was not held responsible. When, on that fateful night, Rachel McAllister had whispered faintly in her father's ear, "McLaren–", it was inevitable that the cousins would be hunted down and shot in atonement for their crime.

But the elusive pair continued to keep out of sight. They were impossible to find. Willemeyer, Whiteman and the McAllister men combed the countryside throughout the following months, believing the McLarens to be holed up in an obscure tilt along some unfamiliar mountain stream.

Two Way spread word among the band that the two men must be captured if located, and brought before the residents of Skaha Crossing; or, he pointed out, the same could happen near their village, to one of their women. Messages were passed by trappers and traders who passed through the valley, but by the beginning of 1858, no trace of the two McLarens had been found.

Then, without warning, provocation, or notice, the cousins returned to Skaha Crossing. They descended upon the cabin of Mercy Bright on a dark, stormy night in July 1859. Heavy thunder rumbled overhead. Long forks of lightning struck the earth with a sizzling force that lent impending violence to the hot, steamy air. Boss and Happy McLaren burst through the entrance of the cabin, sending the door flapping crazily against the wall. From his bed they dragged the kicking, screaming, Bright outside onto the ground and bound his hands.

In a grove below the spring, Boss McLaren quickly located a substantial pine and tossed a rope over the lower limb. "Here's where all yer blasted screamin' comes ta 'n end, little darkie!"

"An' yer rapin'!" Happy McLaren danced around the crouched figure of Bright, kicking and slapping uncontrollably. "You know what happens ta a nigger what touches a white woman? We takes this knife here, see? An' we cuts off–"

"Shut up, you fool!" Boss bellowed as the thunder rolled above him. "Bring 'im over here. Yer wastin' time!" He pulled on the rope, testing its tightness.

Mercy Bright's dark, luminous eyes bulged in fear. His small body shook outrageously. The pain where Happy had kicked his spine was excruciating. He was completely helpless and he realized the finality of his life that night. Mercy Bright hung his head and pleaded silently for a quick end to it. "I ain't no brave man, Lord. No, I sho' ain't brave, Lord." he whispered in forlorn resignation. Then, his eyes rolling heavenward, Mercy Bright slipped into blessed unconsciousness.

Happy McLaren was furious. "Now look what the bastard's gone an' done!" In a rage of feeling cheated, he reached impulsively for his gun and, placing the barrel at Mercy's temple, pulled the trigger.

The sound of the explosion was followed by a thunderous clap above them, the residual rumble echoing against the mountains. The contorted, bound, brainless young body of Mercy Bright lay in a crumpled heap at their feet. The smell of burnt powder filled the air. Nausea suddenly gripped Boss McLaren and he turned away, retching into the weeds. Rain began to fall. As Boss pulled the rope from the tree, he glanced across at his cousin.

Happy McLaren now stood in sober silence, staring down at the rifle in his hand as though it had committed the murder of its own accord. Boss knelt and felt for a throb in Mercy's chest, but he knew the Negro was dead, that there was no brain, so there could be no pulse. He stood up, kicked his cousin into action, and together they lifted the limp body and carried it into the thick brush where they buried it. They did not have to clean away the blood. The deluge of rain soon washed away all trace of the murder that had been committed that night.

The blacksmith, Holinger, was the first to realize that something was amiss. "I ain't seen young Bright today," he told Duncan when the younger McAllister led his horse into the corral.

"He's around for sure, somewhere," Duncan called back. "I took Rachel to her folks early this morning and came straight up to Two Way's. We're moving the cattle up a little higher today. My father's riding with us, too. Good rain, last night!" Duncan continued. "We need all the water we can get."

"Well, jus' seems odd he ain't here. Always here at daylight, that boy is." Holinger rummaged about his shop, beginning his day.

Bright did not turn up at Holinger's shop, nor at Parr's store. Nor had he been seen at the Lodge or in the granary. At one o'clock in the afternoon Billy Willemeyer sent his eldest son galloping off on horseback in the direction of Bright's cabin, then on to Hackett's farm if necessary. When the Willemeyer boy returned with Linas Hackett riding beside him, Skaha Crossing was alerted to the disappearance of Mercy Bright.

"His cabin was broken into. The door's wrung off its hinges,"

Hackett announced solemnly. "Looks like he was dragged from his bed." Linas Hackett did not need to be told by whom. He organized an immediate search. "Get my dog. That one found Rachel!"

The men of Skaha Crossing prepared to carry out a thorough search of the area. When Duncan, Two Way and McAllister returned to the settlement that evening, the body of Mercy Bright had been located by the hound. It was lifted to the surface from its soggy grave in the trees near Mercy's Spring, bathed, freshly clothed, and laid upon his bed, awaiting a proper burial.

A profound sadness lingered among the residents of Skaha Crossing through the hot, summer months and into the winter. No cheerful singing could be heard from behind the store where Bright had chopped the winter's supply of wood for Parr and Holinger. The elderly blacksmith missed the constant companionship of Bright about the barn and his shop. Linas Hackett blamed himself for the tragedy. He believed that if he had insisted that young Bright remain under his protection and the McLarens mercilessly hunted down, the murder would not have happened. As well, there were few words which could console Duncan and Rachel. There was no compensation for the loss of the young man who had been their friend.

With the burial of Mercy Bright, the cemetery was determined. On a warm, sunny day in May 1860, Linas Hackett and his wife visited the grave, taking with them a piece of lilac root and a small painted cross with the young man's name carved into the wood.

Duncan and Rachel cleared out Mercy's cabin that spring. Until now, no one had wanted to go there.

"Look at all these little trinkets he kept," Rachel exclaimed opening Mercy's cupboard drawers and boxes. "What're we to do with them?"

Duncan carefully considered the possibilities. "We can burn them, bury them or keep them. I think I'll keep them in that old deerskin water bag my father gave me when I went to Spokane House." The contours of Duncan's face softened and he leaned against the table, thinking, remembering and holding some of Bright's collection in his hands. "When I was there, Mrs. Walker took me to a fine house once, where the gentleman displayed some sketches of the wagon trains that moved west. There were tools and tins and dishes set on wooden pack boxes for display. Furniture made by his own hand filled the house. Some of the things the old fellow sold, but mostly he just let people come and look."

Rachel smiled and recalled one of Mrs. Willemeyer's school books. "I read once about places in Europe like that. They're called galleries. Even in Virginia and South Carolina, the mansions there have furniture that has been brought across the ocean, and huge paintings hanging on the walls."

Duncan stared across the room at his wife. "I think that old man at Spokane House had the first gallery in the west." Suddenly his eyes brightened as he looked down at the contents of the box in his hand. "Rachel, you do something for us. You find my old waterbag and put these things in it. Write on a paper that they belonged to Mercy Bright and that he was killed because his skin was dark, and that he was shot by the McLaren cousins. We all know they did it. They've been hunting him long enough." He scrambled about the cabin, placing other articles upon the wooden table attached to the wall below the window. "Fix a date on his death, too. Put down where he came from. Talk to your father about that. Here's a little sketch of him. He must have made that himself. Write his name on the back of it."

"What about the bag?" Rachel enquired in a teasing way. "What do I mark on that old piece of rawhide?"

Duncan smiled into her eyes. It was so good to hear her laugh and tease once more. "You write, my sweet wife, that it was given to Rayne McAllister, a trapper from Fort St. James in New Caledonia, by an Indian woman from a village called Penti'ktɛn. He told me that's how he got it. Then we'll put all these things away. Someday when I take you on a trip to Spokane House we'll take this stuff for display."

Rachel paused, feeling a little sad. "Seems like we shouldn't take it so far away," she murmured sentimentally.

"We'll put everything away for now. There's a few things of Father's that should be saved. He must have some things that belonged to my mother. He has a sea otter cape. It belonged to his father."

Methodically, Rachel labelled some of Bright's personal articles and a few pieces of his clothing and stuffed them into the doeskin waterbag. Enthused by the project of preserving a bit of their way of life, she called on Catherine for assistance in locating McAllister's otter cape, Willow's wedding dress and several pieces of old jewellery.

"We can only presume some of this belonged to Willow's mother," Catherine explained. "Rayne says Duncan can have it."

McAllister's miniature pocket knife also fell prey to Rachel's preserving nature and, although the trapper spent weeks in search of it, he was never able to locate it. Rachel hid it among the other articles, making no mention of the knife to anyone. In her home once more, she placed all that she had gathered from Bright's cabin and McAllister's house into the wooden trunk at the foot of her bed, locked it tight and nailed the key onto the bottom.

35

In 1862, smallpox ravaged Shoshen-eetkwa. At an alarming rate the epidemic had spread from the coastal tribes into the interior and eventually to the Okanagan.

Two Way forbid Waneta to visit the village and ventured there himself only when news of his mother's death reached him. He discovered to his horror that Nahna was ill and dying like the others. Upon his return home, Waneta went to stay with Catherine and Rayne while Two Way quarantined himself until it was positive that he was not a carrier of the disease.

While Two Way struggled with the loss of family and old friends, Duncan and Rachel were rejoicing in their announcement to their parents that Rachel was, at last, with child.

Waneta remained quiet at the news. Her heart suddenly felt empty. She thought of Two Way alone in their cabin, surrounded by sorrow. She knew that Two Way needed her close by at this difficult time for him, and the loss of their baby girl suddenly crowded her mind. She rose from the chair, excused herself from the others, and left the house.

Catherine watched with a saddened heart full of feeling, as Waneta crossed the yard to her own home. She understood the emptiness a woman could feel without a child.

Later that evening, together in their comfortable house, Rachel confided in Duncan, "I'm sure it will be a boy." The statement was full of excitement and confidence. "I just feel it in my heart." Outside, a freezing wind howled about the corners of the log building and rattled against the windowpanes, causing Rachel to burrow deeper beneath the quilts over their bed and move close to the warmth of Duncan's body.

"You don't know that," Duncan smiled in the dark.

"Yes, I do, and we'll call him David after your wonderful father. He never uses his first name, so our son will. Your father is very kind to me."

"He never had a daughter. Maybe he's discovered how darling girls can be, all the while they're getting their own way about things." He leaned over and kissed her gently, his lips soft against her forehead as Rachel lay cradled in his arm. "Anyway, he likes you. We all know that."

David entered his parents' world quietly, without great stress to his mother or anxiety to his father, and thrived without fuss or fever, throughout his months of infancy. Catherine was thrilled to be a grandmother. Memories of conversations with Evan Dubrais surfaced in McAllister's mind, bringing a smile of satisfaction to his face. Waneta watched Rachel and the child with a touch of envy, for the hurt of having lost the only baby she had borne, was still with her.

Eighteen months later, the McAllisters presented to their families a second child, a girl whom they named Mary. Mary arrived following twenty-nine hours of labour which nearly spent her mother, and thereafter altered the peace and tranquillity of the McAllister and Hackett households daily with colic and constant crying. It seemed to Rachel, and to her mother and mother-in-law, that their lives would never again know the calm of days gone by. Even little David, nearing the age of two, leaned over the crib from time to time to view the bundle from which came constant wailing, and resisted the urge to reach across and choke his sister, thereby putting an end to the noise and all the attention that went her way.

Although he generally avoided the baby and therefore the fuss stirred by her, Rayne McAllister often reassured Rachel, "You have given me a real family, my dear. A friend once told me that I would go to my grave and leave no sons to keep my name." He felt a deep affection for Rachel. "Dubrais never counted on you."

"Really," corrected Catherine with a mischievous smile. "I do believe Duncan had something to do with it, too. Such miracles don't just happen, you know."

McAllister placed an arm about his wife's shoulders. "You're right, you're right. Now, we'll leave you children. An old man must get his sleep. Catherine?"

They stepped out into the autumn evening. The air was warm and calm, lending contentment to the settlement. "Imagine me," the trapper said, unable to conceal his pride, "with two grandchildren. Who would've thought it!"

Catherine and Rayne shared their pride and pleasure as they walked together across the fields, her arm looped through his, their strides equal. Frisky, young foals galloped and kicked their way across the pasture, turning, wheeling toward the fence, as if they could frighten the intruders away. The last of the daylight descended behind the distant mountains when they reached the steps of their home. When Catherine went inside to light the lamp, McAllister took it from her, circling her waist with an arm.

She smiled up at him. "What are you up to, David Rayne McAllister?"

"I love you," he said softly, setting aside the lamp. A nostalgic mood gripped him. He brought her gently against him, his arms holding her tight. "I have so much to thank you for," he whispered against the silky softness of her hair. "You brought me to life again. You help me to understand my family. You work beside me. And you're always there, warm and wonderful when I go to my bed. What more could I ask for?"

Catherine was astonished at his rush of words. It was unlike him to express, so freely, his innermost feelings. "Remember that you gave me my life, Rayne," she said. "I owed you a great deal with no way to repay. What happened was, I fell in love with you and everything just moved along naturally. I don't think I knew what real tenderness was until after you found me in the cave. I was terribly afraid of you then." Catherine reached up and brought his face down to hers. Lying her cheek against his for a brief moment, she moved her mouth to kiss him softly at first, then with the wonderful feel of his body against her own, Catherine allowed the kiss to tease her senses. The lamp remained on the shelf, unlit and unneeded in the quiet evening.

In November, the trapper and Two Way loaded the pack horses with supplies to stock the winter cabin, grain for the horses and trapping gear. They rode across the valley floor of the South Okanagan and up into the hills of the eastern ridges, following the route to the meadows where Two Way's uncle Rattler had earlier hunted furs for McAllister. Later McAllister and Horace Whiteman built a solid, warm cabin and, together, trapped the creeks and many ponds of the vast meadows, reaping a greater number of pelts annually than he had from the Okanagan River.

The icy stillness of the forest through which McAllister and Two Way rode echoed the sounds of the horse's hooves upon the crusted snow, the jingling of bits and creaking of saddles. When the forest was left behind, deer were spotted on the open slopes, standing in silent watchfulness of their passage. Sparrows flitted between the trees. From the branches of fir and pine, the snow fell in clumps behind them as their packs brushed against the branches. McAllister's one-room winter cabin stood near the stream which fed the meadows. Protected from the wind by the hillock behind it, and banked by snow already, the cabin afforded far greater comfort for the trapper than his small tilts and sod huts of the past. The door, hung on wide pieces of hard leather, was only five feet high and fit snugly to its casing. One window allowed only a little light into the dark interior, but with several tallow candles, McAllister had all the light necessary.

Prepared to isolate himself as he had done all the winters of his life, the trapper bid Two Way farewell and the Indian left the meadows to return to Skaha Crossing. Without apprehension of any kind, McAllister watched him disappear. The temperature would soon drop miserably below zero. Snow, however, would drift three and four feet deep against his cabin, providing welcome insulation. Stacks of wood for his stove, left from the previous year, stood along the face of the cabin. To this pile, McAllister would add more in the following days. He was totally at home in the mountains, still indifferent to the deprivation of the normal comforts of everyday living.

At the age of sixty-one, McAllister still appreciated the challenge the mountains presented. There, in the stark white wilderness of winter, he remained comfortable with Nature, treading the banks and shores of the streams and ponds, setting and emptying his traps.

Winter settled upon the meadows. The snowfall was heavier than normal. Hoar frost clung in beautiful patterns on the trees. McAllister's horses snorted through frost-crusted nostrils and impatiently pawed the snow-covered ground of their corral. McAllister kept only his saddle horse and one pack horse with him, sending the rest back to the ranch with Two Way. Grain was doled out to them in small amounts to make it last. Throughout the daylight hours McAllister allowed them to hunt for short grass beneath the snow. Each night they returned to the corral for their grain, where they remained overnight in the windbreak.

The trapper's advancing age and his continuing pre-occupation with trapping in the mountains was a constant concern to Catherine, Duncan and Two Way. Duncan could not explain why his father absented himself from the warmth of his home each year, returning from the hills for the brief Christmas season, only to be gone again until March or later. The farm was operating well. There was no longer the demand for furs as there had been. The financial need for the trapper to house himself in the mountains every winter no longer existed. It was just his way of life. Only Two Way understood it.

All were acutely aware that there would come a time when the trapper might not return. It was in the spring of 1866 that fear of the worst lay heavily upon Two Way's mind.

"Do you think something's happened?" asked Catherine, anxiety filling her eyes, as she searched Two Way's face for a sign of his thoughts.

"No. He is good at what he does. No harm will come to him." It was weak reassurance he gave her, Two Way knew, but what else could he say? Twice during February and March he had ridden into the eastern mountains, taking supplies to the trapper and bringing out pelts. However, it was now the end of April and springtime at the ranch, and each day as Two Way saw the snow disappear from the face of the far mountains, a gnawing apprehension began to work on him. Soon it was the beginning of May and the trapper was long overdue. Two Way rode to Mercy's Spring to confer with Duncan.

"He is several weeks late this year," he reminded Duncan. "Certainly ten days at the least."

Duncan refused to show his concern, which had also been growing. "How d'you know that? He comes home whenever he feels like it," he replied.

"Many Rains is always home by now. I know that things are not right," Two Way stated flatly, not amused by Duncan's hedging on the subject.

For a tense moment Duncan pondered his father's situation. He saw the warning in Two Way's black, piercing eyes, and nodded his assent. "Alright," he murmured low, "we'll go."

The following morning before sunup, Two Way and Duncan, accompanied by a cousin of Two Way's from Shoshen-eetkwa, rode into the eastern mountains toward the meadows.

36

McAllister squinted his eyes against the morning sun as he watched two men ride below him along the narrow canyon. He had followed them since the noonday before. So had the Sanpoil Indians, hunting in the territory while visiting Soi'yus. He figured the riders to be the McLarens and had deliberately searched them out. Two weeks earlier, while McAllister gathered his traps for the close of the season, all the pelts he had baled for travel had been stolen from his camp. He began to track the thieves. The thought easily crossed his mind that it might be the McLarens. The cousins had trapped in the region several years before and McAllister considered it reasonable to suspect their presence in the country again. He could not know that the cousins had, in a daring manoeuvre, stolen two horses from the Sanpoil camp, to carry the hides.

From his position across the canyon, McAllister stood watching the small group of Sanpoil appear from time to time, their spotted ponies silhouetted brilliantly in the bright sunshine against the cloudless, blue sky. As he leaned against his horse, resting from the saddle, he pondered what their move would be. Perhaps they were waiting for him to make his.

McAllister knew the McLarens rode ahead of them. They had grown careless of their trail in their haste to cross the border. He pulled his wide hat forward to shade his eyes from the sun's brightness and stepped into the stirrup of his saddle. Untying the rope of his pack mare, McAllister moved down the trail to cross the bottom of the canyon and follow the Sanpoil.

By dark, the Indians had beat him to the McLarens. They did it at sundown and cheated the trapper of his personal revenge. When McAllister found the McLarens at their camp, Boss lay sprawled upon the ground, his skull split open, bone and brains a meal for magpies and ravens. Around him, the dirt and pine needles were wet and brown with his blood.

Cautiously McAllister dismounted and stood beside his horse. Happy McLaren had to be near, he warned himself; the worst of the two and the one most likely to escape the Indians. The horses and bales of furs had been confiscated by the Sanpoil. A slight noise alerted the trapper to Happy's position. When McAllister crept up on him, he instantly saw that the man was dying.

While he leaned against a log in deeper brush, Happy clutched both hands to his abdomen. Blood rolled over his hand, onto his clothes, to disappear into the scuffed dirt and leaves. Clearly, the wound had been made by a knife. Happy McLaren was just barely alive. He stared at the trapper with disbelieving eyes. McAllister pulled back one of McLaren's hands, taking a quick look at the depth of the wound.

"This is the end, you know," McAllister told the little bandit solemnly. "Your life means nothing to me, nothing to anybody. Everyone is hunting for you. I would've shot you cold, both of you, had I found you first." Nodding his head in thought, he added through clenched teeth, "Maybe this way is even too good for you. You deserve the worst!"

Blood gurgled thick and profuse in Happy's throat. He was beyond pain. He was incredulous at the trapper's fierce statement. "For your skins?" he coughed. "You'd kill for those-- stupid-- skins?"

Coldly, McAllister stepped back and stared venomously down at the dying man. The urge to kick a boot into his ribs was resisted. "For the pelts. For Rachel Hackett. For Mercy Bright." An angry, hurt feeling rose within him and his fists involuntarily balled. "You hunted Bright down like he was the lowest thing on Earth! And killed him like he was the lowest!"

"Boss--"

"Shut up!" McAllister's lip curled. He stabbed his big hands deep into his pockets so that he might curb the urge to reach out and finish McLaren off. "What you did to Rachel Hackett was just as bad as death! It was the same as hunting her down, too--" The trapper cleared his throat and spat down at Happy McLaren's boots. "That's what you are! Garbage! Nothing more!"

Suddenly McLaren's eyes widened, bulging in shock. His shoulders jerked. His head flew back against the log. His body stiffened, then stilled. Calm and composed, McAllister watched the blood-crusted hands slowly slide away from the gaping wound, falling from McLaren's hips to rest against the ground where he sat. The second McLaren cousin was dead.

For a long while, the trapper sat beside the dwindling fire. His thoughts rolled and meandered. All his life the threat of attack and possible death had been bantered about by trappers and traders, around campfires and in forts, but had seldom been a concern for McAllister. As he watched the last dancing flames of the fire, he thought about the isolation and emptiness that death left behind. It surrounds me now, he told himself, and he could not explain why the passing of a McLaren would mean that to him.

Eventually, and for no reason that he could have explained, McAllister laid the McLaren cousins side by side. In the darkness of late evening he placed branches over their stiffening bodies. Then he made a better camp for himself further along the canyon floor near the creek. He was glad to finally rest. His body protested its weariness.

Lately, McAllister had felt a good deal of weariness. Often his shoulder bothered him. It was as though the knife wound of years ago was fresh again, seizing the muscles of his chest and halting his breath. He had said nothing to his wife, his son, or Two Way. The old wound was of a life long before their time with him. In the darkness he smiled to himself. Two Way, with the slightest of hints, would have ferreted it out of him.

Slow in rising the following morning, it was several hours before McAllister had eaten and finally broke camp. When he was in his saddle and searching the canyon walls for evidence that the Sanpoil might have returned, he spotted Two Way, Duncan and a third rider. He waved his hat to catch their attention, but realized they must have been watching him for some time. They raised their arms in acknowledgment.

McAllister reined his horse onto the northward trail and dallied the rope of the mare over the saddle horn. It was a relief to be away from the glare of the sun. With his back to it, its mid-morning warmth penetrated his clothing and felt good to his skin. McAllister felt very tired, so rode easy in his saddle, comfortable and familiar with the pace of his horse.

Strangely, the trapper cared not that the Indians had his pelts. He did not know they were Sanpoil visiting for the winter in Soi'yus. In fact, for awhile he had even forgotten about the hides. Not like the old days! He smiled, remembering Rattler's game of thievery. Of course, he reminded himself, given the chance, the Babines up north would have sacked his canoe. And the Snakes– oh, they were a breed to contend with, though he himself had suffered nothing at their hands. He decided, as he rode the canyon floor, that the only time in his life when a twinge of fear had ever really gripped him, was the three years he trapped the Clearwater in Shoshone territory.

As McAllister led his pack horse along the trail toward his son and Two Way, he wished only to be home. He decided that he was finished with the mountains. The time had finally come for him to say goodbye to the rivers and ponds, to the beaver, mink and muskrat; to the rustic, but warm tilts he had built, and to the marvellous eerie stillness of the forest in wintertime.

Before his mind passed the image of a young Indian boy perched on a ledge high above the rolling twin waterfall. He smiled.

Then pain seized McAllister's chest, exploded and, cascading through his body, ended his life.

As Duncan waved again and called to his father riding below, he saw McAllister slump over the saddle and the horses cease their steady pace. Duncan sank his heels into the side of his horse and called to Two Way. "Something's happened! He must be hurt." Their horses leapt down through the rocks and brush to the canyon floor. Two Way raced past Duncan, furiously kicking the sure-footed mare he rode.

McAllister's horse remained immobile, lest it shift the weight of the man in the saddle. Duncan and Two Way lifted the trapper down and laid him gently upon the new spring grass. Duncan felt for a pulse, tore at the shirt and pressed his ear against his father's still chest. Hope quickly diminished. When he looked up to meet Two Way's dark eyes, he realized the Indian already knew.

"He's dead," Duncan whispered, his mind reeling, unable to believe it and not wanting to. He knelt one knee against the ground beside his father for several anxious moments, listening again for some sign of life. Finally he reached out and gently closed his father's eyelids. Then he rose to his feet, pulled his hat low over his forehead, shoved his hands deep into his pockets and remained silent.

Staring toward the mountains beyond, to the sun and into the trees and rock faces of the great canyon walls, Duncan wondered at the timing. The warming spring sun crept behind new clouds moving up from the south. He turned his gaze toward Two Way, who stared gravely down at the body of the trapper. When Two Way looked up, Duncan saw that his dark eyes were moist; saw that Two Way let the tears fall without shame.

Two Way whispered, "He was your father, Duncan, but he was my brother."

Duncan nodded, understanding. "I know. I know about that, Two Way." He turned toward Two Way's cousin, indicating a need for assistance in getting the trapper over the horse's back.

"I remember an old buffalo hide he had," Duncan told them. "All his life he carried that hide with him. Told me once he had two of them, that him and his father each had one and they travelled the rivers in their big canoe and trapped together as far back as he could remember, up north and back east. He never went to school much, you know. I guess he just learned everything by experience. He taught me many things."

Two Way watched as Duncan tested the security of the rope that held his father's body on the horse.

"No Indian ever really feared him," Duncan continued, "but neither was he afraid of them. He just wanted to be their friend, he always said. He was one brave man--" His voice broke. "Two Way, will you lead this old trapper home?"

Two Way handed the rope of the pack horse to his cousin and swung into the saddle of his own horse. "Many Rains was a man of the rivers and mountains." He spoke softly, with a voice full of sorrow. "It is fitting that he should die here. It is right."

Two Way took the lines of Rayne McAllister's horse, kneed his own forward onto the trail and began the steep climb out of the canyon. They rode in single file, solemnly through the forest, down from the high mountains toward the great river of the valley below.

37

Trapper and settler, David Rayne McAllister, was lowered into a deep grave beside that of Mercy Bright. Two Way immediately departed the site. He walked along the trail, through the ravines, down the hillside toward his village at Lac du Chien. Many times he had travelled this trail with the trapper. It was comforting at this time to walk there. He felt the friendly presence of McAllister beside him and knew that it would always be so. He stood above the twin waterfalls where he had sat as a young boy and watched the trapper's entry into the valley. An early evening breeze played about the length of his dark hair, tossing the unbound strands across his shoulders. In the eastern distance, the mountain ridges from whence he had brought McAllister's lifeless body were awash with amber hues of the setting sun.

In the dusk of evening, Two Way returned to his home at the Crossing. He had not remained long in the village. There were few left to visit. Smallpox had ravaged Shoshen-eetkwa. Most of Two Way's family were gone. Only a few remained to rebuild life in the devastated village.

As he walked, head bowed, eyes intent on the trail in the growing darkness, he murmured sadly, "You are with me still, Many Rains, and it will continue so, my brother."

EPILOGUE

During the next decade, Skaha Crossing became the hub of the area. The McAllister ranch prospered under Two Way's careful management, assisted by Duncan, who also took over the settlement's store and trading centre. Lenny Parr had taken his wife to Spokane House to see a physician. While there, Mrs. Parr died, and the heart went out of Lenny. He never returned to his store at the Crossing. Consequently the sale of his stock which took place between Duncan and Parr, was carried out by mail and took seven months to complete.

In the meantime, Duncan found he enjoyed the operation of the store. Catherine and Rachel gave him assistance when Two Way called on Duncan's help for the ranch or when the McAllister youngsters were in school. As David and Mary grew up, they were expected to work following their lessons, Mary in the store and David on the ranch.

One day, in the spring of 1871, while plowing the hilly fields of his property, Billy Willemeyer's work team spooked and raced away. Willemeyer was dragged to his death when the reins wrapped around his wrists. Stunned and bewildered, Mrs. Willemeyer gave up teaching the children of Skaha Crossing, and moved her four daughters to Kamloops. Teaching duties were taken over by Heather Carmichael.

For every family that moved away from Skaha Crossing, two more arrived. Beef, grain and dairy products were in demand by miners operating in the area. Gold had been discovered twenty miles south of the Crossing by a man named One-Arm Reed and the town of Fairview had sprung up where the pugnacious, troublesome McLaren cousins had sworn no gold was to be found. Across the valley, gold bearing quartz was revealed, and Camp McKinney was built. The decade of the 1880's spelled prosperity for farmers who could provide meat and fresh produce to such a ready market.

It was the start of a prosperous era for Skaha Crossing, Duncan McAllister felt, for the settlement had lingered in limbo after the fur brigades had ceased. As he stood in the open doorway of the store watching Two Way and David, astride their horses, moving the cows and new calves to spring range, Duncan smiled in contentment.

It was adventure, he realized, that had drawn his Scottish

grandfather westward, and compelled him to stay and raise his young son in the wilderness of early New Caledonia. But what was it that had drawn his father to the Okanagan Valley to build his life and therefore, Skaha Crossing. Peaceful integration with the Indian people of the valley? His close friends among them? A world where he was comfortable and at peace with every aspect of his life? Yes, all that and more, Duncan decided, and maybe the surroundings: the mountains, high but not towering or overwhelming, cradling their lakes with a living wilderness beyond, and a bountiful river near which a man could live well.

And perhaps, Duncan considered, the contentment that he, himself, now felt with these particular surroundings.

Welcome to all, he thought, with great pride and anticipation of a bright future at the Crossing; to all who travel our way and pause to wonder about us. "Come in," he whispered. "Come in to the valley."

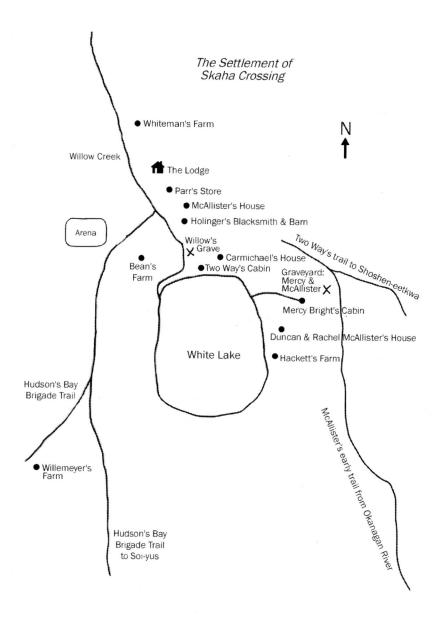

*The Settlement of
Skaha Crossing*

N

● Whiteman's Farm

Willow Creek

🏠 The Lodge

● Parr's Store

● McAllister's House

● Holinger's Blacksmith & Barn

Arena

Willow's
Grave ✗

Two Way's trail to Shoshen-eetkwa

● Bean's
Farm

✗ Carmichael's House

● Two Way's Cabin

Graveyard:
Mercy &
McAllister ✗

Mercy Bright's Cabin

● Duncan & Rachel McAllister's House

White Lake

● Hackett's Farm

Hudson's Bay
Brigade Trail

McAllister's early trail from Okanagan River

● Willemeyer's
Farm

Hudson's Bay
Brigade Trail
to Soɪ-yus

ISBN 141203785-9